7 May 98

BEGGARS RIDE

Also by Nancy Kress

NOVELS
The Prince of Morning Bells
The White Pipes
The Golden Grove
An Alien Light
Brain Rose
Beggars in Spain
Beggars and Choosers

STORY COLLECTIONS
Trinity and Other Stories
The Aliens of Earth

BEGGARS RIDE

NANCY KRESS

A TOM DOHERTY ASSOCIATES BOOK
NEW YORK

This is a work of fiction. All the characters and events portrayed in this novel are either fictitious or are used fictitiously.

BEGGARS RIDE

Edited by David G. Hartwell

A Tor Book
Published by Tom Doherty Associates, Inc.
175 Fifth Avenue
New York, NY 10010

Tor® is a registered trademark of Tom Doherty Associates, Inc.

ISBN 0-312-85817-5

Printed in the United States of America

For Jill Beves, R.N., CCRN,
who could never be replaced by a nursing 'bot

BEGGARS RIDE

Prologue

The prison door swung open and she stepped through.

The aircar waited in the parking lot a hundred feet away. She had asked her husband this: *Don't come for me. Let me come to you.* Will Sandaleros had understood. He waited in the car, alone.

Jennifer Sharifi stood still, surveying the outside. Grass. Trees. Flowers, genemod marlilies and silver roses, sweet william and moonweed. It was full summer. The warden, beside her, said something. She didn't hear him.

Twenty-seven years.

Everything had changed. Nothing had changed.

Twenty-seven years since she had been tried, convicted, and imprisoned for a crime she most certainly had committed, treason against the United States of America. Except that it had not been a crime. It had been a revolution, a fight for freedom from the Sleepers that had tried to plunder and destroy Jennifer's people. The government had used that modern weapon of destruction, ruinous taxes that eviscerated productive life, and Jennifer in turn had used one even more modern: genetic terrorism. Jennifer Sharifi and her eleven Sleepless allies had held five American cities hostage to genemod retroviruses, until the Sleepers let her people go.

Only they had not done so. But not because the Sleeper government could outwit Sleepless. Jennifer's defeat had come from another quarter. And Jennifer and the others had gone to prison with varying sentences, Jennifer's the longest. Twenty-seven years.

A second groundcar pulled up beside Will's. Reporters? Maybe not, in this changed world. An old woman got out of the car, walked in the opposite direction. Jennifer watched dispassionately. The old woman—in her eighties, from her face—moved with the smooth-jointed walk and fluid arm swings they all had now. Since the Change. But the woman was still old: used up, nearly finished.

Jennifer Sharifi was 114. She looked thirty-five, and would continue to look thirty-five. But twenty-seven years had been lost. And her world.

The warden was still talking. Jennifer ignored him. She concentrated on her rage: massive, molten, welling up like slow thick lava from the planetary core. Coldly she walled it off, contained it, directed it. Undirected rage was a danger; directed rage was an inexhaustible force. It was an engineering problem.

Not a muscle of her beautiful face moved.

When she was ready, Jennifer walked away from the gabbling warden, away from Allendale Maximum Security Federal Prison, where she had spent twenty-seven years for treason against a government that, by now, barely existed.

Will didn't kiss or embrace her. But he reached for her hand, and he sat motionless a moment before he started the car.

"Hello, Will."

"Hello, Jenny."

No more was needed.

The car rose. Below her, the warden dwindled, and then the prison. Jennifer said to the comlink, "Messages?"

"No messages," it answered, which wasn't surprising. The link wasn't shielded. Her messages would be waiting on Will's link, wherever he was living temporarily. There would be a lot of messages, and more in the days to come, as Jennifer gathered up once more the strands of her enormous, tangled corporate and financial web. But not in the United States. Never again in the United States. There was one call to make on an unshielded link.

"Connect to Sanctuary, public frequency."

"Signaling Sanctuary, public frequency," the comlink said. Will glanced at her, returned his gaze to the car.

Jennifer's screen flashed the access codes, immediately replaced by her granddaughter's face. So Miranda had been waiting, had known the hour, the minute, of Jennifer's release. Of course.

"Hello, Grandmother," Miranda Sharifi said, from 200,000 miles above Earth. She and the other third-generation Sleepless had been in possession of Sanctuary orbital for years now. Of Sanctuary, which Jennifer had built to keep the Sleepless safe. Jennifer didn't enjoy irony.

Miranda did not say *Welcome home.* Her plain face, with its oversize head and unruly black hair, did not smile. Jennifer looked at her granddaughter, and remembered, and held back the walls around her rage. It was Miranda who had sent Jennifer Sharifi to prison.

Jennifer said in her clear cold voice, "I am resuming possession of Sanctuary. It is legally mine. Your father's authority of guardian-in-law is void by my release. Both of you will vacate the orbital, along with the twenty-six other SuperSleepless and all those who have any formalized business arrangement with you, within twenty-four hours. If you do not, I will bring against you all the corrupt legal force of government that you brought against me."

Miranda said expressionlessly, "We will vacate Sanctuary." The screen blanked.

Will took Jennifer's hand.

The car approached a Y-energy security dome in the middle of an Appalachian upland. Old, worn hills, rounded on the top, gentled to leafy dark green, ungenemod. Will signaled the shield and it let the aircar through. He landed on the roof of a stone house, nanobuilt, on a low hill. They got out.

Below Jennifer stretched a meadow of clover and daisies and bees, bounded by a shining stream that broke at the north end into a waterfall. Beyond, mountains rose in blue mist like smoky cathedrals. The sky arched milky white, faint gold at the western edge.

Will said softly, "You're home."

Jennifer looked at it, all of it—house, meadow, mountains, sky, country. Her face didn't change, except that she closed her eyes, the better to see the meticulously engineered rage.

"This, home? Never. This is only a battleground."

Will nodded slowly, and smiled, and they went inside.

I

NOVEMBER 2120–JANUARY 2121

If wishes were horses, then beggars
might ride.
—John Ray, *English Proverbs,* 1670

One

There it was. Lying on a sidewalk on Madison Avenue in the Manhattan East Enclave. Almost it could have been a fallen twig overlooked by a defective maintenance 'bot. But it wasn't a preternaturally straight twig, or a dropped laser knife, or a truncated black line drawn on the nanocoated concrete, going nowhere. It was a Change syringe.

Dr. Jackson Aranow picked it up.

Empty, and no way to tell how long ago it had been used. The black alloy didn't rust or dent or decay. Jackson couldn't recall the last time he'd seen one lying around outside. Three or four years, maybe. He twirled it between his fingers like a baton, sighted along it like a telescope, pointed it at the building and said "Bang."

"Welcome," the building said back. Jackson's extended arm had brought him within sensor range. He put the syringe in his pocket and stepped into the security portico.

"Dr. Jackson Aranow, to see Ellie Lester."

"'Alf a minute, sir. There you go, all cleared, sir. 'Appy to be of service, sir."

"Thank you," Jackson said, a little stiffly. He disliked affected accents on buildings.

The lobby was expensive and grotesque. A floor programmed with a yellow brick road whose bricks shifted every thirty seconds to a different path, all ending up at blank walls. A neon-green Venus with a digital clock in her belly, sitting on a beautiful antique Sheraton table beside the elevator. The elevator spoke in a high, singsong voice.

"Please to be welcome, sahib. I am being very happy you visit Memsahib Lester. Please to look this way, allow me humble retina scan . . . thank you, sahib. Wishing you every gracious thing."

Jackson didn't think he was going to like Ellie Lester.

Outside the apartment door, a holo of a black man materialized, wearing a faded calico shirt, barefoot. "Sho is glad you here, sir. Sho is. Miz Ellie, she waiting on y'all inside, sir." The holo shuffled, grinned, and put a translucent hand on the opening door.

The apartment echoed the lobby: a carefully arranged mix of expensive antiques and ugly, outrageous kitsch. A papier-mâché rat eating her young atop an exquisite eighteenth-century sideboard. An antique television polished to a high gleam under a diamond-filament sculpture covered densely with dust. Faux chairs, all dangerous angles and weird protuberances, impossible to sit on. "In an age of nanotech, even primitive nanotech," said the latest issue of *Design* magazine, "the material presence of objects becomes vulgar, even irrelevant, and only the wit of their arrangement matters." The two goldfish in the atrium were artfully dead, floating beside a small holo of a sinking *Pequod.*

Ellie Lester strode out of a side door. She was genemod for size, which gave Jackson her age: female children engineered to top six feet had been briefly fashionable in the late eighties, when material presence hadn't yet been irrelevant. Now that *Design* had decided it was, Ellie compensated for her height with wit. Over her bare breasts she wore a necklace alternating glowing laser beads with nanocoated animal turds; her draped skirt was red, white, and blue. Jackson remembered that tonight was election night.

"Doctor, where the hell have you *been?* I called you ten minutes ago!"

"It took me four minutes to get a go-'bot," Jackson said mildly. "And you did tell me that your grandfather was already dead."

"Great-grandfather," she said, scowling. "This way."

She walked five paces ahead, which gave Jackson a good view of her long, long legs, perfect ass, asymmetrically cut red hair. He thought of pointing the Change syringe at her and whispering "Bang." But he left the syringe in his pocket. Parody displays weren't actually as witty or intriguing as *Design* thought.

Coward, jeered the Cazie in his mind.

They passed through room after grotesque room. The apartment was even larger than Jackson's on Fifth Avenue. On the walls hung elaborately framed, programmed burlesques: the Mona Lisa laughing like a hyena, *A Sunday Afternoon on the Grande Jatte* in frantic, dot-dissolving motion.

The dead man's bedroom was much different, painted white and undecorated except for some small, predigital photographs grouped on one wall. A nursing 'bot stood silent beside the bed. The old man's lips and cheek muscles had gone slack with death. Not genemod, but he might have been handsome once. His skin was deeply lined but nonetheless had the healthy look of all those who'd received the Change syringe, without spots or lumps or rough patches or anything else caused by either abnormal cells or toxins in the body. Neither existed anymore.

Neither did illness. The Cell Cleaner, half of the Change magic, saw to that. Nanomachinery, made of genetically modified self-replicating protein, occupied one percent of everyone's cells. Like white blood cells, the tiny biocomputers had the ability to leave the bloodstream and travel freely through body tissues. Unlike white blood cells, the Cell Cleaners had the ability to compare indigenous DNA with non-standard variations and destroy not only foreign substances but aberrant DNA variations. Viruses. Toxins. Cancers. Irregular bone cells. Furthermore, the Cell Cleaner spared a long list of preprogrammed substances that belonged in the body, such as essential minerals and symbiotic bacteria. Since the Change, no doctors carried antibiotics or antivirals. No doctor carefully monitored patients for infectious complications. No doctor needed diagnostic judgment. Jackson, who had graduated from Harvard Medical School the same year that Miranda Sharifi had supplied the world with Change syringes, wasn't a specialist. He was a mechanic.

Jackson's "practice" consisted of trauma, Change syringe injections of newborns, and death certifications. As a doctor, he was as obsolete as a neon-green Venus. A parody display.

But not at this moment.

Jackson unpacked his equipment from his medical bag and turned on the official medical comlink. Ellie Lester settled herself in the room's only chair.

"Name of the deceased?"

"Harold Winthrop Wayland."

Jackson circled the dead man's skull with the cerebral monitor. No electrical activity, no blood circulation in the brain. "Citizen number and birth date?"

"AKM-92-4681-374. August 3, 2026. He was *ninety-four.*" She almost spat the age.

Jackson placed the dermalyzer on Wayland's neck. It immediately uncoiled and spread itself in a dense net of fine synthetic neurons over his face, disappearing under the collar of his silk pajamas and reappearing over his feet. A crawling, probing cocoon. Ellie Lester looked away. The monitor showed no break or other indication of intrusion anywhere on the skin, not even the smallest puncture wound. All feeding tubules were fully functional.

"When did you discover Mr. Wayland's body?"

"Just before I called you. I went in to check on him."

"And you found him as he looks now?"

"Yes. I didn't touch him, or anything in the room."

The dermalyzer web retracted. Jackson snaked the lung hose into Wayland's left nostril. As soon as it touched the mucous membrane, the hose took over and disappeared down the bronchial tree into the lungs.

"Last lung expansion at 6:42 Eastern Standard Time," Jackson said. "No evidence of drowning. Sample tissues secured. Now, Ms. Lester, tell me and for the record everything you can remember about the deceased's behavior in the last few days."

"Nothing unusual," she said flatly. "He didn't leave this room much, except to be led to the feeding room. You can access the nursing 'bot's records, or take away the whole 'bot. I tried to check on him every few days. When I came in tonight, he was dead and the 'bot was on standby."

"Without having signaled distress signs to the house system? That's not usual."

"It did signal. You can access all the house records and see for yourself. But I wasn't home, and the connection to the comlink was malfunctioning. It still is—I didn't touch it, so you could see."

Jackson said, "Then how did you call me?"

"On my mobile link. I also called the repair franchise. You can access—"

"I don't want any of your records," Jackson said. He heard his own contemptuous tone, tried to modify it. The official link was still open. "But the police might. I only certify death, Ms. Lester, not investigate it."

"But . . . does that mean you're going to notify the authorities? I don't understand. My great-grandfather clearly died of old age! He was *ninety-four!*"

"Many people are ninety-four now." Jackson looked away from her eyes. Rich genemod brown, but flat and shiny as a bird's. "Ms. Lester, what did you mean when you said that Mr. Wayland left this room only when the nurse 'led him to the feeding area'?"

Her shiny eyes widened, and then she shot a look of sly triumph at the comlink. "Why, Dr. Aranow—didn't you access your patient's records on the way over here? I told you I'd authorized your access."

"The go-'bot ride was short. I only live three blocks away."

"But you had four minutes of idle waiting for a go-'bot!" From her chair she gazed at him with brow-raised triumph. He'd bet anything she wasn't genemod for IQ.

He said calmly, "I did not access Mr. Wayland's medical records. Why did the nurse have to lead him to your feeding room?"

"Because he had Alzheimer's, Dr. Aranow. He'd had it for fifteen years, long before the Change. Because your much-vaunted Cell Cleaner can't repair damage to brain cells, can it, Doctor—only destroy abnormal ones. Which left him with fewer every year. Because he couldn't *find* the feeding room, much less take off his own clothes and feed. Because his mind was gone and he was a drooling, vacuous, empty shell. Whose damaged brain finally just gave up and killed his body, even if it had been senselessly Changed!"

She breathed hard. Jackson knew she was goading him, daring him to say it: *You killed him.* Then she'd probably sue.

He didn't let himself be provoked. After marriage to—and divorce from—Cazie Sanders, Ellie Lester was a stupid amateur. He said formally, "The cause of death will, of course, have to be made by the medical examiner for the City of New York, after autopsy. This preliminary report is concluded. Comlink, off."

He put the link in his bag. Ellie Lester stood up; she was an inch taller than Jackson. He guessed the autopsy would show one of the Chinese or South American inhibitors that simply make the brain forget what to do, make it stop sending signals to the heart to beat or the lungs to breathe. Or maybe the autopsy wouldn't show it, if the drug was enough ahead of the detection technology. How had she delivered it?

She said, "Perhaps our paths will cross again, Doctor."

He knew better than to answer. On his mobile he made the call to the cops and took a last look at Harold Winthrop Wayland. The wall screen came on. The house system must have been pre-set.

". . . final election results! President Stephen Stanley Garrison has been reelected by a narrow margin. The most startling feature of the results, however, is the number of Americans casting ballots. Of ninety million eligible voters, only eight percent voted. This represents a drop of—"

Ellie Lester gave a sharp crack of laughter. " 'Startling.' God, he's a disease. Why would anyone bother to *vote* anymore?"

"Maybe as an act of witty parody," Jackson said, and knew that by his saying it, she'd won after all. And it was no comfort that she was too stupid to recognize that.

She didn't see him out. Maybe *Design* had decided that manners, too, were irrelevant. But as he left the dead man's bedroom, he looked closely for the first time at the small framed photos on the wall. All but the last were predigital copies, faded and uneven in color.

Edward Jenner. Ignaz Semmelweiss. Jonas Salk. Stephen Clark Andrews. And Miranda Sharifi.

"Yes, he was a doctor, too," Ellie Lester said maliciously. "Back when you people were really necessary. And those are his heroes—four Livers and a Sleepless. Wouldn't you know?" She laughed.

Jackson let himself out. The holo of the black man had been replaced by a naked Roman slave, heavily muscled, handsome but clearly not genemod. A Liver. The slave knelt as Jackson passed, lowered his eyes, and opened his mouth. Translucent manacles of holographic gold bound him to Ellie Lester's doorknob.

"She's the far end of a bell-shaped curve, I know that," Jackson said to his sister Theresa. "So it shouldn't bother me. Actually, it doesn't bother me."

"It bothers you," Theresa said in her gentle voice. "And it should."

They sat in the atrium of their apartment, having drinks before dinner, which would be old-fashioned mouth food. The atrium wall facing the park was a transparent Y-shield. Four stories below, Central Park rioted with autumn color under its invisible energy dome. The Manhattan enclaves had recently voted to restore modified seasons, although the vote had been close. Above the shield the November sky was the color of ashes.

Theresa wore a loose flowered dress that fell in graceful folds to her ankles; Jackson had the vague impression that it was out of fashion. Her face, without makeup, was a pale oval under her silvery blonde hair. She was twelve years younger than Jackson's thirty.

Theresa was fragile. Not in her slender genemod body, but in her mind. Jackson's private belief was that something had gone wrong during her embryonic engineering, as something sometimes did. Genemod was a complicated process, and once the zygote had become blastomeres, no further permanent engineering was possible. Not, at least, by anyone on Earth.

As a child Theresa had hated to go to school and had clung, weeping in a quiet and hopeless way, to her bewildered mother. She didn't like to play with other children. For days she stayed in her room, drawing or listening to music. Sometimes she said she wanted to wrap herself in the music and melt into it until there wasn't any more Theresa. Medical tests showed high reactivity in her stress-hormone response system: high cortisol levels, enlarged adrenal glands, the heart rate and gut motility and nerve-cell death associated with presuicidal depression. Her threshold for limbic-hypothalamic arousal was very low; she found anything new intensely threatening.

In an age of custom-engineered biogenic amines, nobody had to stay fragile. Throughout Theresa's girlhood she had been on and off neuropharms to rebalance her brain chemistry. The Cell Cleaner would have made that problematic, since it destroyed everything in the body that it decided didn't belong there, that didn't match either the DNA patterns or approved set of molecules stored in its tiny, unimaginable, protein-based computers lodged in and between human cells. But by the time the Change brought the Cell Cleaner, it no longer mattered. At thirteen Theresa announced—no, that was too strong a word for Theresa, she never "announced"—she had said that she was finished with neuropharms "for good."

By that time, their parents had both died in an aircar crash and Jackson was his sister's guardian. Jackson had argued, reasoned, begged. It had done no good. Theresa would not be helped. She didn't argue back; intellectual debate confused her. She simply refused to allow a medical solution to her medical problems.

However, at least she didn't—Jackson's secret fear—attempt suicide. She became even more reclusive and more elusive, one of those gentle pale women from an entirely different century. Theresa embroidered. She studied music. She was writing a life of the martyred Sleepless woman, Leisha Camden, of all irrelevant pursuits—another woman who had been entirely eclipsed by a different generation of far more ruthless females.

When the Change occurred, Theresa was the only person Jackson knew who refused the syringe. She could not ground-feed. She could become infected by viruses and bacteria, and did. She could be poisoned by toxins. She could get cancer.

Sometimes, in his darker moods, he thought that his sister's elusive neurological frailties, so divorced from her intelligent sweetness, were the reason he'd become a doctor. Just lately it had occurred to him that Theresa's frailties were also the reason he'd married someone like Cazie.

Watching his sister pour herself another fruit juice—she never drank sunshine, alcohol, or any of the synthetic endorphin drinks like Endorkiss—Jackson thought that it was wrong to have his life so shaped by a younger sister who was softly, stubbornly, unnecessarily crazy. That he was weak to have allowed it to happen. And that around Theresa what he felt was strong, probably in comparison, which was itself a weak way to look at it.

"People like Ellie Lester," Theresa said, "they're not whole."

"What do you mean?" He didn't really want to know—it might lead to another of Theresa's tentative, tortuous discussions on spirituality—but the sunshine in his drink was pleasantly affecting him. His bones were starting to relax, his muscles to sway, the trees below to hum in a nondemanding harmonious background. He didn't want to talk. Certainly not about the data he'd looked up on Ellie Lester when he got home, which included discovering that she would inherit control of her great-grandfather's enormous fortune. Let Tessie babble instead. He would sit in the humming twilight and not listen.

But all Theresa said was, "I don't know what I mean. I just know they're not whole. All of them. All of us."

"Ummm."

"There's something wrong inside us. I believe that, Jackson. I do."

She didn't sound as if she believed it. She sounded unsure as always, with her hesitant soft speech and loose flowered dress. It occurred to Jackson that in an enclave where dinner parties often ended up naked for communal feeding, he hadn't actually seen the shape of his sister's body for years.

But then Theresa spoke in a sudden rush. "I read something evil today. Actually *evil*. I sent Thomas into the library deebees, for my book. Because of something Leisha Camden wrote in 2045."

Jackson braced himself. Theresa often sent her personal system, Thomas, trawling through historical databases, and she often misinterpreted what she found there. Or she became indignant over it. Or she cried.

"Thomas brought me a sentence from a famous doctor who knew Leisha. Hans Dietrich Lowering. He said, 'There is no such thing as the mind. There is only a collection of electrical and physiological operations we collectively call the brain.' He said that!"

Pity flooded Jackson. She looked so distressed, so ineffectually indignant, at this piece of old and nonstartling non-news. But his pity was laced with disquiet. As soon as Theresa had said the word "evil," Jackson had a sudden flash of Ellie Lester, taller than he was, teeth bared in a fury that she could not allow into the official medical comlink. She had looked evil—an evil, beautiful giantess, and under the unwrapping of sunshine Jackson could admit what he had denied before: he had wanted her. Even though she was not really evil, only greedy. Not really beautiful, only obvious. And no more a giant than the sinking miniature holo of the *Pequod* beside the dead goldfish in the atrium pool.

He shifted uneasily on his chair and took another sip of his drink.

"It's evil to deny the mind," Theresa was saying. "Let alone the soul."

"Tessie—"

She leaned forward, a pale insubstantial blur in the gloom, her voice close to tears. "It *is* evil, Jackson. We aren't just sensors and processors and wiring, like 'bots. We're humans, all of us."

"Calm down, honey. It was just a sentence written a long time ago. Musty data in an old file."

"Then people don't believe it's true anymore? Doctors don't?"

Of course they did. Only Theresa could get this upset over a clichéd statement seventy-five years old, based on other clichés two hundred years old.

"Tessie, sweetheart . . ."

"We have *souls,* Jackson!"

Another voice: "Oh, Christ, not another babble-on about souls!"

She came in smiling, mocking, filling the large room with her larger, five-foot-three, utterly vital presence. Cazie Sanders. His ex-wife. Who refused to depart his life, the divorce she'd taken from him just one more thing she casually disregarded now that she had it. On the excuse that she was Theresa's friend, Cazie came and went in the Aranows' apartment as she pleased, took up and discarded the Aranows as she pleased, pleased herself always.

With her were two men Jackson didn't know—was one of them her current lover? Both of them? One glance at the older man and Jackson knew he was on something stronger than sunshine or Endorkiss. Sleek, long, unmuscled, he had the deliberately androgynous body of a vid star, dressed in a rough brown cotton tunic like a pillowcase, already eaten into small holes by the feeding tubules on his skin. The younger man, whose genemod handsomeness uncomfortably reminded Jackson of Ellie Lester's slave holo, wore an opaque holosuit that appeared to be made of thousands of angry, crawling bees. His mouth curved in a permanent sneer. Would Cazie actually sleep with either of these diseases? Jackson didn't know.

It was difficult to explain why he'd married Cazie, but not very. She was beautiful, with her dark short curls, honey-gold skin, and elongated golden eyes flecked with pale green. But all genemod women were beautiful. Certainly Cazie wasn't as lovely or loyal or kind as Theresa—who, next to her ex-sister-in-law, faded. Nearly disappeared, flickered weakly like a malfunctioning holo.

Cazie burned with some vital, ungenemod force, darkly intelligent, primal and erotic as driving rain. Whenever she'd touched him—feverishly, or languorously, or tenderly, with Cazie there was no predicting—Jackson had felt something iron and cold dissolve in his center, something he usually didn't even know he was carrying around. He'd felt connected to nameless, powerful, very old longings. Sometimes during sex with Cazie, her fingernails raking him and his penis moving blind within her like a hot living missile, he would be amazed to hear himself weeping, or shouting, or chanting—another person entirely, the memory of which embarrassed him afterward. Cazie was never embarrassed. Not by anything. After two years of marriage, she had divorced Jackson for being "too passive."

He had been afraid, during the messy weeks of her moving out, that nothing in his life would ever again be as good as those two years. And nothing had.

Looking at her now, dressed in a short green-and-gold drape that left one shoulder bare, Jackson felt the familiar tightening in his neck, his chest, his scrotum, a complex of desire, and rage, and competitiveness, and humiliation that he had somehow not been strong enough to swim in the dark currents of Cazie's inner sea. He put down his drink. He needed his head clear.

"How are you feeling, Tess?" Cazie said kindly. She sat down, unasked, beside Theresa, who both shrank back minutely and put out one hand, as if to warm herself at Cazie's glow. Their friendship was inexplicable to Jackson; they were so different. But once someone had come into Theresa's life, she clung to that person forever. And Theresa brought out the protective, tender side of Cazie—as if Tess were a helpless kitten. Jackson looked away from his ex-wife, and then refused to allow himself that weakness, and looked back.

"I'm fine," Theresa whispered. She glanced at the door. Strangers increased her agitation.

"Tess, these are my friends, Landau Carson and Irv Kanzler. Jackson and Theresa Aranow. We're on our way to an exorcism."

"To a what?" Jackson said. Immediately he wished he hadn't. Irv drew an inhaler from a pocket of his consumable tunic and sniffed more of whatever was rearranging his neural chemistry. That was the problem with the more toxic recreational drugs: the Cell Cleaner busily removed them almost as soon as they entered the body, so users had to keep renewing every few minutes.

"An ex-or-cissssm," Landau drawled in a phony accent. He was the one wearing bees. "Haven't you *heard* of them? You must have *heard* of them."

"Jackson never hears of anything," Cazie said. "He doesn't leave the enclave and go down and dirty among Livers."

"I leave the enclave sometimes," Jackson said evenly.

"I'm delighted to hear it," Cazie said, helping herself to a glass of sunshine. The fingernail on her left ring finger was sheathed in a holo of a tiny chained butterfly frantically beating its wings.

"An ex-or-cisssm," Landau said with exaggerated patience, "is simply nova. A genuine brain trot. You'd die laughing."

"I doubt it," Jackson said, and vowed that was the last thing he'd say to this toxin. He folded his arms across his chest, realized that probably made him look as stuffy as Cazie had implied, and unfolded them.

Landau said, "Surely you've heard of the Mother Miranda cults? They're sort of a Liver religion—so typical. Miranda as the Virgin Mary, interceding with the Divine. And for *what?* Not salvation or grace or world peace or any of those dreary eternal verities. No—Mother Miranda's followers are praying for *immortality.* Another Change. If the SuperSleepless could deliver the first syringes, goes this risible theology, then they can just as well go deliver another miracle that makes all the grubby little Livers go on forever."

Irv laughed, a sudden bark like ice cracking, and sniffed again from his inhaler. Direct pleasure-center excitation, Jackson guessed, with hallucinogenic additives and a selective depressant to lower inhibition.

Cazie said, "God, Landau, you're such an unoriginal snob. It's not only Livers involved in the Mother Miranda cult. There are donkeys in it, too."

Theresa shifted on her chair, a small agitated gesture that was the kinesthetic equivalent of a whimper. Jackson took her hand.

Landau said, "But it's *mostly* Livers. Our newly self-sufficient, self-disenfranchised eighty percent. And Livers are the only ones who do ex-orcisssms."

Theresa said, so low that at first Jackson thought nobody else heard her, "Exorcising what? Demons?"

"No, of course not," Landau said. His bees buzzed fractionally louder. "Impure thoughts."

Cazie laughed. "Not exactly. More like ideologically incorrect thoughts. It's really a political check to make sure all the good little Mother Mirandites are convinced of her semi-divinity. They just call it an exorcism because they drive out wrong ideas. Then they all create yet another broadcast to beam up at Sanctuary."

"Real brain-trot entertainment," Landau said.

Jackson couldn't help himself. "And this ritual is open to the public?"

"Of course not," Landau said. "We're crashers. Humble novices in search of some faith in our pointless and overprivileged lives."

Theresa's quiet agitation increased. Cazie said, "What is it, Tess?"
Theresa burst out, "You shouldn't!" Immediately she shrank back
into her chair, then stumbled to her feet. Jackson, still holding her
hand, felt her fingers tremble. "Good night," she whispered, and
pulled free.

Cazie said, "Wait, Tessie, don't go!" But Theresa fled toward her
own room.

"Nice going," Jackson said.

"I'm sorry, Jack. I didn't think she'd react like that. It's not real
religion."

"She's religious? My condolences," Landau said. "And in the immediate family, too."

"Shut up," Cazie said. "God, you bore me sometimes, Landau.
Don't you ever get tired of supercilious posturing?"

"Never. What else is there, really? And may I remind you, Cassan-
dra dear, that you too are on your way to this ex-or-cisssm, hmmmm?"

"No," Cazie snapped. "I'm not. Get out!"

"A sudden mood shift into anger! How exciting!"

Jackson stood. Landau touched a point on his chest; his bees
buzzed louder. For the first time Jackson wondered if they were all
holos, or if some of the bees were weapons. Certainly Landau would
wear a personal Y-shield.

"Out!" Cazie screamed. "You heard me, you infection! Out!" Her
dark eyes blazed; she looked as much a caricature as Landau. Was she
posturing as well, amusing herself with the drama? Jackson realized
he could no longer tell.

Landau stretched lazily, yawned ostentatiously, and rose to his feet.
He drifted toward the door. Irv followed, sniffing his inhaler. He
hadn't said a single word.

When Cazie returned from slamming the apartment door, Jackson
said quietly, "Nice friends you have."

"They're not my friends." She was breathing hard.

"You introduced them as friends."

"Yeah, well. You know how it is. I'm sorry about Tessie, Jack. I
really didn't know Landau was so stupid."

If this humility was a posture, it was a new one. Jackson didn't trust
it, didn't trust her. He didn't answer.

Cazie said, "Should I go after Tess?"

"No. Give her some time." But from behind him came Theresa's
soft voice; she must have heard the door slam and crept out.

"Did they leave?"

"Yes, pet," Cazie said. "I'm sorry I brought them here. I didn't think. They're real asses. No, not even that—just assholes. Fragments. Partial people."

Theresa said eagerly, "But that's just what I was saying earlier to Jackson! There's something . . . not whole about people now. Why, this afternoon Jackson saw—"

"I can't discuss a confidential medical case," Jackson said harshly, although of course he already had. Theresa bit her lip. Cazie smiled, humility already replaced by mockery.

"A murder, Jack? I can't think what else they'd need you for that you can't discuss. A little off your usual practice of the once-monthly accident and the twice-monthly newborn Change?"

He said evenly, "Don't needle me, Cazie."

"Ah, Jackson darling, why couldn't you be so assertive when we were married? Although I really do think we're better off as friends. But Tess, honey"—she turned back to his sister, suddenly kind again, while Jackson was left wanting to hit her, or convince her, or rape her—"you have a point. We donkeys are just coming apart since the Change. Joining Liver cults, or doing brain-deadening neuropharms, or marrying a computer program—did you hear about that? For dependability. 'Your AI will never leave you.'" She laughed, throwing back her head. The dark curls danced, and her elongated eyes narrowed to slits.

Theresa said, "Yes, but . . . but we don't have to be that way!"

"Sure we do," Cazie said. "We're bred to be forthrightly self-serving, even the best of us. Jackson, did you vote today?"

He hadn't. He tried to look condescending.

"Did you, Tess? Never mind, I know you didn't. The whole political system is dead, because everyone knows it isn't where power is anymore. The Change took care of that. The Livers don't need us, they're managing quite well in their own lawless little ground-feeding pseudo-enclaves. Or they think they are. Which is, incidentally, why I'm here. We have a crisis."

Cazie's dark eyes sparkled; she loved crises. Theresa looked frightened. Jackson said, "Theresa, did you show Cazie your new bird?"

"I'll get him," Theresa said, and escaped.

Jackson said, "Who has a crisis?"

"Us. TenTech. We have a factory break-in."

"That's impossible," Jackson said. And then, because Cazie usually had her facts straight, "Which factory?"

"The Willoughby, Pennsylvania, plant. Well, it's not exactly a break-in yet. But somebody was just outside the Y-shield this afternoon with bioelectric and crystal equipment. The sensors picked them up. If you'd check your business net, Jack, you'd know that. But oh, I forgot—you were out investigating murders."

Jackson kept his temper. Cazie had received a third of TenTech in the divorce settlement, since her money had kept the company afloat during the disastrous year when a nanodissembler plague had attacked the ubiquitous alloy duragem, and businesses had died like Livers. He said evenly, "Nobody got inside, did they? Nobody can breach security on a Y-energy shield. At least, not . . ."

"Not Livers, you mean, and who else would be out in the wilds of central Pennsylvania? I think you're probably right. But that's why we should go have a look. If it's not Livers, who is it? Kids from Carnegie-Mellon, sharpening their datadipping skills? Industrial espionage by CanCo? SuperSleepless like—gasp!—Miranda Sharifi, obscurely interested in our little family-owned firm? What do you think, Jack? Who's messing with our factory?"

"Maybe the biosensors are malfunctioning. Another failure like duragem."

"Maybe," Cazie said. "But I checked around. Nobody else is having sensor failure. Just us. So I think we better go have a look. Okay, Jackson? Tomorrow morning?"

"I'm busy."

"Doing what? You're not busy—that's the trouble, none of us are busy enough. Here's something to do, something that impacts our finances, something with actual substance. Come with me."

She smiled at him, full voltage, her long golden eyes full of the sly pleading missing from her brash words. Jackson knew that later, when he lay in bed going over and over this conversation, he wouldn't be able to re-create the compelling quality of her. Of her eyes, her body language, her tone. He would remember only the words themselves, without grace or subtlety, and so would curse himself for saying yes.

Cazie laughed. "Nine o'clock, then. I'll drive. Meanwhile, I'm starving. Oh, Tessie, here you are. What a pretty little genemod bird. Can you talk, cage bird? Can you say 'social dissolution'?"

Theresa held up the Y-energy cage and said, "He only sings."

"Like most of us," Cazie said. "Desperate discordant tunes. Jackson, I *am* hungry. And not for mouth food, either, tonight. I think we should keep Tessie company while she eats, and then you should invite me to dinner in your so-tasteful feeding ground."

"I'm going out," Jackson said quickly. Theresa looked at him in quick surprise, as quickly veiled. He never knew how much she knew, or guessed, about his feelings for Cazie. Theresa was so sensitive to distress; she must intuit that it would be impossible for Jackson to go calmly with Cazie to the dining room, take off most of his clothes, and lie on the nutrient-enriched soil while his Changed body absorbed everything it needed, in perfect proportions, through his feeding tubules. Jackson couldn't do it. Although the lure was powerful. To lie there under the warm lights, their changing wavelengths carefully selected for a relaxing effect on the mind, to breathe the perfumed air, to turn on one elbow to talk casually to Cazie, to watch Cazie feed, lying on her stomach, her small firm breasts bared to the earth . . .

Impossible.

He waited until his erection had subsided before he stood and stretched with elaborate nonchalance. "Well, people are waiting on me. Good night, Cazie. Theresa, I won't be late."

"Be careful, Jackson," Theresa said, as she always did, as if there could be any danger inside the Manhattan East Enclave, protected by a Y-shield from even unwanted weather. Theresa had not left the apartment in over a year.

"Yes, be careful, Jack," Cazie mocked tenderly, and his heart caught when it seemed he heard regret mixed with the tenderness. But when he turned back, she was fussing again over Theresa's bird, and didn't even look at him.

There was tomorrow.

Damn tomorrow. It was a business trip, to find out what was going wrong at the Willoughby plant. He owned the damn company—or at least a third of it—he should check the factories' printouts more, give orders to the AI running it, link with the TenTech chief engineer, check up on problems. He should be more responsible about his and Theresa's money. He should . . .

He should do a lot of things.

He walked out into the cold November night, which under the dome felt like a warm September night, and tried to think up someplace he might actually want to go to dinner besides home.

TWO

Lizzie Francy halted on the rough grass of the dark Pennsylvania field and put a warning hand on Vicki Turner's arm. A cold wind blew. A hundred feet ahead the TenTech Y-energy cone factory loomed in the moonlight, a windowless foamcast rectangle, blank and featureless as a prison.

"No farther," Lizzie said. "The security shield starts four feet ahead. See the change in the grass?"

"Of course not, I can't see *anything*," Vicki said. "How can you?"

"I was here in daytime," Lizzie said. "We have to move, a little left . . . I left a marker. You're shivering, Vicki—you cold?"

"I'm freezing. We're all freezing. That's the point of this whole illegal nocturnal burglary, isn't it? God, I must be crazy to do this . . . How far left?"

"Right here. Don't go any closer, the infrared detectors will pick us up."

"Not me, I'm too cold. I'd register as rock. No, I don't want your cape, you need it."

"I'm not cold," Lizzie said. She opened a gunnysack and started pulling out equipment.

"That's your hormones surging. Pregnancy's little Y-energy cones. All right, I'll take the cape . . . How come your skin doesn't eat clothes as fast as mine? Or does it just seem that way . . . Lizzie, baby, don't get too excited. This isn't going to work. Nobody, no matter how good a datadipper, can break into a Y-energy factory."

"I can," Lizzie said.

She grinned at Vicki. Vicki didn't know. Vicki was smart, was educated, was a donkey, those people who used to run the world. Vicki had given Lizzie her first terminal, and taught her to use it. Lizzie owed Vicki everything. But Vicki didn't *know*. Vicki was old, maybe even forty, and she'd grown up before the Change, when everything was different. Lizzie had spent the last five years on datanets, and she knew how good she was. There wasn't anything she couldn't dip (except of course Sanctuary, which didn't count). It was Lizzie's world now, and she could do anything. She was seventeen.

The two women unwrapped Lizzie's equipment from more rough-woven sacking. Crystal library, system terminal, laser transmitter, full-body holosuits. Some of the equipment was jerry-fitted, some was stolen, all was old. Lizzie, her enormous belly pushing out the woven tunic already eaten into holes, worked at fitting the equipment together and aiming it at the building. Vicki, wrapped in Lizzie's cape, suddenly chuckled. "I met Jackson Aranow once."

"Who's Jackson Aranow?"

"The owner of this factory we're about to rob. Or at least his family is. Know your unwitting and unwilling patrons, I say. The Aranows are old-line conservative, stuffy, boring. And rich as Sanctuary."

Lizzie looked up from the decryptions on her screen. "Really?"

"No, of course not really. God, don't be so literal. Nobody's as rich as Sanctuary."

"Okay, we're ready," Lizzie said. She grinned, a flash of white teeth in the gloom. "You got your sack? Now remember, the shield will only be down for ten seconds before the system resets. You armed?"

"If you call this 'armed,' " Vicki said, hefting the metal pipe she carried in her right hand. "Did you have to make it so heavy? If I'm going to die, I want to die light."

"You're not going to die. And you're all but naked, isn't that light enough?" Lizzie laughed, a low reckless giggle, and her fingers flew over her equipment. "Okay—*now!*"

A laser beam pierced the darkness, straight and hard-looking as a diamond-filament rod. It shot through the invisible energy shield to an exact, virtually indistinguishable site high on the building. A second beam followed. Multiple data addresses, their bioelectric molecules excited by the first laser array, absorbed additional energy from the second in a different region of the spectrum. The absorbed energy initiated a branching reaction, a sequential one-photon architecture— a set of wavelength keys fitted across the darkness into a self-repairing chromophore lock originally built of bacterial protein. The night filled with invisible information, some of it sent to other reception sites, farther relays, terminals in other states. There was nothing Lizzie could do about that; security systems, by their nature, alerted other systems. But the air shimmered briefly, and the Y-energy security shield dissolved.

In ten seconds it had reset itself into other codes, other patterns.

Lizzie and Vicki, carrying their sacks, had already run across the rough grass and through the information failure.

It was all done in silence. No floodlights came on, no alarms sounded. Factories were fully automated, managed by systems based in distant enclaves, which the owners could consult and direct. Or not.

The first security 'bot skimmed toward the two women almost immediately, terrifyingly fast, a soundless metal shape speeding over the grass. Vicki pointed her EMF disrupter at it and it stopped, sank to the grass, and fell over. Vicki laughed, a little too wildly. "Die, impudent upstart!"

"Come *on!*" Lizzie urged. She scrambled a second security 'bot and raced for the factory doors.

They had locked, of course, when the Y-shield went down. Lizzie punched in the manual overrides, and held her breath. It had taken months to dip the TenTech security data, and even though she could do anything, somehow she had never quite found the resets for the manual overrides if the security breach had automatically reset them. She hoped that meant there weren't any resets, that the designers were so arrogant or so cheap they'd gone with faith that the complex Y-system was enough, that no one could breach it. Except, of course, Sanctuary, who had no reason to try.

Sanctuary, and Lizzie Francy.

The doors opened, and Lizzie took a precious moment to squeeze her eyes shut in a brief prayer of thanksgiving to a God she didn't believe in. Billy's God, her mother's God. Lizzie didn't need Him. She'd done it.

Actually *done* it—broken into a donkey factory where energy cones were manufactured, to steal enough of them to take her tribe through the winter. They had everything else they needed, since the Change. A plastic polymer tarp for the feeding grounds. Water that no longer had to be clean. An abandoned soy-processing factory from before the Change, with more than enough space to house their tribe. A weaving 'bot that could easily turn out enough clothes and blankets for everyone, even young people whose bodies ate clothes fast. But they had no Y-cones, and winter in the Pennsylvania hills was cold. Now that donkeys no longer shipped things like cones and blankets in exchange for votes, tribes just had to take care of themselves. Nobody else would.

Lizzie opened her eyes. Another security 'bot darted from an alcove, and she zapped it with the disrupter. Hidden monitors were of course recording the break-in, but both she and Vicki were enveloped in head-to-foot holosuits. To the monitors, Lizzie appeared to be a twelve-year-old blonde girl eight months pregnant. Vicki was a red-headed male donkey dressed in a business suit. And all the infrared detectors would get were two heat patterns of human shape, female gender, a certain size and mass and metabolism—but not a certain identity.

It was so easy! Dart in, stuff seven or eight cones from the end of the line into their sacks, run back outside to wait for her equipment to fire a second laser array and bring down the shield for another ten seconds, dart back out. Pretty good for a Liver brat! She ran down the short corridor to the factory floor, her belly swaying from side to side like a bonga rhythm.

And stopped dead, in front of a place gone mad.

Two forklifts rolled across the floor. One lifted, stacked, sorted, and removed nothing at all—batches of empty air. The other carried a single packing case to the end of the robotic line, placed it there, received empty energy cones, carried the same case to the center of the factory and dumped the cones out. Then the forklift rolled through them, sending them clattering over the floor, while it carried the empty case back to the end of the line. The case was dented in a hundred places, folded in at one corner, missing both sealing flaps. It looked as if it had been through a war. On the line itself, robotic arms lifted the delicate cone innards fed to them from the sealed cold-fusion unit—and missed stuffing the power packs into the cones by six inches. The packs, crushed, dropped to the side of the line. The empty cones sailed on, to the waiting demented forklift at the end, which packed, transported, and spilled them before going back for more.

Vicki said, "What . . ."

"The ranging algorithms are messed up," Lizzie said, with great disgust. "God, the *waste* . . . your owner friends must only check the output figures, not the quality control or even the—Vicki, it's not funny!"

"Of course it is!" Vicki said. She doubled over with laughter, barely able to get the words out. "It's . . . hysterical. The high-tech donkey world . . . it looks like a 'bot Holy War on Endorkiss . . . and . . . that stuffed shirt Jackson . . . Aranow . . ."

"We only have a few more minutes, and we need cones! Help me find the cones packed before this all went diseased, it can't have been going on that long . . ."

"No? Look . . . at the dust on everything!" And she was off again, holding her belly, laughing like some crazy in a bedlam holo. Sometimes it seemed to Lizzie that *she* was the adult and Vicki, with her weird donkey humor, was the child. Then, other times, Vicki became the woman Lizzie remembered from her childhood: scary, knowing, poised, a being from that other world that ran the world. Why couldn't people be as easy to dip as systems? Lizzie jabbed Vicki in the shoulder.

"Come on! Help me look!"

Vicki did. The two women raced to the packing crates stacked by one of the forklifts before (when?) they went crazy. Fortunately, the sealer 'bot must have malfunctioned as well: none of the crate flaps were fastened, which made it easier to yank them open. The first crate on the top tier was empty. So was the second. The third was stuffed with crushed energy packs, smeared against and around cone casings like smashed yolk on unsmashable eggshells. Lizzie marveled. What could have messed up the programming this bad?

"Vicki—time is running out! The laser array only fires once more, resets are paired but the next pair is random-generated, I couldn't program for it—"

"Here!" Vicki said, no longer laughing. "This crate is good. Grab three or four cones—go! Go!"

They stuffed cones into their sacks, then ran for the corridor, dodging rolling empty cones from the forklift. At the corridor's end, the factory doors were closed.

"What—Lizzie! They locked automatically!"

Lizzie clawed at the manual override, punching in various standard "open doors" codes. Nothing happened. The security system had reset the door closings, but not the openings. It made sense. If the shield was breached, let whoever had breached it go in—but not out.

Vicki said, "Can you get in and get the code?"

"Not before the shield collapses. That happens right . . . now."

Lizzie slumped against the door. Slowly her body sank to the floor, like a rag doll, the sack of precious Y-cones clutched in her arms. She hadn't done it, after all. She had failed—she, Lizzie Francy!—and now Vicki and she were trapped inside the cone factory, an impenetrable foamcast building. And even if they could get out of the building, they were stuck inside a ten-foot dirt moat around that building by a Y-energy shield that no molecule larger than air could get through. Trapped.

"Vicki," she whispered, and she wasn't the girl-genius datadipper, she was a scared seventeen-year-old girl clutching at an adult, "Vicki—what are we going to *do*, us?"

"We're going to wait," Vicki said matter-of-factly. She settled down beside Lizzie, her back also to the door. "Until somebody shows up."

Lizzie reached out one hand to a patch of floor just beyond the door. She scraped her finger across the foamcast. It came up dusty.

"And how long you think it's been, you, since anyone was here, them?" She heard her speech sound Liver again, the way it did when she was upset. She hated that.

Vicki said, "Someone will come to check on the security breach. Some tech supervisor dispatched by TenTech. The dust isn't significant—it doesn't mean no one ever comes. The whole air filter system could have blown at the same time as the rest of the 'bots, and spewed all its accumulated dust back in again."

Lizzie frowned. Arguing made her feel less hopeless. "But the 'bots been malfunctioning, them, for a long while. Look at all them ruined cones . . ."

"Not that long. We found the whole cones in the top tier of crates, remember."

"And how do we know, us, that these cones even work?" Lizzie demanded. She sat up straighter, hauled one out of her sack, and turned it on. Immediately it radiated heat. She switched it to light, then both at once. "It works."

"Well, good."

"Maybe whoever comes will let us keep these few cones."

Vicki just looked at her. The hopeless feeling washed back over Lizzie again. No, of course they wouldn't let her keep the cones. They were donkeys. They would arrest her and Vicki for breaking in, and stealing, and whatever else they decided to, and Lizzie and Vicki would go to jail. Her baby would be born in jail. And the tribe wouldn't have heat after all for the winter, and so would have to migrate south, like most other tribes had already done. Well, that wouldn't be so bad, the weather was warm in the south and there weren't so many people left after the awful Change Wars that there wasn't room . . . but Lizzie's mother and Billy wouldn't go. Not if Lizzie were in jail here in the north. Would it be up here? Sometimes they sent people to distant prisons. The donkey cops could send her anywhere.

She said miserably, "They still control us, them, don't they? Despite the Change. And the Cell Cleaner. And . . . everything."

Vicki didn't answer. She just sat there, a renegade donkey herself, living with Livers, watching the insane forklift lift and transport and stack empty air while damaged cones rolled past and clattered into corners.

They waited all night, sleeping a few hours on the factory floor. Toward morning a cone rolled into Lizzie and nudged her from fragmented dreams into fragmented wakefulness. She shoved the cone away and considered disabling the forklift. But why bother? She curled up tighter around the still-unfamiliar mass of her swollen belly. The factory floor was cold. Beside her, Vicki snored gently, but Lizzie couldn't make sleep return.

She sat up. During the night more of her tunic had disappeared. The belt she wore tied under it, now riding high over her belly, was made of a nonorganic synthetic from before the Change. From it hung a pouch of the same material, holding her tools. If only she had a tunable lasersaw! A lasersaw would have cut them out of here in no time. But only donkeys had lasersaws. That had been true even during the Change Wars, when there'd been warehouse looting and fighting and what Vicki called "the monumental civil upheaval of a dying order." Donkeys stayed in their impenetrable enclaves, and their lasersaws stayed right in there with them. Besides, a lasersaw wouldn't get them through the outer security shield. Nothing but a nuclear weapon shattered that kind of Y-shield.

The factory lights had stayed on all night. Probably they were programmed to do that whenever the building detected human presence. In the soft glow the 'bots performed busily, doing everything wrong. Stupid machines.

But no stupider than Lizzie had been, her.

As long as she could remember, Lizzie had felt to herself like two people. One of them had always been asking questions, pestering her mother and Billy and later Vicki, tearing through the pathetic educational software at school, taking 'bots apart whenever she could, listening, listening, listening. There was so much she wanted to *know*. And until Vicki and the Change, no way to find it out. So when Vicki Turner had left the enclaves and come to live with Livers and given Lizzie a good terminal and crystal library, there was everything to learn. Lizzie—one of the two Lizzies—grew almost frantic, working the terminal every waking minute, trying to make up for lost time. And when she had—when she'd first learned how to use the Net, and then how to master it, and finally how to dip it for any information she wanted, anywhere—when she'd learned all that, it was like she was drunk. Drunk with power, drunk with doing. She'd designed the weaving 'bot for the tribe, and dipped unshielded warehouses until she found all the necessary parts to build it, and located the abandoned factory for their winter home, and gotten pregnant by a boy she'd never see again and didn't need to. Lizzie Francy had decided she wanted a baby, just like she'd decided she wanted a weaving 'bot, so she got it. She could do that, she could do anything, and nobody better tell her otherwise, them!

But every minute, underneath, there was this whole other Lizzie that nobody saw. Who was scared all the time. Who knew she was going to mess up eventually, it was only a matter of time. And then everybody would know that she was really a fake, and couldn't do anything right, and didn't belong. This second Lizzie was frightened to datadip important corporations like TenTech, and afraid that once her baby was born she wouldn't be able to take good enough care of it, and terrified that Vicki and Billy and her mother would somehow go away and leave her all alone. Alone with a baby. Which two other girls her age in the tribe, Tasha and Sharon, managed just fine, but which Lizzie Francy couldn't. Because Lizzie—this other Lizzie—only wanted to curl up in a ball and stop being the person a whole tribe looked to for answers stolen from a Net she didn't really own after all. Donkeys owned it. Just like they always had.

Sitting with her back against the cold foamcast wall, watching 'bots destroy Y-cones, she suddenly couldn't take the two Lizzies inside. Both making her throat tight and her head hurt. *I can do anything! I can't do anything right!* Both pressing on her chest. She had to get up, get away from them both.

She left Vicki sleeping. Vicki looked beautiful sleeping—she always looked beautiful. Genemod. Lizzie would never look like that. She was too short and her chin looked funny and her wiry black hair stuck out in all directions because she pulled at it while she was dipping. But Vicki was asleep and Lizzie wasn't, so it was up to her to *do* something about their situation. Something, anything.

Restlessly she prowled the perimeter of the huge room, where fewer cones rolled underfoot. Past the main doors, that she had spent a futile hour last night trying to dip. Past the panel over the narrow air-filter ducts, which Vicki had pried open. The air-filter system had indeed blown with the rest of the programming. Lizzie's bare feet smeared dirty tracks on the floor.

But then on the far wall she noticed something that, in her exhaustion and discouragement, she'd missed last night. Eight feet up from the floor, a metal panel about a yard square, the exact color of the gray foamcast wall.

Not storage, not way up there. Not the sealed Y-energy housing; that was clearly marked and anyway impenetrable. This panel didn't look impenetrable, at least not from down here. Small bolts secured each corner.

Lizzie stalked the second forklift, busily lifting and sorting and packing empty air. When it rolled to a stop at the end of the assembly line for another nonexistent load, she climbed aboard its flat squat motor housing. It took her three minutes to reprogram the machine to carry her to the wall, lift her up seven feet, and stand motionless while she unbolted the nearly invisible panel, putting the bolts in her pouch. The panel, made of some light alloy, she set carefully behind her on her metal pedestal.

Behind the panel lay a foamcast indentation shaped like a squared funnel. About four feet deep, it narrowed at the far end to a square only eight or ten inches. The indentation hadn't been on the building plans Lizzie had dipped while planning this raid. At the end of the funnel was another bolted panel.

She leaned into the indentation. But she couldn't quite reach the small panel, especially over the awkward bulge of her belly. She heaved herself into the opening and crawled forward.

These bolts wouldn't unscrew. If only she had a lasersaw! Doggedly she worked the bolts, but they wouldn't loosen. Yet they weren't nano-fitted; the building was sixteen years old, too old for most nanotech.

Finally, in frustration, Lizzie whacked the panel with the butt of her screwdriver. "Damn it all to stinking hell!" Billy's favorite oath.

"Awaiting instruction," the panel said.

She stared. She'd never even considered that the thing might be a screen or voice-activated. Stupid, stupid. What if she'd damaged it by her pounding?

"Awaiting instruction," the panel repeated.

"Run test sequence." Find out what she was dealing with.

"Running test sequence."

The lights in the factory turned off. Five seconds, ten, then back on. Next the noise of the robotic line ceased—a silence shocking as an explosion. Before the din started again she heard Vicki yell, "Hey! Lizzie?"

Lizzie, intently studying the small screen, didn't answer. Elation ballooned in her. It was running the entire sequence—including the outer security shield. She knew what it was now. Part of the backup system, minimally accessible from the outside of the building for safety control but physically unreachable by any of the line 'bots—which, as Lizzie had just demonstrated, were all too easy to reprogram. Some of the old-style factory systems had experimented with all sorts of weird redundancies to take physical control back from mischievous disablers. If she could dip this auxiliary system, she could control the Y-shield from here.

And she *would* be able to dip the system. She was the unbeatable Lizzie Francy.

"Repeat test sequence," she said, intending to call out to Vicki at the next silence. But right after the lights check, the little wall panel blanked. Then it flashed, without vocals, TEST SEQUENCE ABORTED. 65-B.

65-B. A standard industrial code for a microwaved master signal from a supervising, physically present source outside all systems. It was a common fail-safe for any process involving radiation. The entire operation could be halted by the right signal from a handheld remote at close range. Donkeys had arrived at the factory.

Lizzie backed out of her cramped hole eight feet above the floor. Her feet felt for the metal platform of the forklift. It wasn't there.

Frantically she twisted her pregnant body until she faced outward. The forklift had rolled three feet away from the wall, probably as part of the machinery test sequence. Balancing precariously, Lizzie stretched out both arms full-length. She could just grasp the edge of the alloy panel resting on the forklift's raised platform. But the panel wasn't fastened to the forklift itself, and she couldn't use it to pull the machine forward. And then suddenly the forklift came to life again and started to roll toward the line, returning to its normal work, and Lizzie was left with the alloy panel dangling from her fingers eight feet above the floor.

Below, the demented nonwork continued: 'bots assembled Y-energy works and then smashed them against misaligned cones; cone shells rolled across the floor; forklifts stacked air. From behind a pile of packing crates Vicki raced into view, yelling something over the din. Probably Lizzie's name. And then the main doors, on the adjacent factory wall, sprang open and two donkeys walked in, a man and a woman, with drawn guns.

Immediately, not even thinking about it, Lizzie pulled the alloy panel back into place, holding it from the inside with her fingernails. Heart hammering, she cowered high inside the foamcast wall.

INTERLUDE

TRANSMISSION DATE: November 4, 2120
TO: Selene Base, Moon
VIA: Toledo Enclave Ground Station, GEO Satellite C-1494 (U.S.), Satellite E-398
    (France)
MESSAGE TYPE: Unencrypted
MESSAGE CLASS: Class D, Public Service Access, in accordance with Congressional Bill
    4892-18, May 2118
ORIGINATING GROUP: "Roy L. Spath's tribe," Ohio
MESSAGE:

Mother Miranda! Blessed are the poor in spirit, them, for theirs is the Kingdom of
    Heaven! We are the poor, us, and we beg you for mercy! You gave us God's
    gift, you, with them Change syringes, and we honor you! Blessed are thou
    amongst women! You gave us freedom from the Horsemen of Famine and
    Pestilence, and so now we ask you, us, for freedom from Death! Give us this day
    our immortal life, and send syringes that can Change us to live like you do,
    forever and ever world without end amen! Pray for us, you, that we have no
    hour of death! Thank you!

ACKNOWLEDGMENT: None received

Three

Fifty miles from Willoughby, Cazie said, "The factory security shield's down."

Jackson glanced at his ex-wife, her face intent on the screen of her handheld mobile. The aircar flew on automatic and he had been half-asleep, secretly pleased with his ability to doze in her presence. That meant her effect on him was lessening—didn't it? Or maybe it just meant he wasn't used to being awake and in the air at 6:29 in the morning. In the east the sky was lightening, and in the pearly light Cazie's profile looked pure and luminous. Theresa would say Cazie looked like a saint. At this thought, Jackson snorted.

She said, "You don't believe me? Look for yourself." She thrust the mobile at him.

He thrust it back. "I believe you. The program must be malfunctioning. Nobody can break into a Y-shielded factory."

"God, Jackson, your faith in technology is touching. Especially for a scientist. The program is *not* malfunctioning. The shield went down for a thirty-second manually controlled test sequence. Not only that, it went down last night as well, that time triggered by an outside system with the proprietary aircar signal. I wonder why they collapsed the shield entirely, instead of just opening a car passage?"

"Nobody has the proprietary signal but you and me and the chief tech. Who, you told me, is in the Mexico complex this week."

"He is. Somebody must have dipped the data banks. God, that dipper must be good. Maybe we can hire him. He's in there now."

"In there *now?*"

"Two human bodies recorded on infrared," Cazie said. She was smiling, presumably at the drama. In the face of her enjoyment, Jackson felt ashamed to say he wasn't keen on confronting two possibly armed intruders. Who were probably crazy. What could anybody want inside a cone factory? Cones were cheap; TenTech shipped all over the northeast (or so Cazie had told him); no donkey would break in just for the hell of it. Except kids, of course. It must be hotshot kids, counting datadipping coup.

He said, "What are they doing in there?"

"Jackson, infrared scans aren't detailed enough to show what people are *doing*. I thought doctors were supposed to be good at machines."

"I'm good at the machines I need to be good at. They don't happen to include factory robotics."

"Well," said Cazie sweetly, "maybe you should broaden your horizons."

Jackson folded his arms and resolved to say no more. Cazie could always make him feel like a fool. Well, this was her party. Let her run it.

She opened a passage through the shield for their aircar. His laser signal lit up the bioelectronic receiver high on the factory facade. The car landed on the ground in front of the main doors.

"Locked," Cazie said, with relish. "There's an off-line security redundancy. Evidently our young dippers aren't *that* good."

"Ummmmmm," Jackson said, noncommittally.

She reached inside her shirt, a nonconsumable synthetic, and drew out two pistols. Grinning, she handed one to Jackson, who took it with what he hoped was lofty indifference. He didn't like guns. Did Cazie remember that? Of course she did. Her IQ was genemod. She seldom forgot anything.

"Okay," she said, "let's reclaim the Alamo."

"You shoot anybody and I'll bring charges against you myself. I swear it, Cazie."

"Good old Jackson. Champion of the underdog. Even when the underdog is overprivileged kids guilty of criminal trespass. Come on, let's go."

She unlocked the doors and strode down the corridor. Jackson hurried to catch up with her, so it wouldn't look as if he was cowering behind. At the factory floor he stopped. The whole place had gone crazy. Robots malfunctioning, debris all over the floor . . . how long had this been going on? Why hadn't the chief tech picked it up?

Cazie laughed. "Jesus Christ, look at it! Just look at it!"

"It's not—"

"Funny? Of course it is. Wait . . . look over there."

A man raced toward them. Jackson's grip tightened on his gun, until he saw the man wasn't armed. Then he saw it wasn't even a man, but a woman or boy dressed in a head-to-toe holosuit of a man dressed in a brown business suit. The figure spotted them and stopped running.

Cazie raised her gun. "Come here. Slowly, and with your hands high in the air. Now."

The figure put his hands over his head and walked slowly forward.

"Now turn off the holosuit," Cazie said. "One hand only, moving slowly."

The button was at his waist. The holosuit vanished and Jackson saw not the college kid he'd expected but a woman in her thirties, genemod, dressed in a skimpy homespun eaten into fresh-looking holes. Tall, violet eyes, small nose . . . Jackson was good with faces. "I know you! We met years ago someplace . . . at some party . . . Diana Something."

"Not anymore," the woman said sourly. "Look, Jackson, this is all lovely and social, but if you'll excuse me, I've got a crisis on my hands just now."

Cazie laughed. Her dark eyes shone with malicious pleasure. "You certainly do. Criminal trespass. How'd you pull it off? You don't look like a dipper."

"I'm not. But my friend is, and she's lost someplace in here . . . she's just a kid."

"Ah, a kid after all," Cazie said. "Well, let's find her." She did something with her mobile and all activity in the factory ceased. Robots froze in midmotion. The noise cut off. In the silence, Cazie yelled, "Yoo hoo, Diana's young friend! Come out, come out, wherever you are! Allee allee oxen free!"

Diana smiled; Jackson had the impression it was in spite of herself. No one answered.

Cazie said casually, "Is your friend armed?"

"Only with hubris," Diana said, and for half a minute Jackson wasn't sure which of them had spoken. It was something Cazie might have said. Then Diana called, "Lizzie! Where are you? It's all right, Lizzie, come on out. We're not going to gain anything by postponing the inevitable. Lizzie?"

No answer.

"Lizzie!" Diana called again, and this time Jackson heard the note of fear. "This is Vicki! Come on out, honey!"

Behind them, something clattered to the floor. Jackson turned. Eight feet up the wall, a hole had appeared, framing a scared brown face and crouching body. The girl had wiry black hair sticking out in all directions. She looked about fifteen. And she wasn't the donkey college dipper he'd expected; she was a Liver.

"Good God," Cazie muttered.

Diana/Vicki—what the hell was her name?—called, "Lizzie? How did you get up there?"

"Programmed the forklift," the girl said. Her voice was less scared than her face. Bravado? She glared at the three below her. "Send it back over."

Nobody moved. Jackson saw that none of them knew how to do that—even Cazie could only manipulate the commands she knew, not reprogram on the spot. How come this girl could? A Liver?

Cazie put her mobile and gun in her pocket, walked over to the closest motionless forklift, and pushed it. Her face turned red; the machinery barely budged. Diana/Vicki and Jackson joined her. Together they hauled the cumbersome thing to under the hole in the wall. Nobody spoke. Through his annoyance Jackson suddenly felt weird—the three donkeys performing manual labor in the silent factory to rescue a criminal Liver. The whole situation was surreal.

He suddenly thought of something Theresa had once said to him: *I never feel anyplace is really normal.*

"Okay," Diana/Vicki said when the forklift was against the wall, "come on down, Lizzie. And for God's sake be careful."

The girl was facing outward. Carefully she turned herself in the narrow cubbyhole. As her bottom came into view, Jackson saw that she was mostly naked. Of course Livers didn't seem to care that their bodies consumed their clothes, at least not the Livers who'd grown up since the Change. When they didn't wear pre-Change synthetic jacks, they went half-naked in their wandering "tribes." Sometimes it seemed to Jackson that Miranda Sharifi had reversed evolution, turning a stationary industrial population back into hunter-gatherer nomads. Who neither hunted nor gathered—at least, not food.

The girl in the wall stretched out her legs, feeling with her feet for the forklift behind her. She extended her body full-length, unrolling from the cubbyhole like a printout, and Jackson saw that she was heavily pregnant.

"Careful," Diana/Vicki repeated.

As the girl's toes touched the forklift, it began to roll away from the wall. No other machinery in the factory resumed operations.

Cazie grabbed for the forklift and tried to shove it back against the wall. After a moment of shock the other two sprang forward to help. It was too late. The forklift rolled back to its pointless duties as if the humans weren't there. The girl screamed and tumbled eight feet to the foamcast floor.

She landed on her right arm. Jackson dropped beside her and restrained her from moving. His voice was level and calm. "Cazie, get my bag from the car. Now."

She went immediately. Jackson said, "Don't move. I'm a doctor."

"My arm," the girl said, and started to cry.

Jackson checked her pupil reaction: both pupils round, the same size, equally reactive to light. He didn't think she'd hit her head. The arm was a compound radial fracture, the bone sticking whitely through the skin.

"It hurts, me . . ."

"Just lie still, you'll be fine," Jackson said, more confidently than he felt. He put a hand on her abdomen. The fetus kicked back, and he breathed out in relief.

Cazie returned with his bag. Jackson slapped a pain patch on the girl's neck and almost instantly her face relaxed. The patch was a potent mixture of pain-nerve blockers, endorphins, and the highest legally allowable dose of pleasure-center stimulators. Lizzie began to grin idiotically.

He palpated her arm and asked her to shift her shoulders through a range of motion. She could. Her other limbs were undamaged. He bioscanned her neck, spine, and internal organs: no damage. The portable trauma unit imaged the fracture, guided the two pieces into alignment, and sprayed instacast from elbow to wrist and between two fingers for anchor. Jackson rocked back on his heels.

That was it. The cast, Cell Cleaner, and the girl's own body would do the rest.

"Lizzie . . ." Diana/Vicki said, reminding Jackson that she was there. Her voice broke. Jackson looked at her. He had no idea what the relationship between them was, but on the older woman's face was naked fear and love. It gave him a little shock. Could the girl be her daughter . . . an ungenemod Liver? From before the Change? It didn't seem likely.

"Lizzie, are you all right?"

"Of course she's not all right, her arm's broken," Cazie said tartly, at the same moment that Jackson said with professional soothing, "Everything's under control." Diana/Vicki swept them both a look of scorn.

"Lizzie, honey?"

Cazie said sarcastically, " 'Diana, honey'? You have some explaining to do here, both of you. Public records show you changed your name to 'Victoria Turner.' It doesn't say what you're doing trespassing in my factory."

Vicki, who'd been kneeling beside the dreamy girl, stood up and faced Cazie. Vicki was taller, older, wilder-looking in her eaten Liver tunic and cropped, sleep-matted hair. Her jaw hardened, and Jackson had the sudden impression that she had faced challenges that he couldn't imagine. There was a nasty lift to her eyes as she squared off with Cazie.

To Jackson, it looked like an even match.

"What I'm doing 'trespassing in your factory,' " Vicki said distinctly, "is seeing that an entire tribe doesn't freeze this winter. Not that I would expect that to concern you."

"You have no idea what does or does not concern me," Cazie said coolly. "What should concern *you* is felony charges. Breaking and entering, criminal trespass."

"Oh, I'm terrified. Look, Cazie Sanders, how long is your kind going to—"

" 'My' kind? Unlike you, I suppose?"

"—going to go on blind to what's happening all around you? The easy answers are over. No more trade goods, colored beads and energy cones, in return for the votes that keep your kind in power."

"Oh, my God, recycled Marxism," Cazie said scornfully. "Seize the means of production, right? And you two are the advance army."

"I don't think—"

"That's obvious. Who are you, anyway? Some renegade donkey gone native among the Livers to feed her own ego? A white goddess among the savages, hmmm? Pathetic."

Vicki looked at Cazie a long time. Her face changed. Then she said quietly, "Who am I? I'm the person who led the Genetic Standards Enforcement Agency to arrest Miranda Sharifi. And then led the citizen legal fight to free her."

It was the first time Jackson had ever seen Cazie at a disadvantage. Her small vivid face registered shock, disbelief, reluctant acceptance. Something about Vicki Turner compelled belief—the way she stood with her feet braced wearily apart, as if she'd been resisting strong winds a long time. Or the way she stood guard over Lizzie, lying on the floor in a glowing stupor from Jackson's painkillers. Or maybe just Vicki's face, full of a complex regret. Not the expression Jackson would have expected.

Vicki said quietly, "We still need Y-energy. It's the only thing we do need from you. And we'll try to take it, and you'll try to stop us, and a lot more lives will be lost in the process. Just as in the Change Wars. Lives that might have gone on, with the Cell Cleaner, for a hundred years. You have the weapons, the enclaves, the sophisticated electronic security systems you've never let Livers learn. But they *are* learning, Cazie Sanders. I didn't datadip your system—*Lizzie* did. There are a lot of young Lizzies out there, learning more every day. And we have the numbers on our side. There are ten of us for every one of you."

She had said it—every donkey's nightmare. The fear that rested under the frantic parties and disdainful fashions and stupid time-wasting social competition: *Don't look behind you. They may be gaining on us. There are a lot more of them than us.*

"And you know the worst part?" Vicki said, still in that quiet deadly voice. "You can't even see it. Not from stupidity, God knows. From willful blindness, for which you are going to deserve exactly the price you end up paying."

"Oh, God, spare me the melodramatic rhetoric," Cazie said. She had recovered from the unexpectedness of Vicki's attack. "The law is perfectly clear. And you're in violation of it."

To Jackson's surprise, Vicki smiled. "Law only works if the majority agree to let it. Don't you know that? No, of course you don't. You're a simple binary code. On for your own interest, off for everybody else. You could be dipped by a child. And you were."

Cazie said angrily, "Ad hominem sophistry isn't argument."

"You're not a hominem. You're not even a synonym. You're redundant code in the human information, and you're already obsolete."

The woman was *playing.* Standing there, laughing at his ex-wife, this ragged renegade was playing with Cazie, with the situation. How much self-assurance did it take to play like that? Or was it not self-assurance but self-righteousness? Suddenly Jackson wasn't sure he could recognize the difference.

Cazie said, "Defiant words. Not power." She keyed her mobile, and a security 'bot came to life. It lifted itself off the littered factory floor and sped toward them. A faint shimmer marked the edges of the energy bubble it threw over Vicki.

"You are intruding on TenTech private property," the 'bot droned. "You are being held immobile until further instruction."

Vicki went on smiling. Jackson saw Cazie's face darken.

"You are intruding on TenTech private property. You are being held—"

"Shut it off," Jackson said, before he knew he was going to. Both women looked at him; it was clear that, absorbed in their battle, they'd forgotten he was there. Cazie smiled and keyed her mobile; the 'bot stopped reciting.

"No," Jackson said. "I meant—turn it off completely. We're not arresting her."

"Oh, yes, we are," Cazie said.

Reaction welled up in Jackson, a gush of pure hormones he couldn't label. Or didn't want to. It poured out in a single sentence, which even as he said it, he knew didn't mean what the words said: "You don't run TenTech."

She said, "That's exactly what I do. Who else? You? You never even look at the financial dailies, let alone the operational data. Leave this to me, Jack. Stick to your medical knowledge."

His obsolete medical knowledge, she meant. Baiting him again, but this time not affectionately, which meant she felt cornered. Cazie cornered. Suddenly he loved the idea.

"I'm not leaving this to you, Cazie. I'm overruling you. Turn off the security bubble."

She keyed her mobile. The 'bot started to move toward the entrance. Vicki, encased in the shimmering hollow energy field as if in a translucent box, was carried along toward the factory doors.

"Cazie. Turn the 'bot off."

"Bring that stuffed and trussed child, Jack. We're leaving."

"Turn it off. I own TenTech, not you."

"We each own a third of TenTech," she said evenly. The 'bot continued to move toward the door, encapsulating Vicki.

Jackson said, "I'm voting Theresa's third." And just like that, just that easily, he reached out and took the mobile from Cazie's hand before she knew he would. Or could.

"Give me that back!"

"No," he said, and gazed at her steadily, and saw the storm coming. Despite himself, his own blood surged. God, she was beautiful . . . the most desirable woman he'd ever seen. She grabbed for the mobile in his right hand. He gripped her upper arm with his left hand and held her off easily. Why hadn't he ever thought about how much stronger he was than Cazie? He should have gotten physically assertive with her years ago. His penis stiffened.

"I. Said. Give. Me. That. Now."

"No," Jackson said, smiling. Damn, he didn't know the codes or he would turn it off himself. Well, he could figure it out. Or—strange thought—ask Lizzie. Cazie stood still, not struggling in his grip, her golden skin flushed with anger, the green-flecked eyes burning.

He had never felt such power over her.

Cazie bent her head toward his left hand, which was still clenched on her upper arm. Pain tore through him, surprising him into opening his fingers. Blood poured over them. She had bitten him. Below him, the girl on the floor said something.

"That's your trouble, Jackson," Cazie said. "You're never prepared for the counterattack."

Two long slashes slanted across the back of his hand. Clean slashes, not tooth-jagged, and deep. Cazie had retractable blades implanted between her teeth.

Venous blood pooled dark red on the floor beside Lizzie, who again said something. Jackson couldn't take it in. Was he going into shock? No, no light-headedness or nausea, and the wound wasn't serious. Cazie must be able to control the retraction of her blades. His shock was all emotional; no one was behaving consistently.

Including the girl on the floor. She looked up at him—dopey-eyed, in a smiling haze of neuropharms—from a sudden pool of water between her legs, and chuckled. "The baby's coming."

"Oh, Christ," Cazie said. "All right, you fly the girl back to her 'tribe,' and I'll stay here with Ms. Champion-of-the-Downtrodden until the cops arrive. There must be somebody in the Liver camp who can do whatever it is they do for childbirth."

"That someone is me," Vicki said, kneeling beside Lizzie, holding both her hands. Something in her tone moved Jackson. Or maybe he was moved by nothing more than his need to oppose Cazie on medical grounds, his only sure landscape.

"Ms. Turner's right, Cazie. She needs to stay with the girl."

"Charming maternal solicitude," Cazie said. "So what do you want me to do, Jackson, arrest them both?"

"Neither. Not until this is over."

"And you're just going to deliver a baby here on the factory floor."

"Of course not. She's not going to deliver for hours yet." Jackson's hands probed gently. And found that the baby was a breech.

The Change, he reflected grimly, had not reversed certain key aspects of human evolution. The birth canal was still considerably narrower than an infant head, and the cervix still not designed for anything but headfirst delivery. And Lizzie, prima gravida, was only eight months along.

Still, it could have been worse. Jackson's fetal dermalyzer showed a frank breech presentation—buttocks first, hips flexed, knees extended, feet up near the shoulders—rather than the more dangerous footling or complete breech. The head was flexed forward, ballottable in the fundal region. The fetus, a boy, weighed a viable 2800 grams, heart rate a steady 160, growth normal. The cord wasn't prolapsed, and the placenta wasn't previa; it would decently follow the birth, which, Jackson estimated, was still a few hours off. Although she was already five centimeters dilated. Halfway.

It could have been much worse.

"Lizzie," Jackson said, "I'm going to lift you. We're going to take you somewhere more comfortable."

"Which is where?" Cazie said. "You're not taking her—them—to the enclave!"

Lizzie said, without urgency, "I want to go home." She didn't look like a mother-to-be; she looked like a smiling, slumberous child. Jackson sighed.

"All right. We'll take you home. But, Lizzie, listen to me, I'm going to stay there with you. The baby is upside down—do you understand? I'm going to stay with you so I can rotate him at the proper times."

The girl looked up at him. In her drugged black eyes, Jackson was startled to see a flash of coherent relief. He had expected her to protest, however languorously, against having a donkey doctor attend her. Hadn't she grown up with mechanical medunits, when politicians still supplied those? But maybe Lizzie was different from most Livers, because of this Vicki Turner. Or maybe Jackson didn't know as much about Livers as he thought.

Cazie said, "You're just going to walk into a Liver camp with nothing but a pistol? Accompanying a criminal that I'm damn well going to have arrested?"

Jackson stood, lifting Lizzie in his arms. She could walk, but pulling her upright would hasten delivery. He didn't want to deliver a breech, even a frank breech, in an aircar. He faced Cazie. "Yes. That's exactly what I'm going to do. And you can come with me or not. Just as you choose."

Cazie hesitated. In that moment of her hesitation, Jackson felt a surge of hope. Was that actually respect in her eyes? For him? Whatever it was, it vanished.

"It's a two-person car, Jack."

He'd forgotten that. "All right . . . I'll take them both to their camp—three can squeeze into my car. You stay here and call for another car."

"I'll call for the cops, is what I'll do."

"Fine. Call for the cops. They can come to the camp, too. We'll have a party."

He carried Lizzie across the factory, now frozen except for the forklift Lizzie had reprogrammed, which went on lifting nothing. Had it resumed work because Lizzie had made an error? Maybe she wasn't as good a dipper as Vicki claimed. Or maybe Cazie's signal from the aircar had set up some kind of interference or override. Jackson didn't know enough about industrial systems to guess. Behind him he heard Cazie on her comlink. "Police emergency, code 655, damn it, Robert, answer me . . ."

Vicki sat on the passenger seat cradling Lizzie on her lap. Two half-naked women in tattered clothes, wet from Lizzie's burst water, hair matted, smelling of blood and sweat and dirt and amniotic fluid. It was close in the car.

Vicki had a mocking tendency to catch his thoughts. As the aircar lifted she said, "And when was the last time you played doctor to Livers, Doctor?"

He didn't answer. The car flew through the passage he opened in the security shield. Lizzie said dreamily, "Another one's coming. It's so weird, I feel it but I don't . . ."

Jackson looked at the aircar console. The interval between contractions had shortened: ten minutes. That *fast*. He speeded up. "Fly west," Vicki said. "Follow that river . . ."

The "camp" turned out to be an abandoned soy-processing factory. Only Livers had ever eaten soy; now no one did, and all the soy franchises had gone bankrupt. The building was windowed gray foam-cast, decayed and badly patched. All around stretched fields returning to weeds, bushes, saplings of maple and sycamore. Their scrawny branches were bare. Jackson had forgotten how ugly ungenemod nature was in November, especially in these high hills, or low mountains, or whatever they were.

He set the aircar down in front of the building's main door, which had fallen—or been torn—off its hinges, and then clumsily wired back on. Inside, Jackson knew, the machinery would have long since been removed for retooling. Or looted during the Change Wars. Or vandalized. Nothing was less necessary now than large-scale agriculture.

The moment the aircar landed, they were surrounded. The horde—it seemed like a horde, even though Jackson counted only eleven people—shoved their faces against the windows, grimacing. Dressed in warmer clothes than Vicki and Lizzie, they nonetheless looked primitive: old synthetic jacks in garish colors over or under woven tunics; ungenemod faces with a weak chin or low beetling brow or too broad forehead or small squinty eyes. An older man was actually missing a front tooth. And this was post-Change. What had these people looked like before the Cell Cleaner?

"Lizzie!"

"It's Lizzie and Vicki!"

"They're back, them."

"Lizzie and Vicki . . ."

Vicki said, "Release the door, Jackson." How had she come to be the one in charge?

The horde threatened to spill into the car itself. Vicki handed Lizzie out; the girl grinned dopily as her all-but-naked belly tightened in another contraction. Jackson made himself climb out the other door. A young man—large, heavy, strong—glared at him. A teenage boy scowled and clenched his fists.

Vicki said, "He's a doctor. Leave him alone, Scott. Shockey, you take Lizzie. Carry her carefully, she's in labor."

The boy said, "I don't care, me, if he's a doctor. What'd you bring one of *them* here for, Vicki? And where's the cones, them?"

"Because Lizzie needs him. We didn't get any cones."

The crowd made a subverbal noise Jackson couldn't interpret.

The inside of the building was dark—Jackson realized that the lights no longer worked, and the only illumination came from the plastic windows. It took his eyes a minute to adjust to the gloom. The room was large, although not as large as the Willoughby factory. Three sides of the perimeter had been divided into curtained cubicles made of shelving, of old furniture, of broken sections of foamcast, of dead and gutted machinery, even of roughly cut logs. Inside each cubicle were makeshift pallets and personal possessions. Through the south window Jackson saw a tent of clear flexible plastic, probably stolen, stretched four feet above the churned-up earth. A natural-light feeding ground.

In the open middle of the floor sprawled dilapidated sofas, chairs, tables, all surrounding a small portable Y-energy cone of the sort used on camping trips. This communal room was warmer than the outside, but nowhere near what Jackson thought of as room temperature.

Vicki said, "That's the only cone still working in the camp, and it's not designed for a space this big. Fires are problematic because it's so hard to ventilate properly through foamcast. Although we have a design for a Franklin stove, which is our auxiliary plan to TenTech cones. Meanwhile, we share the one cone we have. You, of course, would simply have had it seized by the richest family among you."

"You could have migrated south," Jackson retorted.

"Safer here. Everybody else is migrating south for the winter. We're not heavily armed."

"Ooohhhhhh," Lizzie said, in hazy appreciation. "Ooohhhhh . . . I feel another one coming . . ."

A handsome middle-aged black woman came running across the floor. "Lizzie! Lizzie!"

"It's all right, Annie," Vicki said. "Doctor, this is Lizzie's mother."

Lizzie's mother didn't even glance at him. She grabbed whatever portion of Lizzie, still carried in the enormous young man's arms, she could reach, and held on tight. "You bring her in here, Shockey— careful, you! She ain't no gunnysack, her!" Jackson saw Vicki smile, an unamused, turned-down smile. Some history between the two women. Three women. Shockey concentrated on maneuvering his swollen, limp, smiling burden into one of the sleeping cubicles.

Annie blocked the narrow passage with her ample body. "Thank you, Doctor, but you can leave now, you. We don't need no help, us, with our own. 'Bye."

"Yes, you do, Ms. . . . You do. It's going to be a breech birth. I have to rotate the fetus at the proper times to—"

"Ain't no fetus, it's a baby!"

Vicki said, "For God's sake, Annie, get out of the way. He's a doctor."

"He's a donkey, him."

"If you don't move, I'll move you myself."

Despite himself—the scowling boy had moved closer—Jackson felt a surge of impatience. Were Livers *always* threatening physical violence? It was tiresome. He said firmly, "Madam, *I* will move you if you don't let me at my patient."

"Why, Jackson," Vicki said, "I didn't know you had it in you." Her tone, so much like Cazie's, infuriated him. He pushed Lizzie's mother aside and knelt beside Lizzie, who lay smiling on her bed. A thin mattress of nonconsumable plastic, blankets of recycled plastic jacks. The only other furniture was a battered chest and a molded plastic chair that looked like it had once been used for target practice. The walls were hung with the kind of gaudy-colored metal-on-fake-wood art that Livers liked, depicting a scooter race on fluffy yarn clouds. On the bureau lay a Jansen-Sagura terminal and crystal library, of the kind used by the most well-funded scientists. Jackson blinked at it.

Lizzie's dark eyes were merry with cheating pain. "It don't hurt at all, me. When Sharon had *her* baby, she hollered, her . . ."

"No meds for Sharon," Vicki said. "No profit in it for donkeys."

Jackson said, "You people shouldn't have destroyed the warehouses."

"Why not? You people had stopped shipping to them."

He hadn't come here to argue politics with a renegade donkey. Jackson reached inside his bag. "What's that, it?" Annie said. She loomed over the bed like an avenging angel. A strong female odor came from her, musky and strangely erotic. Jackson thought about what it would have been like trying to maintain asepsis in these conditions. Before the Cell Cleaner.

"It's a local muscle-relaxant patch. To expand the vaginal opening as much as possible and prevent tearing before I do the episiotomy."

"No knife," Annie said. "Lizzie'll be just fine, her! You get out!"

Jackson ignored her. A hand gripped his shoulder and jerked him backward just as he applied the patch to Lizzie. Then Vicki grabbed Annie and the two women tussled until behind him Jackson heard a voice say, "Annie. You stop that, love."

Lizzie still smiled at Jackson in drugged serenity, while her enormous belly stretched and contracted, shuddering with fleshy quakes. She held his hand. Jackson turned to see a stately black man, at least eighty years old in the strong and healthy mode eighty had become, leading Annie firmly from the cubicle. Behind the retreating Annie stood a whole crowd of Livers, silent and hostile.

He turned back to Lizzie.

"What can I do?" Vicki said briskly.

"Nothing. Stay out of the way. Lizzie, turn on your left side . . . good."

It was another hour before he had to do the episiotomy. Through his quick, large cut—there would be no infant head out first to widen the passage—Lizzie smiled and hummed. The old man, Billy, had miraculously kept Annie quiet. There, but quiet.

"Okay, Lizzie—push." This was the drawback of the neuropharms swarming through her system. They were selected to not cross the placental barrier, but they vastly reduced Lizzie's need, or desire, to do anything as focused as pushing. "Come on, push . . . pretend you're shitting a pumpkin!"

Lizzie giggled. The baby's little ass presented itself, through his mother's blood. Jackson waited until the infant's umbilicus had passed the perineum, then grasped the baby's hips and applied downward traction until the scapulae appeared. Carefully he rotated the baby so its shoulders were anterior-posterior. When the shoulders were delivered, he rotated the squirming small body back, for a facedown delivery, the least likely to cause head trauma.

"Push again, Lizzie, harder . . . *harder* . . ."

She did. The baby's head finally squeezed out. No visible head trauma, good muscle tone, minimal ecchymosis and edema. Cradling the baby's soft wet buttocks in his hand, Jackson felt his throat suddenly tighten. He checked the child with his monitor and then laid him, slimed with blood and vernix, on his mother's chest. The cubicle was again full of people. Privacy was evidently not a Liver value. He delivered the placenta, cut the cord. And drew a Change syringe from his bag.

The entire crowd drew a collective breath: "Aaaahhhhhhhh . . . !" Jackson looked up in surprise.

Vicki said, in a voice completely different from any he'd heard from her, "You *have* one!"

"A Change syringe? Of course—" Then it hit him. "You don't. Outside the enclaves."

"Our birth rate is higher than yours," she said wryly. "And our supply less. When the syringes just stopped appearing a few years ago, you donkeys scavenged and stockpiled them all."

"So your children—"

"Get sick. Some, anyway. Could die. Don't you know armed battles are being fought over the remaining syringes?"

He did, of course. But watching it on the newsgrids was different from seeing this crowd eye the syringe hungrily, from feeling their tension, smelling their desperate avidity. He said quickly, "How many unChanged children are in your . . . your tribe?"

"None yet. But we only had one syringe left, for Lizzie. Next pregnancy . . . How many syringes have you got, Jackson?"

"Three more . . ." He almost added *with me,* saw his mistake in time. "You can have them."

He injected the baby, who predictably started yelling. Somewhere outside the cubicle, a man's voice said harshly, "Donkey cops here, them!"

Vicki smiled at him. The smile surprised him: frank, weary, and yet somehow comradely, as if his delivering Lizzie's baby and handing over the other syringes had changed things between Jackson and the Liver tribe. It took him a minute to realize the smile was a put-on. But she said softly, "You going to let that bitch arrest your patient, Jackson?"

Lizzie lay laughing maniacally over her baby—either the neuropharm company had put too much pleasure stimulant in the patch or Lizzie was especially maternal. The baby wailed loudly. People called and argued in the tiny space, some congratulating Lizzie, some threatening the cops (absurd—they'd be armed and shielded like fortresses), some demanding to know why there weren't new Y-cones. The smell of packed-in humanity was overwhelming. Jackson looked at Vicki's smile. He thought of Cazie's anger, her mockery of him.

Vicki said, under cover of the din, "You told Cazie that you vote two thirds of TenTech stock—yours and your sister's. You could drop the charges."

"Why would I want to do that?"

She merely waved her hand to indicate all of it: the baby, the cold room, the ragged Livers, the arguing, the cops he knew must be standing beyond the wall of people who were biologically impervious to disease and hunger but not to cold or violence or other people's greed. Suddenly he thought of Ellie Lester. Who thought that natives, second-class subjects, slaves—Livers—were ever so witty. Who thought that powerlessness was funny. Unlike Cazie, who merely thought it was boring.

"Yes," he said. "I'll drop the charges."

"Yes," Vicki echoed, and stopped smiling, her eyes narrowing as she regarded him closely, as if wondering what use it might be possible to make of him next.

Four

*T*oday, Theresa thought. *Today's the day.*

Lying in bed in the early morning, she felt the familiar dark cloud descend over her mind. Heavy, queasy, hopeless. "The black dog that doesn't let go," somebody from old times had called it. "The dark woods than which death is scarcely more bitter." That was "Dante"—she remembered that name. "The gnawing beast in the brain." She didn't remember that one. Thomas, her personal system, had found the quotes for her in some deebee, and now Theresa couldn't forget them. Dogs, beasts, woods, clouds—she had lived with the darkness for so long she no longer needed names for it, yet she had them. Like the fear itself.

But today the queasy fear wouldn't stop her. She wouldn't *let* it stop her. Today was the day.

"Take a neuropharm," Jackson always urged her. "I can prescribe . . . Tessie, it's an imbalance in brain chemistry. No different from diabetes or anemia. You right the chemistry. You *fix* it." And Theresa could never find the words to make him understand.

Because words weren't important. Action was. She had come to see that only recently. When she had realized it, a deep shame had swept over her. How could she have been so self-indulgent, so pampering of her own weak soul? It had been over a year since she'd even left the apartment . . . and she'd never left Manhattan East Enclave. Never, her whole life. No wonder she was what Jackson called "clinically depressed."

Today.

Jackson had gone with Cazie, very early, to check on a factory someplace. Theresa had heard him leave. She was uneasy whenever he left the apartment, but she tried very hard not to let him see that. It wouldn't be fair. Jackson already stayed home too much for her sake. Hovered over her, worried about her. *I can prescribe . . .* He worried about her, but he didn't understand. He didn't see what he called a "brain-chemistry imbalance" really was. Only Theresa knew what it really was.

It was a gift. Her soul's way of telling her that she had better change her ways and pay attention to what really mattered.

Theresa swung her feet over the side of the bed and waited for the daily anxiety to subside. If she let herself, she could stay in bed all day. It was so safe there. Instead, she walked into the sonar shower, took a thirty-second wash, and walked out again. In the bedroom she caught sight of herself naked in the long mirror on the west wall, and stopped.

She didn't even *look* like everybody else. Her body was beautiful, she supposed—everybody was beautiful. But she somehow looked . . . not there. Pale hair and eyes, pale small face, pale skin—what had her parents been thinking of? A fairy. A ghost. An insubstantial holo, fuzzy at the edges. No wonder she didn't belong anywhere, didn't know even a single person who could understand her struggle for what it really was. Not even Jackson, loving brother though he was.

Even Jackson thought that Theresa had been born wrong. That she'd been damaged somehow during her in vitro genemod. Even Jackson couldn't see the nature of the gift that Theresa had been handed. Because it *was* a gift, no matter what anyone said. Pain always was.

Pain meant that you had to change something, had to learn to think differently about the world. Seeds, Theresa imagined, felt tremendous pain when they burst their husks in the cold dark earth and began to push blindly toward a light they had never seen. Pain was what made you grow. No one seemed to understand that. Everyone she knew, as soon as they were in pain, did everything they could to make it go away. Medicine. Recreational drugs. Sex. Frantic parties. Which were all, when you got right down to it, the same thing. Distractions from pain. How come nobody else in this century thought like that? Only her.

"Each environment," Jackson had said once, in the slow, careful way he always talked to her, "rewards different personality profiles. Ours rewards vivaciousness, aggressiveness coupled with the appearance of not caring, a certain careless cruelty . . . you're not like that, Tess. You're a different kind of person. Not a worse kind, just different. It's all right to be different."

Yes, it was. But only because she'd come to believe that her differentness had a *point*. The black cloud in her brain, the fear of everything new, the attacks of anxiety so strong that she sometimes couldn't breathe—their point was to make Theresa break her lazy husk and push blindly toward the light. She believed that. Even though she'd never seen it and didn't know quite what she was pushing toward. Even though sometimes she despaired that the light was even there. But that was part of the gift, too. It made her question everything that happened around her, in case she missed a vital clue to what she was supposed to do next.

She hadn't told Jackson that part. He already worried too much about her, and he wouldn't understand anyway. That was actually funny—Jackson was the smart one, Theresa the one whose IQ modification hadn't quite worked. Certainly she'd never been very good at school software. But Jackson wouldn't understand that although he had been right about different personalities being rewarded in different cultures, he hadn't taken the idea far enough.

Theresa had. She'd spent thousands of hours at her terminal, slowly and laboriously sending Thomas to search through the history deebees. And she'd found the place that would have rewarded who she was: the Age of Faith.

She should have been born Catholic. In the late Middle Ages, when men and women had been honored for devoting their lives to the uses of pain in the service of spiritual growth. She would have belonged. To enter an abbey, to have a reason for a cloistered life, joined with others in constant prayer . . . But she had been born into an age when no one she knew even believed in God. Including her.

Tears filled Theresa's eyes. She dashed them away impatiently and moved away from the sight of her naked body in the mirror. It was stupid to cry. She had been born now, not then, and that must be part of the gift, too. She was meant to find another way, a different push toward the light she so often despaired of finding. And after months—years—of meditation and false starts, she had come to see what that way was.

She must go out.

Out of the apartment, out of the enclave. Jackson usually urged her not to watch the newsgrids because they made her feel so much worse, and until a few months ago Theresa had been glad to do what Jackson wanted. But lately she had watched holovid whenever Jackson wasn't home, and although most of the news had of course been about donkeys, there had been glimpses of Livers, too. Between the stock market reports and enclave politics and even an occasional national report from Washington, which nobody seemed to think anymore was anywhere near as important as internal enclave affairs. Just glimpses of Livers, and those Livers were suffering. Not from hunger—not that, ever again. But from lack of things like energy cones and decent clothing and replacement parts for terminals. While people like Theresa and Jackson and Cazie and those loathsome friends Cazie had brought by last night had more *things* than they knew what to do with. That's when shame had burned her.

And then Theresa had seen something on the holovid that made her know she was *meant* to go outside. There were Livers actually trying to organize into spiritual groups! And the news channel had shown where one of those groups was wintering. The holovid had been sneering, of course . . . but it had given district coordinates.

She dressed in one of her long, loose, flowered dresses. Theresa designed them herself, sending sketches and her measurements to a tailoring franchise that would still work in cotton. She found a warm coat—they didn't have weather voting, outside—and an old pair of boots. But then she hesitated.

What should she take to give them? Energy cones, yes—she'd already ordered a dozen on the TenTech account, and the mail 'bot had delivered them last week. Theresa hadn't understood the account very well. Usually Jackson took care of these things. She had used a "proprietary password" he'd once given her, but it must have been the wrong word because the system thought she'd wanted access to factory records. She'd mucked around in them awhile before realizing her mistake; she only hoped she hadn't caused malfunctions in any system anyplace. After she'd found the household accounts, though, she'd been able to figure out how to order what she wanted. It gave her an odd sense of power, which she immediately distrusted. "Pride goeth before a fall." Her mother used to say that.

Clothing. She should bring decent clothing. On the holovid the Livers wore these awful homespun things, or else jacks in truly terrible colors . . . but all her clothing was cotton or silk. That wouldn't do. The Livers were all Changed, of course. They needed nonconsumables.

She went into Jackson's room and looted his wardrobe. Shirts, pants, tunics, coats, farrells, shoes. He could always order more. And next trip she'd bring some nonconsumable women's clothes.

What else? Oh! Money, of course. But how did that work, for Livers? They didn't use money, or at least they hadn't, before the Change. They'd all had meal chips and ID cards and the politicians had given them everything free in exchange for votes. Nobody voted anymore, except for enclave elections. Well, of course not . . . that's why the Livers were in this position! They didn't have any money to buy the things they needed. So most of them just went south, where they didn't need heat or clothes, and fed out in the open, and got into stupid wars, and forgot civilization entirely. But not all of them. The ones Theresa was going to visit could surely use money. But how do you sign over credit to people who don't have accounts?

She'd bring a handheld terminal. A mobile. Maybe they had some sort of group account for the organization, or something. Or maybe she could figure out how to set up one in their name, but with access to some of her money. That shouldn't be too hard. People must set up accounts on the Net all the time. She could leave them the mobile.

She could do this. She really could. For the first time in her life, after so many false starts, she—Theresa Katherine Aranow—could actually be useful to something larger than herself.

The black cloud in her head didn't lift. But it lightened a little, and Theresa smiled.

On her way out, she passed her main terminal. It was on, holding a screen of her book about one of the first Sleepless, Leisha Camden. Another false start. Theresa knew she wasn't much of a writer; the book wasn't very good. But she had wanted to write about Leisha, that outsider from her own people who'd fought so hard to keep Sleepless and donkeys from splintering into two armed camps. Leisha had tried to keep the Sleepless from withdrawing into armed retreat in Sanctuary. She'd tried to keep Sleepers from boycotting all corporations invested in by Sleepless. She'd tried to keep Miranda Sharifi from the same kind of isolation that had driven Miranda's grandmother to treason.

Leisha had failed, at all of it. And then the Sleepless had engineered the SuperSleepless and everything got even worse. But Leisha had at least tried. What had driven Leisha, Theresa wondered, before she'd been murdered by outlaw Livers in a desolate Georgia swamp? Something must have driven Leisha. Some light she could see more clearly than Theresa had been able to do.

At the elevator to the roof, her arms filled with a load of Jackson's expensive and perfectly tailored clothes, Theresa hesitated. It was so hard to go outside. So many new things . . . what if she had an attack? Maybe if she first watched a Drew Arlen concert, the one about taking risks . . .

Drew Arlen, the Lucid Dreamer. There had been a period, several months long, during which Theresa had watched an Arlen concert two or three times each day. She'd let Arlen hypnotize her, with his subliminals and programmed graphic shapes that seized the unconscious mind, into a different kind of dreaming. Deep, personal, massaged into shape by Drew's art of mass hypnosis and universal symbols to which he seemed to have easy access. The dream became whatever the listener wanted it to be, needed it to be, and the dreamer awoke cleansed and stronger. Like any other temporary drug.

No. Not today. She was not going to watch a Drew Arlen concert today, not use it like just another neuropharm. She could do this alone. She could. Today was the day.

"Good morning, Ms. Aranow," the elevator said.

She let it swallow her.

"Why you doing this, you?"

"I wanted to . . . I saw you on the newsgrid. About your . . . the attempts you're making to . . ." Theresa took a deep breath. The man wasn't tall, but he was thick and bearded and sunburned and scowling. He stood too close to her. Three of them, two men and a woman, had run toward the car as soon as it landed, a respectful distance away from their building. What she hoped was a respectful distance. Her heart raced, and her breath snagged in her throat and wouldn't come out. Oh, not now, not *now* . . . She breathed deeply. The air outside was colder than she'd expected, and grayer. Everything out here—air, trees, ground, faces—looked cold and gray and hard.

Theresa turned to the woman. Maybe a woman would be easier. "I know you're trying to find . . . to do . . . the newsgrid said this was a 'spiritual experiment.' " What the newsgrid had actually said was a "quasi-spiritual attempt at a completely irrelevant human delusion."

The second man's face softened. He was younger, maybe Theresa's age, skinnier, unbearded. "You're interested, you, in our ways?"

"Don't be taken in, Josh," the woman said sharply. "She's donkey, her!"

"Let's see, us, who she is," said the first man. From his pocket he pulled a mobile—were Livers supposed to have those? "On. ID check. Aircar number 475-9886," followed by code authorizations. How did he know those?

The terminal said, "Car registered to Jackson William Aranow, Manhattan East Enclave." It added a citizen number and address. Theresa hadn't known those were public.

"I'm Theresa Aranow . . . Jackson's . . . sister." She tried to breathe normally.

"And you brought us supplies, you," the woman said. "Out of the goodness of your heart."

"Yes," Theresa whispered. "I mean, no, I don't think . . . I'm that . . . good . . ."

"You all right, you?" the younger man said. Josh. Theresa slumped against the car and he touched her arm. She flinched.

"I'm . . . yes. Fine."

"Josh, unload the supplies, you," said the other man. "Might as well have them, us."

Theresa made herself breathe normally. She had come this far. "Could I . . . please see what you're doing here? Not in exchange for the supplies, but just because I'm . . . interested?"

The woman said, "We don't need no spies, us," at the same moment that Josh said, "You really interested? In bonding?"

"Shut up about that!" the woman snapped.

The two glared at each other. Theresa didn't remember anything about "bonding" in the newsgrid. She shivered in a sudden gust of wind. It was so cold.

The older man made a sudden decision. "She can know, her. It's time people knew. We're doing what's right, us, and it's working, and we know that. We should spread the word, us."

"Mike—" the woman began angrily.

"No, it's time. And if a donkey's really interested, her . . ." He eyed Theresa speculatively.

"I say no, me," the woman said.

"I say yes, me," Josh said. "Patty, grab some of those cones, you."

Patty grabbed, with bad grace. Theresa pulled some of Jackson's clothes from the car and walked with Josh toward the building, staying as far away from Patty and Mike as she could.

The building was a huge, flat, windowless rectangle. Maybe once a warehouse of some kind. They didn't take her inside. Instead, they ducked in one by one to drop off their loads of cones and clothing. Then they led her around to the back of the building. Several more people followed, until there was a small crowd.

Behind the building a tent of clear plastic stretched over churned-up ground. The tent, held up at its center by spindly poles four feet high, sagged rapidly to edges held to the ground with temporary-look-ing stakes. Inside was a Y-cone, a feeding ground, and six naked people, in two groups of three each.

"See, you?" Josh said, not ungently. "Bonded groups, them. Feeding in harmony. That six months ago were enemies, them."

"Not enemies," Patty said sharply.

"Not friends," Josh countered. "We had a lot of fighting, us. Like most tribes. It almost made us blow apart, us, go off alone . . . be isolated."

"Which would mean, it, that we was denying our humanity," Mike said. "Humans are meant to be together, us. Isolated, we ain't whole."

"Oh," Theresa said. Was he right, this ragged healthy-looking Liver? Was that why her life had felt so empty—because she'd isolated herself? Disappointment seeped through her. It seemed too simple, too . . . easy. All those isolated ecstatic mystics she'd read about in her library, who saw visions and suffered for truth—they'd needed more than just more company! She searched for something to say that wouldn't offend her hosts.

"How did you stop the fighting and . . . get to be so unified?"

"Bonding!" Josh said triumphantly. "It was given to us by Mother Miranda, her, and we took it, and now look!"

"Mother Miranda?" Theresa said. "Are you the same as those people who insist Miranda Sharifi develop an immortality drug?"

"No," Mike said. "We don't insist, us, on nothing. We don't ask for nothing. But we took the gift, us, when we found it."

The gift. "What gift?"

Josh answered, fervor in his voice. "At first we thought, us, it was more Change syringes. But the new syringes were red, them, not black, and there was a holo to play on our terminal. Miranda Sharifi telling us, her, that this was a gift to start with us, then later go to everyone. The gift of bonding. To make up for the isolation of the Change!"

"A holo of Miranda Sharifi," Theresa repeated. Jackson had said that Miranda and her fellow Supers had nanobuilt themselves a lunar base, Selene, after Jennifer Sharifi got out of prison and threw Miranda out of Sanctuary. That had been over a year ago. How was Miranda sending new syringes from the moon?

"With a *new* Change," Mike said. "Bonding. So we can't ever be alone, us, again. So we *have* to develop the spiritual aspect of ourselves and get along together. In threes, like the Father and Son and Holy Ghost, them."

Theresa looked again at the tented feeding ground. Three people at one end, two women and a man. Three at the other, a man and a woman and a young boy. Around her in the crowd people stood grouped in threes, some groups holding hands. Patty and Mike and Josh had imperceptibly moved from opposite sides of Theresa to form a small huddle facing her.

"A syringe," she said. "It held a new drug, and you took it, and—"

Patty spoke directly to Theresa, looking her full in the face, smiling brutally. "And the drug made us one, it. We *can't* move, us, too far away from each other. We are each other's life!"

The crowd suddenly intoned, "We are the life and the way. We are the life and the blood. We are the life and the chosen."

Josh said eagerly, "You see now, you? We're a real community, us. The Change syringe divided people, everybody able to go off by himself, them, to eat and be healthy and live, nobody needing anybody else. But the bonding syringe unites. If Mike or Patty or me get too far away from each other, us, we die."

"Die?" Theresa faltered. "Really die?"

Patty said triumphantly, "Really die. And a bonded group did, them. In another tribe. I *saw* it, me. The fools didn't believe Mother Miranda, and the Holy Ghost moved away, her, and in one night the other two died."

"But . . . but what if you have a baby? Does the baby—"

"We got lots more red syringes, us," Josh said. "A baby ain't no problem. It just stay with its mother, him, until it's old enough to bond with his own group."

Theresa felt sick. They wanted so badly to have a reason to need each other, to be a community . . . but *this*. It must be done with pheromones. Jackson had explained pheromones to her. Chemicals given off into the air and smelled by other people, even if they didn't realize. And the chemicals affected people's behavior . . . Maybe without the new smell, some poison was set off in the bonded person's body. But wouldn't the Cell Cleaner destroy any poison? Wasn't that what the Cell Cleaner was *for?* Of course, if Miranda Sharifi had really made them both . . . would Miranda Sharifi do that? Why?

A part of Theresa's mind said softly, *Because they remade human bodies in their own image. Now the Supers want to own human brains.* No. That was Theresa's own brain, the part that was so afraid of new experiences and new things, the part that never wanted to leave the apartment. Xenophobia. Inhibition. Agoraphobia. Novelty anxiety. Jackson had taught her the words. It was she who was mistaken, was blind, didn't recognize a path up to the light when she saw it . . .

No. It wasn't her. What these people were doing was *wrong*.

Her breath went ragged, her heart raced. She felt the attack coming—nausea, dizziness, the terror of not being able to breathe—and flailed one hand, as if she could physically ward it off.

Patty misinterpreted her gesture. "You don't believe me, you? Then come see the holo!"

"No . . . I . . . please *don't* . . ." Patty seized her arm and dragged her around the building and inside.

Livers were there, in threes, crowding close to her and breathing in her face and it was dark and her gorge rose and . . .

"Mother Miranda time!"

The holostage sprang to life. A pretty, meaningless swirl of color, and then Miranda Sharifi appeared, head and shoulders only, the background a plain dark recording booth designed for anonymity. Miranda wore a sleeveless white suit. A red ribbon held back her unruly black hair.

"This is Miranda Sharifi, speaking to you from Selene. You will want to know what this new syringe is. It's a wonderful new gift, designed especially for you. A gift even better than the Change syringes were. Those set you free biologically, but also led to much isolation when you no longer needed each other for food and survival. It's not good for man to be alone. So this syringe, this wonderful gift—"

Beyond the holostage, in a corner of the warehouse, Theresa saw an unChanged child.

About two, the child sat propped in a corner, thin flabby legs straight out. One side of its head was empty of hair, the skin eaten into circular patches oozing pus. Rheum trickled from its filmy eyes.

Theresa's throat closed entirely.

"You, my chosen people, the first to know the life and the way—"

The child whimpered. A girl no older than Theresa darted forward and picked it up. A strong, healthy Liver girl, free of hunger and disease, who could stand by herself and see from clear eyes . . . Was the unChanged child . . . could it be in *actual pain?*

"—spiritual gift, the life and the way—"

She couldn't breathe. No matter how hard she tried, she couldn't breathe . . .

"—building on the work of the Change syringe I first gave you years ago when—"

. . . couldn't *breathe* and she was going to die, this time she would really die . . .

"What's the matter with the donkey, her?"

"What's wrong, you?"

"Give her some room!"

"She's dying, her!"

"People don't die, them, you asshole! Holo's done! Inject her!"

"There ain't nobody, them, to be in her group . . ."

"Yes! The two new people, them! Cathy and Earl!"

"Inject them, all three! Inject them!"

The room spun crazily. It went black in a deep swooping wave, as if someone had jerked the far wall, and the wave rushed toward her in a minute it would take her . . . *Put your head between your knees*, Jackson's voice said inside her head. *Breathe deeply. Take a neuropharm*

. . . She doubled over. Two people pulled her upright, one on either side of her, her new bonded group . . . In the spinning room a syringe whirled into view, in somebody's hand, bright red.

"No!" Theresa screamed. "No . . . d-d-don't . . ."

"It's all right, honey," a woman's voice said soothingly. Her coat was pulled off. "It don't hurt. Just like another Change needle, you won't hardly feel it, you. Mother Miranda says, her, that it just builds on the first Change . . ."

The red syringe swam closer to her arm. The room whirled and the dark wave washed over her . . . dizzy faint she was going to throw up . . . At the last minute she pulled the words somewhere out of herself.

"I'm . . . not . . . Changed!"

And the blackness took her.

Outside. She was lying on the ground outside, and it was cold. She wasn't wearing her coat. She opened her eyes and the sunlight hurt them. People stood around her in groups, their ugly faces gazing down at her. In a group . . . Cathy and Earl and Theresa . . . She was bonded.

"She's coming back, her."

"Give her some room, damn it!"

"Don't give the bitch nothing, us."

"Theresa . . . you're not bonded, you. We didn't do it." Josh, squatting beside her, not touching her. Theresa concentrated on her breathing. Sometimes the attacks came in twos, or even threes . . . The very thought made her heart race and her breath shorten.

"I said, me, that we didn't bond you."

Josh's face was kind. How could that be, kindness from a Liver? He couldn't understand what happened to her . . . not even Jackson understood. Theresa tried to breathe deeply.

Patty said, "It must be true. What we heard, us. That even the enclaves don't have no more Change syringes." Her tone was slyly pleased.

Theresa sat up. Home. She had to go home. Would they let her go home? What would they do to her? Tears filled her eyes.

"Oh, God, she's crying, her," Patty said. "Let the bitch go."

Mike said, "No. Wait. She's got a mobile. She knows entry codes we could use, us."

"She don't know nothing, her—look at her! She ain't even Changed!"

"So? She's got stuff in her head, she's a donkey—"

Josh leaned close to her. Theresa flinched. His breath was sweet and warm but somehow alien. He said, very low, "Get up, you, while they're arguing. Get in your car and go."

She looked at him wildly. He nodded once, pulled her to her feet, and whispered something in her ear. Mike and Patty had started pushing each other, their faces contorted, their words coming out in spittle at the corners of their mouths. Theresa ran toward her car.

"Stop her!" Mike called. "Stop, you!"

Theresa lurched and fell. Her breath came hard, the ground shook and grasped . . . *not again*. Not another attack. She forced herself to her feet and looked back over her shoulder.

Patty and Mike were trying to chase her, but every time they got a few yards from Josh they stopped, ran back, and tried to pull him along. Josh made himself heavy and limp as rags. And Mike and Patty couldn't chase Theresa without him.

She stumbled to the car and collapsed inside. "Door lock. Automatic . . . takeoff . . . Home coordinates." The car lifted.

Below, she saw Patty slug Josh.

Theresa fell back against the seat, trying to control her breathing, trying to stop the world below from spinning into another of the sickening black waves. Home. She had to get home. She should never have left, should never have come out of the enclave, should never have thought she was strong enough or worthy enough to actually find out something about the light . . . She was just a defective overprivileged donkey . . . no, those *people* were wrong, that wasn't the way, courting death to force you into community, no no no . . . Not like that. The answer wasn't like that.

She closed her eyes. It shut out the spinning world, but it couldn't shut out the thing scarier than that. The most terrifying thing she'd seen, in an afternoon of terror, inner and outer . . . Josh's face, whispering a final sentence. Kind, regretful, horrifying. His words.

"You ain't ready, you. Least, not yet."

Theresa shuddered. She never would be ready, for that. Bound forever ten feet from two Livers, death if she left them . . . No. It was wrong. A dead end.

But what was Miranda Sharifi *doing*?

And what was Theresa going to do?

She was again alone with her empty life.

INTERLUDE

TRANSMISSION DATE: December 1, 2120
TO: Selene Base, Moon
VIA: San Diego Ground Station, GEO Satellite C-988 (U.S.), Holsat IV (Egypt)
MESSAGE TYPE: Unencrypted
MESSAGE CLASS: Class B, Private Paid Transmission
ORIGINATING GROUP: San Diego Parents' Coalition
MESSAGE:

Dr. Miranda Sharifi and Associates—
    Knowing, as we do, that you firmly embody the principle that people are never more themselves than when they make choices for others, we approach you with a request. Your gift of Change syringes has transformed our lives. Thanks to your efforts, our children are healthier and stronger. But the supply of Change syringes in our enclave— as in the others—is dwindling. Soon it will be nonexistent. Children born after that must be vulnerable to disease, to accidental poisoning, to danger.
    Dr. Sharifi, please don't permit this to happen. Our children are so precious to us. They are all of our futures. You have been so compassionate and benevolent to your fellow beings that we, the parents of San Diego Enclave, ask you to be so again. We ask for more Change syringes for the children as yet unborn to us. Let this be, from your deep knowledge of humanity, your first scientific goal. We ask not for ourselves, but for the children.

ACKNOWLEDGMENT: None received

Five

They had been flying over Africa for less than half an hour when the plane began to descend. Jennifer Sharifi gazed out the window. In the pink dawn the outlines of a city blurred, as if the buildings might or might not actually be there. Heisenberg Uncertainty Principle, she thought, and didn't smile.

"Atar," Will Sandaleros said, and stretched as much as he could in the cramped confines of the four-seater Mitsu-Boeing. Two days ago Jennifer and he had come down from Sanctuary, their first time down in the four months since they'd returned from Earth to the Sleepless orbital. All signs of Miranda and the other Supers had been obliterated from Sanctuary. The friends convicted with Jennifer had also returned to Sanctuary, their shorter sentences long since finished: Caroline Renleigh and Paul Aleone and Cassie Blumenthal and the rest. Back to finish the fight for freedom.

But only Jennifer and Will had made this trip down to the international shuttleport in Madeira. They had gone directly to the Machado Hotel, built and owned by Sanctuary through a complex series of blind holding companies, a luxury business hotel guaranteeing unbreakable security for orbital and Terran executives. For two days they had stayed in their Y-shielded room while hotel staff—half Sleepless, half well-paid Norms—had determined the identity of all the agents, reporters, terrorists, and nuts inevitably trailing Jennifer Sharifi. Last night Jennifer and Will had left the Machado by an underground tunnel built along with the hotel, and so well shielded that only ten people in the world knew it existed. A car had taken them to the coast and the Mitsu-Boeing. Will, used to exercise, was restless after three days in vehicles and shielded rooms.

Jennifer was never restless. She had learned to sit completely still and retreat into her thoughts for hours, for days. For months. Will would have to learn, too. It was a necessary discipline to gather everything inside and bring it to a single point, like sunlight focused by a motionless magnifying glass. A burning point.

"They'll be waiting?" she said over the back of the seat to the pilot. He nodded. His brown hair, gray eyes, stolid features, could have come from five different continents. He never spoke. Beside him the Sleepless bodyguard, Gunnar Gralnick, checked his weapons.

The plane landed on a dusty, unmarked landing field in the desert, Atar barely visible on the dawn horizon. The only building, a window-less foamcast rectangle curiously pristine and dustless under a Y-shield, might have existed anywhere in the world. The air was colder than Jennifer remembered, this close to the equator. But the sun wasn't up yet. Later, the air would be hot.

Three men awaited them, dressed in light Arab robes. Nonconsum-able synthetics, Jennifer saw. They were all Changed. In Africa, you never knew. The men had swarthy, sunburned skins, but light eyes: two green, one blue. The one with blue eyes had red hair, neither genemod nor fashion augment. Berbers.

"Welcome to Mauritania," the oldest of the men said to Will, in nearly unaccented English. He did not glance at Jennifer. She had expected this. She said nothing. "I am Karim. This is Ali, and Beshir. Did you enjoy a good flight?"

"Yes, thank you," Will said.

"No complications?"

"We were not followed."

"We detected nothing at this end," Karim said. "But it is best not to linger. Please follow me."

The pilot remained with the plane. The other six climbed into a large aircar, Will and Jennifer in the back seat with Gunnar between them. They flew low, traveling deeper into the Sahara, which grew more sunlit every minute. Rocks, scrub vegetation, an occasional oa-sis, its green stopping with the irrigation system as abruptly as if sheared with scissors. Then no vegetation: just rock and sand. They landed beside a small foamcast building whose domed shield was half-buried in drifting sand.

The Arabs landed the car inside the dome, on hard-packed ground free of blowing sand. The building opened through retina scan, Jen-nifer noted. An underground German company had recently devel-oped software to duplicate retina coding. The Berbers would need to update their security.

The elevator spoke briefly in Arabic. Will gave no sign he did not understand the language. Jennifer understood Arabic although she, too, gave no sign. But of course the Berbers knew what languages she spoke or understood. They knew everything about all three of their Sleepless visitors, everything in any data bank anywhere. Which was never the information most crucial to have. Sleepers never understood that.

Jennifer stood close to them, for the discipline, and made her hatred focus calmly, a controlled burn. For the discipline. The elevator— *"The peace of Allah go with you"*—might or might not be a piece of satirical programming. If satire, it was a weakness; satire indicated the ability to stand outside your own endeavors and mock them. If not satire, it indicated the strength of tradition.

Mauritania had a lot of traditions. Proud Berber nomads. Islam. Colonial oppression. Collapse and drought and plague and warfare and brutality, like all of Africa but more so. Mauritania had been the last country in Africa to outlaw slavery, less than two hundred years ago. The slavery had persisted, joined by newer outlaws and newer genetic and technological slaves. Mauritania had no government left to speak of; what did exist was easily bought.

The elevator stopped far underground. It opened directly into a conference room, all gleaming nanobuilt white walls and the fragrant smell of strong coffee. Doors led, presumably, to the labs and living quarters. On the gleaming teak table surrounded by comfortable chairs stood a silver coffee service. More chairs ringed the walls. A low side table held a holostage.

Jennifer took a chair at the side of the room, sitting with downcast eyes. This had been the result of negotiation, carried on through Will. The Berbers, shrewd businessmen in their unforgiving environment for three millennia, had adapted easily to being brokers for the international underground. They were less willing to adapt to female entrepreneurs. Had Jennifer been any other woman in the world, she would not have been allowed in the room at all.

Any other woman but one. Miranda, who had betrayed her people and made this interaction with Sleeper scum necessary in the first place.

Will and the Berbers sat at the polished teak table. Gunnar remained standing, back to the wall, between Jennifer and the elevator, so that he could survey everything.

"Coffee?" Karim asked.

"Yes, please," Will said. "Where is Dr. Strukov?"

"He will join us in just a few minutes. We are a bit early."

The coffee looked dark, rich, bitter. Jennifer's mouth watered. She made the saliva stop. The three Berbers drank leisurely, not talking, seemingly completely at ease. But even Karim stiffened slightly when a door opened and Serge Mikhailovich Strukov entered.

The legendary Russian genius was huge, clearly genemod for size. His skin had the characteristic glowing health of the Changed. The syringes had, of course, been dropped in Ukraine as well as everywhere else on Earth, but how widely they were used wasn't known; not only had Ukraine closed all its borders tight, but the weird antitechnology cults that had flourished there since the Limited Nuclear Wars had greatly slowed any use of the Net. What wasn't on the Net couldn't be dipped. Much of eastern Europe and western Asia was unknown even to Sanctuary.

But not Strukov. He was known everywhere, seen nowhere.

He had escaped from Ukraine at seventeen, ignorant of microbiology but, somehow, genemod for IQ. He never spoke of his parents, his background, his adolescence, or how he came to speak not only Russian but idiomatic Chinese and fluent, although accented, French. By twenty-two he had a Ph.D. in microbiology from the Centre d'Étude du Polymorphisme Humain in Paris. At thirty-one he won the Nobel Prize in medicine for his work on genetically modified excitotoxins in neural mitochondria. He never showed up in Stockholm to accept the prize. Three months later he walked out of his lab in Paris and disappeared.

Over the next decade, odd reports of Strukov surfaced on the underground Net: hints that he was working for the Chinese, for Egypt, for Brazil, always on biological warfare, always on genemod projects that never quite surfaced on the world newsgrids. Or never quite went away. A microbiologist in the San Francisco Bay Enclave declared that he recognized Strukov's hand in a nasty piece of genemod sent him from a doctor in the Chilean conflict: a deadly retrovirus that destroyed memory formation in the hippocampus. A week later the microbiologist drowned in the Bay.

Strukov sat at the head of the table. Then, pointedly ignoring Will, he swiveled his chair to look directly at Jennifer. She didn't raise her eyes to his, but he went on looking anyway: five seconds, ten. Fifteen seconds. She could feel the tension in the room shoot upward.

Finally Strukov turned back to the men at the table. He was smiling faintly. "What is it that Sanctuary desires next of me?" His English carried a heavy Russian accent, but the sentence structure was not Russian. Mentally translated from French, Jennifer guessed.

Will looked less composed than Strukov. "You've already been informed what we want."

"I wish to hear your words."

"We want," Will said, a little too sharply, "for you to modify the genemod virus you've already developed. The trials we received aren't satisfactory."

"And why is it that Sanctuary, in possession of the most fine laboratories of the science in the solar system, yourself cannot modify this virus?"

"There are reasons," Will said, "that we prefer not to."

"I am able to guess. Sanctuary is run by the communal decision, isn't it? And many of your people must be opposed to whatever it is you plan. Many more must be in ignorance of your plans. Also, your labs on Sanctuary are arranged for the genetic modifying of the embryos, and for the research into that area. You are not arranged for the creation and the delivery of the deadly viruses."

Will said nothing. Strukov threw back his head and laughed, a great open laugh that filled the room. Karim smiled. Jennifer Sharifi and Will Sandaleros had gone to prison for trying to hold five American cities ransom with a deadly genemod virus.

Strukov said, "Twenty-eight years changes much, isn't it? And not only in the microbiology. And yet, even so, *Plus ça change, plus c'est la même chose.* You wish to try again this assault on the American government?"

"No," Will said. "But what we do with the virus is our business. Yours, as we initially agreed, is to deliver it."

"Piece of the cake," Strukov said, clearly savoring the cliché. Karim laughed.

"Maybe not," Will said. "You don't yet know everything our modification requires."

"Permit me, then, to show to you the modifications I already have created," Strukov said. "Angelique, *commencez. Le programme de démontrer.*"

"*Oui,*" said the system. The holostage came to life. A three-dimensional model of the human brain, in light gray, surrounded by a ghostly outline of skull. Two almond-shaped areas the size of a baby's thumbnail, located just behind the ears, suddenly glowed red.

"The right and left amygdalae," Strukov said. "They rest themselves on the interior underside of the temporal lobes. Both amygdalae are in essentials identical. Angelique, *ça va.*"

The left amygdala suddenly expanded, filling the whole deck and replacing the brain. It became a complicatedly elaborated tangle of neurons, densely packed, with input and output nerves branching outward.

Strukov said, "The neurotransmitter of dominance in the

amygdalae is glutamate. It is an interesting amino acid. Subtle metabolic changes can turn glutamate into an excitotoxin that kills neurons in the hypothalamus, a part of the brain one uses in memory formation. Poor transport of glutamate can kill neurons in the brain and spinal cord. Overstimulation of glutamate production leads to many chronic diseases of degeneration."

Jennifer's expression did not change. This was basic, common information. Strukov was overestimating her ignorance. Error? Or insult?

Will said, "But any metabolic changes that created a toxin would be dealt with by the Cell Cleaner. It would destroy toxins as fast as they were created. And overproduction is the result of faulty DNA coding that would be corrected by the Cell Cleaner as soon as it was detected."

"True," Strukov said. "This is why the diseases such as Huntington's and ASL have disappeared themselves. Also the accidental poisoning. But the amygdala does more. Angelique, *ça va*."

The holomodel changed to a cluster of a dozen magnified cells, long axons and dendrites curling close to each other. Structures in and on the cell membranes glowed yellow and orange.

"The yellow receptor sites are called AMPA receptors. The orange ones are NMDA receptors. AMPA receptors activate themselves in response to glutamate and cause the startle reaction."

Suddenly the cell holo disappeared. In its place a laser cannon appeared, swiveled, and fired directly at Will. A blast of noise deafened everybody. Gunnar reacted instantly, throwing a Y-shield around Will and Jennifer, drawing his own gun. The laser cannon was only a holo. Strukov threw back his head and bellowed his huge laugh.

"Like that. You reacted with the fear: pulse, blood pressure, adrenaline rush, isn't it? Your AMPA receptors lit up like the trees of Christmas."

"I don't appreciate being made part of your demonstration," Will said stiffly. Jennifer watched.

"But it demonstrates the issue, yes? However, more exists here. The AMPA receptors that created your fear response clear themselves rapidly after the fear is finished. The neural reaction is temporary. You did not stay afraid after you realized that the cannon was not real. And your NMDA receptors did not activate themselves. Those receptors are different. What it is that activates them is a fear response of the high and prolonged stress. And then the NMDA receptors bond the experiences together. The neural pathways created in this fashion are permanent."

"What do you mean, 'bond experiences together'?"

"Watch. Angelique, ça va. This is real-time recording."

The laser cannon was replaced by a large transparent Y-energy cage outlined by thin black plastic struts. The cage held two white mice. At the far end, the shield collapsed and a cat wearing a bright red collar rushed in. The cat pounced on one of the mice, which let out an agonized squeal. The cat bit down. Blood spurted from the mouse, which screamed at such a high pitch that Jennifer's ears hurt. With one paw the cat reached out and carelessly, almost nonchalantly, raked its extended claws across the back of the other mouse cowering in a transparent corner.

"Now," Strukov said. "A week later."

The same cage, with the same mouse. Its back showed fresh scars. The same cat entered, wearing the same bright red collar. The mouse immediately showed intense fear, both cowering and baring its teeth. Evidently a Y-energy shield invisibly divided the cage in two; the cat could not advance more than halfway toward the mouse, which continued to exhibit fear.

"Three months later," Strukov said. Same mouse, the scars further healed. A hand entered from the top of the cage, holding a bright red leather collar. Immediately the mouse exhibited intense fear.

"Now, this is merely the Pavlov response, yes? The mouse associates the collar with the fear. This is the same as a man in the combat, who twenty-five years later hears a loud noise and throws himself flat on the ground. The experience of the loud noise and the deadly danger are bonded in his brain, and the amygdala is the place this happens. But now it becomes interesting. The mouse's amygdalae have both been removed."

Same mouse. The cat entered. The mouse looked up, saw the cat, went back to sniffing aimlessly at its cage. It wandered toward the cat, which immediately pounced and killed it.

Will said, "No amygdala, no fear."

"No remembered fear," Strukov said. "The instinctive fear is still able to be induced, as for example throwing the mouse from a great height and monitoring its bioresponses on the way down. The fear of the falling is instinctive. But the remembered fear depends on the NMDA receptors in the amygdalae. They lay down a permanent neural pathway, the same as some drugs of the street, which in turn permanently alters the reaction. The organism cannot *not* feel the fear at the proper stimulus. Angelique, ça va."

The cluster of amygdala neurons reappeared. Now glowing lines connected various yellow and orange receptor sites.

"In addition," Strukov said, "I am able to make the process go the other way. With the correct viral modifications to trigger, injected into the blood or the cerebrospinal fluid, the natural excitatory transmitters such as glutamate—among many others—can be turned into the excitotoxins. Thus, the fear pathways can be created even without a prior experience. Of course, they are not memory-specific, since there has existed no memory. There is no input from the hippocampus. But the fear pathways are permanent, because they do not depend on the molecules remaining in the brain. The Cell Cleaner can come along two minutes after injection, but voilà! The NMDA pathways have already been forged.

"Also, the metabolic process that changes the neural structure is marvelously complex, and so the variations possible are marvelously varied. I am able to create the permanent reactions for the fairly specific fears, if the basic instinctual response is genetically encoded. Angelique, *ça va*."

Another real-time recording; Jennifer could tell from the quality of the holo. An Arab teenage boy, not genemod for appearance: pimply, gangly, shuffling his feet. He sat in a small nondescript room, playing a game on a holoterminal. Strukov entered the room and pressed a wall button. An entire wall dissolved, opening the room to a garden with an inviting stream and tall date palms. The boy turned ashen. His breathing raced and his chest rose and fell. In panic he whirled away from the garden and pushed his face against the opposite wall, trembling and moaning. "No no no no . . ."

"The agoraphobia," Strukov said.

"Permanent?" Will asked.

"Probably. Unless he undertakes either the intense personal behavior modification or the corrective pharmacology. Which his Cell Cleaner will of course destroy unless it renews itself constantly. One will need either another genemod virus or many, many patches each week."

"How hard would that be to create?"

Strukov shrugged. "For whom? For the usual doctors? Impossible. For a good research facility of the medicine? Difficult, but not impossible. For your granddaughter Miranda Sharifi and her SuperSleepless? Who can tell? Angelique, *ça va*."

The display showed a young girl, eleven or twelve, not Arab, with uncombed hair and skinny arms. With her was a woman in her sixties, who sat placidly reading. The girl roamed restlessly around the room, touching the walls, windows, terminal, toys, but stopping to use nothing. Every few seconds she touched the woman, as if reassuring herself that the other was still there. Her face, ungenemod but pretty, crinkled in constant anxiety.

"The fear of the abandonment," Strukov said with satisfaction. "She cannot bear to be alone by herself. Watch."

The older woman rose from her chair, laid down her book, and said, *"Nathalie, je vais à la cabinet de toilette."*

"Non, non, Émilie—s'il vous plaît!"

"Une minute, seulement, chérie."

"Non! Vous ne sortez pas!"

The girl clutched desperately at Émilie. Gently the woman unwrapped her clinging arms. Nathalie threw her arms round Émilie's legs, starting to cry. Émilie detached herself and went into a bathroom, closing and locking the door. Nathalie burst into loud sobbing and curled into the fetal position on the floor. Jennifer glimpsed the girl's face. It was a mask of anxiety and fear.

After a few moments Émilie came out of the bathroom. Nathalie crawled over to her and again threw her arms around the older woman's knees.

Strukov said, "The fear of being alone."

Will said, "Does she have to be with this particular person?"

"But no," Strukov said, smiling. "She is exactly the same with anyone in the room. She is comfortable and free of the anxiety only when the room holds many people, and all appear prepared to stay for many hours. Then, and only then, the fear of the abandonment is eased. Angelique, *ça va*—but this one you have already seen, isn't it? You have decided against this."

An American Liver town in early fall: trees blazed with color. Three ragged people stood close together on an empty nanopaved road. From their contorted faces and waving arms, they were arguing fiercely. One man shoved the other. The woman stalked away, shouting at them both over her shoulder, into a nearby woods. There was a close-up of her shocked face as two holosuited men grabbed her and forced her into a small aircar.

"They called it 'the bonding,'" Strukov said mockingly. "But you know that better than me, isn't it? You yourself made the holo the peasants have watched. After they saw it, they injected themselves with the red syringes, and so they became bonded. Now then, this is three hours since the woman is carried away."

The abducted woman sat alone in a comfortable room. Abruptly she gasped, clutched her chest, and slid off her chair. Her eyes stared in death. The holo superimposed a robocam shot of the two men who had bonded with her, also dead.

"An electrical event in the heart," Strukov said. "A very clean mechanism, very elegant. I like this technique to control your peasants. Render them very dependent on each other and their actions can be only very limited, yes? A good design. But you do not choose this design. You tell me, leave this attempt, give me something different."

Will didn't answer directly. "This whole range of fears you can induce permanently—the biochemistry dictates they're all as pronounced as these two examples?"

"But no. These NMDA receptors have been strongly activated. They have created the neural pathways of the great strength. It is possible to create the lesser effects."

Will said, "Is it possible for *you* to create them?"

"But of course. Angelique, *ça va.*"

The holostage switched to screen mode. Screen after screen of charts, equations, molecular diagrams, chemical formulas, tables of variables, and ion reaction schematics flashed past, as maliciously complex as the previous demonstrations had been simplistic.

Strukov said, "Much of the work on the fear and the anxiety has concerned itself with the synapses, the neurotransmitters, and the receptor subtypes. I have concerned myself more with the processes of the cellular stress inside the nerve cells, where the neuropeptides form themselves. Here is where the chemical reactions originate and conclude. Each pyramidal neuron receives as many as a hundred thousand contacts from those neurons to which they connect. One therefore begins with models of the nerve transmission.

"And with one other thing. There exist the peptides that form themselves only under the pathological conditions. It is possible to instigate a chain reaction of the complex amines, beginning inside a cell. Some amines in the chain are pathological; some are normal; some are the endogenous excitatory amino acids transformed into the excitotoxins. This chain, it has its beginning in the altered pathways of the amygdalae.

"From there, it extends itself through the central nerve nucleus to the interiors of the cells in many other places—in the brain, in the muscles, in the glands and the organs. The chain ends in affecting many bioamines, including the acetylcholine—look at this chart, here—the norepinephrine, the CRF, the glutamate, the critical gamma C—many many amines.

"Moreover, that chain will go on constantly, once begun by the triggering virus. And since the chain consists of the substances entirely created by the brain itself, the stupid Cell Cleaner does not attack them. It will destroy the virus, but by that time, it is too late. The chain has begun. And according to the stupid Cell Cleaner, the chain belongs there. According to the stupid Cell Cleaner, the chain is *native*." Strukov laughed. "And so it is."

Will said, "And all human brains will respond the same way to the initiating virus?"

Strukov shrugged. "Of course not. The people always differ in their response to anything that impacts the biogenic amines. Some will sicken. Some will respond too strongly. A few will not respond at all. But most will become what you have requested me to make them: inhibited, fearful of anything new, filled with the anxiety at any separation from the familiar. Like the babies with the stranger anxiety. In the essence, my chain reaction brings forward as primary a more primitive function of the brain, which human growth suppresses in favor of the more complex functions. I reverse that."

Strukov looked directly at Jennifer and smiled. "I will, in its finality, turn your target population into a nation of the fearful children."

Jennifer gazed back. She had to fight showing her revulsion for the huge bearded giant completely absorbed in his own genius, completely at ease with its demonstration on his own people. Jennifer had always known that Sleepers had no loyalty to their own, no moral sense. They would do anything to each other, if enough money was involved. Nor were they capable of distinguishing between the prison term served by Jennifer, a penalty borne of the Sleepers' fear of her and of her own sense of moral obligation to safeguard her own, and the prison term that would be served by this brilliant vermin if his brain tampering was discovered by Sleeper authorities. Strukov was a disease. She would use a disease to protect her people, if she had to. But she would not give a disease the moral courtesy of tradition.

She stood, eyes meeting Strukov's. "And you can deliver the triggering genemod virus by injection, without detection?"

"I have said so," Strukov said, amused, as the three Arabs rose angrily to their feet. "The vector contains sixteen different proteins, five of which never before have existed. All will be destroyed by the Cell Cleaner long before any scientific authorities can isolate and culture them."

Karim said to Will, "We had an agreement about who will speak at this meeting!"

"Injection will not do for us," Jennifer said to Strukov.

He answered, smiling, "Your granddaughter remade the human body, and you will remake the human mind, isn't it?"

"What we do is not your concern," Jennifer said, at the same moment that Beshir said hotly to Will, "Control your wife!"

Strukov said, "Do you speak always in the first-person plural, Madame Sharifi? What delivery of the virus do you require? And on what schedule?"

"Two different delivery modes. One developed and tested as soon as possible, the other to follow a month later."

"And those two modes of the delivery are : . . ?"

She told him.

Six

Jackson woke to the sure knowledge that someone was moving around his bedroom in the dark.

A dream? No. The intruder was real. And not a 'bot. A dim human blur across the room, passing briefly in front of the semi-opaqued window. Theresa? She didn't come into his room at night, and if she did, she'd turn on the light.

He lay still, simulating the deep breathing of sleep, and considered his choices. He could call for building security, but not even the neuropharm option would take effect before the intruder shot Jackson at the sound of his voice. He could roll off the bed, keeping it between himself and the window, and try to reach the personal security shield in the bottom dresser drawer. Or was it in the second-bottom drawer? He pictured himself fumbling naked through his socks and underwear, groping for the thing while the intruder politely waited. Yes, sure. He could lunge off the bed and try to tackle the intruder, counting on surprise to keep from getting shot.

In the seconds it took him to decide, the intruder said, "Lights on," and the room lit up. "Hello, Jackson darling," Cazie said.

She was naked, and covered with mud. It caked on her pubic muff, smeared across her full breasts, fell off in wet globs onto his white carpet. Immediately Jackson felt his penis stiffen. What if he'd made an idiot of himself by calling for security?

"God damn it, Cazie, what the hell do you think you're doing?"

"You're going to like what I'm doing, Jack. We're going to a party. I left it just to come and get you."

She moved closer to the bed, and he could see her green-flecked eyes. She was on something, and it was a hell of a lot stronger than Endorkiss. She caught his frown and held out the inhaler. "Want a whiff?"

"No!"

"Then let's go to the party." She yanked the blanket off Jackson's bed. Mud from her hands smeared the nonconsumable fabric. "Oh, look, you're all ready! You always could get hard fast, Jack. I do like that. Come on, let's go. They're waiting."

He yanked the blanket back from her, feeling like a fool. "I'm not going anywhere."

"Oh, yes, you are," she purred. She let go of the disputed blanket, threw herself on top of him, and kissed him ferociously.

He couldn't help himself. His arms went around her and his tongue shot into her open mouth. His cock felt ready to burst. Cazie laughed, her mouth still on his, and pushed him away. She was stronger than he remembered. Clumsily, still laughing, she rolled off the bed and started for the door.

"Not here, Jack. Come on, you don't want to miss the party."

"Cazie! Wait!" He heard her run lightly through the apartment and tell the front door to open. Jackson grabbed his pants and pulled them on. Barefoot and bare-chested, he ran after her, hoping they didn't wake Theresa. Cazie had disappeared. Jackson yanked open the front door.

"Have a good evening, Dr. Aranow," the door said to him. "Shall I cancel your wake-up call?"

"Yes," Jackson said. "No. Cazie!"

She'd already gone into the elevator; it closed. As he watched helplessly, the door opened again. She stood there, naked and muddy and smiling, lowering the inhaler. "Come on in, Jack, the water's fine."

"Shall I wait, Dr. Aranow?" the elevator asked. "Or are you staying on this floor?"

Jackson stumbled into the elevator. Cazie laughed. "Sixth floor, please."

"Cazie, you're naked!"

"And you're not. But we can fix that. Isn't it lucky the party's right in your building?" She reached out one hand, hooked it into the top of his pants, and pulled him toward her. She undid the single clasp he'd had time to fasten when the elevator stopped and the door opened.

"Sixth floor, Ms. Sanders," the elevator said. "Have a nice evening."

"*Cazie . . .*"

"Come on, Jack! We're late!" She ran down the hall, shedding mud. Cursing, Jackson followed.

He should go home right now.

The cheeks of her ass, smeared with mud, flashed alternately—*left right left right* . . . Her ass was firm but not so firm that it didn't jiggle as she ran. Jackson followed.

The party was at Terry Amory's. Jackson knew Terry, but not well.

The door was open. Cazie led him through a pseudo-Asian minimalist decor to the dining room. "He's here! Let the games begin!"

"And just in time," Terry drawled. "We were going to start without you. Hello, Jackson. Welcome to the psychobank."

Six naked people, three men and three women, lolled on a feeding ground the size of Jackson's bedroom. Water had been churned into the custom-mixed organic loam; the resulting mud was thick, rich, and subtly perfumed. The wall program displayed earth tones, grays and tans and ochres, with dissolving and re-forming cave paintings. Stalactites—probably holos—hung from the ceiling. Two of the women sprawled carelessly across one of the men who, Jackson saw, was Landau Carson, tonight not wearing bees. Landau and Terry were the only people Jackson recognized.

The woman not lying on Landau, a tall, slim redhead with bright blue eyes, said to Jackson, "Well, take your pants off, darling. They don't look very edible."

Jackson considered leaving. But Cazie inhaled again from whatever was scrambling her brain. The little fool. Did she even know what was in the inhaler? Didn't she know there were street drugs that did permanent damage to the brain, altering neural pathways before the Cell Cleaner had a chance to destroy them?

"Give me the inhaler, Cazie."

To his surprise, she did, holding it meekly out to him. When he reached for it she shoved him into the feeding ground.

Fury tore through Jackson. Let her warp her brain. Let her fuck every single one of these diseases, of both genders. She was sick, less mentally healthy than Theresa, and with far less reason. Let her go to hell . . . He had hauled himself out of the mud to leave, when he saw the knives.

Twelve of them, stuck in an orderly blades-down row into a molded stand. The hilts were all shaped differently, ornamented with crudely carved animals that echoed the cave paintings of the wall programming. Throwing knives, but not well balanced. Deliberately.

"I've got the paint," the redhead said. She sniffed from an inhaler. "Who's first?"

"Neophytes first," Cazie said. "First me and then Jackson."

"Here," Terry crooned, "let me assist you, as said Cro-Magnon to the Neanderthal. Ummmmmm, nice." He dipped his hand in the pot and smeared paint the color of dried blood on both Cazie's nipples. Then liberally on the fuzzy muddy mound between her thighs. Cazie smiled.

The redhead handed her a belt with a small dark button in the front. Fumbling, laughing, Cazie strapped it around her waist and pushed the button. Jackson saw the faint shimmer of a personal Y-shield spring around her.

Cazie slogged through the mud to the opposite side of the room. She stood flat against the wall, under a stalactite, arms straight at her side after one more whiff from the inhaler. Terry said, "Host's prerogative, ladies and gentlemen," and reached for the knife stand.

Jackson thought rapidly. If the shield was standard—and it looked like it was—a knife would not pierce it. Terry might aim for the painted areas of Cazie's exposed body, but the exposure wasn't real. It was just playacting, a fake thrill, the simulation of danger.

"Pleasure or pain?" Terry mused theatrically. His hand hovered over one knife after another. "Pain or pleasure? And for such a beautiful body, too . . . so full and ripe . . . pleasure or pain?" He chose a knife.

As Terry pulled it free of the stand, Jackson saw that the knife blade, too, was encased in the shimmer of a Y-energy shield. Sudden cold prickled the base of his spine.

The redhead sank into the mud on her belly, wriggled in the depression her body made, and rolled onto her back, streaked with mud. She raised herself on her elbows to get a better view of Cazie. Her conical breasts rose and fell with her breathing.

Terry threw the knife, and Cazie screamed.

Jackson scrambled forward across the mud. But Cazie wasn't hurt; the knife was embedded in the dining-room wall and Cazie laughed down at Jackson. "Fooled you, darling!"

Before he could react, Terry threw another knife. Jackson saw it fly through the air—it *was* unbalanced, the knives were designed to be hard to make a hit with—and strike Cazie's left breast, to the left of the painted nipple. The knife bounced off her shield and fell into the mud.

"No points!" the redhead said. "Bad, bad, bad aim, Terry darling."

"One more throw," said the man Jackson didn't know. "Cazie's friend, get out of the way, please. We can't see, and some of us are too entangled to move."

"I may never move again," said one of the two women lying twisted around Landau Carson. "Oh, do that again, Landau."

A third knife whistled through the air, missed Cazie, and embedded itself in the wall.

"Three strikes and you're out, Terry," Landau said. "I'm next."

"As thrower?"

"Garrote the thought. As target, of course."

Landau took Cazie's place against the wall. Cazie flopped down in the mud on her belly and used her inhaler. Jackson watched the green-eyed redhead select a knife, with much dramatic deliberation, and hurl it at Landau's genitals. It hit and bounced off into the mud.

"Uuummmmmmmmm," Landau said. "Nice."

Cazie said, "You know you can't feel it through your shield, Landau. Irina, three points." She lifted the inhaler again. Her eyes were shiny.

Irina threw a second knife. It missed.

"Oh, don't hiccup now," Landau said. "Hit me, lover."

She did. The third knife struck right above Landau's erect cock. Everyone laughed and cheered. "Six points!" Terry called. "Irina, what do you choose?"

Irina gazed, smiling, at Landau. He looked back expectantly. Jackson felt the subtle shift in the room: a different kind of tension, tauter and hotter.

Irina said, "I choose to take the knife myself."

Landau looked disappointed. But there was something else in the disappointment, Jackson thought, something incongruous. Relief? He looked again at the stand of knives, encased in their shimmering shields. Why shields?

"Wait," Cazie said. "Don't choose yet, Irina. Terry, help me, you slug."

Cazie and Terry gathered the six thrown knives from the mud. As they squished through the thick sludge, Terry smeared a quick, proprietary glob across Cazie's back. Suddenly Jackson knew that Terry had already had sex with Cazie, earlier. As part of the general mud-rolling foreplay to the knife game. Jackson's chest constricted and burned.

"Okay, that's all of them," Terry said. "Irina, choose."

Twelve knives, six gleaming and six muddy, stood phallic in their stand. Irina knelt before them in the mud, lips pursed, drawing out her moment of choice. The others watched, mud frosting their beautiful genemod bodies, faces keen and hot-eyed. Landau rubbed his fingers across his clavicle. One of the women caught her bottom lip between her teeth.

"This one," Irina said.

She drew a clean knife, its hilt carved with a crude mammoth head. Irina's thumb did something to the hilt. The shimmer of Y-shield disappeared.

"Pleasure or pain, pain or pleasure," Landau chanted softly. "Pleasure or pain . . ."

Irina smiled at each face in turn. Then she drew the knife across the soft, mud-smeared flesh of her upper arm. Blood spurted out. A woman winced. Landau bared his teeth.

For a long moment no one moved. Then Irina collapsed onto the mud, facedown, writhing. Cazie grabbed her and pulled her to a sitting position.

"Pleasure!" Landau crowed.

Irina's face transformed. Her head tilted back; her back arched; her whole body shuddered. Then she collapsed against Cazie, trembling. Her eyes closed.

"A strong dose," Terry said. "Lucky Irina."

Cazie laughed. Jackson couldn't watch her. He half turned away, standing ankle-deep in mud.

It must be a selective nerve stimulator, going right to the pleasure center. Addictive, degenerative, illegal. Blood still dripped from Irina's soft arm. The Cell Cleaner would take care of it: repair the cut faster than could the unaided body, destroy any infectious bacteria, consume the mud in the wound. No risk.

He said, "What's on the 'pain' knives?"

Terry said, "Just that. The stimulator works directly on the brain."

Landau said, "*Very* unpleasant. And it seems to last an eon."

"You're all sick," Jackson said. "Every one of you."

"Oh, dear," Landau said. "More morality."

"Jackson, it's a *party*," Cazie said. "Don't be so grim."

He gazed bleakly at her. Smiling back at him, tenderly cradling Irina. These people were biologically underaroused. Underarousal produced thrill-seeking behavior. He could recite the neurochemistry: deficient levels of monoamine oxidase, serotonin, and cortisol. Slow heart rate, low skin conductance, high threshold for nerve triggering. Excess of dopamine, imbalance of norepinephrine and alintylomase. Plus, of course, whatever imbalances they were creating with the inhalers.

Knowing the biochemistry didn't modify his disgust.

"Come on, Cazie. We're leaving. You and me. Now."

She went on smiling at him, naked and covered with mud, the dreamily comatose Irina in her arms. She would refuse to go with him, of course. She had always refused anything he demanded. His mood shifted suddenly, to a fearful elation. She would refuse. And then, after seeing her like this, with these underaroused diseases . . . after this, he would be free of her. Finally. It would be over. He would be free.

"All right, Jackson," Cazie said. "I'm coming."

She laid Irina carefully on the mud and stood up, wiping a thick glob of mud off her wrist.

"Hey, Caz, you can't go now!" Terry said. "The party's just starting!"

"And I'm up next," a woman said. "Who wants to throw?"

"Loser's prerogative," Landau said. "Since Irina didn't choose me for the knife."

"Cazie! Don't go!"

"Good night," Cazie said. "Tell Irina I'll call her tomorrow." She took Jackson's hand. He dropped hers: bleakly, angrily, with trapped love.

She followed him meekly to the elevator, down the hall—they met no one, it was 3:00 A.M.—into the apartment. Into the shower. Jackson saw that she'd left her inhaler behind.

"I'm sorry, Jack," Cazie said when they were both clean. "I didn't think well. Of course you wouldn't like such a party. It's just that . . . I missed you."

He stared at her, trying to maintain his disgust, knowing he failed. "You didn't miss me. You just wanted more thrills. The only experiences you've ever thought worth having were intense thrills."

"I know."

"That's not normal, Cazie. Normal people don't need constant dangerous excitement to feel happy!"

"Then there are a hell of a lot of donkeys who aren't normal. Not anymore. Hold me, Jack."

He stood stiffly, not moving. She put her arms around him and pressed against him. His naked cock rose into her belly. Her soft breasts breathed gently into his chest.

"Oh, Cazie . . ." It was a groan, half desire and half defeat. "No . . ."

"I'll be sweet," she mumbled against his neck. "You're so good to watch out for me . . ."

She did stay sweet. And tender, and gentle—a vulnerable Cazie, holding back nothing, giving everything. Afterward she fell asleep against his shoulder, curled into him like a child. The sheets were wet from the bodies they hadn't dried after their shower, from the sweet juices of lovemaking.

Jackson lay awake in the dark, holding her, wishing that she hadn't come with him from the party, wishing that she would never leave his bedroom, wishing that he were a different kind of person from what he was. More resolute. More able to sustain anger. More able to write her off.

There were neuropharms that would do that. Modify his neuro-chemistry, rebalance transmitters and hormones and enzymes. Less CRF. More testosterone. Less serotonin. Fewer dopamine reuptake inhibitors. More ADL.

Like the people at the party. Terry and Irina and Landau.

No.

He couldn't sleep. After thrashing and turning for half an hour, he eased himself out of bed. He kissed Cazie's cheek, put on a robe, and padded to the library.

"Caroline, messages, please."

"Yes, Jackson," said his personal system in the slightly formal voice he preferred. "You have four messages. Shall I list them in the order received?"

"Why not." He poured himself a whiskey from the sideboard.

"Message from Kenneth Bishop, from Wichita. Subject: Willoughby plant." The TenTech chief engineer. He had finally checked on the deranged factory. A week late. Maybe TenTech needed another chief. Christ, Jackson hated dealing with this shit.

"Message from Tamara Gould, from Manhattan. Subject: party." The last thing Jackson wanted tonight was another party. Would Cazie want to go? If he took her, would Cazie stay with him a little longer?

"Message from Brandon Hileker, from Yale. Subject: class re-union." Oh, God, had it been ten years since his B.A.? A reunion. *And what do you do, Jackson? A doctor? Isn't that a little . . . superfluous?*

"Message from Lizzie Francy. Subject: baby project." *Baby? Project?* What did that mean? Had something happened to the baby Jackson had delivered last week? Why call it a "project"? But, then, what did Jackson really know about what Livers called anything?

"Caroline, give me that message, please."

Lizzie's face formed on the wall screen. Unlike the last time he had seen them, Lizzie's expression was alert and her hair neatly combed. Her black eyes sparkled. Her speech, he noted, sounded donkey, not Liver. Victoria Turner's doing?

"This is Lizzie Francy for Dr. Jackson Aranow. Dr. Aranow, I'm calling because I need your help. It's a project connected to the ba-bies' health—not just my baby that you delivered, but all babies in the tribe. And maybe other tribes." She hesitated, and her voice changed. "Please call back. It's really really important." Another hesitation, then a curiously stiff little bow of the head. "Thank you."

"End of message," Caroline said. "Do you wish to reply?"

"No. Yes." If the baby had had some kind of accident . . . "proj-ect"? "Record message."

"Recording."

"Dr. Jackson Aranow for Lizzie Francy. Please give me more details about your problem. Is the baby in need of medical attention? If so, then—"

To his surprise, Lizzie's face in real-time interrupted his recording. It was 4:30 in the morning. What was she doing, overriding his personal system? And how was she doing it?

"Dr. Aranow, thank you for calling back! I—we—desperately need your help. Could you—"

"Is the baby all right?"

"The baby's fine. See?" She enlarged the screen scope; he saw that she was nursing her infant son.

"Then why did you say this 'project' was for the baby's health?"

"It *is*. But long-term. I didn't know who else to ask. It's a really important project!"

Jackson had the feeling he should hang up. Livers. It was always a mistake to get involved with them. Provide the basic necessities out of human charity, yes. Donkeys had tried to do that; it wasn't the donkeys' fault if Livers had rejected the social contract—goods for votes—that had provided for their needs. Beyond that, Livers were difficult. Uneducated, demanding, ungrateful, dangerous. And the sight of Lizzie's full breast in her child's mouth made him oddly uncomfortable. He thought of Cazie, asleep in his bed.

Lizzie said, "Did you ever hear of a woman named Ellie Sandra Lester?"

Jackson drew in a breath. "Yes," he said. "Go on."

INTERLUDE

TRANSMISSION DATE: November 28, 2120
TO: Selene Base, Moon
VIA: Boston Ground Station, GEO Satellite 1453-L (U.S.), Luna City Ground Station
MESSAGE TYPE: Encrypted
MESSAGE CLASS: Class B, Private Paid Transmission
ORIGINATING GROUP: GeneModern, Inc., Boston, Massachusetts
MESSAGE:

Ms. Sharifi:

As we said in our previous two transmissions, GeneModern is interested in pursuing a commercial partnership with Selene Base in developing viable extensions of your patented product, the Cell Cleaner ™. We believe that our research facilities, among the best in the world, have succeeded in duplicating some of the nonpatented aspects of your groundbreaking work in cellular biology (see attached documents). The rest remains not only proprietary but—let us be frank—beyond our current capabilities. What we *can* bring to a partnership with Selene is unparalleled manufacturing abilities, superb international distribution, and high-quality investment interest. The former two attributes may be more necessary to you than formerly, since your relocation at Selene. The latter would relieve you of the financial exposure your first venture must have entailed. In addition, our data security system, designed by Kevin Baker, ranks among the most excellent anywhere (see attached documents).

We believe that the ROI opportunities in a GeneModern/Selene partnership are without precedent. Therefore, GeneModern invites your earliest reply.

Yours very truly,
Gordon Keller Browne, CEO.
GeneModern, Inc.

ACKNOWLEDGMENT: None received

Seven

W hy didn't you ask *me?*" Vicki said. "I could have helped you with this just as well as *Jackson Aranow!*"

"He's a donkey," Lizzie said. She hated it when Vicki was mad at her. Vicki was supposed to be Lizzie's champion. That was her program.

"Lizzie, *I'm* a donkey," Vicki said.

"But you don't live, you, with donkeys. You don't know anybody anymore. Dr. Aranow knows other donkeys, him." Lizzie heard her speech sliding back, into Liver, which happened only when she was excited or upset. She rolled over onto her back and crossed her arms on her chest.

The two women lay under the feeding dome, having a late breakfast. They were alone except for Dirk, sleeping beside them on the warm, dry ground. Four feet above their heads the weak November sun was so magnified by the special plastic of the tent that the new Y-energy cones Dr. Aranow had sent from TenTech hadn't even been turned on. Sunlight soaked into Lizzie's skin; it seemed to her she could *feel* her body absorbing nutrients from the ground, energy from the air. She resented Vicki for interfering with this usually lovely feeling.

Lizzie said, "I thought Dr. Aranow might know about Harold Winthrop Wayland and Ellie Lester. And he did know."

Vicki pushed her hair off her face and frowned. "Okay—what did Jackson say about Wayland? What information that I couldn't have discovered for you just as competently?"

"That District Supervisor Wayland was dead, and so—"

"We already knew that!"

"—and the person who was supposed to notify the state government was his great-granddaughter. Ellie Lester."

"Great-granddaughter? How old *was* the district supervisor?"

"I don't know. But she's his next-of-kin, and she should have notified the state so that they could arrange a special election to fill his position. And she didn't."

"Well, of course she didn't," Vicki said. "Why bother, when nobody votes anymore because the Livers are all moving around like nomads? Nomads don't have voting addresses. Or district warehouses. No votes, no warehouses, no need for a district supervisor. It was always an entry political office, anyway. It conferred no power among donkeys themselves."

Lizzie said stubbornly, "She was still supposed to tell the state capital they needed a special election."

Vicki smiled. "I'm perpetually astonished by the rules you think should be honored and the ones you're willing to break. No hobgoblins in your inconsistent mind."

"What?"

"Never mind. Although . . . it *is* strange that the system wasn't programmed to automatically advise the government of official deaths among elected officials. Then again, maybe it *did* advise Harrisburg. What else did Jackson Aranow say about Ellie Lester?"

Lizzie said, "Not too much. But he sounded . . . funny about her."

"Funny how?"

"I don't know. He also said that he's going to help us."

"We don't need him."

"Well, he's coming anyway. This afternoon."

"And is he again bringing the ferocious Cazie Sanders with him, for protection?"

"I don't know."

"I think," Vicki said, "that if you felt such an overwhelming need to pick an additional champion among the donkeys, you could have done better than Jackson Aranow."

Lizzie didn't answer. She cradled Dirk, hoping he'd wake up and nurse. Dirk didn't criticize her. And he was an unfailing delight: a calm, unfussy baby already starting to smile. Mama said it was gas, but it wasn't gas—nobody got gas anymore. That was just Mama, poking at Lizzie's pleasure, just like Vicki was doing. She, Lizzie, would never do that to Dirk.

She would never tell him he was wrong, never nag him, never let that hook in her voice that just snagged a child and unraveled all their plans. Lizzie was going to be a perfect mother. She wouldn't make a single mistake with her precious son. When Dirk nursed, his dark blue eyes fastened unwaveringly on Lizzie's face and his compact little body solid in her arms, she felt she could die from happiness. She kept him wrapped in nonconsumables, just so his little body wouldn't ground-feed and so cut down her nursing time. She would never never let Dirk down. And she was going to make the world safer for Dirk— no matter *how much* Vicki poked at her plans.

Vicki said, "Speak of minor devils. Here comes an aircar."

Dr. Aranow landed behind the building, beside the feeding ground. Lizzie and Vicki pulled on jacks, nonconsumables years old and a little tattered but still warm and bright. Jacks didn't fade. Lizzie's were marigold, Vicki's turquoise. Vicki smiled as she pulled on her shirt, a smile that to Lizzie looked amused and superior. Sometimes Lizzie thought she didn't like Vicki as much as she had when she was a child.

"Lizzie. Ms. Turner," Dr. Aranow said, from just inside the door flap of the feeding tent.

"The good doctor," Vicki said back, still smiling. Dr. Aranow flushed. Lizzie felt she'd missed something. She plunged right in.

"Dr. Aranow, we need your help. We have a plan, but we need you to carry it out."

"So you said on comlink. How is the baby doing?"

"He's wonderful, him." Lizzie heard her own voice change tone, and saw the softened way both donkeys looked at her. She felt a little better about Vicki. "He nurses like a vacuum pump."

"Good," Dr. Aranow said. "I'd like to examine him in a bit."

"What for?" Vicki said. "Infection? Diaper rash? Varicose veins?"

"There still exist structural and endocrinal deficiencies," Dr. Aranow said stiffly. "The Cell Cleaner only eliminates malfunctions, it doesn't build what isn't there."

Lizzie said, "But Dirk doesn't have deficiencies, him!"

"No, I'm sure he doesn't," Dr. Aranow said soothingly. "Just routine. But first, what is this plan you need help with?"

"It's . . . no, come someplace else," Lizzie said. A small crowd was heading toward them, Tasha and Kim and George Renfrew and old Mr. Plocynski, while Scott and Shockey inspected the aircar. So far Lizzie hadn't discussed her plan with anyone but Vicki. And what if her mother came out? Lizzie didn't want to answer any questions from Annie.

"Whereplace else?" Vicki said. She was smiling again.

Dr. Aranow said, "Let's get in the aircar and lift."

"Nervous, Jackson?" Vicki said. "We're not Luddites, you know. What you see on Shockey's face isn't rage, it's envy."

"Yes, the aircar, it," Lizzie said. Would anyone stop her from getting into it with Dr. Aranow?

They didn't. And it was a bigger car than last time; this one had four seats. Lizzie climbed in front with the baby, Vicki in back. In silence

Dr. Aranow lifted the car, flew it a mile to the river—so fast!—and set down on the bank. Withered grass and the thick stems of dead asters. Gray rocks and cold water. On the opposite bank, a mangy-looking rabbit darted away. Lizzie wished the car had landed someplace else, but she was afraid to say so. Fear made her angry with herself, and she heard her words come out loud and bossy and Liver.

"District Supervisor Wayland is dead, him. We called his office and demanded he open a warehouse for us 'cause we're staying, us, in one place over the winter. The program said we weren't registered voters for Willoughby County and couldn't get warehouse chips without being registered. So we said we'd register. Then the program said there was a three-month county residency requirement. So we listed ourselves and waited three months. That was up yesterday. Then we called back, and the program said Supervisor Wayland was unavailable."

" 'Dead' is pretty much unavailable," Vicki said from the back seat. Lizzie ignored her.

"So I dipped a little to find out where the supervisor was. He wasn't anyplace. Finally I checked the death deebee. He died a month ago. You were listed as the 'certifying physician.' "

"Yes," Dr. Aranow said. His face was blank.

"So then I dipped, me, to find out why Harrisburg wasn't holding a special election, like they're supposed to when an elected servant dies. And it turned out the state government didn't know the district supervisor was dead."

Dr. Aranow said, "I checked on this after your call. Everyone is claiming a systems malfunction."

"Oh, yes, certainly," Vicki said. "Let me guess, Jackson. In Wayland's unexplained absence, no district services were authorized, costing nobody any money. Wayland's great-granddaughter has control of his entire, not-inconsiderable fortune, which is quite a coincidence, considering that her house system is the one that developed the comglitch with Harrisburg."

Dr. Aranow twisted in his seat to look at Vicki. "Do you know Ellie Lester?"

"No. But I know donkeys."

"From the viewpoint of one who left? Like Lord Jim knowing the merchant marine?"

"More like Horatius knowing the Roman legions."

What were they talking about? Lizzie had lost control of the conversation. She said loudly, "So I told Harrisburg they were supposed to hold a special election, and they said they planned to. On April first.

There's two candidates, and they both filed campaign speeches on Channel 63. But—"

Vicki interrupted. "Both speeches, naturally, make the same tired promises, the same meaningless avowals of providing consistent and reliable service. Meanwhile, there are exactly two hundred sixty registered voters for non-enclave elections in Willoughby County. Our tribe here, plus a few in the mountain enclaves that hold those donkeys who moved permanently out of Manhattan and into their summer places during the Change Wars. Fleeing the revolution. Workers unite, you have nothing to lose but your warehouses."

Lizzie said, "So we—"

Vicki said, "The idea here, in part, is that you and your impeccable donkey credentials can discover the inside politics of these two candidates. For purposes of—"

Lizzie said, "I'm telling this!" so loudly that Dirk woke up and blinked. "Vicki . . . I'm telling this. It's my idea. It's mine."

"I'm sorry, baby," Vicki said, putting a hand on Lizzie's shoulder. That was almost as bad.

"I'm not a baby. I told you that before!"

And then Vicki and Dr. Aranow exchanged a look, and Lizzie saw that they were both amused at her, and she was so angry she didn't even care that it was the first time they'd looked like they agreed on something. Didn't even care that it was good for the plan. They both thought she was still a baby. And they both were just damn well going to learn better. She was Lizzie Francy, she was the best datadipper in the country, she was a mother, and she was going to make the world a better place for her baby. By herself, if she had to. *That* would serve them right. Because her plan was going to work, and not even donkey laws could stop her this time.

She said icily, "We're going to elect our own candidate, us, to district supervisor. Somebody from the tribe. A Liver."

There, that was better. Dr. Aranow was looking at her like she'd really surprised him, her. Like she was somebody for even a donkey to notice!

But then his expression changed. He said gently—too gently, "But, Lizzie—even if you brought that off . . . even if you got a Liver elected to district supervisor . . . don't you know that donkeys pay taxes by providing services out of their own money? In exchange for votes? That way they get—used to get—the power to make laws that suit them, and you people got the goods and services to stay alive. But if a Liver was elected—how would he fill a warehouse? You don't have the money in the first place. You see, my dear—"

"Don't talk to me like a baby, you son of a bitch!"

Dr. Aranow's eyes widened. Behind her, Lizzie could hear Vicki shake with badly contained laughter. At that moment she hated them both. But at least she had Dr. Aranow's attention. In her arms, Dirk stirred and whimpered. Lizzie lowered her voice, and the baby again drifted into sleep.

"I know more, me, than you do about it. Not all the warehouse supplies come from the politicians themselves. There's a pool of tax money they all pay into, and it gets divided among the counties of Pennsylvania, and you can spend it on what you need. That money—I want it."

"There, Jackson—not up on our governance procedures, are we," Vicki murmured. "Medicine is such a demanding mistress."

"I want those credits," Lizzie repeated, because Dr. Aranow looked impressed for the first time. Or stunned. Was he stunned? Was it really so hopeless for a Liver to get elected? Again doubt attacked her. Maybe this couldn't really work . . . Yes. It could. She would make it work.

Dr. Aranow said, "You? Personally? You want to run for district supervisor?"

"Not me," Lizzie said. "I'm not old enough. You got to be eighteen."

Dr. Aranow looked over his shoulder. "Ms. Turner?"

"Oh, certainly," Vicki said. "A donkey gone native. Nobody in either camp would vote for me. But don't look so terrified, Jackson . . . we're not going to ask you to run."

"Course not," Lizzie said. "Billy Washington is going to run. Only he don't know it yet, him."

Dr. Aranow said, "Billy Washington? That elderly black man who pulled your mother off me when I was trying to deliver your baby?"

Vicki said, "You have a good memory for names. Almost a politician already."

"Yes, that's Billy," Lizzie said eagerly. "My stepfather, him. He'll do it, if *I* ask him. He'd do anything for me and Dirk."

"The 'plan for the health of babies,' " Dr. Aranow said. His mouth twisted. It wasn't quite a smile. "I see. Well, your campaign should be quite interesting. What do you plan to do, register all the nomad Liver voters in Willoughby County at least three months before the election, promise them warehouse access if they vote for Mr. Washington, and just overwhelm the divided donkey candidates by sheer numbers?"

"Yes," Lizzie said eagerly. "I know we can do it!"

"I'm not so sure. Both established political parties will mobilize their own voters, you know."

"We figured that out. We'll get all the voters lined up, but none of them will register until 11:30 P.M. on December thirty-first, the last day before the three-month deadline. It'll be too late for the donkey candidates to get more people registered. They'll never know what hit them."

"And do the numbers indicate—"

"There are only four small enclaves in Willoughby County," Lizzie said. Her confidence returned in a rush; this was data. "And they're summer enclaves. The total of voters registered here even for internal enclave elections is only four thousand eighty. That's *all*. We don't know how many Livers are in the county right now, but more probably than we guess, in abandoned towns and farms and factories like ours. Staying out the winter. We can get them registered here, or reregistered here."

"Out of their vast civic pride," Vicki said. But Lizzie saw that she didn't smile.

"Well," he said, "good luck. But one question: How do you know I won't just go tell everyone I know about this, so that more donkeys register in Willoughby before December first?"

"You won't, you," Lizzie said. The baby stirred in her arms and she shifted his solid little body. "We need you."

"For what?" He looked nervous, and again Lizzie felt that rush of confidence. She could make a *donkey* nervous.

"Two things. We need you to find out about these two candidates. Susannah Wells Livingston and Donald Thomas Serrano. How their voters are split up, like."

"Because," Vicki said, "if one candidate is going to get one hundred percent of the vote, Lizzie will need to register a lot more people than if she can be confident the vote will be split up like cannibals and missionaries. Or if, say, one of the candidates should happen to be as dead as Harold Wayland."

Dr. Aranow turned in his seat to face her. "You're not taking any of this very seriously, are you?"

"On the contrary," Vicki said, "this is how I sound when I'm serious. When I'm frivolous, I make pontificating speeches of great pretentiousness. Such as this one: There's a way of looking at history that traces all enormous events back to the nature of key personalities shaped by very limited environments. This theory says that Napoleon, Hitler, Einstein, and Ballieri changed the world so profoundly precisely because of the strictures or hardships of their childhoods."

"Who's Napoleon?" Lizzie asked. "Or . . . what name did you say? Ballieri?"

"You don't know who Ballieri was?"

"No."

"*Lewis* Ballieri? Last century?"

"No! And I don't care, me!" Why couldn't Vicki behave like normal people? But if she had . . . If she had, she'd never have come to live with Livers, and Lizzie wouldn't ever have gotten . . . She thrust that line of thought away from her.

Vicki said to Dr. Aranow, "I prove my point."

Lizzie changed her grip on Dirk and leaned toward the doctor. "There's a second thing that we need you for, us."

"What's that?"

She couldn't read his expression; his face never seemed to change. She drew in a deep breath. "We need your aircar."

"My *aircar?*"

"To borrow. We need to go look for other Livers, us, and we can't contact them by comlink because the link might be dipped. Our plan has to be secret. So we need to cover the county by air to find everybody's tribes in all the mountains and valleys, and then visit them. Vicki can drive. She knows how. Please. We just need it, us, for a few weeks. And when Billy is elected, we're going to use the tax credits to get Change syringes as well as Y-cones. It's for the *babies.*"

Dr. Aranow sat silent. Outside the car, the wind picked up, whipping the cold river into small frothy waves. A crow landed on a gray rock, cawing. Finally Dr. Aranow said gently, "Lizzie . . . You can't get Change syringes through a warehouse. What few are left are not for sale, at any price. Every donkey organization in the country has been trying to reach Miranda Sharifi at Selene to beg for more . . . didn't you know that? Selene never answers. Electing Billy Washington to district supervisor of Willoughby County won't change that."

"Then we'll get the old-fashioned 'bot medunits for the babies," Lizzie said. Her arms tightened on Dirk. What if he hadn't been Changed, what if she had to worry all the time about infections and bad water and worms . . . For the first time, Lizzie glimpsed what motherhood must have been like for her own mother. Why, Annie must have been afraid every single minute that something would happen to Lizzie! How could parents live like that, them? Lizzie shuddered.

Dr. Aranow said, "I don't think—"

"Yes, you do," Vicki interrupted, and her voice had changed yet again, to something Lizzie hadn't heard in a long time. Vicki was talking to the doctor like she used to talk to Lizzie herself when she was a child, small and sick. "In fact, you probably think too much, Jackson. But this time—don't. Just act. You'll feel better if you do this one thing for the Livers. Without first worrying it to death. And it will cost you so little."

"Don't try to bully me, Ms. Turner."

"I'm not. I'm only trying to present our case—Lizzie's case—in all its aspects. You're an aspect now. You didn't ask to be, but you are. If you say no, that's just as much a statement as if you'd said yes. There's no fence to sit on here. The choices are yours. All I'm trying to do is articulate that."

Vicki's eyes locked with Dr. Aranow's. Lizzie wondered if Vicki was going to bring up Mrs. Aranow, or whatever her name was—the woman that Vicki said was the doctor's ex-wife. She still owned him, Vicki said. Lizzie didn't see how that could be—your family owned you, maybe, and your tribe, but not somebody who'd chosen to leave your tribe. Why, that would be like saying that Harvey could influence Lizzie's decisions just because he was Dirk's father! The world didn't work like that. Still, if mentioning Mrs. Aranow would help the doctor choose against the donkeys . . . but maybe Lizzie better leave this to Vicki. Vicki was the donkey, after all. Although no one in the tribe would dream of holding it against her.

Vicki said, in a different voice, "Don't you ever wish, Jackson, that the class war had turned out differently? That both sides weren't paying the price we are?"

To Lizzie, the words made no sense. What price were the donkeys paying? Donkeys were public servants, they did the work of running things so the Livers could enjoy themselves—or, they used to do that. Now they had so much less work to do. Didn't they like that? How had they paid any sort of price for not supplying warehouses and medunits and food lines and all the other things? It saved them money and work. Vicki wasn't making sense.

But Dr. Aranow was gazing straight ahead now, through the car window. Lizzie had the feeling he wasn't seeing the river or the fields or the cold woods. He was seeing some other place, some other people besides her and Vicki. Who?

"All right," Dr. Aranow said. "On one condition. Not this car. I don't want it spotted and traced and my system jammed with irate messages from people who used to be my friends. I'll furnish you with an aircar leased to some nonexistent company in another state."

"Oh, thank you, Doctor!" Lizzie said. She leaned over and kissed Dr. Aranow on the cheek. Her motion pushed her breast into Dirk's

face, and sleepily he started to suck. When he discovered cloth between his mouth and her nipple, he whimpered and screwed up his
face. Lizzie opened her shirt and gave him her breast.

She'd done it. She'd managed to people-dip an aircar.

She said, "And you'll find out, you, about the other candidates?
Please?"

"Why not." He didn't sound as happy as Lizzie had hoped.

"Cheer up, Jackson," Vicki said. "Commitment only hurts while the
first rope goes on."

"You're quite a pastoral philosopher, aren't you? Could part of this
deal be that you just stop lecturing me?"

"But you like it so much. Look at Cazie."

"Vicki," Lizzie said. But then the doctor smiled. It wasn't a very
sweet smile, but it was a smile. He wasn't mad at Vicki for her nasty
comment. Why not? Lizzie would never understand donkeys.

But she didn't have to. He'd promised to do it. Lizzie had *won*.

Now all she had to do was convince Billy. But that would be easy—
Billy had never denied her anything, not in her whole life.

"No," Billy said.

"No? *No?*"

"No, I won't, me."

"But . . . but it's for Dirk!"

Billy didn't answer. He and Lizzie sat on a fallen log in the November woods, their coats open to an afternoon that had suddenly turned
warm. Billy loved the woods. Before the Change he was the only one
in East Oleanta who used to go off into the woods by himself, just to
be alone with trees. Now more people did, but Billy was still the only
one who'd go in winter for days at a time. Or as many days anyway as
Annie'd let him. And just when Annie got to grumbling and com-
plaining about his absence—just at that very minute, it always seemed
to Lizzie—Billy would come home again. Walking into camp with the
strong walk he had since the Change, not the old-man shuffle from
before. There'd be wet leaves stuck to Billy's jacks, and twigs in his
hair, and Annie would squeal when Billy hugged her because he
hadn't shaved in so long. But she'd hug back, hard and tight, before
she started scolding and grumbling again.

Lizzie had known that Billy would be in the woods, checking his
rabbit traps, and she had followed his tracks in the mud. When Billy
wanted to hide, nobody could track him, but his time he hadn't both-

ered. Lizzie had left Dirk with Annie. Now she wished she'd brought the baby. Maybe Dirk would have changed Billy's stubborn old mind.

Billy was too old, him. That was the trouble. Even if the old people were healthy and strong since the Change, they were still old in their brains. They *thought* old. Lizzie made herself calm down to reason with Billy.

"Why won't you run for district supervisor, you? Don't you see that it will help us get all the things we need, us, like more 'bots and medunits for any more babies and better boots? Don't you see that?"

"I see that, me."

"Well, then, why don't you run for election? It will work, Billy!"

"Not if I run, me."

Lizzie stared at him. The old man broke a branch off a dead maple and poked at the ground with it.

"Lizzie, you see this dirt? It should be frozen, it, by this time in November."

"What's that got to do with—"

"Wait. The reason the ground ain't frozen is 'cause we had us a mostly warm autumn. Nobody could predict that, them. It just happened. But we didn't know it would happen, so we got all ready, us, for a hard winter. All the blankets and jacks we could scrounge, caulking the tribe house airtight, them cones you and Vicki got us from TenTech."

Lizzie waited. There was no use rushing Billy, him. He always did what she wanted, but it sometimes took him a long time to get there.

"We prepared, us, for the hardships we could see coming, even if they didn't come. Anything less is just stupid. Right, dear heart?"

"Right," Lizzie said. Billy's stick continued to poke at the ground.

"If you and Vicki do this donkey election, you got to see coming what you can, you, and prepare for it. Donkeys ain't stupid, and they don't play as fair as the weather. Where Livers be concerned, us, donkeys are always cold."

Not Vicki or Dr. Aranow, Lizzie wanted to say, but she didn't interrupt.

"If I run for district supervisor, me, we'll lose. Nobody will vote for me, them. Not just no donkeys—no Livers neither, outside our tribe. Just like they wouldn't vote for you or Annie. We was the first ones who got Changed. Who tracked down Miranda Sharifi in her underground lab and demanded, us, that she help you when you was so sick. Who actually saw Miranda and talked to her."

"But those are all good things, them!"

"Yes. But they all *different* things, them. Different from most folks.

And most folks don't like too much different. It makes them uneasy, them. Don't you listen on the talk channels in the county, you?"

Lizzie didn't. She had too many more important, more interesting deebees to explore, without listening to the endless intertribe gossip and rumors and tiny plans on local comlinks. *Somebody said, them, that a friend heard on a donkey channel in New York that some folks in Baltimore got a scooter track powered up and running . . . Then if you're from Glenn's Falls, you, do you know my second cousin Pamela Cantrell, she's oh five foot six with . . . We got a feeding ground, us, big enough for . . .*

"People talk, them," Billy said. "And even with the Change, people don't trust ideas and plans that feel too different from what they're used to. Maybe because of the Change. We already had so much new, us. And here you come with another new idea, maybe a dangerous idea, if you get donkeys mad at you. If different-type folks like me are running for public servant, too—well, everybody's gonna be so uneasy, them, they won't vote for me."

"But—"

"Besides," Billy went on in his gentle voice, "we're the family, us, who got Miranda arrested by the Genetic Standards Enforcement Agency, even if we didn't mean to and even if they let her go, them. *Miranda Sharifi.* No, Lizzie, dear heart, ain't nobody gonna vote in a donkey election for me. Or Annie or you or Vicki. Nobody, them."

"Then who?" Lizzie cried. "Who would they vote for, them?"

"Somebody that ain't too unfamiliar." Billy stood. "Somebody who used to be a mayor, maybe. Livers are used to a mayor, them, being sort of part of the government."

This was true. Lizzie considered. The mayors of the Liver towns—when there'd been settled towns—had always been Livers talking donkey. They'd been the ones to talk on the comlinks, back when each town only had one, before the Change Wars. The mayor had been laughed at and teased for working like a donkey when everybody else just enjoyed themselves, even though mayors then hadn't worked as hard as everybody did now. Still, the mayor had been considered sort of dumb to do it at all; a real aristo Liver didn't serve—they were served. By donkeys. Or so everyone Lizzie knew had thought then.

But a mayor was a familiar person to negotiate with donkeys. To report something broken, to present voter demands to newly elected public servants, to send for police or game wardens or techs when they'd been needed. Maybe Billy was right. Maybe Willoughby County Livers would be more likely to vote for somebody who used to be a mayor. But would a mayor agree to run for election?

"You know any leftover mayors, Billy? Our tribe doesn't have any, us."

Billy smiled down at Lizzie, still sitting on the log. "Yes, we do, us. Don't you know? That's what comes of dipping all your fancy data instead of talking to people."

A little flame warmed Lizzie. Billy was proud of her ability to datadip. Billy had always been proud of her, even when she'd been a little girl piecing together broken 'bots, trying to learn without any real system.

"Who's a mayor, Billy?"

"Who *was* a mayor."

"Okay—who *was* a mayor, them?"

"Shockey," Billy said, and Lizzie felt her mouth open into a round "O." Billy smiled. "Ain't it surprising what people, them, turn up in what places? That's the biggest thing the Change taught me, dear heart. The biggest thing. We just don't ever know, us. Hardly nothing."

"It's not at all surprising," Vicki said. "Here, take Dirk, he wants to nurse."

Lizzie took the baby. The familiar warmth ran through her at just getting her arms around him. She scrunched into a sitting position against the foamcast wall of her cubicle and opened the shirt of her marigold jacks. Dirk's hungry little mouth fastened onto her nipple like a heat-seeking missile. The thrill, half mommy and half sexy, ran through her body, from nipple to belly to crotch. Lizzie was still a little ashamed of that thrill—it didn't seem right to get heated up from her own baby! But it happened every time, and she finally settled for just keeping the feeling to herself. But it increased her irritation with Vicki, sitting there beside Lizzie on Lizzie's pallet, looking like she knew everything. *Vicki* had never birthed and nursed a baby.

Lizzie said, "Well, *I* was surprised, and so was Billy. Shockey! He just doesn't seem like the kind of person who'd been a mayor anyplace."

Vicki smiled. "What kind of person do you think goes into politics?"

"Somebody like Jack Sawicki was. Interested in helping his village, and not caring if people made fun of him sometimes. Shockey gets mad if you tease him even a little, and I don't think he ever wanted to help other people in his life."

Vicki said innocently, "Is that why you're backing this daring political venture? Because you have a burning desire to help other tribes in Willoughby County?"

"Of course I—" Lizzie began, and stopped. Vicki smiled again.

"Lizzie, honey, the people who go into politics are ninety-nine percent exactly like Shockey. They want personal gain, and they want power, and they want to make the world wag their way. Just as you want warehouse goods and power over tax money for yourself and your tribe. The only difference between—"

"But I don't want it for myself! I want it for Dirk and Billy and Mama and—"

"Really? If Billy and Annie went south tomorrow, and if the ever-beneficent Jackson Aranow hand-delivered any goods you wanted to you, and also set up a credit account in Dirk's citizenship number, would you just drop this kingmaker scheme entirely? Hmmmm?"

Lizzie said nothing.

"I didn't think so. There's nothing wrong with that, Lizzie—with looking out for your own self-interest. As long as that's not all you're looking out for. Someone I once knew told me—"

Here we go again, Lizzie thought. She shifted Dirk, sucking greedily, to a more comfortable position.

"—that there were five states that any human relationship could exist in. Any relationship—an international treaty conference, a marriage, a police department, whatever. Only five possible states. One, healthy negotiation from a basically allied position. Two, complete detachment, without any mutual-aid pacts or significant interaction. Three, dominance-and-dependence, like the Livers used to be with the donkeys. Four, covert struggle for dominance, without much outbreak of actual fighting. Or, five, actual war. As long as you try to stay within the election laws, you're in a covert struggle for your own interests. Nothing wrong with that. But so is Shockey, only more crudely than most politicians. I'll bet he was only mayor of his old town briefly, wasn't he?"

"I don't know."

"Bet on it. As John Locke once pontificated—"

"Isn't there anything you don't think you already know, you!"

Vicki looked at her. Lizzie dropped her eyes to the baby, then raised them angrily to Vicki. Well, it was true. Vicki was always *telling* her things. Like Vicki knew everything and Lizzie was some kind of datadumb . . . Liver.

"Actually," Vicki said quietly, "I hardly know anything, which is peculiarly startling when you consider that just a few years ago I thought I understood it all."

"I'm sorry," Lizzie muttered. Was she sorry? She didn't know. Lately Vicki confused her, and she used to think Vicki was so wonderful . . . nothing was the same, it.

"Don't be sorry." Vicki stood, stretching the kinks out of her legs. "Here's looking at you, Karl Marx."

"What?"

"Nothing, dear heart. I'll see you at dinner, okay?"

"Okay," Lizzie mumbled. She watched Vicki stroll out of Lizzie's cubicle and disappear around the battered plastic upended table that formed one of its walls. Vicki didn't look back. Lizzie hugged Dirk, wishing she hadn't said that about Vicki knowing everything. Vicki'd been so good to Lizzie when Lizzie was just a kid, her. But . . . Vicki *did* act like she knew everything. Every idea that came up, every plan or . . . Why was Vicki like that? Because she was a donkey?

Lizzie reached upward, trying not to disturb the baby, until her fingers groped at the top of her chest of drawers. She pulled down her terminal. "Library search."

"Ready," the system said.

"Three-sentence definitions of two things. First—'Here's looking at you.' Second—'Carl Marks.'"

" 'Here's looking at you,' was a famous line from a pre-holo entertainment recording titled *Casablanca*. It was said as a drinking toast by the male lead to the female lead. In the 2090s the phrase enjoyed a renewed vogue as an ironic expression roughly meaning 'I guess you won that contest.'

" 'Karl Marx' was a political theorist whose writings were used by many twentieth-century revolutionaries as a basis for rebellion. He advocated a socialism that included collective ownership of the means of production. The mechanism he foresaw for achieving this was class warfare."

"System off," Lizzie said.

"System off."

Class warfare. Was that what she, Lizzie, was asking for? Was that what Vicki really felt about Lizzie? And Billy and Annie and . . . Dirk?

A sour taste filled Lizzie's mouth. She swallowed, but it didn't go away. She'd been going to ask Vicki to go with her to explain the plan to Shockey. Maybe now she wouldn't. Maybe she'd just go alone, if that was the way Vicki felt.

The baby had finished feeding and had fallen asleep again. Lizzie hugged him close and bent over to smell his sweet, clean baby smell. But even then the sour taste in her mouth and nose didn't go away.

* * *

She found Shockey with Sharon and Sharon's baby, nine-month-old Callie, fishing by the river in the mild weather. Sharon and Shockey wore winter jacks with the coats unbuttoned. Lizzie saw that Sharon's shirt was unbuttoned as well. So that's how it was.

Callie sat on the riverbank in a blue plastic clothes basket, turning a grimy plastic duck over and over in her fat little fists. She was a pretty baby, with Sharon's soft brown hair and big eyes, but when she caught sight of Lizzie, she screwed up her face to cry and looked frantically around for her mother. Annie said babies got this way at Callie's age. They got shy of strangers and nervous about new things. Callie would outgrow it, Annie said. Well, Lizzie didn't spend a lot of time with Sharon but she wasn't exactly a stranger, either; they belonged to the same *tribe*. She hoped Dirk didn't go through a stage like this when he was older. She moved out of Callie's line of sight.

Sharon and Shockey bent over their fishing lines. Sharon giggled and guided Shockey's hand from his line to her open shirt.

"Hello!" Lizzie said loudly.

"Hey, Liz," Shockey said, straightening. "If we catch anything, us, want to share a real meal for a change?"

There was nothing wrong with the words. The tribe ate by mouth often: berries or nuts, roasted rabbit, wild apples. Sometimes Lizzie got a longing in her mouth that nothing but the sharp bite of wild onions would satisfy. The Change just meant that nobody had to bother with getting food; not that they couldn't. There was nothing wrong with Shockey's offer of fish. It was the *way* he said it—his eyes bold on Lizzie, his mouth half smiling, half sneering, his hand still on Sharon's bare breast. Sex bareness was different from eating bareness; it should be private. And Shockey acted like he owned Sharon. Well, he didn't own Lizzie.

But she made herself smile. "Sure, if you catch anything, you. But that's not why I'm here. I have an offer, me, to make to you."

Shockey's smile widened and his dark eyes blinked slowly. Lizzie said quickly, "Billy told me you used to be mayor of a town someplace."

Shockey's smile vanished. "Yeah? So what? Somebody had to be mayor, them."

"You're right, you," Lizzie said. She looked levelly into Shockey's face. "And somebody still does."

Sharon said, "We don't need no mayors, us, anymore."

"But we need a district supervisor, us. Harold Winthrop Wayland is dead."

Sharon's voice scaled upward. "Shockey ain't no donkey, Lizzie Francy, and don't you forget it, you!"

"Of course he ain't," Lizzie said. "He's a Liver, him—that's the whole point."

"What whole point?" Sharon said, so loudly that Callie, alarmed, looked up from her rubber duck. "Livers don't work, them, at no jobs like district supervisor!"

"A district supervisor controls the warehouse distrib. Willoughby County ain't got no supervisor, us, so there ain't nothing in the warehouse. But if we elect one of our own, then—"

"Then there still ain't nothing in the warehouse! Dip your brain, you, for a change, instead of donkey nets! Shockey can't put no goods in no warehouse!"

"Yes, he could," Lizzie said. She was suddenly tired of talking Liver to this stupid girl. She'd known Sharon all her life, and Sharon had always been stupid. "There's a tax pool of credit from the state, collected from corporate taxes, that's divided up between all the counties. A credit base that donkey taxes add to. But if we can get enough Livers registered and get Shockey elected, he can use Willoughby's share to stock a warehouse for us."

"But if he—"

"Shut up, Sharon, and let Shockey talk." Lizzie hoped this would make Shockey mad—the hint that Sharon was controlling him. But Shockey wasn't mad. His bold eyes, under heavy brows, had a faraway look, and his hand moved from Sharon to stroke his dark beard. Both women stared at him.

Finally he said, "Yeah."

" 'Yeah'?" Sharon shrieked.

"Shut up, Sharon. Yeah, I'll do it, Liz." Abruptly he swooped down on the baby and lifted her high above his head. "How about it, Callie—you want, you, to see your big buddy a district supervisor?"

The baby squealed happily. Apparently little Callie didn't consider Shockey a "stranger." Sharon sulked. But Lizzie, watching, thought that Shockey wasn't seeing either of them. His eyes gazed at something else, and he smiled the same half sneer as when he offered Lizzie the fish. What was it Vicki'd said? In her list of kinds of human relationships? *A covert struggle for dominance, without much outbreak of actual fighting* . . .

"Liz, you just tell me what to do first. I'm all ready, me, and I'm all yours."

Eight

When the security alarm sounded, Theresa was sitting in her new study, working at a terminal.

She had made the study from a maid's room in the middle of the apartment's upper floor, unused probably since before house 'bots. Theresa had chosen it because it had no window, only a skylight set small and high on the wall and angled into an airshaft, from which she could see nothing but a patch of artificial sky. She'd had the building 'bot clean the room and paint it white, and she had moved in a terminal and an old-fashioned, inflexible chair. The only other thing in the room were the printies.

They were tacked on every wall, full-color flat printouts of whatever holoscenes she selected from the newsgrids. In one, three abandoned Liver children huddled together, dead, in a snowbank, their frozen and well-fed faces smooth with Cell Cleaner health.

In another, a baby lay in its grieving Liver mother's arms. The mother, who looked about fifteen, was clearly Changed. The baby's face was ravaged by some disease; its skin had turned mottled and pulpy, and blood oozed from its closed eyes. The camera had caught the mother with one cupped palm upraised, empty of a Change syringe.

In a wide-angle shot from an aerial camera, a shimmering Y-shield enclosed a beautiful valley in the Ozarks. The entire valley. One rich donkey lived there, a former financier whom no one had seen since the Change, when he gave a press conference exulting that now he would never need to have contact with another human being again.

In a small printie on the far wall, four emaciated adults, elbows like chisels, ate meager bowls of mush and drank water under a cross wood-burned with the words THE DAILY BREAD HE MEANT FOR US. Malnutrition marked their bowed legs and thin hair. All four smiled beatifically at the camera, smiles with missing teeth and swollen gums.

A large printie behind the terminal stand showed Miranda Sharifi's face, overlaid with a blue veil, three lilies, and an open prayer book. Beside it an equally large printie showed the same holo, overlaid with gravestones and coffins and black candles and implements of torture along with the words WHEN IMMORTALITY, BITCH?

The pictures went on. Two donkey children lying naked and laughing on the corpse of a slaughtered deer sliced open from breast to tail, body-feeding directly on the blood and flesh. Another diseased Liver child, in a French town where there had been no Change syringes for four years. An ad for Endorkiss, the colors glowing and seductive, in which three incredibly perfect donkey bodies ground-fed quietly, their faces blissful, nobody looking at anyone else and clearly not needing to.

Jackson had not seen the room. Theresa went there only when he wasn't home, and she'd asked Jones, the house system, to admit no one but herself to this room. Of course, Jackson probably knew how to override that, but even if he could, maybe he wouldn't. Jackson wouldn't understand the room. He would think it was a medical problem, like what he called Theresa's "neurochemical anguish." He wouldn't see that the room was necessary.

The system in front of Theresa was in screen mode, its flat energy "surface" divided in half vertically by a thick black line. Above the line was a quote in severe dark blue letters: " 'Even an animal can get lost in unfamiliar terrain, but only men and women can lose themselves.' Christopher Caan-Agee, 2067." Below was the last paragraph Theresa had written in her book on Leisha Camden:

Leisha had a friend. His name was Tony Indivino. Tony was much angrier than Leisha about a lot of things. It didn't seem right to Tony that some people had so much money and others had so little. Leisha had never thought about that before Tony made her think. Leisha wrote later that Tony said to her, "What if you walk down a street in a poor country like Spain and you see a beggar? Do you give him a dollar? What if you see a hundred beggars, a thousand beggars, and you don't have as much money as Leisha Camden? What do you do? What should you do?" Leisha didn't know answers to Tony's questions.

Theresa studied her paragraph. She said to her personal system, Thomas, "Put 'important' before 'friend.' " It did, changing the "a" to "an." Leisha studied her sentence again. Then she looked at the sentence above: *Even an animal can get lost in unfamiliar terrain, but only men and women can lose themselves.* She said, "Thomas, bring me the second quote in my list."

Thomas brought up the words, reading them aloud in its rich male voice: " 'But man, proud man, drest in a little brief authority, most ignorant of what he's most assured, his glassy essence, like an angry ape plays such fantastic tricks before high heaven, as make the angels weep.' William Shakespeare, 1564–1616."

"The next quote."

" 'Man's unhappiness comes, as I construe, of his greatness; it is because there is an infinite in him, which, with all his cunning, he cannot quite bury under the finite.' Thomas Carlyle, 1795–1881."

Again Theresa read her own paragraph, with "important" inserted before "friend." Then she listened again to Carlyle's sentence.

Why was it so hard to write a book? She could see so clearly what she needed to say about Leisha Camden, could feel it so clearly. She could even talk about it, at least with Jackson. But when she sat down in front of the terminal, the words she spoke were stiff and cold and it would be better if she never tried to show the world at all why Leisha Camden mattered, why a life given to something as large as keeping Sleepless and Sleepers as one people *mattered*. Even if Leisha had failed. Despite Leisha's efforts, the Sleepless had gone to Sanctuary. The country had gone into a long bitter divide. Jennifer Sharifi had gone to prison. And Leisha had gone to her death in a Georgia swamp, murdered by Livers who despised Sleepless even more than Theresa despised herself.

But Leisha had at least tried. And so saved herself from what the rest of them had become. No, Theresa had to write this book about Leisha. She *had* to. But why was it so hard to find words as wonderful as Thomas brought back when she sent him out on a quote search?

Theresa rubbed tears from her cheeks and looked again at the printies around the walls . . . *most ignorant* . . . *like an angry ape plays such fantastic tricks before high heaven, as make the angels weep.*

"Take a neuropharm," Jackson would say. "I can custom order you one that—"

"Building security has been breached," the house system said loudly from Theresa's terminal. "This is not a drill, Ms. Aranow. Repeat, building security has been breached and this is not a drill. What would you like me to do?"

Breached? How could building security be breached? There were Y-shields, there were locks . . . What should she do? Jackson was gone somewhere with Cazie. Theresa didn't know what to tell the system. It wasn't supposed to be breachable.

She said, "Lock all the doors!"

"They are always locked, Ms. Aranow."

Of course they were. Theresa thought wildly. "Show me the breach!"

Prose, hers and Carlyle's, disappeared from the screen. It went holo and transmitted a wide-angle view of the building foyer. People—Livers!—pushed toward the elevator, which said, "I'm sorry—this elevator opens only for authorized residents and guests." A man with a handheld terminal did something to it and the elevator door opened.

Theresa stood, knocking over her chair. Her heart thudded. Five Livers, four men and a woman, people with squat foreheads or knobbly chins or hairy ears or thick necks, dressed in old winter jackets. In her building. Their faces were focused and intent, and one had a mobile. Where had he gotten it? The Change Wars? But those were over years ago . . . weren't they? What should she *do?*

"What . . . what should I do, Jones? Is there a standard security procedure?"

"A standard intruder-repellent sequence exists, in escalating stages. Shall I begin it? Or do you wish to speak to the unauthorized intruders first?"

"No! No . . . I . . . what do they want?"

"Shall I put front-door visual and audio through to Thomas?"

"No . . . yes. And start the intruder-repellent sequence!"

"All levels, on automatic?"

"Yes!"

The display stage showed the corridor outside the apartment door. Three of the people, including the woman, now held guns. Theresa felt her throat close and she gasped for breath. No, not now, not now . . . The Livers weren't shouting. The one with the mobile spoke calmly but loudly, in their street talk: "—get for our kids, us, more Change syringes. That's all we want, us. We won't hurt nobody. I tell you again, me, that all we want is more Change syringes, we know you got them, Dr. Aranow, you're a doctor, you—"

"Go away!" Theresa called. The words came out strangled, unable to force themselves past her panic attack. She tried again. "Go away! No Change syringes here! My brother doesn't keep them at home!" Which wasn't true. There were sixteen Change syringes in the house safe.

"What? Is that Dr. Aranow, you? Open the door!"

"No," Theresa whimpered. She couldn't breathe.

"Then we're coming in, us!"

The front door clicked open. The security procedure . . . why wasn't Jones responding? What had these people had time to do to Jones . . . and how did they know how to do it? Theresa wrapped her arms around herself and rocked back and forth. Jones said, "You are unauthorized intruders. If you don't leave immediately, this system will activate its bio-based defenses."

"Wait, Elwood, don't—"

"I knocked out the defenses, them. Come on!"

"But you—"

"The syringes—"

"Activating now," Jones said, and abruptly the holostage was full of a dark yellow gas, coming from everywhere at once. And it *was* everywhere. Theresa's study was suddenly full of it. Gasping for air, she drew gas into her lungs and—

—and her arms and legs fell off.

Theresa tumbled to the floor. She could see her arms and legs lying beside her, clearly detached . . . But, no, they couldn't be hers, because there was no blood. They were somebody else's arms and legs . . . the intruders'? But how had they gotten as far as her upper-floor study, without their legs? How odd! But interesting, actually. Although maybe they weren't the intruders' arms and legs. But, then, whose could they be?

She pushed the nearest leg away from herself. Really, the disgusting thing shouldn't be lying around on the floor. Where was the cleaning 'bot? Perhaps it was broken . . .

As she shoved the stray leg hard, Theresa was astonished to feel her own body jerk. Now, what was that all about? Nothing seemed normal today. Although Jackson always said that normal was a huge warehouse . . . he must be right, if "normal" had to include arms and legs that weren't even hers cluttering up her study.

Theresa grasped a detached arm and tried to throw it across the room. Again her torso jerked, and pain tore through her shoulder, which didn't make sense. And how had the intruder dressed his arm in one of Theresa's flowered sleeves? He must have gone first to her bedroom, changed clothes, and then come in here to fall apart. Maybe Leisha had sent him. Yes, that would make sense—Leisha was always compassionate to Livers. Compassionate and unafraid.

"Theresa!" someone called. *"Tess!"*

Although now that she thought of it, Theresa wasn't afraid either. Really, she was very calm. Jackson would be proud of her. She was staying calm and thinking what to do. First, get the cleaning 'bot to clear up these extra arms and legs off the floor. Then, notify the enclave police about the intruders. Third, figure out what made Thomas Carlyle's sentences so good, so that she could write ones just as good. Or so her personal system could. Yes, that made sense—she would ask her system to duplicate Carlyle's prose. After all, they both were named Thomas.

"Tess! Where are—oh, my God!"

Theresa looked up. Cazie stood over her, wearing a Y-shield helmet with air filter. Cazie seemed to have all her arms and legs. This was interesting . . . how had Cazie hung on to hers when both Theresa and the intruders hadn't been able to? Fourth on her list would be to ask Jackson about this. It was probably a medical problem.

"Here, breathe deep . . . hold still, Tessie, just breathe as deep as you can, the gas only needs a few minutes to leave your body . . . just breathe . . ."

There was something over her head, although it must be made of Y-energy because through it Theresa could still see Cazie. Cazie looked so concerned . . . but she needn't, really. Theresa was fine. Jackson would be proud of how fine she was, staying calm in an emergency, breathing normally, making a rational list of what to do and what order to do it in . . . But she should speak the list to Thomas. That way she would be sure to remember everything on it. Thomas could write it down.

She crawled toward her terminal to do this. "Breathe deep," Cazie said again, but before Theresa could, everything went black.

She awoke on the living-room sofa. Jackson and Cazie stood over her. Cazie said, "How do you feel, Tessie?"

"I . . . there were Livers . . ."

"Gone now. No, don't get upset, Tess, it's all right. Enclave security has them all, and nobody was hurt. It won't happen again."

"But how . . . what . . ."

Jackson sat beside her and took her hand. "They dipped the building entry codes, Theresa. Nobody knows how they got into the enclave. But all our systems have been reprogrammed—building, elevator, and Jones. Cazie's right, it won't happen again."

His voice sounded hollow. He was lying to her.

Cazie said, "Nothing was stolen. Maybe they didn't even intend to steal anything but Change syringes. They knew Jackson was a doctor. Other medical types were breached, too. The cops will take care of the whole thing. Nobody was hurt."

"But there were arms and legs all over the floor!" Theresa cried. She could see them, horrible detached limbs . . . she shuddered and gasped. "And *my* arms and legs—"

"Easy, Tess," Cazie said. "It's all right now. There weren't any arms and legs on the floor, and yours are all right, too. It was just the system biodefense. Why didn't you put on your mask when you activated it?"

"You're upsetting her," Jackson said. "She didn't know. Tess, it's all right now, we're right here. You don't need to think about it anymore."

"But . . ." Theresa said. Her fingers tightened and loosened on Jackson's, tightened and loosened. "But tell me . . . what did I breathe in? Please tell me, Jackson."

Jackson said reluctantly, "It was a gas that acts directly on the parietal cortices, inducing anosognosia. The parietal cortices control how the mind perceives the sensations and movements of the body. In anosognosia the mind is incapable of recognizing its own limbs, and also incapable of recognizing that anything is wrong. So the victim invents elaborate scenarios to explain the perceived limb paralysis. It makes a good security method to incapacitate without increasing the anger and panic that can lead to reckless response. And it doesn't harm anyone."

"The arms and legs on the floor were your own," Cazie said. "The Livers never got past the foyer."

Jackson said, "You just breathed a temporary neuropharm. Even without the Cell Cleaner, it doesn't last long. You might have a tingling in your limbs for a while, but it's not harmful."

A neuropharm. She had breathed in a neuropharm, and become a different person. A person without arms and legs, a person who thought other people's arms and legs cluttered the floor, a person who hadn't been upset by that but rather had planned a calm list of ways to deal with it. Not Theresa. Someone else entirely.

She looked up at Jackson, and for the first time she could remember, Theresa didn't want him close. "You . . . you made me somebody else."

"No, I didn't, the house system—"

"But you want me to take neuropharms always. To be somebody different from me."

"Theresa, you can't compare—" he began, but she interrupted him.

"That's not the answer. I don't know what is, but not that." She let go of Jackson's hand and struggled to stand.

Cazie said, "Tess, honey, you're not really being fair to Jack. He just—"

"I know what he just," Theresa said, and somehow she left them there, Jackson looking stricken and Cazie rueful. Staggered to her room really, her walk was so unsteady, her arms and legs did tingle and once she thought they might buckle under her.

But at least they were her own.

The building sat on the side of a mountain high in the Adirondacks. Theresa landed the car, which of course flew on automatic, on an artificially flat stretch of nanopaved ground that she assumed was a parking lot, although no other cars rested on it. Then she stood for a long time in the cold just gazing up at the Sisters of Merciful Heaven.

The convent, not foamcast but built of genuine stone, blended into the mountain. Gray rock, scantily covered with withered ivy vines that matched the withered winter vegetation growing at angles on the steep ground. It was the first donkey building Theresa could remember ever seeing, even in newsgrids, that wasn't surrounded by the faint shimmering bubble of a Y-shield. Only snow, heaped in clean drifts. A little wind skirled the light powder around Theresa's legs, and she shivered. She started toward the door.

It was opened by a middle-aged woman, not a security system or a 'bot. A woman—a sister?—dressed in a straight gray robe of what looked like cotton. *Cotton.* A consumable. The sight almost overcame Theresa's usual shrinking from strangers. She clutched her two hands tightly together and forced herself not to step back.

"I'm . . . Theresa Aranow. I called . . ."

"Come in, Ms. Aranow. I'm Sister Anne." She smiled, but Theresa couldn't smile back. Her face felt too tight. "I'm the one you talked to on comlink. Come with me to where we can talk."

She led Theresa through a gloomy stone foyer and opened a heavy wooden door. Sound flowed out.

"Oh! What . . . What *is* it?"

"The sisters, singing vespers."

Theresa stopped, transfixed. She had never heard singing like that. Not from any sound system, ever. A glorious outpouring of sound, without instruments—just human voices, every one genemod for musical ability, raised in fervent ardor. She couldn't make out the words, but the words didn't matter . . . it was the passion that mattered. Passion for something unseen but—but what? Felt. The passion . . .

Sister Anne said gently, "You said on comlink you were not raised Catholic. Have you heard vespers sung before?"

"Never!"

"Well, neither have most Catholics. Or what passes for Catholics now. Come in here, where we can talk."

Theresa followed her into a small, white-walled room furnished only with a desk, terminal, and three chairs. Wooden chairs. She blurted, "You're not Changed. Any of you."

"No," Sister Anne said, smiling. "We must eat, and drink, and depend on our own efforts and His grace for our daily bread."

"Is it . . . is it . . ." She was trembling. But she made herself get the words out, because they were so important to her. "Is it a spiritual discipline?"

"It is. Suppose, Ms. Aranow, you start by telling me why you're here."

"Why I'm here." Theresa looked at the nun. Theresa had had Thomas do background. Sister Anne was fifty-one years old, had entered this semi-cloistered order at seventeen, was one of only eight hundred forty-nine Sisters of Merciful Heaven left in the world. Born Anne Grenville Hart in Wichita, Kansas, she had inherited three million dollars from her mother, cofounder of a bakery franchise, Proust's Madeleines. The entire three million had been donated to the order. Why was Anne Grenville Hart here? But Theresa couldn't ask that. Obediently, she tried to answer the sister's question, knowing even before she began that the answer would be inadequate, wouldn't really say at all what Theresa could never find words for in the first place.

"I'm here because I . . . I'm looking for something." And waited to be asked what. The unanswerable question, which would only lead to stammering and muddled words and puzzled looks from the sister, growing more impatient, until Theresa collapsed into hopeless silence.

But Sister Anne said, "And you've looked everywhere else you could think of, couldn't find it, and so have tried here, in desperation. Even though you can't begin to define what you're looking for, and are afraid it isn't the Catholic conception of God at all."

"Yes!" Theresa gasped. "How . . . how did you know?"

"You're not the first to come to us," Sister Anne said serenely, "and you won't be the last. But I think you may be different from most. Ms. Aranow, why aren't you Changed?"

"I can't."

"Can't? You mean, there is some physical difficulty?"

"No, no. I mean I just . . . can't."

"You're afraid of making your own life too automatic. In physical need, you think, begins spiritual questing. Its roots and wellspring."

"Yes!" Theresa gasped. "Oh, yes! Only . . ."

"Only what, Ms. Aranow?" Sister Anne leaned forward on her chair, a chair of hard mellowed natural wood that her unChanged body would not consume molecule by molecule until the solid had been turned into a holed skeleton of itself. Sister Anne's chair would stay a chair. Sister Anne's expression was as warm as Jackson's and Cazie's but different somehow, not . . . not what? Not careful with Theresa, not pitying, not condescending. Sister Anne didn't think that Theresa Aranow was weak, or crazy.

The words spilled out. Looking at the calm, understanding face, Theresa's fear of strangers somehow disappeared and the words tumbled out, tidal-waved out, unstoppable.

"I've always wanted something, looked for something, my whole life . . . only I don't have any idea what it is! And nobody else has ever seemed to need it, or to even know what I'm talking about, even good people that I know are good people. People I love. They look at me like I'm crazy . . . actually, I am crazy. I'm depressed, agoraphobic, and severely neurologically inhibited. I haven't left our apartment in over a year except once and that was—nobody else I know feels like this. I want there to be something . . . large. Larger than myself. Something in the universe to hang on to, to give my life some kind of meaning . . . I'm a fraud, you know, agreeing with you that I'm un-Changed because I don't want things too automatic. They *are* automatic for me. I'm rich, and I have a loving brother who stands between me and the world, and I never have to worry or struggle for anything, certainly not my daily bread, which is delivered and cooked and served by 'bots that—while most of the people in this country are out there without safety or enough Y-cones or medical care for their children who are born without enough Change syringes . . . Not that I think the Change is a good—I'm confused about the Change. I know it. But the reason I've always been different is that I want something nobody can have—Jackson says nobody can have it because it doesn't exist. I want the truth! The truth that is real and solid and you can use to help you figure out how to live your life and what that life is supposed to mean. Oh, I know there's no such thing as that kind of truth—absolute truth—and it's stupid and naive to go looking for it . . . but I *did.* I tried to, anyway. I had Thomas help me search through Christianity and Zen and Yagaiism and Hinduism and the Text of the Scientific Change . . . I'm not very smart, Sister, something may have gone wrong with my in vitro fertilization and maybe I don't understand much of what Thomas brought me. But I did try. And it seems to me that those beliefs all contradict each other, all say different things, and if so, how can they all be true? And then they also contradict themselves internally, with different parts of their own beliefs that don't fit with each other, or don't fit with what I see all around me in the world, so how can *any* of them be true? They're not! But then I'm left with nothing except this longing, and nobody else I know seems to feel it so I end up so alone I think I'll die. I've seriously thought of suicide. But what that would do to Jackson, who already feels so responsible for me . . . I can't. I can't. It wouldn't be right. Only . . . how do I know what's 'right' if I can't find out what's true? And so I go on living in this . . . this *void,* and sometimes the emptiness is so big and dark and thick I feel that I'll suffocate, or that I'm so lost I can't ever be found . . . can't find myself, I mean, except that myself isn't what I want! It's too small, to find nothing but myself!"

Theresa stopped, gasping. What had she been saying? Pouring out all that to this stranger, this poised woman whom she didn't even know, like some sort of whining baby . . .

"You are right in your search," Sister Anne said, "but wrong in your conclusions."

She spoke with utter conviction. And yet Theresa felt confused; she didn't think she'd stated any conclusions, hadn't been able to come to any. Wasn't that the problem?

"I don't understand, Sister."

"How old are you, Ms. Aranow?"

"Eighteen," she said, and waited for the smile. It didn't come.

"You say the beliefs you've examined—from Yagaiism to Zen—all contradict each other, as well as being either internally inconsistent or inconsistent with your observed experience, and therefore all cannot be true. That is your error."

"What?" Theresa cried. "What's my error?"

"They are all true. Every last one of every belief you named. Plus atheism, Druidism, cannibalism, and devil worship."

Theresa gaped at her.

"The fact is, my lost child, that truth is not so simple. It is solid, and large, and bright enough to banish the darkness—but it is not simple."

"I don't understand," Theresa faltered. She had a sudden picture of Cazie watching Sister Anne from the corner of the white-walled room: Cazie with her head tilted, her golden eyes scornfully bright, smiling at them both. Always smiling. *Irony, Tessie. Don't lose your irony.*

"Everything is true, under difference circumstances. Men are good, and men are sinful. God is all-powerful, and God cannot choose for each soul. Love is greater than justice, and justice greater than love. How else could the Church have changed over more than two millennia, and still be the Church? Sometimes heretics must be rooted out and destroyed, and sometimes heretics must be embraced, and sometimes heretics are we ourselves. All of it is true. But humankind cannot see all of truth at once, and so in each age we see what we can. There are fashions in truth, as in all else. And under the fashions, the largeness abides."

"But, Sister . . . but if everything is true . . ."

"Then the task of the searcher is to set aside the egotism of perception and see as much of God as each can."

The egotism of perception. Theresa struggled with the concept. "You mean . . . we can't see it all, so we must trust the rest is there? On faith?"

"That's part of it. But there's more involved. We must literally set aside the smallness of our perceptions—the limits of our perceptions—and see what was hidden to us before."

"But *how?*" And then, more quietly, "How?"

Sister Anne stood and walked to the door. She opened it and the glorious sound swept back into the room: thirty, fifty voices raised in song, ardent and pure, a rush as heady and perfumed as the smell of summer nights. Theresa closed her eyes and leaned forward, as if the singing were a physical stream and she lowering herself into it.

"Like that," Sister Anne said.

Irony is always the best defense against self-delusion, Cazie said.

"It's also the best defense against the risk of any genuine feeling," Sister Anne said quietly, and Theresa's eyes flew open and her heart sped, until she realized she must have spoken Cazie's words aloud.

Theresa stood, too, although she couldn't have said why. Vespers rose and fell around her, a sea of sweet sound, palpable and powerful as a rush of fresh water. Again her heart sped, but this time without any risk of an attack. Her breathing was calm and deep. *Yes,* something said inside a deep part of her mind. *Yes yes yes!*

The nun watched her closely. "Very few people actually belong in this order, Ms. Aranow."

Theresa said, "I do," and it seemed to her she had never spoken with such confidence in her life. It was over, then: the uncertainty, the lostness, the tremendous fear. Above all, the fear. Of the strange, the alien, the different. Over. She was home.

Sister Anne smiled; to Theresa, her smile blended with the glory of the music, was the music. "I think maybe you do. Would you like to have the preliminary blood and cerebral-spinal tests now?"

Theresa smiled back. "Tests?"

"To use as an eventual base for your customized neuropharms."

"My . . . what?"

"We customize the mix for each postulant, of course. Our lab, which we share with the Jesuits in Saranac Lake, is as advanced at this work as any in the world. Your mix will match anything available in Boston or Copenhagen or Brasilia, for any purpose."

Theresa said woodenly, "I don't take neuropharms."

"You have never taken any like these, certainly. For this purpose, with this result. Not yet."

"I don't take them at all." Dizziness rushed over her, displacing the music. She reached for the back of the chair with both hands.

"I see," Sister Anne said. "Just as you are unChanged. But, Theresa, they are not the same thing. Neuropharms for the greater glory of God . . . What did you think I meant when I said we set aside the egotism of perception? That's a cortical-thalamic function."

"I don't know what I thought," Theresa mumbled. The dizziness grew worse. She clutched the back of the chair.

"Our neuropharms modify activities in the mammillothalamic tract, cortical association areas, and dorsomedial nucleus—no different from modifying biochemistry through fasting or frenzied prayer in other ages. We merely break down the neural barriers to increased levels of attention, perception, and integration of various conscious states. To better know and glorify God."

"I have to leave now," Theresa gasped. The room whirled, and her throat closed. She couldn't breathe. There was no air . . .

"But, my child—"

"I have . . . to go! I'm . . . sorry!"

She stumbled through the open door of the room. Vespers rose around her, stronger as she staggered blindly along the corridor: glorious, fervent, heartbreaking. Theresa yanked at the convent door; it wouldn't open. She couldn't talk to order it open. Gasping, she beat on the wood, until someone she couldn't see through the whirling confusion, someone behind her, opened the door for her and she fell through.

The door closed, cutting off the music.

When she could breathe again, Theresa sat for a long time in her car. Then she lifted it and flew south.

The first tribe she came to had housed itself for the winter in the remains of a pre-Change-Wars Liver town. The three undestroyed buildings were Liver colors: fuchsia, mint, and bright red. Behind the red building stretched a huge sheet of heavy plastic over churned-up earth: a feeding ground. Beyond it lay a pile of broken machines, scooters and 'bots and what looked like water pipes. People, made small and nonthreatening by the aircar's height, stopped moving and looked up, hands shading their eyes against the cold winter sun. Theresa couldn't see their faces.

She didn't try to go down to them, or even to lower her altitude. Instead she powered down the window and dropped out the package of Change syringes. Sixteen of them, all that Jackson had had left in the house safe. The syringes were wrapped in nonconsumable flowered dress cloth. The cloth might tear when it landed, but nothing could shatter Miranda Sharifi's Change syringes.

As soon as the packet hit ground, Livers ran toward it. Theresa didn't wait. She flew south, back to Manhattan East, knowing she was a hypocrite. She didn't believe Change syringes were good for people, but she was giving them to Livers for their children. She didn't believe neuropharms could be the path to meaning, but the Sisters of Merciful Heaven felt that their lives were meaningful whereas she, Theresa, felt her life was shit. She believed that pain was a gift, a signpost to the soul, but she let herself be fed by 'bots and coddled by Jackson and protected by bio-weapon security systems, so that she didn't have to fear too much pain.

And all the while Cazie rode with her in the front seat of the car, scornful and concerned and impatient and loving and dangerous, saying *Irony, Tessie. Don't lose your irony.*

I never had any to lose, Tess thought, and opaqued the car's windows so she didn't have to see outside. So she could put her head in her hands and wonder what, if anything, could be left for her to try next.

"You did what?" Jackson said. He spoke very slowly, as if his words were slippery and he had to keep a firm hold on them.

"I gave them to a tribe of Livers," Theresa said.

"You gave all the rest of my Change syringes to a tribe of Livers? What tribe?"

"I don't know. Just a random tribe."

"Where?"

"I don't remember."

Jackson laced his fingers together tightly. *"Why?"*

"Because they need them. Or their babies will get sick and die."

"But, Tessie, I needed them, too. For babies born to my patients . . . did you know they were the last syringes I had?"

"Yes," she whispered. She had never seen her brother like this. So quiet. No, that wasn't right, Jackson was usually quiet. But not like this.

"Theresa. I need the tools of my trade to help people. I need syringes. And Miranda Sharifi isn't providing any more . . . you know that. Every doctor in the country is running out of Change syringes. And can't get any more. How am I supposed to help my newborn patients without the syringes?"

"You can doctor them, Jackson." She'd had time to think about this; she was calmer than when she'd first arrived home. A little calmer. "The people in our enclave have you. Those Liver babies out there don't have anything. And I wanted—" She stopped.

Jackson said, with a choking noise in his voice, "You wanted to give them something."

"I need to give *somebody* something!" Theresa cried.

Jackson turned away, toward the window. He stood with his back to her, looking out at the park. Theresa took a step toward him, halted. "Don't you see, Jackson?"

"I see," he said, which made her feel a little better, even though he didn't turn around.

"And you can help the people in our enclave, too," Theresa said. "You can help them the way you went to school to learn to do. After all, you're a doctor, aren't you?"

But this time Jackson didn't answer her at all.

INTERLUDE

TRANSMISSION DATE: January 5, 2121
TO: Selene Base, Moon
VIA: AT&T Comlink Satellite 4, Holsat 643-K (China)
MESSAGE TYPE: Unencrypted
MESSAGE CLASS: No class. Not a legal transmission
ORIGINATING GROUP: Not identified
MESSAGE:
You give us Change syringes so we become dependent on you non-humans. Then you withdraw the syringes so we'll starve and sicken. What's that but genocide? You think no one knows what you're really doing. Not so, bitch. There are groups all over America that know what's really going on. What your plan is. Weaken us, control us, and then attack. It won't work. Some of us, undeluded by the fucking cowards that call themselves our government, will be waiting for you to come down from your hiding place. Sleepers are stronger than you think, and we value our God-given and Constitution-given freedoms. Too many Americans have died the past 350 years for us to let our freedoms go without a fight.

Remember that.

ACKNOWLEDGMENT: None received

Nine

On December 31, Jackson sat in his apartment watching news-grids he didn't really want to see, and resisting the idea of going to Willoughby County on this last day of legal voter registration for the April special election.

"Yesterday's bloody conflict in San Francisco's Bay Enclave may have lasted less than an hour," said the handsome genemod journalist over holos of the attack, "but the aftermath continues. Enclave Police Chief Stephanie Brunell expressed both outrage and puzzlement at that attack, allegedly motivated by a search for Change syringes, by the terrorist group calling itself Livers For Control. Police investigation is concentrating on how both Y-shield and biodefense security systems could have been overridden by the underground group—"

By datadipping, you dips, Jackson thought. But nobody wanted to believe that, because it meant you had to believe Livers were capable both of learning to manipulate sophisticated computer systems and of seizing power. And so much donkey effort—decades of effort—had gone into ensuring otherwise. Rotten educational software. Lavish handouts of material goods. Simple government-funded amusements that simply distracted. A political agenda that convinced those at the bottom that because they didn't have to work, they were actually at the top. Jackson changed the channel.

"—Year's Eve celebration at the Mall Enclave in the nation's capital. Warmed to a summery seventy-two degrees in deference to this season's stunning bare-breasted evening gowns, the Mall itself has been transformed for the sight of this most lavish gala. President and Mrs. Garrison will divide their time between dancing at—" He changed the channel.

"—of the match. International chess champion Vladimir Voitinuik, here pondering his fourth move against challenger Guillaume—" He changed the channel.

"—heading rapidly toward the Florida coast where, unfortunately, a great many so-called Liver tribes have chosen to winter. Although Hurricane Kate occurs late in the tropical hurricane season, winds of up to a hundred thirty miles per hour . . ."

Robocam of terrified Livers, many almost naked, trying to dig safety ditches with shovels, sticks, even pieces of metal from what looked like broken 'bots. A close-up of a child being blown away from its screaming mother—

"Jackson?" Theresa said. He hadn't heard her pad, barefoot, into the room. Quickly he offed the newsgrid.

"Jackson, I need to ask you something."

"What, Theresa?" She looked terrible. She'd lost even more weight. Anorexia nervosa had all but disappeared since the Change—feeding directly, the body knew what it needed—but Jackson thought that Theresa, unChanged, was on the verge of it. Below the hem of her loose flowered dress he could see the long light outline of her tibiae, and above the neckline her clavicle stood out against the pale floaty mass of her dry hair like twigs against cloud. He despaired of what a proper workup would show. Deficiencies in bone density, white and red blood count, cerebrospinal transmitters, metabolic processes— nothing in balance. Cardiac, cortical, and even cellular-level stress clean off the scale. Plus biogenic amines the body produced only under pathological conditions—the kinds that signaled accelerated nerve-cell death and permanent changes in the neural architecture.

"Tessie . . . you need to eat more. I've told you. You promised."

"I know. I will. But I get so wrapped up in my book . . . I do think it's going better. Some of the paragraphs almost say what I feel. What Leisha feels. Felt. But now could you recommend a good program on Abraham Lincoln? Something not too hard, but clear about his life and politics?"

"Abraham Lincoln? Why?" But the second after he said it, he knew.

"Leisha Camden wrote a book about Lincoln. I think, from what Thomas told me, that it was considered important. And I know hardly anything about President Lincoln."

Theresa had never been interested in history—had never, in fact, gone past the primary-grades software. Jackson said, "Why not just use the Camden book, then?"

His sister blushed. "It's not adapted. And when I had Thomas read it to me . . . well, I think I need something easier. Will you help me?"

"Of course," he said gently. And then, because he couldn't help himself, "How is your book on Leisha going?"

"Oh, you know." She swiped vaguely at the air with one hand. "There's always a gap between the book in your head and the one in the page."

It sounded like something Thomas had found for her in an indexed quotation program. She was fond of those. Did they give her the illusion of understanding? His heart ached with pity. "Try Clear and Present Software. Their hypertext explains things well. I don't remember the exact title you need, but Thomas can find it for you."

"Thank you, Jackson." She smiled at him, looking fragile as spun glass. "Thomas can find it. Clear and Here Software?"

"Clear and Present."

He could see the knobby calcaneus in her bare heel, uncushioned by flesh, as she left the room.

Jackson sat in front of the empty wall screen for several minutes. Syringe wars. Attacks on enclaves. Desperate Livers. Theresa. Abraham Lincoln. He remembered a speech of Lincoln's, floating up from the mental flotsam of his own schooldays: *The ballot is stronger than the bullet.*

Nobody believed that anymore. Nobody he knew.

Except Lizzie Francy.

He landed his car a couple hundred feet from the tribe building, remembering how, nearly two months ago, scruffy Liver young men had been all over it. Now, of course, one of those scruffy young men was supposedly a candidate for public office.

Someone sauntered toward the car. Vicki Turner. Jackson rolled down the window. Cold winter air gusted in.

"Dr. Jackson Aranow. What an honor. I would have expected you to be at a New Year's Eve party somewhere. Have you come to share the final push toward democratic voter registration? Or to satisfy yourself that we actually went through with it, instead of just giving up in typical Liver fashion after our initial burst of ephemeral enthusiasm?"

Jackson frowned. "I'm here to see how the project is going."

"Such non-evaluative language. Your med school psych professors would be proud of you. Actually, we're on our way to try one more time with a particularly recalcitrant group of non-registrants. Perhaps you could give us a lift."

"Ms. Turner—I checked on your credit rating. It's rotten, presumably as a result of your arrest by the GSEA and the subsequent . . . unpleasantness. But I don't believe for a minute that you don't have accounts stashed under other names in other places. Why not just buy your . . . your tribe an aircar?"

"You're wrong, Jackson. I don't have money stashed anywhere. I spent it all."

"On what?"

She didn't answer, smiling at him faintly, and suddenly Jackson knew. On the Change Wars. Whatever part Vicki Turner had played in that struggle to convince Americans that the syringes were not a Sleepless plot to enslave Livers, to convince Americans to stop killing each other over radical changes in biology, to convince Americans to stop attacking Washington because, now, they *could*—whatever Vicki had done, it really had cost her all her credit. And she didn't regret it.

He blurted, "You make me feel ashamed."

For an instant, her face softened, and he saw something behind the brittle mask, something wistful and a little lonely. Then she smiled as before. "Then you can atone for your deep civic shame by giving us a surreptitious lift to these reluctant voters."

Jackson didn't answer. In that instant of unwitting vulnerability, she had again reminded him of Cazie. And he had again reminded himself of a bumbling dolt.

Lizzie and Shockey walked toward the car. Lizzie carried Dirk, well wrapped against the cold. Shockey wore screaming yellow jacks and a lime coat, with antique soda-can jewelry in his ears. On his right shoulder sat an odd lump. As he got closer, Jackson saw that it was a red, white, and blue flower, made of layers of plant-dyed rough-spun cloth wired together into a rosette.

Vicki murmured, ". . . and they never even heard of Jacobins." But the affectionate look she gave Lizzie was real.

Shockey said, "Doctor. Coming along, you, for the last big push? You might learn something."

"True, Doctor," Vicki said. "We are, after all, making startlingly new political history with our grass-roots movement toward democracy."

"Damn right," Shockey said. The young man seemed to expand, raising the rosette on his broad shoulder another two inches. *Hot air,* Jackson thought.

Lizzie almost danced with excitement. Her black hair stood out in more directions than Jackson imagined possible. "If we can get these people to agree to register tonight, Dr. Aranow, we'll have ninety-three percent Liver participation. Four thousand four hundred eleven Liver voters in the county for the winter. Now, you said that Susannah Wells Livingston wasn't a real candidate, just someone to run against

Donald Thomas Serrano, and Serrano would get the vote of nearly every registered donkey. That's four thousand eighty-two votes. Even if we can't convince this tribe to register, we should still win."

"*I* should still win," Shockey said.

"All right—*you* should still win," Lizzie said. Jackson saw that she was too elated to bother arguing with Shockey. "We're going to do it!"

Jackson glanced at Vicki. She nodded. "You tell them, Jackson. Maybe she'll listen to *you.*"

"Lizzie . . ." Jackson said, and stopped. He hated to puncture her. How long had it been since he'd seen genuine enthusiasm, for anything constructive? "Lizzie, getting the edge in number of voter registrations won't guarantee you a win. There's three months before the actual April first election. In three months, Donald Serrano is going to do everything in his considerable power to convince your Liver voters to vote for him. And every single donkey politician is going to help him, including Sue Livingston. Because if you win, it will set a potentially devastating precedent for electing outsiders to government."

"We're not outsiders, us!" Shockey flashed.

"To the donkey political establishment, you are. They do not want you and your kind making decisions that affect them and their kind. Not even the tiny peripheral decisions that a district supervisor gets to make. They want to keep you out. And they'll try to do that by buying the votes of every legally registered voter in Willoughby County. With Y-cones and music systems and medunits and luxury foods and scooters, and every other material pleasure they can offer right now and you can only promise to try to obtain, maybe, in the future."

Lizzie scowled over the sleeping baby. "And you think we'll fall for that? Be bought like that?"

Jackson said quietly, "You were bought like that for nearly a hundred years."

"But no more! We're different now, us! Since the Change! We don't need you no more!"

"Which is why we want you to give us a ride now," Vicki said. "Earn your keep, Jackson. Lizzie, Shockey, get in the car."

They did. Vicki gave him directions, and the four flew in silence for several minutes over rough country littered with the debris of winter. Wind-fallen branches, withered scrub, soggy dead leaves, dells of deep snow. Finally Jackson said, "Do you want me to land right by their . . . camp? Or shouldn't they see a donkey associated with this Liver enterprise?"

"No," Lizzie said, surprising him. "You come, too. These particular people, they should see you."

The tribe, like so many, had passed the winter in an abandoned food-processing plant. Jackson guessed this one had once processed apples from the gone-wild orchards covering the low hills. No one came out to meet them. Lizzie, carrying the still sleeping Dirk, led the way around to the back of the building, where, under the usual plastic-tent feeding ground, lunch was in progress.

Sixty or seventy Livers lay or sat naked on the churned-up ground, soaking in both nutrients and sun. For a second Jackson flashed on Terry Amory's party that Cazie had taken him to. But there was no danger of confusing the two. These Livers were—well, Jackson hated to admit it because it echoed the worst kind of dehumanizing bigotry—the Ellie Lester kind. But it was the truth. The Livers were repulsive.

Hairy backs, sagging breasts, flabby bellies and thighs, graceless proportions, faces with features too squished together or too spread apart or not well matched to each other. It didn't even matter that everyone's Cell Cleaner skin was smooth and healthy and blemish-free. Since his internship had ended, Jackson had seen mostly perfect genemod bodies. Now he remembered how purely ugly most of humanity was in comparison.

Vicki murmured by his ear, "Kind of a shock, isn't it? Even for a physician. Welcome to homo sapiens. 'The aristocrat among the animals,' as Heinrich Heine remarked."

Lizzie said, without preamble, "We're back, us, to talk to you some more about this here election. Janet, Arly, Bill, Farla—you listen, you."

"Do we got any choice, us?" said a flabby, grinning, naked middle-aged woman with buttocks like deflated balloons. "Lizzie, you hand me that there sweet baby."

Lizzie handed over Dirk and stripped off her clothes. Shockey and Vicki, with complete unself-consciousness, followed. Vicki grinned at Jackson. "When in Rome . . ."

He wasn't going to let her—let any of them—intimidate him. He stripped off his jacket and shirt.

"Oooooh, nice," the middle-aged woman said, and laughed at Jackson's discomfiture. "But, Lizzie, tell us, you, why you brought this pair of donkeys, them, along with your so-called candidate."

"Ain't nothing so-called about me, Farla," Shockey said good-naturedly. "I'm the next Willoughby County district supervisor, me."

Farla grinned. "Sure you are."

Jackson was having trouble. He stood slowly unfastening his pants . . . as slowly as he could. Livers were used to communal feeding nudity. So were donkeys—but ground feeding, done in softly lit and perfumed private feeding rooms, was very often sexual. Here, young men like Shockey were relaxed naked. Comfortable. Flaccid. Jackson, for no good reason he could discover, had an erection.

"Go on, Jackson," Vicki said softly. "Unveil the genemod family lavaliere."

He turned to her angrily—why did she always try to make things worse?—and immediately things were worse. Her naked body was dizzyingly beautiful. Smaller breasts than Cazie's but higher, narrower waist, slim hips, and long legs . . . Her pubic hair was reddish-blonde, a pretty light fuzz, a veil over . . .

"Oh, my," Vicki said. "Your family got their money's worth." And then, a moment later in a different voice, "Come on, Jack. Laugh. It's funny, don't you even see that?"

He laughed hollowly, trying to exaggerate the hollowness, trying for irony. He knew he failed.

Lizzie was giving her pitch. "If you all register, you, between 11:15 and 11:50 tonight, like we told you, then no other donkeys can register themselves for the election. We got enough Livers to win. If we win, us, we can get the tax pool money and stock the warehouse at the county seat with whatever we need. You going to tell me, you, there ain't stuff you need?"

"Course there is," said a small, scowling, elderly man. "And hell, I'd vote for you, Shockey. You been a mayor, you. 'Sides, I can remember when not all candidates was donkeys, them, long before you kids was even born. But what I want to know, me, is what price the donkeys going to make us pay for electing one of our own."

Shockey said, "Ain't going to be no price."

"Ah, son, there's always a price. They always make a price, them."

Shockey bristled. "Like what, Max? What could the donkeys do to us, them?"

"What couldn't they do, them? They got weapons, police, they can change the goddamn climate, I hear, me—at least a little ways. We're better off, us, the way we are. We got everything we really need, and we don't attract no attention."

"But that way things will never change, them!" Lizzie cried. "We'll never get anyplace!"

The old man said, "Just as well. You keep your eyes on the sky, you, you're bound to stumble over the rocks."

"But—"

"But they got donkeys with them," another man said suddenly. "They ain't just Livers, them, stumbling along with the rest of us."

Lizzie said, "Vicki and Dr. Aranow aren't—" but Vicki interrupted her. Vicki looked right at the man.

"That's right. They have donkeys with them. I'm Victoria Turner, formerly with the GSEA. And this is Dr. Jackson Aranow, a physician, and owner of TenTech, a major corporation. Lizzie's not fighting alone. Any paybacks the donkeys try for beating them in the election, Dr. Aranow and I have the resources to counter."

Jackson stared. The man said bluntly, "Why? Why you on Lizzie's side, you?"

"*My* side," Shockey said, scowling.

"Because," Vicki said, "I believe in this country." She reached over to the pile of Shockey's discarded clothing and tore the red-white-and-blue rosette off the jacket shoulder. She held it out to the man: with overt sincerity, with cynical irony, with what Jackson finally perceived to be a protective camouflage over genuine belief. But Vicki didn't believe this election could really succeed—she'd said as much. She must believe in some deeper political commitment, of which this was only a first necessary defeat.

The man snorted. But he took the rosette. The older man, Max, grinned. Farla said abruptly, "All right, Shockey, tell us, you, what you gonna do if we elect you."

Someone in the crowd giggled. "Yeah, Shockey. Make a campaign speech, you."

"Well, I will, me! Now you Livers listen, you! Everybody!"

" 'Let arms yield to the toga,' " Vicki murmured. "Jackson, get comfortable. The people speak."

It was dark before they left Farla's tribe. The debate went on all afternoon and early evening, as much, Jackson suspected, out of relish for the fighting as desire for information. People shouted and insulted and threatened and blustered. They moved indoors after feeding, to the dark, warm den of battered chairs, sleeping cubicles created by makeshift partitions, craft projects and skinned rabbits, and an expensive terminal with a label from one of TenTech's subsidiaries. Stolen? Vicki grinned at him. Y-cones kept the huge depressing place warm—were the cones some of the ones he'd sent Lizzie's tribe from TenTech? Maybe Shockey, too, understood the value of voter bribery.

At sunset, Dirk grew fussy. "He should be home," Lizzie said finally. "Grandma Annie's gonna get worried, her. Dr. Aranow, drive us home, please."

Jackson could see that the others were impressed by Lizzie's order-

ing him around. He had become a campaign asset. Plus public trans-
portation—without his aircar they would have faced a long cold walk
over the mountains. No . . . without his aircar, they wouldn't have
stayed so late, or argued so hard. Vicki grinned at him.

"I'm so excited," Lizzie said in the car. "Just a few more hours!
Dirk, hush, sweet baby. Hush, dear heart. A few more hours and four
thousand four hundred eleven—at least!—Willoughby County Livers'll register all at once!"

Shockey said, "You're sure, you, that all them bumpkins know the
on-line procedure, them?"

"Sam Bartlett and Tasha Herbert told all the tribes twice. Everybody knows what to do. It will *work*."

And, to Jackson's faint surprise, it did. At 11:00 P.M., everyone except small sleeping children gathered around Lizzie's terminal. She'd
programmed a running tally sheet: WILLOUGHBY COUNTY VOTERS, divided
into two columns: LIVERS and DONKEYS. The number under DONKEYS, in
glowing three-dimensional Univers Gothic, remained constant. Every
time the other tally added another hundred voters, an American flag
flashed, music played, and a tiny figure pressed a ballot button on a
tiny voting net. The entire display sent out holo streamers ending in
simulated fireworks.

Behind Jackson's left shoulder, Vicki said, "Sort of a blend of New
Year's Eve, Scooter All-Stars, and Tammany Hall."

"Get ready, everybody!" Shockey said. "It's 11:48!"

Jackson watched the screen. Suddenly the LIVER number jumped,
then jumped again, passing the DONKEY number. Flags flashed. People
cheered, almost drowning out "Sometimes a Great Nation." Annie
Francy said, "Oh, my dear Lord." The numbers jumped again, then
again, and then came so fast that they looked animated, while projected holo fireworks exploded and all around him Livers screamed
and hugged each other and jumped up and down.

Midnight. LIVERS: 4,450. DONKEYS: 4,082.

"We did it, us!" Shockey yelled.

"Hooray for the next district supervisor of Willoughby County!"

"Shock-ey! Shock-ey!"

Shockey was lifted up by his feet and walked around the floor on his
hands—some Liver triumphant ritual, Jackson assumed. All at once,
he felt very tired. His mobile rang.

"Jackson, answer me. Now."

Cazie. How had she heard about this so damn fast? It was only
12:06. Did she just happen to be monitoring obscure voter registrations, or did she have a flag program to alert her to unusual political

ripples? Suddenly Jackson wanted to talk to her. He was going to enjoy this. He moved to a relatively quiet corner and stood facing the wall, holding the small screen so Cazie couldn't see the room.

"Cazie. What are you doing up so early?"

"Where are you, Jackson?"

"With friends. Why?"

"Willoughby County, Pennsylvania, has just registered an additional four thousand four hundred fifty voters minutes before the registration deadline. They're Livers. Plus, a petition was filed to run a third candidate for Ellie Lester's vacant position as district supervisor."

Jackson said, "You mean Harold Winthrop Wayland's position?"

"He was senile; his granddaughter ran the office. To, I might add, TenTech's considerable advantage. District supervisor, as you know, does more than stock warehouses, behind the scenes the office controls—no, you probably don't know. But, Jackson, this is serious. Certain people anticipated something like this, that's why I found out about it immediately. It can't be allowed to become a trend. Livers in office. Jesus Fucking Christ."

"The voter registration was legal, wasn't it?"

Cazie ran her hand through her dark curls. "That's the problem. It *is* legal. It's too late to register more donkeys—and we can't jig the program directly, the media will be all over this one. Just because it's a story. I've called Sue Livingston and Don Serrano and their campaign programmers, and I think you should be at our meeting, too. If only because TenTech is potentially affected. Do you know how deeply we're invested in county and state bonds, just to give one aspect of the situation?"

"No," Jackson said slowly, "I don't."

"Well, I'll brief you. Ordinarily I wouldn't bring you in on the political side of the company at all, but this time—Jackson, you've just never realized how important the political side is. TenTech *is* political connections!"

"I thought TenTech was a corporation for manufacturing necessary goods."

Cazie sighed. "You would. Anyway, the meeting is at nine in the morning. My place."

Jackson said nothing. Behind him, the celebratory roar had muted to a happy babble. He felt someone's eyes on him, turned, and saw Vicki three feet away, unabashedly listening.

"Jack?" Cazie's image said on the mobile's small screen.

Vicki said softly, "If you don't tell her you helped us, she'll probably never know."

"Jack? Are you still there?"

Vicki said, "You can just go to work again for the other side, protecting TenTech's political tentacles. And losing . . . what? Do you think you'd be losing anything, Jackson?"

"Jack!"

Jackson lifted the mobile. He angled the lens so that Cazie could see the tribe building, then Vicki, then himself. "I'm here, Cazie, at Willoughby. And, yes, tomorrow morning I'll be at that meeting, to disentangle TenTech interests from voter results. But not to undo the voter results."

Cazie gasped. Jackson broke the link before she could speak and instructed the mobile to disregard all calls for the next six hours. He turned to Vicki. "But I want you to know that if I'm not a vote-tamperer, neither am I a political reformer. I'm a *doctor.*"

She said, "The situation doesn't require a doctor."

"And do you always just become whatever the situation requires? No personal choice?"

"That's right. I'm just a bunch of brain chemicals responding to stimuli."

He said, "You don't believe that."

"No. I don't. But do you?" she said, and walked away.

Having had, he noticed, the last word.

The Livers sat in rows now on scarred chairs, interrupting as Lizzie and Shockey and Billy Washington planned aloud. Jackson scanned the slouching bodies—misproportioned, ungraceful, uneducated, contentious, rude. Dressed—barely—in tasteless garish free-issue plastic and homespun rags. Shouting stupid suggestions at each other motivated by greed, or unrealistic expectations, or orneriness, or a complete ignorance of governmental structure.

He left the political meeting and went home.

II

MARCH–APRIL 2121

Affiliation requires boundaries; a "we" must
be defined on some basis if there are to be any
obligations to the "we"; and once there is a
"we," there will be a "they."
—James Q. Wilson, *The Moral Sense,* 1993

Ten

Jennifer sat at her desk in Sanctuary, drawing with a black calligraphy pen. It was amazing how relaxing she found this trivial art, using not a drawing program but actual ink, on paper. She allowed herself twenty minutes twice a day to draw whatever she chose, whatever came into her mind. *A means of focusing your attention?* Sanctuary's communications chief Caroline Renleigh had said, which merely showed how little Caroline understood her. Jennifer's attention did not need focusing. The drawing was a refreshing break in relentless attention.

Her office, at the cylindrical orbital's arbitrarily designated "south" end, shared dome space with the Sanctuary Council chamber. To the "north," farms and living domes and labs and parks made a pleasant, orderly vista that curved gently into the sky. To the "south," the office abutted the transparent, super-tough plastic sealing the orbital. Jennifer's desk faced space.

When she was younger, she had kept her console turned away from that blackness. In her office, at Council meetings, Jennifer had always faced Sanctuary, and its soft artificial sun. She had come, over the long years in prison on Earth, to understand that this was unallowable weakness. Now she placed her chair so that she always confronted space. Sometimes she faced a void, with stars too far for even Sleepless technology: the unreachable escape. Sometimes she faced Earth, oppressively filling the window, reminding her of why her people needed escape. Jennifer contemplated both views. For the discipline.

She could take her people no farther from the enemy. The moon, yes—but Miranda had gone there, with her traitors. The genemod generation who were supposed to be the way around genetic regression to the mean, ensuring that the Sleepless continued to expand their superiority over Sleepers. And who instead had betrayed their creators and loving parents, sending them to prison for treason.

Mars was colonized by several nations, but most ambitiously by the

New Empire of China, powerful and dangerous. Sleepless there received a bullet in the back of the head.

Titan belonged to the Japanese. They were spreading to the other moons of the solar system as well. More reasonable than the New Empire, they nonetheless had never taken well to ethnic outsiders. In one generation—or two, or three—they might turn against a Saturn- or Jupiter-orbit Sanctuary, just as the United States had turned against the original Sanctuary, on Earth. And then Jennifer's great-great-grandchildren would have to dance the whole bloody dance again.

No, she could take her people nowhere else but this orbital, this fragile haven of titanium and steel, built even before nanotechnology. Nor could she challenge Earth directly. She had tried that, and failed, and spent twenty-seven years in prison. When you had an enemy that hounded and reviled and murdered your people, an enemy that you could neither fight nor flee, then you must operate underground. Use cunning. Stealth. Turn the enemy's own weakness against him, and arrange it so he never knew what robbed him of his effectiveness. There was no overt triumph that way, but Jennifer had learned that she could do without overt triumph. Provided that she gained what was most important: safety for her people. That was her responsibility.

Responsibility, self-control, duty. The moral virtues, without which no accomplishment was possible, and no greatness. They had forgotten those virtues on Earth. Strukov, the classic mercenary, betrayed his own kind every time he engineered pathological viruses for money. The aristocrats of the New Empire of China settled Mars, but left their own poor to struggle in the genemod-virus hell that warring factions had made of West China. And the American donkeys, who kept Sanctuary legally and financially tethered to the United States for the huge taxes the orbital paid, had abandoned their own morals to pursue empty pleasures in the Y-sealed enclaves.

That left space.

Sanctuary orbital, the last bastion of responsibility to one's own. Of responsibility, self-control, duty. Of a morality that was able to look beyond the pleasure of the moment, the individualistic needs of any one person, to the needs of the community. The rest of the world had forgotten that "community" had a biological base as well as a social one. A human being belonged not only to those communities he chose, professional and geographical, but to that into which he was born. His first obligation must be loyalty to the community that had nurtured him, or the entire chain of nurturing generations broke down. And that loyalty must be a choice, not a mindless dogma. That was, finally, what it meant to be fully human: not the pack loyalty of wolves, but that people *could* choose other than their pack—and choose not to. The moral choice.

The Sleepers, dazzled by the technology that should be servant and not master, had forgotten that kind of morality. Too bad for the Sleepers. They would destroy themselves. It was Jennifer's task to make sure they were incapable of destroying Sanctuary first.

She completed her ink drawing. An intricate geometric figure, the lines and angles as precise as if she'd used a protractor. She always drew geometric figures. But there were four minutes left in her drawing time. She started another figure at the bottom of the page.

"Jennifer? Something here you should see." Paul Aleone, Vice President of Finance for Sharifi Enterprises, stood in the doorway. Paul, like Caroline Renleigh, had been one of the twelve Sleepless behind the plan to force the United States to allow Sanctuary to secede. He, too, had been betrayed by his own grandchildren, had been convicted, had served ten years in Allendale Federal Prison. He could be trusted. Jennifer swiveled her chair to fully face him, and smiled.

"Look," Paul said, handing her a sheaf of printouts. Genemod handsome, he still moved with the lightness of a young man. But, then, he was only seventy. "Caroline's newsgrid program flagged these among the Earth channels. The flag was 'Billy Washington.' He's the Liver who—"

"I remember who he was," Jennifer said. Sanctuary always monitored the Genetic Standards Enforcement Agency data banks, of course, along with most other governmental agencies. Billy Washington, his wife Annie Francy, and her child had been the first guinea pigs for Miranda's biological experiments. Along with a donkey GSEA agent in such deep cover that not even Sanctuary had been able to find out who he or she was.

Paul said, "The program also flagged 'Lizzie Francy,' Washington's stepdaughter. She's now seventeen. She and her so-called tribe are trying to elect a candidate to governmental office."

"A Liver candidate?" Jennifer scanned the printouts. Although they reflected the usual Sleeper sensationalism, she was able to discern the facts under the bombast. Livers in Willoughby County, Pennsylvania, had registered to vote—something Livers used to do faithfully, but did no longer since Miranda Sharifi had turned eighty percent of civilization back into nomads who followed neither game nor herds, but merely the sun. These Pennsylvania voters planned to elect their own candidate to county office in a special election April 1. A Liver candidate.

Jennifer sat motionless, considering. Paul said, "In terms of our interests, there are two ways to look at this. One is that the more dissension among the Sleepers, the more attention they'll devote to struggling with each other and the less attention they could ever devote to us—no matter what we choose to do. The other, negative view is that Livers in power creates a second entity we have to protect against, and an unknown and less predictable one than the Sleeper aristocracy. And those newsgrids do seem to assume that Liver power is a possibility. Even allowing for their hysterical exaggerations."

Jennifer glanced again at the printout headlines:

THE THREAT TO EFFECTIVE GOVERNMENT: "WE WANT TO RUN THINGS THE LIVER WAY FOR A CHANGE" SAYS PA CANDIDATE FOR DISTRICT SUPERVISOR

LETTING THE CHILDREN RUN THE ORPHANAGE:
A REVERSAL OF FOURTEENTH-AMENDMENT PRIORITIES

**LEGAL OLIGARCHY: A GOVERNMENT WHOSE BIOLOGICAL
TIME HAS FINALLY COME?**

*HOW DID IT HAPPEN? INDEPENDENT COMMISSION
TO INVESTIGATE PA CAMPAIGN OUTRAGE*

"LET MY PEOPLE GO"—THE INAPPROPRIATE FORMULA THAT
MASKS GOVERNMENTAL DISASTER

"TIME TO RECONSIDER VOTER REGISTRATION TESTS,"
DECLARES MAJORITY LEADER BENNETT

Paul said, "I ran the probabilities through an Eisler significance program. If this Liver candidate wins the election, the system effects come out far more far-reaching than one county. It has an event index of 4.71. A Liver win stands an eighty-seven percent chance of becoming the nucleus of a fundamentally transformed system."

"Can he win?" Jennifer said.

"No."

"Money?"

"Of course. The donkey candidates will buy the election."

"Then our concern is . . ."

"A test site." Paul ran his hand through his hair, still thick and glossy brown. Sanctuary men wore their hair short and simply cut; so did Sanctuary women. Jennifer's long black hair was an anomaly. She kept it in a knot low on her neck; Will said it made her look like a Roman matron. This was one of the few things Will had said lately that pleased her.

Paul continued, "I know we'd planned on testing Strukov's compound on a donkey enclave. After all, they're the target population. But using this Liver tribe may be even better. We've had nothing to do with the election, neither incumbent nor challenger. No one would have reason to think us involved."

"But don't the Liver voters winter in widely scattered places? Delivery of the compound would be much more difficult."

"Not really," Paul said. "Willoughby County is mostly hills and low mountains. The winter climate is tedious. There are only twenty-one Liver camps in the county. All of them have plastic-tented feeding grounds, easily penetrated by drones. And none of them have any kind of radar, which of course the donkey enclaves do. There's a map on the last page of the printout."

Jennifer studied the map, and then the page of Eisler equations. She nodded. "Yes. I see. If the Livers lose this election, the system effects are negated?"

"Everything is as it was before. And then we can go ahead with the enclaves."

"Yes. Go ahead. This will make an interesting little pre-test, as well as averting a large-scale systems change."

Paul nodded. "We want as few variables as possible for the big campaign. I'll advise Robert. He's handling the delivery negotiations. He'll have a report for you by the end of the week."

"Not Arab, Russian, French, or Chinese. And no one who is known to have ever before worked, however remotely, with Strukov."

"These men are Peruvian."

"Good. La Guerra de Dios?"

"No. Freelancers."

"And Strukov has agreed to work with them?"

"He has. Although only with his procedures, his locations, his security team."

"Naturally," Jennifer said. "Schedule a meeting with Robert."

"For you and me and Caroline?"

"Also Barbara, Raymond, Charles, and Eileen. I want everyone to know everything the others do."

Paul nodded, less happily, and left. He didn't understand, Jennifer thought. Paul would rather apportion knowledge according to each individual's contribution, as if it were money. Why was it so hard for some of them—Paul, even Will—to grasp the moral principle of this?

Sanctuary was a community. Those who led the community must act from responsibility, duty, loyalty. And no one could owe one-third less loyalty or duty than the others. Therefore, all twelve of the people who were going to make Sanctuary safe from the United States must share equally in the risks, the planning, and the knowledge. Anything less was to act not from morality, but from a desire for rank. That was what the Sleepers did. The immoral ones.

Jennifer swiveled her chair back to face her office window. It was full of stars: Rigel, Aldebaran, the Pleiades. Suddenly she remembered something she'd once said to Miranda, so long ago, when Miri had been just a little girl. Jennifer had lifted Miri to the window in the Sanctuary Council, and a meteor had streaked past. Miri laughed and reached out her fat little arms to touch the beautiful lights in the sky. "They're too far for your hand, Miri. But not for your mind. Always remember that, Miranda."

Miranda had not remembered. She had used her mind, yes, but not to reach outward, upward. Instead, she'd used her boosted intelligence—which Jennifer Sharifi had given her—to wallow in the muck and dirt of Sleeper biology. For the benefit of the Sleepers who had betrayed Sanctuary. As had Miranda herself.

"The friend of my enemy is likewise my enemy," Jennifer recited aloud. Beyond the window, Earth moved into view. Sanctuary orbited over Africa, another place the Sleepers had ruined.

Her screen brightened. Caroline again. But this time the communications chief looked shaken. "Jennifer?"

"Yes, Caroline?"

"We have some . . . new data."

"Yes? Go ahead."

"Not on link," Caroline said. "I'll come to you. Immediately."

Jennifer didn't allow her composure to slip. "As you wish. Can you say what the new data concern?"

"They concern Selene."

The screen blanked. While she waited for Caroline, Jennifer wiped the nib of her calligraphy pen. Her twenty minutes were long since up. Looking down, she saw that while thinking about Miranda she had gone on drawing, not even aware of what her hand sketched. On the thick white paper, outlined and crosshatched, were the frontal, temporal, and parietal lobes of a human brain.

INTERLUDE

TRANSMISSION DATE: February 12, 2121
TO: Selene Base, Moon
VIA: Lyons Ground Station, Satellite E-398 (France), GLO Satellite 62 (USA)
MESSAGE TYPE: Unencrypted
MESSAGE CLASS: Not Applicable; Foreign Transmission
ORIGINATING GROUP: Unnamed group, Ste. Jeanne, France
MESSAGE:

Nous sommes les gens d'une petite ville en France qui s'appelle Ste. Jeanne. Nous n'avons plus de seringues de la santé. Maintenant, ici, il n'y a pas beaucoup d'enfants qui ne sont pas changés, mais que ferons-nous demain? S'il vous plaît, Mademoiselle Sharifi, donnez-nous plus de seringues de la santé. Que somme-nous obligés faire pour vous persuader? Nous sommes pauvres, mais vous aurez les remerciements. Commes les riches, nous aimons les enfants, and nous avons peur de l'avenir.

S'il vous plaît, n'oubliez-nous pas!

ACKNOWLEDGMENT: None received

Eleven

Y ou *can't,*" Lizzie said to the sullen Liver. Jackson, standing seventy-five yards away in a stand of oak still tattered with last
year's withered leaves, wore zoom lenses and a receiver the size
of a pea. He watched Lizzie's face struggle not to set itself into ridges
of disapproval. She smiled the most hollow smile he'd ever seen.

The man said, even more sullenly, "Shockey said, him, that I can."

"*Shockey* said you can?"

"Yeah."

"Just a minute, please," Lizzie said. She walked away from the man,
who stood just outside his tribe's feeding area, the usual stretched
plastic tent. Inside, twenty naked Livers were having lunch. It seemed
to Jackson that every time he checked on Lizzie's tribe, he ended up
watching naked Livers have lunch. This time, however, three donkey
reporters with cameras stood outside the enclosure, fully clothed, recording the meal. More robocams hovered inside. This particular
group of Livers, unlike some other tribes in Willoughby County, was
enjoying its temporary notoriety. Jackson noted that two of the
women had gold barrettes in their hair. Another, he suddenly saw,
wore a necklace with what looked to the zoom like a diamond. More
trouble.

Lizzie walked up to Jackson, who was disguised as a Liver. In the
last three weeks he'd grown a scraggly beard. He wore baggy blue
jacks, a battered hat pulled low over his forehead, and the heaviest
boots he'd ever had on in his life. The ground was a sea of mud; it had
rained for two days straight, a hard-driving late March rain that
threatened to resume. Jackson's boots were caked with mud. He'd
walked with Lizzie over a mountain to this tribe; Livers didn't use
aircars, and he was passing as a Liver. So far, none of the swarming
reporters had noticed him. He felt ridiculous.

Lizzie leaned close to him in despair and whispered, "He says
Shockey said it was all right for them to accept the scooters!"

"Well, do you think Shockey really said it?" Jackson asked. His own opinion was yes. Shockey hadn't seemed to grasp Lizzie's idea that if the Livers were going to vote for their own candidate on April 1, they couldn't accept material objects or credit accounts from the other two candidates on March 25. "Reparations," Shockey called them, and where had he even learned the word? "Bribes," Lizzie said, and she was right.

Lizzie chewed her bottom lip. "Harry Jenner says Shockey told him to accept the gifts, make no real promises, and then just vote for Shockey anyway."

That was the way donkeys had done it for decades. Jackson said as much to Lizzie.

"But it isn't *right*," she said, and he was suddenly impatient. For her, so invested in this innocent, doomed legal revolution. For himself, standing here in the concealing shade of trees that didn't offer much shade because it was only March, itching in his nonporous synthetic jacks caked with mountain mud.

"The important thing is," he said, "will Harry and his tribe actually vote for Shockey after accepting scooters and jazzy clothes and perfumed soaps and diamond necklaces? Or will they vote for the candidate giving them all this loot?"

"Diamond necklaces?" Lizzie said blankly.

"That girl closest to the plastic, the one with the long brown hair, is wearing a diamond necklace. Tiffany, I believe."

"Oh, my dear Lord."

Jackson smiled. Lizzie would be upset to know that in moments of stress, even when she didn't talk Liver, she sounded like her mother, the formidable Annie. Jackson didn't tell her. In the last three months, hanging around this ridiculous campaign, he'd become fond of Lizzie. She was an odd combination of toughness and vulnerability. Sometimes, she even reminded him of Theresa.

Which was not nearly reason enough to have gotten involved in this quixotic project. So why was he?

"Look, Lizzie, it's six days until the election. You'll just have to trust Harry Jenner and all the rest of them that they'll vote for Shockey despite the . . . gifts." Gifts. Bribes. Reparations.

"Do *you* think they'll vote for Shockey?" Her black eyes pleaded.

"Actually," he said slowly, "I do. I think the hatred left over from the Change Wars is stronger than Liver greed." Or Liver gratitude. Livers were exactly the opportunists that donkeys had made them.

"That's what Vicki says, too," Lizzie said.

Jackson didn't want to discuss Vicki, who'd been left behind to keep order in "campaign headquarters," and who was so much a part of Shockey's tribe that she didn't have to stand here in the mud dressed like something she was not. *We don't need the adverse effect of your known presence,* she'd said to Jackson, *and you don't need the adverse effect on your, ah, medical career.* Yeah. Right.

"Okay," Lizzie said. "I won't tell them to give back the scooters and other things. But I *will* tell them again how much they need to vote for Shockey!"

"Well, do it now. That reporter is starting to look interested in you again. And in me."

"See you back at camp."

"Right," Jackson said, and tramped off back through the woods.

After a few miles, he was hot enough to open his jacket, and then to remove it. The hat he kept on; reporters with no better story to pursue had used aircars and zoom cams to record this campaign. Which was, depending on the newsgrid channel, an outrage against common sense, a threat to what remained of civil order, an unimportant footnote to political history, or a cosmic joke. Sometimes all at once.

Even to Susannah Wells Livingston and Donald Thomas Serrano. Last week Jackson, a spy in the enemy camp, had attended a fund-raiser for Don Serrano. He'd learned that the donkey candidate wasn't really worried. "I've spread around all kinds of 'benefits' to my constituency," Serrano told him. "Since when can't you buy a Liver?" Jackson had just nodded. Wasn't that exactly what he himself had believed, until Lizzie Francy tumbled into his life from eight feet up a factory wall?

The election, however, was not a cosmic joke to Cazie. To avoid her, Jackson had temporarily moved out of his apartment and, under another name, into a hotel in Pittsburgh Enclave. Not a luxury hotel, the place served mostly techs, those marginal donkeys whose parents had been able to afford only limited genemods, usually for appearance. Techs worked for a living but never ran anything. Jackson came and went quietly among them. He talked to Theresa, the only person with his physical address, daily, on what he hoped was a sufficiently shielded link. That Cazie couldn't find him gave Jackson an odd satisfaction, almost as great as the satisfaction of knowing she was looking.

It took him three hours to hike back to Lizzie's tribe. The late afternoon sun slanted over the mountaintops, dark green with pine and white with lingering patches of snow. The other "voter checking teams" would be straggling in as well, after arduous trips to check the loyalty of the other voters.

So why was he involved in all this? Because Cazie hated it? Not reason enough, not nearly enough.

Because he was sick of his life, his class, his pointless activities? Not reason enough.

Because babies without Change syringes were dying across the country? This election wouldn't help those suffering infants. Even if Livers won every goddamn election for the next six years and controlled every political office from President to game warden, ungenemod carpetbaggers in their own appalled capitals, it wouldn't create more Change syringes. Only Miranda Sharifi and the Supers could do that. And they had not. They didn't even answer the transmissions to Selene, city of exile under the surface of the moon.

Jackson stopped in the shadow of a huge fragrant pine, wiped the sweat off his forehead, and braced himself for the hallucinogenic-holo reality of "campaign headquarters."

It started a quarter mile before the camp, with the candidate.

"Who the hell are you?" the girl said. She raised her face from Shockey's, who chivalrously had chosen to lie underneath, separated from the mud by a blanket of blaring orange. The girl, naked from waist to expensive boots, sat astride him. She didn't move off when Jackson bumbled over a slight rise between the trees and into their barely hidden dell.

Jackson dropped his eyes—not to avoid looking at her, but vice versa. He'd already seen her. Maybe seventeen, with genemod green eyes and long black hair. A donkey girl, slumming. Jackson was supposed to be a Liver; how would a Liver react? Jackson shuffled his feet, as if embarrassed, and kept his eyes on her boots. They were calf-high, Italian leather undoubtedly nanocoated so her feet wouldn't consume them, caked with mud. Above them the girl's perfect thighs prickled with goose bumps. The March air was cool.

She said slyly, "You a reporter?"

Not genemod for IQ, clearly. Jackson mumbled, "No, I'm not, me."

Shockey had recognized him. He pulled the girl back toward himself. "Just a gawker, him, Alexandra. Come gawk instead at me."

She giggled. "In this position?" But she kissed him. Shockey kept his eyes open and glared at Jackson: *Go away.*

He did, wondering if Alexandra was a thrill seeker, a political distraction, a professional bribe, or an attempt at scandal. Jackson hadn't seen any robocams. Still . . . hadn't Vicki Turner warned Shockey? Some of his constituents wouldn't be pleased to see their Liver candidate, the antidote to donkey corruption, rolling around in the concupiscent mud with a donkey who looked like Alexandra.

Jackson turned, cupped his hands, and yelled, "Shockey! Company coming, you! Sharon and the baby!" Maybe that would do it.

At the camp, only two reporters roamed around. One was interviewing Scott Morrison, a buddy of Shockey's. "We're going to win this here election, us. And next year we'll take the goddamn presidency!"

"I see you're wearing a gold chain," the reporter said smoothly. "A contribution from Citizens For Serrano, perhaps?"

"It's an heirloom," Morrison said solemnly. "From my great-grandmother, her. She was a flat-screen actress."

"And the scooter beside you?" The robocam whirred; the reporter didn't bother to hide his sneer.

"Also left over from Great-grandmama."

What had happened to Vicki?

A group of Livers whom Jackson had never seen before slouched sulkily outside the plastic-tented feeding ground. Travel-stained, dirty. The tribe got a few such groups each week. Coming from beyond Willoughby County, they'd seen the fuss on the newsgrids. Some groups looked thoughtfully interested. Some were contemptuous of Livers willing to soil themselves with the donkey work of politics. Some had just heard about the scooters and jewelry and wine from the "non-candidate-affiliated citizen groups for Serrano." Already one scooter had been stolen. Tribe members stuck together now in clumps, which was why all of them were within filming distance of the feeding ground. Except, of course, the candidate, who was enjoying the benefits of fame on his back in the woods.

Where the hell was Vicki?

Annie bustled out of the building, with Dirk in her arms. She saw Jackson, scowled ferociously, and then remembered she wasn't supposed to know him. Immediately she looked disdainfully away, like a fastidious duchess ignoring a dead fish. Her gaze landed on another party of slumming donkey kids, sneering from the safe shadow of a flashy aircar. Two of the kids carried inhalers. The second reporter was interviewing them; fortunately, Jackson was too far away to hear the conversation.

And then another car landed, and Cazie leaped out with the new TenTech chief engineer.

Jackson turned his back. Purposefully he strode toward the building and ducked inside.

What was she doing here? Since the meeting a few months ago about TenTech's political connections, of which Jackson had understood about half, he'd had Caroline, his personal system, do some research. TenTech had a diversified portfolio, but much of it Caroline couldn't trace through legal deebees, even with Jackson's access codes. Jackson had never paid much attention to TenTech. His father had done that until he died, then his father's attorney had managed most of it while Jackson was in medical school; when he'd married Cazie, she had gradually taken over, and Jackson had been glad to let her. Where was TenTech's money, and why was so much of it seemingly connected to the state of Pennsylvania, when TenTech was incorporated in New York? Cazie seemed to have a lot of personal friends in various Pennsylvania corporations and government agencies. Jackson had finally, without telling Cazie, hired an independent accountant, who had yet to report back to him. Maybe Cazie had detected the accountant's inquiries.

Or maybe she came just to look for him.

He cracked the door, peering from dimness into sunlight. Cazie stood talking with Billy Washington, Lizzie's stepfather. At least it was Billy, the sanest person in the tribe. Cazie couldn't follow Jackson into the camp building; Vicki had insisted that no outsiders, under any circumstances, be allowed inside. She'd installed a primitive scanning system; if anyone not carrying a sensitized chip tried to pass the door, an alarm sounded. It was a simple system to fool, but so far no one had bothered. Jackson fingered the chip in his pocket.

Cazie's dark curls gleamed in the spring sunshine. Her high white boots and severe black suit looked fresh and trim. Gesturing at Billy, she flung up an arm, and her full right breast lifted, trembled, fell.

What was she doing here? What was *he* doing here? Through the cracked door, Jackson saw Shockey stroll in from the woods. The donkey beauty wasn't with him. Sharon stormed toward Shockey across the withered grass, her face furious. Annie yelled at a reporter. Billy left Cazie, started toward Annie, and was waylaid by a sneering slummer who ventured away from his aircar long enough to thrust his inhaler under Billy's nose. Billy reeled. Scott Morrison lunged at the donkey kid, tackling him. Both robocams zoomed in on the fight. The candidate jumped another donkey teenager, and Sharon screamed. Annie, still carrying Dirk, rushed to Billy, now smiling emptily. Dirk began to wail. Sharon went on screaming. Cazie threw back her head and laughed, an ugly sound that somehow carried over the other din. She mouthed something at the TenTech engineer, and Jackson read the words on her lips: "The American political process in action."

He closed the battered building door.

All of them were fools. Jackson had been a little surprised to find that so many Livers stuck doggedly to voting for Shockey, even as they accepted bribes from the other side. Shockey would clearly win the election. But in the long run, he was afraid, it would make no difference whatsoever. Shockey would win not because Livers were in the power ascendancy, but because the donkeys had taken this campaign only half seriously. They'd used the carrot but not the stick, spreading around their baubles and assuming the problem was solved. When, on election day, they learned it wasn't, they would retire the carrots. Liver camps were unprotected, untechnological, unarmed. The next Liver candidate for any public office would lose. Jackson was assisting at an historical fluke, an unrepeatable improbability for which he was risking all status with his own people. Which made him the biggest fool of all.

Somewhere in the building, someone was weeping.

He made his way through the gloom, past the decrepit communal furniture, through the maze of makeshift walls of boards, upended sofas, broken shelving, strung homespun curtains. The sobbing grew louder. He passed the tribe's weaving 'bot, patiently turning out yards of ugly dun cloth from whatever raw organic materials were dumped into the hopper. The 'bot hummed softly. Behind them, in the farthest of the ramshackle cubicles against a windowless wall, Jackson found them.

A boy, facing away from Jackson, bent over almost double. The boy's back was thin and, through the holes in the clothing, deeply freckled. Vicki stood beside the boy, one arm around his skinny shoulders, almost holding him up. When the two turned, Jackson saw that the boy huddled over a baby in his arms.

Vicki said somberly, "I was just coming to look for you."

Jackson reached for the baby. He saw immediately that it was dying, probably of some mutated microorganism that had already destroyed the immune system. The infant's mouth was patchy with candidiasis. Its skin was mottled with subcutaneous hematomas. The wasted little cheeks stretched tightly over the small skull. Jackson heard the baby's lungs labor to keep breathing. On its neck stuck two patches, blue and yellow: broad-spectrum antibiotics and antivirals. Vicki always carried them. They wouldn't help; it was far too late.

The boy gasped, "You the doctor? This is my daughter, her. Can you give her a Change syringe? We didn't have none in my tribe . . . no place else neither . . . I heard, me, about this place . . ."

"No," Jackson said, "I don't have any more syringes." Vicki stared at him, stunned. Clearly she had expected a different answer, not of course knowing that Theresa had cleaned out Jackson's meager supply.

The boy said, "You don't have no syringes, you? Really?"

"Really," Jackson said.

"But ain't you a doctor . . . a donkey doctor?"

Jackson didn't answer. No one else spoke. The silence stretched on, painful. Finally Jackson nodded, miserably, and then shook his head. He couldn't meet the young father's eyes.

The boy didn't argue, or explode, or even start sobbing again. In the slump of his thin shoulders Jackson saw resignation: the boy hadn't actually expected real help. He'd never had it. He'd come here because he hadn't known what else to do.

Vicki said tightly, "Will you do what you can, Jackson?"

She had already fetched his bag from its pocket in the tribal junk. Jackson went through futile motions. When he'd finished, the boy said, "Thank you, Doctor," and Jackson's humiliation was complete.

"Come with me," Vicki said, and he followed her, basely glad to go, not caring where. Livers had come in from outside and sat talking animatedly in the communal chairs. Vicki led him around the maze of cubicles, through a curtain stretched between a wall and a long up-ended table.

"No one will come here, Jackson."

"Where's that baby's mother?"

Vicki shrugged. "You know how it is. They get pregnant so easily, nothing can go wrong in their bodies, everyone raises the kids tribally. Anyone who doesn't want to be bothered with an infant doesn't have to be."

"Then it's wrong. This new social organization the Change has created—it's all wrong."

"I know."

"You *know*? I thought you were the biggest advocate of what Miranda Sharifi gave the world!"

"I'm the biggest advocate of adjusting to it. So far, we haven't done that."

He hadn't ever seen her like this: somber, straightforward, unprotected by amused detachment. He didn't like it. She was unsettling, like this. To escape her eyes, he looked around the cubicle, and realized it must be hers. The cubicle held nothing different from any other tribe member's: pallet on the floor, scarred bureau cluttered with handmade jewelry, clothes hanging on pegs. Nothing as expensive or incongruous as the Jansen-Sagura terminal and crystal library in Lizzie's cubicle. Yet the small space looked donkey, not Liver. In the colors, muted and harmonious. In the arrangement of furniture. In the single spray of willow, placed in a black clay bowl with an almost Oriental spareness and grace.

She said, "Did you realize you were crying, holding that baby?"

He hadn't. He swiped at his wet cheeks, disliking her for having noticed, at the same time that he was grateful for her not exposing his tears to the Livers laughing in the middle of the building.

He said, because he had to say something, "They suffer. Not here, in this tribe, but other places without as many resources they live so—"

"The poor have always lived in a different country from the rich. In every age, and no matter how physically close their houses were."

"Please don't lecture me on—"

"Look at this, Jackson." She opened her top bureau drawer, pulled out a holo recorder, and said to it, "Play recording three." When she handed it to Jackson, he took it.

The miniature screen replayed a newscast. From a donkey channel, the tone hovered somewhere between bemusement and contempt. The program, no more than two minutes long, interviewed one of a group of doctors in Texas, who had set up a Y-shielded clinic just outside the Austin Enclave to treat unChanged Liver children. "It's necessary," said a tired-looking young physician who needed a haircut. "They're in pain. What Miranda Sharifi is letting happen here is criminal." The recorder stage went dark.

Vicki snorted. "'What *Miranda* is letting happen.' We still don't take responsibility."

"Who's 'we'?" he snapped. "Sometimes you use 'we' for Livers, sometimes for donkeys."

"So what? Jackson, there are more and more unChanged kids. They need doctors."

He saw again the weary face of the physician in the holo, the security shield around the clinic, the Livers who had attacked his apartment building while Theresa was there. Despite his fondness for the irrepressible Lizzie, he didn't want to practice among Livers. It wasn't what he had trained for.

"Compassion is a lot easier to feel than act on, isn't it?" Vicki said. "But not nearly as satisfying in the long run. Believe me, I know."

He said dryly, "I haven't yet seen you when you thought you didn't."

Vicki laughed. "You're right." She leaned over and kissed him.

It caught Jackson by surprise. What was she doing? Surely she wasn't kissing him just because he'd been crying over a Liver kid . . .

was she? She didn't seem the—but then all thought left him. Her lips were soft, thinner than Cazie's, her body taller and less rounded. Her mouth clung briefly, pulled away, returned. Jackson pulled her to him and a shock went through his torso, sweeping downward from his mouth through his chest to end with a sharp pleasurable jolt in his penis. He tightened his arms around her.

Vicki pulled away. "Give a clinic some thought," she said. "Between your other worries, of course. Here she comes."

Jackson became aware that an alarm was sounding, had been sounding just beyond the edge of his attention. Over it he heard Cazie yelling, "Jackson! I know you're in here someplace! Jack, damn it, I want to talk to you!"

Vicki smiled. Very deliberately she drew back her curtain and called, "Over here, Cazie. We're over here."

Cazie strode through the ridiculous maze of shabby furniture. She took in the scene all at once: Jackson beside Vickie's bed, Vicki standing with one hand gracefully holding back the curtain, Jackson's face flustered and Vicki's sly. Cazie stood very still.

"We're finished here," Vicki cooed. "See you later, Jackson." She winked at him.

He was afraid to meet Cazie's eyes.

April 1, election day, was wet. When Jackson woke in a stuffy cubicle in the tribe building in Willoughby County, he heard the rain clattering on the roof.

He had not planned to be here. But yesterday he'd hiked into a barrage of robocams and reporters, two of whom had tried to pin him against the building wall to identify him. They'd been close enough to see his genemod eyes. He'd shoved them off and escaped into the building, where Lizzie insisted that if he didn't want to be recognized, he should stay all night. Vicki was gone to another tribe. Jackson was just as glad.

He lay on the hard pallet of nonconsumable fabric, staring in the dim gloom at two walls made of foamcast, one of what appeared to be discarded sheet metal braced with broken chair rungs, and one of dun homespun curtain. Hanging on the sheet metal was a handworked sampler in lavender yarn and crimson: WELCOME STRANGER. From this he deduced that he had been put in the tribe's guest room.

He stood up, stretched, pulled on his pants, and followed the general morning noise to the center of the cavernous building.

"Morning!" Lizzie sang. Her black eyes sparkled. She wore outdoor clothes and hiking boots. Dirk lay in a turquoise plastic box on the floor, waving his fat fists and trying to capture his bare toes. "Today's the day!"

"Where's Shockey?" Jackson asked. He badly wanted a cup of coffee, which he was not going to get.

"At breakfast. So's nearly everybody else who wants to be naked on the newsgrid. Are you hungry?"

"No," Jackson lied.

"Good. This would be a good time to get you away, before the reporters really arrive. Most of them went home for the night, and the rest are at the feeding ground. Polls are open from nine to noon. I'm going to duck out the back way to meet Vicki at your car, and then we're both going to check on the Wellsville tribe. Want to come?"

"If you're meeting at my car, I guess I'm walking with you that far. Did you eat, Lizzie?"

"I can't. I'm too excited. Oh, Mama, here's Dirk—I nursed him already."

Annie emerged from her cubicle, frowned at Jackson, and picked up her grandson. The frown wasn't serious. Annie was uneasy around donkeys, but she'd softened toward Jackson when she realized he disliked Vicki. Did he dislike Vicki? He hadn't seen her in the last week, since he'd kissed her. He didn't want to see her. Or Cazie. Or even Lizzie. He wanted to find his car, fly home, and have a cup of coffee.

He knew he was lying to himself.

"Morning, Annie," he said. "Are you headed out for breakfast?"

"Not with them cameras, me," she sniffed. "Billy, he went to fetch us some good soil and bring it inside. We'll eat, us, in decent privacy, thank you very much."

Lizzie hid a grin. She grabbed Jackson's hand and led him to a small door, so far undetected by the robocams, cut by Billy in the back of the building and hidden behind weeds and bushes. The door was so low that Lizzie and Jackson had to crawl through on hands and knees. Foamcast didn't cut easily.

"Lizzie, where did Billy get a tunable lasersaw to cut this door with?"

Lizzie grinned back over her shoulder. "I found a way to dip one. Just last month. But I'm not going to tell you how."

They escaped into the rain, which had lessened to a drizzle. Even so, Jackson was wet and cold by the time they reached the aircar, which was disguised under an opaqued Y-shield. Vicki sat on the shield, smearing mud across it with her jacks-covered rump.

"Morning, Lizzie, Jackson!"

"Vicki! How is everything at Max and Farla's camp?"

"Fine. Everybody up, dressed in their best clothes and finest jewelry, gathered around the terminal and ready for political immortality." She smiled at Jackson, who smiled thinly back.

"Fifteen minutes till the poll opens," Lizzie said. "I guess I'm going to vote at Wellsville."

Vicki said, "Let's do it here."

"Here? How?"

"I'm sure Jackson has a comlink in the car capable of official channels. Don't you, Jackson? We can sit right here in a donkey vehicle and elect the first Liver politician in decades."

Lizzie laughed. "Let's do it!"

Vicki said, "Jackson?"

He looked at all three of their mud-stained, rain-soaked clothing, and decided he must be nuts. "Sure, why not?"

"Oh, I'm so excited!" Lizzie burbled.

He unlocked the car and they crowded in. Jackson activated the comlink, asked for the official government channel, and accessed the polling program. At nine o'clock he looked at Lizzie.

She leaned solemnly forward. "Lizzie Francy, Citizen ID CLM-03-9645-957, to vote in the special election for district supervisor of Willoughby County, Pennsylvania."

"Citizen number verified. Please place your left eye against the icon for retina scan." She did. "Verified. The registered candidates for district supervisor of Willoughby County are Susannah Wells Livingston, Donald Thomas Serrano, and Shockey Toor. For which candidate do you vote?"

Lizzie said clearly, "For Shockey Toor."

"One vote for Shockey Toor. Officially recorded."

"I did it!" Lizzie breathed. "Vicki, you next."

Vicki voted. Jackson, not registered in Willoughby County, felt his chest tighten. Lizzie would have her win, but it was the only one the Livers would get. She had no idea the forces that the established power structure could bring to bear once they took a threat seriously. He looked out at the dreary rain-soaked woods. A bedraggled chipmunk darted by.

"Quick!" Lizzie said. "Get a running total!"

"Lizzie, it's only 9:03!"

"Okay, then, get a newsgrid channel."

Vicki did. Channel 14 was covering the story. Jackson gazed at a robocam shot of the tribe's familiar feeding ground, now empty. Everyone must have gone inside to vote.

A voice intoned, "Here on special election day in Willoughby County, Pennsylvania, citizens are voting for district supervisor in an unusual election. One of the three candidates is unused to public office—and perhaps unfitted for it as well. This is the election that has sparked a national debate on the question of who is best suited to serve the public, how voters are registered, and what safeguards the politically innocent have a right to expect against the politically opportunistic. For the first time, our camera is being allowed to hover at the open door of this . . . 'community' . . . to watch its members line up to vote."

The robocam zoomed toward the building door and adjusted for the dim light within. A wide-angle lens showed the tribe's terminal at one end of the large communal space, on a table covered with a red, white, and blue cloth. At the other end, the tribe lined up to move forward, one at a time, and vote. A hundred sixty-two Livers shuffled forward, carrying babies, holding hands.

"There's Mama with Dirk!" Lizzie squealed. "And Billy. And Sharon with Callie. Shockey must have already voted, he wanted to go first." A moment passed. "Why do they all look like that?"

Jackson leaned closer to the screen.

Lizzie said, "Why do they look so . . . weird?"

The robocam shifted to zoom. Sharon Nugent, Franklin Caterino, Norma Kroll, Scott Morrison—face after face looked strained, unsure. Brows furrowed, eyes dropped, breathing grew rapid as people glanced toward the camera. Sharon huddled closer to her elderly mother, and then Sam Webster moved closer to both.

"What's going on!" Lizzie cried. "Where's Shockey?"

The camera found him crouched in an old lawn chair in a dim corner. Shockey's hands clasped tightly on his lap. When he raised his eyes to the voters, his face clenched. Jackson could swear Shockey trembled.

Someone swung shut the building door from inside.

"In violation of their pre-election agreement, the Livers have just excluded our camera," the newscaster said with strong displeasure. "We switch you now to another tribal polling site in the county . . . No, this building appears to be shuttered as well."

Vicki said, "Turn it off. Switch to the running totals."

It was 9:17. Jackson found the graphic on the governmental channel, a silent unadorned chart:

```
POPULAR VOTE
WILLOUGHBY COUNTY DISTRICT SUPERVISOR—
SPECIAL ELECTION
SUSANNAH WELLS LIVINGSTON: 3
DONALD THOMAS SERRANO: 192
SHOCKEY TOOR: 2
```

As they watched, two more votes registered for Donald Thomas Serrano.

"It's cheating, them!" Vicki cried. "We saw people vote for Shockey!"

"We saw people vote," Vicki said. "We can't really see for whom."

"It has to be cheating!"

Jackson thought rapidly. The results made no sense. But Vicki was probably right that the system wasn't cheating; no one would dare. A system rigged against a Liver candidate today could be rigged against a donkey candidate next time. And the newsgrids would hire top datadippers to find the tinkering. No. Something else was happening.

What? Why?

"Fly home," Lizzie said. "Oh, go quick!"

Jackson exchanged looks with Vicki, lifted the car, and flew back. During the short ride they watched Donald Thomas Serrano capture virtually every vote. Everybody voted early, like dutiful citizens. Jackson landed the car beside the reporters' vehicles; no one paid any attention until Lizzie emerged. She ignored all questions and comments, running toward the front door. Jackson and Vicki trailed behind, stony.

The door was locked.

Lizzie spoke the overrides and flung herself inside.

"Lizzie!" Annie said. "Why you running, you? What happened?" Annie clutched Dirk, who began to wail.

"What *happened?*" Lizzie cried. "Shockey's losing! Nobody's voting for him."

Annie took a step backward and dropped her eyes. *Annie* . . . who always met insubordination with frowns and commands. She shifted Dirk upright to her shoulder. The baby saw his mother and Vicki and quieted, until he glimpsed Jackson. Immediately he began to cry again, burying his head in Annie's shoulder.

Vicki said evenly, "Annie, did you vote?"

Annie shrank back and mumbled, "Yes."

"Did you vote for Shockey?"

Mutely, in distress, Annie shook her head no.

Lizzie cried, "Why not?" while Dirk continued to wail every time he raised his head from his grandmother's shoulder and caught a fresh glimpse of Jackson.

Annie tightened her grip on the baby. "I didn't . . . Shockey ain't, him . . . I'm sorry, honey, but it's just too . . . we're better off, us, with somebody who knows, them, what they're doing."

Jackson stood very still. Annie's manner reminded him of something, something he was too confused to get into focus. In a minute he would remember. Across the vast communal area, now empty of voters, Billy Washington emerged from his and Annie's cubicle. The stately old man took a few hesitant steps, stopped, looked at Annie, took a few steps more, and dropped his eyes. Jackson saw his hand tremble, saw him force himself to move forward.

Theresa. They were all—Billy, Annie, even Dirk—acting like Theresa.

Even Shockey. Today crouching in his lawn chair, nervous and afraid; yesterday full of swaggering innocent corruption, fucking the slumming donkey girl in the woods . . .

The donkey girl sniffing at her inhaler.

"Get out," he said rapidly to Vicki and Lizzie. "Now. Get out of the building right away. Vicki, take Annie."

She looked startled but didn't protest; it must be his tone. Vickie grabbed Annie by the arm and hauled her toward the door. "No, no," Annie said. "No, please. I don't want to go out there, please . . ."

"Come on," Jackson said, grabbing Annie's other arm and hauling her along.

Lizzie said, "What? What is it?" but she followed.

Outside Dirk looked over Annie's shoulder at the outdoors and screamed louder. Lizzie snatched him. Jackson hustled them all, Annie coatless, through the rain toward his car. Robocams descended and reporters in their vehicles, watching the election results, looked up. Jackson shoved Annie into the car and lifted it.

"Okay," Vicki said. "What was it?"

"I'm not sure yet," Jackson said. "A neuropharm, I think. Gaseous. Only . . ." Only Annie's Cell Cleaner should now be working overtime, clearing her body of foreign molecules as soon as she was no longer breathing them in. Instead Annie continued to shrink and tremble, and Dirk to scream and cling to his mother. And if the neuropharm was in the building, he and Vicki and Lizzie would have breathed it. But Lizzie looked furious, Vicki alert, and Jackson himself didn't feel trembly or anxious. So if not in the building . . .

He landed the car and twisted to look at the rear seat. "Annie, did you have breakfast in the feeding ground?"

Annie shook her head and folded her hands together tightly. Her eyes darted from side to side, and her chest rose and fell rapidly.

"Did Billy breakfast in the feeding ground?"

"He . . . he went there, him, to bring in some fresh soil for us . . . privacy . . ."

"But you never went in the feeding ground this morning?"

Annie drew a deep breath. "I . . . later. When no reporters there, and everybody else gone inside, them . . . the sun came out a bit and . . . Dirk needs sun, him. We just sat there, us, with our clothes on . . . we didn't . . ." She trailed off and looked out the window, her pretty plump face terrified. "Please, Doctor, take . . . take me home . . ."

Like Theresa. Jackson said, "Breathe steadily, Annie. Here, put on this patch."

"No, I . . . what is it?" Annie shook her head.

Jackson said, "Vicki, put the patch on her."

He watched closely. Annie—Annie!—didn't struggle.

She cringed against the car window, and put up one hand in a feeble, warding-off gesture that Vicki, wide-eyed, ignored. Vicki slapped the patch on Annie's neck. Annie whimpered.

After a few minutes, she sat up a little straighter, but her hands remained clasped tightly together, her body tense. "Now can we go home? What's going on here, Doctor? Please . . . take us home!"

Jackson closed his eyes. The patch was one he carried for Theresa, who would never use it. It triggered the release of biogenic amines that prompted the body to create ten different neurotransmitters. Those neurotransmitters calmed anxieties about, and lowered inhibitions to, stimuli perceived as threatening. The patch was moderating Annie's symptoms a little—but it was not eradicating them.

He said, "Vicki, put a patch on Dirk. No, wait—don't." Dirk's blood and brain should by now be clear of anything he'd breathed in at the camp, but he nonetheless continued to act like a severely inhibited baby in the throes of full-blown stranger anxiety. And Dirk was not usually shy. Why wasn't the neuropharm wearing off?

Vicki said, "It was in the feeding ground, wasn't it? Lizzie, did you go in there this morning?"

Lizzie demanded, "What're you talking about, you? Did somebody do something to *Dirk?*"

Vicki said, "I didn't feed at the other tribe, either. Too excited. Why isn't the Cell Cleaner undoing the effects on Dirk?"

"I don't know," Jackson said, at the same moment that Lizzie cried, "What effects? What happened to my baby?" and Annie reached across the seat to tap Jackson's shoulder and say tremulously, "If anybody hurt this child, them . . ."

Vicki ignored them all and flicked on the terminal.

POPULAR VOTE
WILLOUGHBY COUNTY DISTRICT SUPERVISOR—
SPECIAL ELECTION
SUSANNAH WELLS LIVINGSTON: 104
DONALD THOMAS SERRANO: 1,681
SHOCKEY TOOR: 32

"Donald Serrano," Vicki said. "He found a way to win the election, without anybody thinking that it was anything but the material bribes they've been spreading around."

"No," Jackson answered. "We don't know how to do this."

"Do what?" Lizzie cried.

He raised his voice to answer over Annie's fear, Lizzie's alarm, Dirk's fussing. "How to create neuropharms that aren't cleared immediately by the Cell Cleaner. The medical journals, my med-school friends who went into research . . . everybody's looking for that. A patentable hallucinogen or synthetic endorphin or other pleasure drug that doesn't have to be inhaled every few minutes . . . For God's sake, get out of the car, Vicki. I can't hear myself think."

Jackson and Vicki climbed out. Jackson locked the doors against Annie's fearful questions, Lizzie's attempts to follow. He stood in the drizzle, water trickling down the back of his neck, and tried to organize his thoughts. "Nobody in the medical establishment is anywhere near that kind of breakthrough. And if they were, it wouldn't be used on a penny-ante election like this. It would be worth billions."

"Then who?" Vicki said. "Miranda Sharifi?"

"But *why?* Why would the Supers do it?"

"I don't know."

The car shuddered. Jackson looked down at Lizzie pounding angrily at the inside of the rain-streaked windows. Looked at an Annie only slightly restored to tolerance for new situations, and then only for as long as the neuropharm in the patch lasted. Looked at the baby acting like a small Theresa, with Theresa's timidity and pervasive fear of anything new, anything risky, any departure from what she'd always done.

Such as electing a Liver to political office.

Vicki demanded. "Who, Jackson? Who's capable of doing this, at multiple sites? And how?"

"I don't know," Jackson said. But it had to be Miranda, nobody else had such advanced neurobiology . . . but it couldn't be Miranda. She didn't make people *less* capable!

Did she?

It had to be Miranda. It couldn't be Miranda.

A whole population of Theresas.

"I don't . . . know."

Twelve

Lizzie clutched Dirk close, and tried to pretend it was for the baby's sake. She had never seen anything like this. Dr. Aranow had taken them into Manhattan East Enclave, just flown through the Y-shield like it didn't exist and landed on the roof of his apartment block. Only it wasn't an apartment block that Lizzie, growing up in the Liver town of East Oleanta and on the road ever since, would have recognized. She didn't recognize the roof as a roof. It was *beautiful*. Bright green genemod grass, beds of delicate flowers, benches and strange statues and stranger 'bots she itched to take apart. But she wouldn't take them apart. She wouldn't even touch them. She wasn't smart enough. She was just a dumb Liver who had fucked up: lost the election and failed her tribe and somehow brought harm she didn't understand to her baby.

"This way," Dr. Aranow said, leading them across the roof that wasn't. The air was warm and cloudless.

" 'Oh what is so rare as a day in June,' " Vicki said, which didn't make sense because this was April. Vicki wasn't smiling, but she didn't look as confused as Lizzie felt. Well, of course, Vicki had once lived this way. How could she have left it to come live in East Oleanta? Lizzie felt obscurely ashamed; she never imagined Vicki had left *this*. Lizzie remembered the times she's lectured Vicki about the world, and the memory made Lizzie writhe. She didn't know enough to lecture donkeys. She didn't know anything at all.

And yesterday, she'd known everything. Just yesterday.

Dr. Aranow had taken Annie back to the camp. Now he led Lizzie, Dirk, and Vicki into an elevator which said, "Hello, Dr. Aranow."

"Hello. My apartment, please. Is my sister home?"

"Yes," the elevator said. "Ms. Aranow is home." It stopped, and the door opened directly into the most wonderful room Lizzie had ever seen. Long and narrow, with smooth white walls, floors of shining silver-gray stone dotted with carpets, a perfect little table with roses on it—only they weren't exactly roses, they had odd silver-gray leaves and a bewitching smell—and a painting lit by an unseen source. Lizzie didn't know what to make of the painting. Two naked women feeding on the grass, and two men dressed in stiff old-fashioned nonconsumable clothes. The men must not be hungry.

"The original Manet, of course," Vicki said, but Dr. Aranow didn't answer. He strode ahead, and when they followed, Lizzie realized that the wonderful white room with the roses had been only a hallway.

Inside the apartment was another hallway, and then a real room. It stopped her cold. A Y-shield made up one wall, looking down on a green, green park. The other walls shimmered with subtly shifting grays and whites—programmed screens, they had to be. Was the park a program, too? The chairs were white and soft, the tables all polished, there were strange plants inside the tables . . . and a girl, sitting on a hard wooden chair and eating food by mouth from some kind of 'bot with a flat top like another shining table.

"Theresa," Dr. Aranow said, and even in Lizzie's chagrined absorption in her surroundings—she knew nothing, nothing at all!—Lizzie could hear the careful gentleness in his voice. "Theresa, don't be alarmed, I've just brought some people here for a business meeting."

The girl shrank back in her chair. No older than Lizzie herself, she looked frightened and uneasy . . . about Lizzie and Vicki? That didn't make sense. The girl had a cloud of silvery-blond hair and was very skinny, dressed in a strange loose flowered dress that Lizzie would have sworn looked consumable. How could that be? The dress had no holes.

"This is Vicki Turner," Dr. Aranow said, "and Lizzie Francy, and Lizzie's son Dirk. This is my sister, Theresa Aranow."

Theresa didn't answer. Lizzie thought she trembled and breathed faster. This was a donkey, and yet unlike Vicki, unlike the reporters, unlike the donkey girls who had liked fucking Shockey when he was a candidate, Theresa looked . . . looked . . .

Theresa looked like Shockey and Annie and Billy looked now.

A glance passed between Vicki and Dr. Aranow, something Lizzie couldn't interpret, and Vicki said softly, "Ms. Aranow, would you like to see the baby?"

Theresa's weird fear seemed to fade a little. "Oh, a baby . . . yes . . . please . . ."

Dr. Aranow took Dirk from Lizzie—fortunately, he was asleep now—and laid him in Theresa's arms. Theresa looked at him with total delight, and then, to Lizzie's amazement, started to cry. No sobbing, just pale lightless tears rolling down her pale checks.

"Could I . . . Jackson, could . . . I hold him while you have your meeting?"

"Of course," Vicki said, and Lizzie felt a minute of resentment. Dirk was *her* baby, this girl, this donkey Theresa who lived surrounded by everything and now wanted Lizzie's baby, too—Theresa hadn't even *asked* Lizzie if she could hold Dirk. And from her looks, Theresa was a weakling. *She* wouldn't last three minutes using her wits to keep a whole tribe supplied with datadipped goods.

"We'll be right there in the dining room, Theresa," Jackson said, and took both Vicki's and Lizzie's arms.

The dining room wasn't a feeding ground, but a table with twelve tall chairs, motionless serving 'bots, and still more huge, strange-looking plants that must be genemod. One wall cascaded with water—not programming, real water. The polished table was bare. Lizzie's stomach suddenly growled.

She said, and it came out angry for some reason, "Don't you even have a feeding ground?"

"Yes," Dr. Aranow said distractedly, "but we'd better . . . are you hungry? Jones, breakfast for three, please. Whatever Theresa was having."

"Certainly, Dr. Aranow," the room said.

"Caroline, on, please."

Lizzie didn't see any terminal, but a different voice said, "Yes, Dr. Aranow."

Vicki said, "You have a Caroline VIII personal system. I'm impressed."

"Caroline, call Thurmond Rogers at Kelvin-Castner. Tell him it's a priority call."

"Yes, Dr. Aranow."

He turned to Vicki. "Thurmond is an old friend. We graduated together from medical school. He's a staff researcher at Kelvin-Castner Pharmaceuticals, his department's fair-haired wonder. He'll help us."

"Help us do what?" Vicki said, but Lizzie didn't hear the answer. In the other room, Dirk cried. Lizzie rushed back to him. Theresa held the baby helplessly, rocking him and crooning, while Dirk wailed in fear and tried to squirm off her lap.

Lizzie took him. All at once she felt better about Theresa. Dirk buried his face in his mother's shoulder and clung to her. Lizzie said, "Don't feel bad. It's just because he doesn't know you."

"Is he . . . is he shy with . . . strangers?"

"Not until this morning!"

The two girls looked at each other. Lizzie saw suddenly how they must look: Theresa genemod beautiful and elegant in her pretty dress, Lizzie with mud and wet leaves clinging to her dirty jacks, in her hair, smeared across her baby's face. But Theresa was the one who was afraid. Lizzie pulled a twig out of Dirk's hair.

"Something happened this morning," she said impulsively to Theresa. "Dr. Aranow said there might have been a neuropharm released into our feeding ground. It made everybody scared of anything new. Even of voting for Shockey! And we worked so hard! Damn it to fucking hell!"

Theresa cringed. But she said, "Scared of anything new? You mean, like . . . like me?"

So that was what was wrong with this girl. She'd breathed a neuropharm like the one Annie and Billy and Dirk had breathed. But . . . Dr. Aranow said he didn't know what the neuropharm was, it was something no Sleepers could invent, so how could Theresa have . . .

"I have to go back," she said abruptly. "Dr. Aranow's calling a research place." She carried Dirk back to the dining room.

The table held dishes of mouth food, although Lizzie hadn't seen a 'bot go past. Strawberries, huge and succulent, bread with fruit and nuts baked on top, fluffy scrambled eggs; Lizzie hadn't had an egg since last summer. Her mouth filled with sweet water. The next second, she forgot the food.

A section of the programmed wall had deepened into a holostage recess. Lizzie had never seen such technology. A man as old as Dr. Aranow, with a handsome face and bright chestnut hair, said, "It sounds incredible, Jackson."

"I know, Thurmond, I know. But believe me, I knew these people before, the behavioral change is both radical and sudden—"

"How could you know Livers that well? They're not patients, are they? Aren't they Changed?"

"Yes. It doesn't matter how I know them. I'm telling you, the change appears neuropharmaceutical, it does not wear off after inhalation stops, and it is not accompanied by gastrointestinal distress or blackout. You want to see this, Thurmond. And I need you to see it."

The holo drummed its fingers on a desktop. "All right. I'll sell it to Castner—if I can. Bring two specimens in, the baby and an adult."

Specimens?

"When?" Dr. Aranow said.

"Well, I can't . . . oh, hell, this afternoon. You're sure, Jackson, that the behavioral effect doesn't wear off when inhalation ceases? Without that, it's not worth my time to—"

"I'm sure. This could be valuable to you, Thurmond."

"Do you want to draw up a percentage contract, if the commercial possibilities pay out? Our standard split—"

"That can wait. We'll be there in a few hours. Alert your security system. Me and three Livers who—"

"Three?"

"The baby's mother has to come, and she didn't breathe in the neuropharm, so there'll be two adults."

"All right. Make 'em take a bath first."

Jackson glanced sideways at Vicki. This Thurmond Rogers—this stupid fucking donkey who thought Livers didn't even wash—said sharply, "Are they there with you now, Jackson? In your *house?*"

Vicki stepped in front of the holostage. She held a strawberry daintily in upraised fingers. Her jacks were as muddy as Lizzie's, and older. Her genemod violet eyes gleamed. "Yes, Thurmond, we're here now. But it's all right, we deloused."

Thurmond said, "Who are you?"

Vicki smiled sweetly and nibbled on her strawberry. "You don't remember me, Thurmond? At Cazie Sanders's garden party? Last year?"

"Jackson—what's going on here? She's a donkey, why is—"

"There'll be five of us coming to Kelvin-Castner," Vicki said. "I'm the baby's nanny. See you later, Thurmond." She moved away.

Thurmond said, "Jackson . . ."

"Noon, then," Dr. Aranow said hastily. "Thanks, Thurmond. Caroline, that's all."

The holostage went dark. Lizzie watched Dr. Aranow and Vicki watch each other. Shifting Dirk to the other shoulder—he was getting heavy—Lizzie waited for Vicki to yell at Dr. Aranow for letting Thurmond Rogers call them "specimens," or for Dr. Aranow to yell at Vicki for fucking up his phone call. But instead all Dr. Aranow said was, "You met Thurmond Rogers with Cazie?"

"No," Vicki said, "I never saw him before in my life. But now he'll surf his brains, wondering where that garden party was."

"I doubt it."

"I don't," Vicki said. "You really don't know how this is played, do you, Jackson?"

"I didn't think we were playing."

"Well, certainly not about the neuropharm. Who's our adult specimen, by the way? Lizzie, don't just stand there glaring and drooling. If you're hungry, have some strawberries. Genemod and exquisite."

Lizzie wanted to say no—how come Vicki was still bossing everybody else around, even in Dr. Aranow's house? But she was too hungry. Sullenly she sat in one of the beautiful carved chairs, Dirk clinging to her shoulder, and helped herself to everything she could reach.

Dr. Aranow said, "We'll fly back to camp and get Shockey."

"Why Shockey?" Vicki said. "Billy breathed in the neuropharm, too, and he'd be much more cooperative. Or even Annie."

"No. Billy's too old. And I already put a patch on Annie, changing the original conditions. Thurmond won't consider them ideal subjects. Also, Shockey's behavioral changes seemed the most pronounced . . . it has to involve the amygdalae."

"The what?" Lizzie said, to remind them she was there. Dirk fretted and she shifted him on her lap to feed him a strawberry.

Dr. Aranow said, "It's a part of the brain that affects fear and anxiety about—what's wrong with Dirk?"

Dirk screamed on Lizzie's lap. He pushed with his small feet and drew his chubby arms in toward his body. His face contorted. He twisted in her arms, trying to get down, trying frantically to escape. In his wailing was the note of pure animal fear as Lizzie held out to him something new in his experience, something he'd never seen before: a ripe red perfect strawberry.

"He's asleep," Vicki said. "Come on, Lizzie."

"Come on where?" She didn't want to leave Dirk. He lay on Dr. Aranow's living room floor on a soft multi-colored blanket Vicki had taken off one of the white sofas. Dirk had screamed and thrashed so much Dr. Aranow had finally put a little patch on his neck. Just to make Dirk sleep, he said. Lizzie sat in the sofa, which had fitted itself around her rump in a comfortable way, and scowled at Vicki. Dr. Aranow hadn't wanted to go alone to get Shockey. Lizzie didn't know what Vicki had said to him to make him agree, or why Vicki wanted to stay behind, or how Lizzie was going to cope for the rest of her life with a child terrified of a strawberry. She was exhausted.

"I want to talk to Theresa," Vicki said. "And don't you want to dip the systems here? Aranow has a Caroline VIII."

A Caroline VIII. Lizzie had only heard about them. Suddenly she wanted to be in that system more than she'd ever wanted anything in her life. She could dip that system. She could understand that system. Unlike everything else that had suddenly erupted in her life.

"Dirk's fine, the patch will last for hours. Come on, Lizzie. Let's establish a beachhead."

Lizzie didn't know what a beachhead was, and didn't ask. But she followed Vicki as far as the dining room, within earshot of Dirk. Mouth food still covered the table.

"Jackson's system will be voice-cued," Vicki said, and Lizzie laughed and reached for a plate.

"Do you really expect that to stop *me*?"

"Apparently not. See you later. I'm going to look for Theresa."

Lizzie ate hungrily. Everything tasted so good! Even the dishes were beautiful, made of some thin material edged with gold. And the glasses. And the silverware. After Lizzie had eaten all she could hold, she glanced furtively around. Quickly she slipped a silver teaspoon into the pocket of her jacks.

Then she began on the house system, Jones. As she expected, it contained direct, laughably protected access to Jackson's personal system. Amateurs. Everything about Jackson was open to Lizzie's hearing.

And everything about Theresa.

Lizzie's eyes sparkled. If Vicki couldn't find Theresa, or couldn't get her to talk, Lizzie could already know everything about Theresa from her personal system. Then, when Vicki said she hadn't been able to learn thus-and-so, Lizzie could casually drop the information. She would actually know more about the situation than Vicki.

Theresa's personal system, Thomas, yielded up calendar files, medical files (had Theresa really been on all these medicines when she was a kid? and what were they?), credit accounts—Lizzie noted the numbers and access paths to those. Wall-programming selections, library requests, comlink calls (almost none—didn't Theresa have any friends?). Orders to Jones, dress designs, didn't she have a diary file? No, but there was a book she was speaking.

Lizzie snorted. The donkey nets were awash with books. Of all the uses for a system, that seemed to her the dumbest. Who wanted to listen to stuff that never happened, or happened a long time ago and was all over? The present had too much stuff in it to absorb as it was. Lizzie quick-tasted the file, until she caught the words, "Change syringe."

She stopped tasting. "Thomas, read me that section."

The system said, " 'Leisha Camden never saw the Change syringes that Miranda made. Leisha was already dead. Everybody thinks Leisha would have liked the Change syringes, because she told Tony Indivino that she would give much money to poor beggars in Spain.

Everybody thinks Leisha would like anything that gives poor beggars like Livers a way to get food. But I don't think Leisha would like the Change syringes. She understood that people need food but they need other things more, like a meaning in life.' "

Poor beggars like Livers? Lizzie had never begged for anything in her life! What she wanted she went out and got, or dipped off the Net. "Thomas, summarize file contents."

"This file is a book spoken by Theresa Aranow. She began the file on August 19, 2118. It is a life of Leisha Camden, 2008-2114, the twenty-first Sleepless genetically engineered in the United States. The book traces Leisha Camden's entire life, starting with her birth in Chicago, Illinois, at the—"

"Enough. File links?"

"One. To newsgrid file 65. Restricted."

Restricted? A newsgrid file? But those were public to begin with. "Where is the file restricted to?"

"To the printer in Theresa Aranow's study."

It took Lizzie three minutes to dip the restriction. "Display on closest screen."

The dining room wall colors dissolved. In their place were pictures with writing under them—horrible pictures, one after another, each displayed for thirty seconds before it dissolved into the next. Lizzie couldn't read the writing, but she recognized the pictures. She'd just never seen so many of them in one place.

Babies with their bellies swollen and mottled. Babies with blood streaming from their eyes. Babies lying still, eyes glazed and scrawny arms limp. Babies shriveled as dried apples, their mouths open on swollen, toothless gums. UnChanged babies, unprotected against disease or starvation . . . so *many* unChanged babies.

Lizzie stumbled back into the living room. Dirk lay asleep on the bright blanket, which—Lizzie now noticed—his chubby little legs were consuming. His rosy mouth made little sucking motions in his sleep.

She went back to the dining room and looked at more pictures. UnChanged babies sick. UnChanged babies dying. UnChanged babies dead . . . all Liver babies. Lizzie closed her eyes. How many unChanged babies *were* there in the United States? If she hadn't had a syringe for Dirk . . . Why wasn't anybody *doing* anything about this?

And why did Theresa Aranow—rich, genemod, protected, safe—care about these Liver babies?

Lizzie realized the answer to that one. Theresa's fear of anything new. Her few friends. The mouth food. The blanket Dirk was consuming. Theresa herself was unChanged.

But how could that be? Theresa was a donkey. And she was Lizzie's age. There had been plenty of Change syringes even two years ago. Were there still plenty for donkeys? Maybe in some places. Lizzie didn't really know. None of it made sense.

The system said in Jones's stiff voice, "Ms. Aranow, Dr. Aranow is in the elevator." At the same time, Lizzie heard Vicki coming back to the dining room.

Immediately Lizzie blanked the system—she didn't know why. But Vicki shouldn't see these pictures. Which was stupid because Vicki was her closest friend in the whole world, Lizzie owed Vicki everything, and besides Vicki kept up with news all the time and probably already knew all about it. But Vicki was still a donkey. Lizzie didn't want her to see these pathetic, horrible unChanged Liver babies. Not in this rich donkey house.

"I couldn't find Theresa," Vicki said crossly. "Or rather, I suspect I did find her, hidden away in a room on the upper floor, but I couldn't dip the lock. Why didn't you come with me? And what's that noise?"

"Dr. Aranow's back."

"Alone? Where's Shockey? Did you get the access codes?"

"Yes."

"Then let's go greet the troops on the upholstered battlements."

"In a minute," Lizzie said. "I just . . . just want a bit more bread."

"You metabolically versatile glutton," Vicki said, and left the room.

"Thomas," Lizzie said softly, "personal message mode for Theresa Aranow. Urgent."

"Go ahead."

"I saw the pictures of the Liver babies. You have to find Miranda Sharifi and make her give us some more Change syringes. You're a donkey, you have all this money, you can get to Miranda, you, in ways we can't, us . . ." Lizzie trailed off. How should she sign it? Why sign it at all? What the hell did she think she was doing, begging help from a donkey girl who was too much of a coward to leave her own apartment?

"Thomas, cancel urgent personal message."

"Personal cancel code, please?"

No time. Jackson and Vicki walked toward the doorway.

"Thomas, close." The wall blanked.

"Let's go, Lizzie," Dr. Aranow said wearily. "This won't be bad, I promise. Some behavioral recording, a brain scan, and then they'll put you briefly to sleep for tissue samples. It won't hurt."

"Where's Shockey?"

"In the car. He wouldn't leave it, even with a tranq patch on. Get the baby and we'll go."

"Are Billy and my mother all right?"

"Yes. No. They're the same as when you saw them."

Vicki said, "How did you get Shockey to come with you?"

"Not easily. He cried."

Lizzie tried to picture Shockey crying. Big, rough, bold-eyed Shockey. "Didn't anybody try to stop you?"

"Yes. Sort of. Billy did, with a few others. But I just started acting very strange, and they all got even more frightened and backed away. I grabbed Shockey and tranqued him and dragged him along. Crying." Dr. Aranow ran his hand through his hair. Lizzie hadn't known a donkey could look so worn-out and . . . well, *upset.*

Vicki said, more gently than Lizzie had ever heard her be with anyone beside Dirk or Lizzie herself, "You should sleep, Jackson."

He laughed shortly. "Oh, yes. That would solve everything. Come on, Lizzie, Thurmond Rogers is waiting."

Lizzie said, before she knew she was going to say anything, "Not until I have a bath. And Dirk, too."

"You can't—"

"Oh, yes, I can. And I will, me."

Vicki smiled at her. It took Lizzie a moment to figure out why. Vicki thought she was having a bath to give Dr. Aranow time for the sleep he needed. Fuck that. She wanted a bath before she faced Thurmond Rogers and his snooty corporation. She and Dirk both. Vicki could show up looking like a piece of the woods, but that was different. Vicki was a donkey.

It seemed to Lizzie that she'd never before realized everything that meant.

"All right, all right," Dr. Aranow said. "Have a bath. Just be quick about it."

"I will," Lizzie promised. She would, too. She was as worried about Annie and Billy as anyone. She would wash herself and Dirk as fast as she could.

And maybe she could dip whatever parts of the system were on-line in the bathing room.

INTERLUDE

TRANSMISSION DATE: April 3, 2121
TO: Selene Base, Moon
VIA: Chicago Ground Station #2, GEO Satellite 342 [Old Charter] (USA)
MESSAGE TYPE: Unencrypted
MESSAGE CLASS: Class D, Public Service Access, in accordance with Congressional Bill
        4892-18, May 2118
ORIGINATING GROUP: American Medical Association
MESSAGE:

An Open Letter to Miranda Sharifi—

    We, the physicians of the American Medical Association, would like to once more collectively request that, as a humanitarian act, you make available to the peoples of the world your proprietary medical substance, Cell Cleaner™. As doctors, all of us witness weekly the personal suffering and social disorder caused by the abrupt lack of this pharmaceutical. It is nothing short of tragic. The long-term consequences for our country—which is also yours—are the gravest possible.
    Please reconsider your decision to withhold the means of alleviating such great suffering.

                  Margaret Ruth Streibel,
                  President, AMA

                  Ryan Arthur Anderson,
                  Vice President, AMA

                  Theodore George Milgate,
                  Secretary, AMA

   . . . and the 114,822 members of the American Medical Association

ACKNOWLEDGMENT: None received

Thirteen

The drone came in low over the trees, no faster than a bird and with no greater mass. The tiny camcorder on its front showed the enclave below, leisurely growing larger. Jennifer Sharifi, alone in her office on Sanctuary, leaned toward the screen.

She had opaqued the office wall facing deep space. For this moment, she wanted no competition from the stars. Just as she wanted no company, not even her husband Will. Especially not Will. The rest of the project team was watching the test from the Sharifi Labs. It seemed to Jennifer that she had earned this personal indulgence.

The California enclave came in closer and closer. Sixteen Liver camps so far, but those had been only trials. This was the first donkey enclave to be penetrated with Strukov's virus, and the first to test the correspondingly more sophisticated delivery drone created by Jennifer's Peruvian contractor. To infect Livers, all one needed to do was puncture a plastic tent. Y-shielded enclaves were a much different matter. The California enclave was a comparatively easy first step.

"Fifty-eight minutes," said an uninflected voice from a different terminal wedged into a corner across the room. Jennifer didn't turn around.

The north California enclave was small, originally a vacation colony clinging to the Pacific coast. Four hundred seventy donkeys lived under a Y-shield that extended a quarter mile over the ocean and well into the ground beneath it. Under the invisible dome were lush genemod gardens, a dazzling and artificial beach, nanobuilt houses of fantastic dimensions and luxuries, and only minor weaponry. During the Change Wars, security had been augmented, but not defense. Why would there ever be any heavy-duty attack on a small vacation enclave of mostly retired people? Thieves couldn't penetrate the Y-shield. Nothing else was necessary.

But the enclave liked birds. Gulls, condors, woodpeckers, swallows, more exotic engineered seabirds. And there was no reason to fear birds—Livers didn't have the technology for biological warfare, and weren't capable of stealing it, or of understanding it if they did. Everybody knew that. Sixty feet above ground the shield admitted birds.

The drone flew slowly through the shield, as slowly as a bird. None of the inhabitants noticed it. Slowly the drone descended, its zoom camera displaying increasingly more detail. The last picture transmitted came from forty feet above a fashionably purple garden: violet-watered swimming pool, masses of violet flowers, even the stems and leaves subtly blending shades of lavender, mauve, lilac, orchid, heliotrope. A genemod plum-colored rabbit turned its violet eyes upward to the sky. The lens showed the dark soft pupils of its eyes, like ink on tinted satin.

The drone exploded soundlessly. A fine mist blanketed a much larger area than would have seemed possible. At the same moment, all remnants of the probe itself dissolved into its component atoms. Artificial breezes inside the enclave, joined by natural ones from the ocean, spread the mist farther. The enclave was always seventy-two degrees; windows in the luxurious homes were open to the flower-scented air. On a screen to Jennifer's right, a chime sounded.

"Ms. Sharifi, you have a call from Dr. Strukov."

Jennifer turned toward the screen. Before she could say she would accept the call, Strukov's holo was there, wordlessly proving the superiority of his overrides. Jennifer let no reaction show on her face.

"Good morning, Ms. Sharifi. Of course you watched the transmission?"

"Yes."

"Without flaw, isn't it? I trust the payment has wired itself to Singapore."

"It has."

"Good, good. And the schedule of delivery remains unaltered?"

"Yes." More test enclaves, better shielded, working up to military and government targets. Those, of course, would be the hardest to penetrate, and the most crucial. If Strukov could infect the federal enclaves of Brookhaven, Cold Harbor, Bethesda, New York, and the Washington Mall, and the military bases in California, Colorado, Texas, and Florida, he could infect anything.

The door to her office opened, closed. Against her express wishes. Will said to Strukov's image, "Very good, so far. But of course there's no proof yet that this version of your virus will work."

She never could teach Will the tactical advantage to not revealing rivalry.

Strukov said, "But yes, it will work." His smile showed perfect teeth.

"Or perhaps you doubt the mechanisms of the delivery. Of course, that responsibility belongs not to me, but to your Peruvian engineers. Perhaps you should discuss your concerns about that technology with your so brilliant granddaughter, Miranda Sharifi?"

Jennifer said, "That's all, Dr. Strukov."

"À bientôt, madame."

"I don't trust him," Will said after the comlink broke.

"There is no reason not to," Jennifer said calmly. She was going to have to think again about Will Sandaleros as partner and husband. If he could not contain his dislike and jealousy . . .

"He still won't release a virus sample to Sharifi Labs for analysis. And our geneticists can't come up with a congruent speculative model. The biochemistry is so damn indirect . . ."

"We asked for indirect effects," Jennifer said. She spoke to her screen. "Newsgrid mode. Channel 164." It was the most reliable of the donkey stations, broadcasting from New York.

"I just don't trust him," Will repeated.

"Fifty minutes," said the terminal in the corner.

"—outbreak of fighting among Livers in Iowa," said the newsgrid. "Security officers have assured all channels that there is no danger to the Peoria Enclave, or to the shielded agri-areas of southern Illinois. Robocam monitoring of the fighting shows several Liver camps to be involved, possibly banded together. The cause, as elsewhere in the country, seems to be the shortage of Change syringes among those unfortunate Liver camps that—"

Jennifer concentrated on the images, transmitted unedited except for rapid-rotation selection among a number of cams. A daylight attack—yesterday?—by thirty or forty Livers on one of their squalid little "camps." The resident Livers sat naked under the clear tarp from which they constructed their feeding grounds. Why hadn't they gone south for the winter, like so many others? It didn't matter. The second group of Livers, dressed in old government-issued synthetic clothing and a bizarre assortment of homespun consumables, rushed into sight and opened fire. People screamed, blood spurted in red jets against the low tarp. A baby shrieked before it was shot.

Jennifer froze the image and studied it. The attackers were armed with AL-72s, a military assault weapon. That meant either they had donkey allies or they'd been able to datadip a federal or state armory somewhere, probably the latter. Their dippers were getting bolder. And as they acquired more knowledge and more weapons, they became more potentially dangerous to not only donkeys but to Sanctuary's financial holdings in the United States, and conceivably, to Sanctuary itself.

"—another group of Doctors for Human Aid have already left for the tri-county area from—"

"Forty minutes," said the terminal in the corner.

Jennifer changed newsgrid channels with metronomic regularity, two minutes for each. Of course, flag programs compiled hourly summaries for her. But it was important to keep personally informed as well, for those nuances of tone that the compilations could not pick up.

A Liver raid on the Miami Enclave; thirty Change syringes stolen, fifty-two people dead. More pictures of unChanged babies in Texas, dying of some unnamed virus or toxin. President Garrison, declaring a state of emergency, which the all-but-self-governing enclaves would ignore. More broadcasts to Selene, pleading with Miranda for additional Change syringes. Another bizarre religious cult in Virginia, this one notable for being made up of donkeys rather than Livers. They believed that Jesus Christ was preparing the Earth for the return of angels from the Orion Nebula.

Jennifer watched composedly, not allowing her emotions to show. What was Miranda doing? Miranda had given the Change to the enemy . . . why was she now withdrawing it?

Inconsistent people were dangerous. You could not anticipate how to block their actions.

"Thirty minutes," said the terminal in the corner.

"Jennifer, it's time for the second penetration," Will said. His voice was high and tight. Jennifer turned off the newsgrid.

This time the target was a less rich enclave, outside the main dome of St. Paul, Minnesota. The enclave housed mostly techs, who kept the machines of the city running and programmed. Techs, skilled and genemod, were part of the donkey economy, although never decision-makers. The drone camera showed rows of small neat houses under an energy dome, genemod lawns and flowers, a playground and a church and community center. The Y-shield did not admit birds. Techs were not much interested in birds.

Nonetheless, the second drone flew through the shield as easily as the first had flown into the opulent retirement enclave by the Pacific. Soundlessly the drone dissolved, and soundlessly the viral mist floated down over houses and playground.

Techs worked for a living. They couldn't be rendered as fearful as Livers or they would refuse to leave their small enclave and would not report to work. But Strukov, learning from the sixteen Liver beta-tests, had refined his product. This version was subtler.

But just as difficult to pin down with biochemical analysis. Not even Sharifi Labs had succeeded. The virus initiated the manufacture and release of a biogenic amine natural to the brain, which in turn caused the manufacture and release of another, which affected multiple receptor sites and caused further electrochemical reactions . . . it was a long and twisted skein of cerebral events. The end result would be that the techs, without realizing it directly, would simply come to prefer the familiar. Routines they already knew, faces they saw every day, tasks they were used to. The old friend, the known line of thought, the conventional attitude, the incumbent politician. It would just feel too unsettling to initiate, or learn, or change.

And then Jennifer Sharifi and the rest of her people would be safe. *Better the devil you know than the one you don't know.*

Safe. Was that actually possible? There had been times, in Allendale Federal Prison, when she'd despaired of ever feeling safe again, or of ever making her people safe. Her previous efforts to safeguard Sleepless had been both crude and naive. Sanctuary, removed from Earth but vulnerable, as all orbitals were vulnerable. Financial power, necessary but not sufficient for protection. Finally, secession from a corrupt government, through terrorism that had only called such blatant attention to itself that it had been bound to fail.

This time would be different. No threats of biological warfare. No demands for freedom. No worldwide broadcasts to try to make the enemy see what they were incapable of seeing. No. This time, stealth and stasis. Freeze the world into biological inhibition, but so subtly that they would never even recognize it. Will was right—they'd never know what hit them.

Except for twenty-seven people.

Those twenty-seven, if they so chose, probably could stop her. As they had once before. That they hadn't interfered yet perhaps meant that their own complex and devious goals dovetailed with hers to a certain point . . . could that be true? *What was Miranda doing?*

Whatever it was, Jennifer would not let it wreck her own plans. Could not let it.

That was the most painful part: Jennifer's lack of real choice. Miranda was her granddaughter; Nikos and Christina the grandchildren of her oldest friend; Toshio Ohmura her great-nephew by marriage. She could not, without pain, simply turn her back on them. That was what Sleepers did: destroyed kinship ties, destroyed community itself, with no sense of loss. That deadened self was what Jennifer fought against.

Still—there was no choice. Not if she was going to make her people safe.

She felt Will's hands on her shoulders. "Jenny—it's time," he said, and she thought he'd spoken the words earlier, but suddenly she couldn't remember. She hadn't heard the terminal in the corner. For a moment the room blurred. She closed her eyes.

"Thirty seconds," said the terminal in the corner. Jennifer forced herself to open her eyes. Her screen had brightened. No drone-mounted camera, this time. The hidden monitor was a mile away, showing only empty desolate landscape, and, on zoom, the faint shimmer of a Y-shield. No, not a Y-shield but something else entirely, designed by genius, unduplicated by anyone else anywhere. Something no drone could penetrate, ever.

"Twenty seconds."

Will's hands tightened on her shoulders. She thought of shrugging the hands off, but somehow she couldn't move. She couldn't think. Her mind, that precision tool, felt clogged with confusion, vaporizing out of the new data Caroline Renleigh had brought her about Selene. Selene, where the traitor Miranda Sharifi hid from the world.

Her granddaughter Miranda. Richard's daughter. Richard, her son, who had chosen to side with Miranda's treachery against his own mother. Richard, who was there with Miranda now.

"Ten seconds."

She couldn't remember Richard as a baby. She had been so young, and so involved in creating Sanctuary, and she had not yet trained herself to the discipline of remembering everything. It was Miranda's babyhood that she recalled. Miranda, with her dark eyes and unruly black hair, laughing at the stars as Jennifer held her to the window in this very room. Miranda.

Miri—

"No!" Jennifer cried, and her cry blotted out the calm voice of the terminal in the corner.

"It's over, Jenny," Will said softly. "It's over." But Jennifer was crying, sobbing so hard she barely heard the system add, "New Mexico operation complete." Later, she would resent that she had sobbed, and resent Will for seeing it. It was a disgrace to her own discipline, but now she cried like a two-year-old because it shouldn't have to be this way, the choices shouldn't have to be so hard. The terrible choices of war.

Miri—

Will held her as if she were a frightened child, and even through her sobbing and resentment and her inexcusable weakness she knew that as long as he, with his despised kindness, still did this for her, she was going to keep Will Sandaleros around.

Fourteen

Light on her face woke Theresa, and she cried out.

A moment later, she remembered where she was. Slumped on the window seat at the end of the upper-floor hallway—since last night? All night? She'd only meant to sit down a minute, look out at the park, escape her study for a little while.

Painfully she uncramped her body from the narrow seat. Her back ached, her neck felt stiff, her mouth tasted horrible. How long since she'd slept, before last night? How long since she'd eaten? She had lost track. Jackson hadn't been home for days. Theresa had been alone, locked in her study, watching the news grids and printing pictures for her wall. Pictures of dying unChanged babies, of adults fighting each other savagely for nonexistent Change syringes, of raids for Y-cones, for furniture, for terminals, on dipped enclaves in Oregon, in New Jersey, in Wisconsin . . . Theresa had watched it all.

I am come to bear witness to the destruction of worlds. Thomas had found her the quote. Theresa had stared at it until her eyes blurred. Then she had stared at the newsgrids some more. Then she had stared at the message on her system, the message that should not have been there:

I saw the pictures of the Liver babies. You have to find Miranda Sharifi and make her give us some more Change syringes. You're a donkey, you have all this money, you can get to Miranda, in ways we can't—

The message had been spoken, of course, but Theresa had asked Thomas to write it out. Then Theresa had stared at it, sleepless, for however many days it had been since Jackson was home. At first she'd tried to pretend that the message was a mistake, a fluke, one of the thousands of messages people all over the country were composing to beam up to Selene, and that it had leaked onto Theresa's personal system through some weird Net error. But even while she told herself that, Theresa knew she wasn't crazy enough to believe it.

Too bad.

The message was from that girl that Jackson had brought home, the Liver girl with the baby made fearful by neuropharms, and the message was intended for Theresa. Jackson always wanted her to face facts; those were the facts. The message was for her.

Of course, that didn't mean she had to do anything about it.

She had been staring at the message, away from it, at the newsholos of the dying babies, away from them, at the walls of her study, away, for two days. Or three. Until last night she'd suddenly thought that if she didn't get out of that room, she *would* go crazy. Crazier. And she'd stumbled to the window seat, and looked down at the night-lighted park and up through the enclave dome at the stars, and she'd started to sob until she couldn't stop. For no reason, no reason at all . . .

Take a neuropharm, Jackson said in her mind. *Tessie, it's biochemical, you don't* have *to feel this way* . . .

"Fuck off," Tessie said aloud, for the first time in her life, and started to cry again.

No. Enough of that. She had to pull herself together, take a bath, eat something . . . She had to return to her study. Babies were dying, little children being scarred and disfigured by horrible diseases, mothers like that girl Lizzie holding babies writhing in pain . . . Why couldn't she forget about it? Other people did! Just push it out of her mind, stay out of her stupid study . . .

Take a neuropharm, Tessie.

"Ms. Aranow," Jones said, "you have a priority-one call."

"Tell them I'm dead."

"Ms. Aranow?"

It could only be Jackson. She mustn't worry him. She mustn't . . . shouldn't . . . couldn't . . .

"Ms. Aranow?"

"Say I'm coming, Jones."

Theresa climbed off the window seat. Her head swam. Leaning against the wall until her vision cleared, she felt her knees wobble. She locked them and took the call in the bathroom, where she wouldn't have to send her image. It wasn't Jackson.

"Tess? Where's visual?" Cazie, looking crisp and fierce in a severe black suit.

"I just got out of the shower." Cazie knew that Theresa didn't like her body on display.

"Oh, sorry. Listen, where's Jackson?"

"Isn't he with you?" Theresa said.

"You know quite well he's not with me; I can hear it in your voice. Don't play games with me, Tess. Where did he take those Livers?"

"I don't . . . which Livers?"

Cazie's face changed. This, Theresa thought, must be the face that Jackson saw when he and Cazie fought: high, sharp cheekbones sprung out of soft skin, eyes as hard as the marble floor beneath Theresa's bare feet. Theresa shrank back a little against the sink.

"Tell. Me. Theresa. Where. Jackson. Is."

Theresa squeezed her eyes shut.

"You won't tell me. All right, I'm coming over there now."

"No! I'm . . . I'm on my way out!"

"Oh, right. When was the last time you went out? Ten minutes, Tess." The screen blanked.

Panic seized Theresa. Cazie would get it out of her, Cazie could get anything out of her, she'd tell Cazie that Jackson had taken Lizzie and the others to Kelvin-Castner in Boston . . . Jackson had said not to say anything. To anyone. Especially not to Cazie. But Cazie was on her way . . . Theresa would order Jones not to let her in.

Cazie would know the overrides. For the apartment, for the building. For Theresa's mind.

All right, then—Theresa wouldn't be here when Cazie came.

The moment the thought came, Theresa knew it was right. She needed to leave before Cazie arrived. Also, she needed to do what the message on her system told her to do—get to Miranda Sharifi and make her give out more Change syringes. You're a donkey, you have all this money, you can get to Miranda, you, in ways we can't—Theresa had spent two days (three?), she now saw, trying to push what she had to do out of her mind. And it hadn't worked—it never did. Ignoring the summons to pain only made the pain worse. The summons was a gift, she'd somehow overlooked that, and not acting on the gift had only made her crazy.

Crazier.

But not now.

Quickly, with a smoothness that surprised her, Theresa darted from the bathroom. No time for a shower now. But shoes—she'd need shoes. And a coat. It was April outside the enclave—wasn't April cold? She grabbed shoes and coat. "The roof," she told the elevator. "Please."

And it wasn't just her muscles that suddenly worked smoothly. Her mind did, too, in efficient autonomous plans that amazed herself. To get to Miranda Sharifi, Theresa needed to start at the last place Miranda had been seen on Earth. That was the Liver compound where people bonded in threes, where Patty and Josh and Mike could never be alone again because they were forced to be with each other. Miranda had been there, leaving a tape explaining the new red syringes. To use the new syringes, you had to be Changed. That's what Josh had said. So Miranda might have also left more Change syringes there than anywhere else. Or, she might even have come back, or sent somebody else back, to bring more, after the fighting broke out over Change syringes. If bonding was Miranda's latest plan for people, then surely Miranda would monitor the place (places?) she was testing it. Even Theresa knew that much about how science worked.

On the roof, she blinked in the bright warm sunshine. Her heart speeded up, and her breath caught in her throat. Outside the enclave, the last time she'd tried that she'd blacked out, the panic had been so bad, seizure after seizure . . .

But Cazie was coming here. If Theresa didn't leave, she'd have to see Cazie.

Theresa closed her eyes, bent over from the waist to put her head between her knees, and breathed deeply. After a few moments, the panic lessened. Or maybe it didn't; maybe it just seemed less because facing a camp full of wild, bonded Livers was less scary than facing Cazie Sanders in a rage.

Maybe that was how people made themselves face dangerous things. By running away from things more dangerous.

In the bright sunshine, walking through the roof garden toward the aircars, Theresa whimpered. Then she climbed into the car and retrieved from its memory the district coordinates for the camp of the biochemically bonded Livers, trying to breathe evenly and deeply, trying not to give in to the chemistry of her own mind.

The Livers hadn't moved camp. Theresa was afraid they might have gone somewhere else—Livers did that—but from the air she could see small human figures moving around in groups of three. How far away could they get from each other before they died? Theresa couldn't remember the exact distance.

She landed, breathing deeply and evenly, but this time no one came running toward the car. Instead, all the triads immediately vanished into the building and closed the door.

She forced herself to get out of the car and walk toward the building, then around it. Under the plastic tarp of the feeding ground sat three naked people who hadn't noticed the aircar: two women and a man. When they saw Theresa their faces froze, and then she saw the kind of look she usually only saw in the mirror.

They were afraid. Of *her*. Like Lizzie's baby had been afraid. This camp had been infected just like Lizzie's had.

"Hello? Is Josh here?" Josh had been kind to her, before.

The three people stood, huddled close together, and clutched each other's hands. In a naked tangle they inched toward the flap of plastic that served as the feeding-ground door. Theresa moved in front of the flap, and they halted.

"I want to speak to Josh. And Patty and Mike."

The names seemd to reassure at least one of the triad. The older woman took a step forward, still holding both her partners' hands, and said fearfully, "Do you know Jomp, you?"

Jomp. It took Theresa a minute to realize this was Josh-Mike-Patty. She felt a flicker of distaste.

"Yes. I know Josh, and I'm here to see him. Take me to him, please."

Despite the pounding in her chest, Theresa marveled at herself. She sounded like Cazie. Well, no, maybe not. But at least like Jackson.

The woman hestitated. She was about thirty, small and fair, with a bony face and short hair as pale as Theresa's own. "Jomp are inside, them. I'll go in, me, and get them."

"You might not come back," Theresa said. "I'm going with you."

"No! No, no. You stay here, you."

Theresa merely stepped aside. The triad squeezed past her. As they left the warmth of the sun-magnified enclosure, their naked skim dimpled and goose-bumped. Theresa watched them pull on the jacks dumped in a pile on a wooden shelf, before she moved closer to the fair-haired woman, who shrunk back.

"It's all right. I won't hurt you, any of you. I just . . . want to see Josh. He'll remember me." Would he? "What's your name?"

"We're Peranla, us." It came out in a whisper.

Peranla. Percy-Anne-Laura. Or Pearl-Andy-Lateesha. Or . . . it didn't matter.

But it should.

"Peranla, I'm going with you to see Josh."

The triad stopped moving. Almost they stopped breathing. What if they went into a seizure, like Theresa did when she got too frightened? What would Theresa do then? But they didn't. After a minute they moved in their huddle past Theresa and broke into a clumsy group run around the corner of the factory. Theresa ran after them.

"Open the door! It's Peranla, us! Open up!"

The door opened, and Peranla tumbled inside. Theresa, astonished at herself, squeezed in with them.

Her eyes took a minute to accustom themselves to the gloom. Over a hundred people, grouped in threes, staring at her. The triads pulled closer together and looked uneasy, but nobody looked terrified. Even Peranla looked less anxious than they had outside. Of course. When Theresa was at home, with familiar people among familiar things, she was less frightened, too. Safer.

Her heart quickened and her throat tightened around her windpipe. "Is . . . Josh here? Josh?"

"You better leave, you," said an old man. Several other people nodded.

"Josh? Jomp?"

He came forward slowly, dragging Patty and Mike by the hand. Mike scowled faintly, but Patty, whom Theresa remembered as a scary bitch, trembled and hid her head in Mike's shoulder. That calmed Theresa's breathing.

Maybe being the least scared person in a group was almost the same as not being scared at all.

"Josh, I'm Theresa Aranow. I was here last fall. I brought you clothes and Y-cones. You told me about the bonding here, and . . . and the red syringes."

Josh nodded, without meeting her eyes.

"And the holo, Josh. You showed me a holo of Miranda Sharifi. She was explaining the new syringes, the ones that she left with you to cause bonding."

Mike growled, "It don't having nothing to do with you."

"I want to see the holo again, Josh. Please. You've all seen it lots of times, haven't you?"

Josh nodded again. Patty looked up from Mike's shoulder.

"Well, then," Theresa said as firmly as she could, "you can see it again. Just like you always do. And I'll watch, too."

"Okay," Josh said. "Everybody, you—it's Miranda time. We are the life and the blood, us."

"We are the life and the blood," the crowd responded raggedly, and Theresa could feel relief running over them, clear as falling water. This was a known routine: comforting, safe. The triads moved and jiggled, settling down in front of an ancient holostage in what Theresa would bet were the same places they always sat. After a minute, she sat beside Josh, nearest to the door.

"On," Mike said. "Miranda time."

The holostage sprang to life. A pretty, meaningless swirl of color, and then Miranda appeared, head and shoulders only, the background a plain dark recording booth designed for anonymity. Miranda wore a sleeveless white suit; a red ribbon held back her unruly black hair.

"This is Miranda Sharifi, speaking to you from Selene. You will want to know what this new syringe is. It's a wonderful new gift, designed especially for you. A gift even better than the Change syringes were. Those set you free biologically, but also led to much isolation when you no longer needed each other for food and survival. It's not good for man to be alone. So this syringe, this wonderful gift—"

Something was wrong with the holo.

Since her first visit to this camp five months ago, Theresa had spent weeks, months, watching newsholos. They replayed at night behind her eyelids. This one was subtly wrong. The voice was Miranda's and words were synchronized with Miranda's moving lips, but not with her body. No, that wasn't it. Her body didn't move very much. That was it. The stiffness of Miranda's body on certain words, plus her movements on others . . . the rhythm was wrong. And the rhythms in the words, too . . . Theresa had perfect pitch. She heard the very slight flattening in the wrong places. The holo had been created, not recorded.

Which meant that Miranda had not given this message. Or these red syringes.

Theresa glanced around. The Liver faces were rapt, almost as if they were watching a Lucid Dreamer concert. There must be subliminals in the holo. She lowered her eyes and listened to the rest of the message without watching the visuals.

If the bonding syringes weren't from Miranda, then who were they from?

Maybe the same people who made the neuropharm these people had breathed in. The neuropharm that made people so afraid of new things. But why?

Jackson had said that nobody except SuperSleepless could create such neuropharms. Nobody but Miranda Sharifi knew enough about the Cell Cleaner to make something that wouldn't be destroyed by the Change nanos in everybody's body. Everybody's but Theresa's.

"—be together in a new way, a way that creates community, that roots that community in biology itself—"

Doubt grabbed Theresa. What did she know about "biology itself," or community, or SuperSleepless? Who was she to decide that this recording wasn't really Miranda? Theresa was a crazy, fearful, un-Changed person who had seizures whenever anything got too unfamiliar, who had left her apartment only three times in the last year, who

was afraid to go home because her ex-sister-in-law, who was also her
only friend, was looking for her. Theresa didn't know anything.

Except every recorded detail of the life of Leisha Camden.

And with that realization, Theresa knew what she was going to do.

She stood up just as the recording ended. All around her Livers
gazed misty-eyed and smiling at their bonded triads. Without which
they would die. Wicked, wicked. It wasn't bonding, it was bondage.

"Give me the holo cartridge, Josh," Theresa said as firmly as she
could manage. She tried to sound like Leisha Camden when Leisha
gave orders. Nobody knew Leisha's life better than Theresa; nobody
knew Leisha herself better.

A hundred misty faces stared at her.

"I'm taking it. I need it. I'll bring it back." Leisha, decisively telling
Jennifer Sharifi that Sanctuary was wrong. Or Leisha telling Calvin
Hawke that his anti-Sleepless movement was finished. Leisha: calm,
firm, cool. Theresa started, knees shaky, toward the holostage.

"You leave our Miranda-time holo alone, you!" somebody said.

"I'm sorry, I can't. I need it." Theresa reached the terminal. But she
wasn't Theresa, she was Leisha. That was the trick. Be Leisha, feel
like her. If Theresa could watch a newsgrid and feel what the mother
of a dying unChanged baby felt—could feel like she *was* that
mother—then she could be Leisha Camden. It was no different. No
different . . .

Now people stood up, some milling fearfully in tight groups of
three, some starting toward her. Mike hesitated, then he and Josh
moved in, dragging Patty with them. Mike's trowel-shaped head was
lowered into his neck, his eyes were terrified. For a second, through
her own trembling vision, Theresa saw them all as they must look
from the outside: four wide-eyed freaks jittering around each other,
smelling of fear. *No, don't think like that, don't see yourself from the
outside, see yourself as Leisha.* She was Leisha Camden.

"Don't stop me," Theresa quavered. Mike broke stride for a moment, then continued toward her.

"I mean it!"

"Mike," Patty whimpered, "don't . . . you can't . . ."

Mike whispered, "She can't take our holo, her . . . she can't have
it . . ." He grabbed Theresa's arm.

The vertigo started, blackness swooping over her brain. Theresa
tried to push the vertigo away—Leisha had never fainted!—along with
Mike's hand. She couldn't. She wasn't Leisha, calm and firm and cool,
she couldn't ever be Leisha, that was more self-control than she could

ever have. Even though being Leisha had seemed to work for a few minutes, Theresa wasn't Leisha—

Then be somebody not calm and cool.

"Let go of that fucking holo or I'll tie you in naval knots!" Theresa yelled, and the words were Cazie's.

Mike dropped her arm and stared at her.

"Get out of my fucking way!"

Part of the crowd drew back; the rest surged timidly forward. Murmurs rose, within and among triads: "Don't let her take it, us" . . . "Stop her, you" . . . "What right does she got" . . .

In a minute they would overcome their fear and grab her again. No—grab *Cazie.* She was Cazie. And these people's brain chemistry now made them afraid of anything unfamiliar, anything they weren't used to.

"I'm going to cry!" Theresa screamed at top volume. "I'm going to melt the floor! There is nanotech you've never seen that lets me do that, I can do that! All I have to do is sing!" She started singing, some song her nanny used to sing to her, only it was too gentle so she started jumping up and down and then spinning around, screaming the words and then changing them to the kinds of obscenities Cazie used when she was mad at Jackson for not doing what Cazie wanted. "You poor deluded son of a bitch, your vision about reality is so limited you don't see even a fraction of it, let alone a fraction of *me,* you lack irony Jackson goddamn it to Liver hell can't you even see that! You pathetic cosseted baby, you'd think you . . . *get the fuck out of my way!"*

They did. The crowd shrank back, and some children started to cry. Triads clutched at each other. Screaming, singing, jumping, cursing, whirling, Theresa moved to the door, the cartridge in her hand, while a hundred people—but there must be ninety-nine, right, or a hundred two—looked at her with the same anxious dread Theresa saw daily in the mirror.

She made it outside just before her own nerve broke.

Still, she was able to stumble to the aircar. "Lift!" she gasped at it. "Home . . ." and then her breath caught and the seizure started and all she could do while it lasted was try to breathe, the car flying itself away from the Liver camp where no small figures sixty feet below came out of the building to watch her leave.

Just before reaching Manhattan East, Theresa gained control of herself. She leaned back against the seat of the car and tried to think.

She couldn't go home. Cazie might still be there. She had the car fly to the first large empty place, which turned out to be a deserted scooter-race field, and set down where she could see in all directions. She sat clutching the holo cartridge of Miranda and breathing as evenly and deeply as she could.

What had just happened?

She had been Cazie. It had only been pretending, of course, but she had been able to pretend powerfully enough to hold off her fear for a little while, and behave in a way she never could have otherwise. But how could that be? Holo actors, of course, pretended to be other people all the time, so they could be convincing in stories . . . but Theresa wasn't a holo actor. And she certainly wasn't anything like Cazie. Her brain chemistry was different, was damaged somehow so that she was always afraid and anxious and what Jackson called "severely inhibited in the face of novelty" . . . Had pretending to be somebody else actually changed her brain chemistry for a few minutes? But how could that be?

She could ask Thomas to find out.

But right now, she had to decide where to go, if she didn't go home. Only she wanted to go home. She didn't know how long this weird borrowed brain chemistry would last, and she wanted her own things around her, her pink bedroom and her crocheted blanket and Thomas. But if Cazie was there . . .

If Cazie was there, Theresa would just become somebody who could tell Cazie this wasn't a good time to talk. Somebody who could say, "I'm sorry, but I'm tired and I need to sleep now." Even if Theresa could only pretend to be that person for a minute. A minute might be enough, surely she could be somebody else for another minute . . . Leisha Camden. Leisha had always been calm and firm. Theresa would be Leisha Camden, calmly arguing the case for Sleepless rights with other lawyers, and Cazie would . . .

Cazie would override Theresa and chew her into tiny bits.

Theresa couldn't be Leisha Camden in front of Cazie. It would be like propping yourself up with drinking straws in front of a hurricane. But maybe she could be Leisha Camden in front of herself. Pretend to have Leisha's brain for just a minute, while she thought where to go and what to do. Leisha, who met problems head-on, trying to use reason to solve them . . .

If Leisha wanted to find out what was known about the fake holo of Miranda, she would go to the place most likely to know. Wherever it happened to be. Even Selene. But Selene wasn't answering messages, and even if Theresa could nerve herself to space travel . . . but she couldn't. She knew that. But maybe she wouldn't have to go quite as far as Selene.

Theresa's grip tightened on the holo cartridge. Could she really do this, even if she was pretending to be Leisha? Fly to an airport, hire a plane all by herself . . . no, it was too hard. Her breathing got ragged just thinking about it.

Then she thought about going home—and trying to avoid telling Cazie where Jackson was.

Theresa put her hands over her face, then straightened. She wasn't Theresa Aranow, she was Leisha Camden. And thinking that would make her feel different, so her brain chemistry would shift just a little . . . She was Leisha Camden. *She was.*

"Manhattan East Airfield. Automatic coordinates," she said to the car, and her voice did sound subtly different to her own terrified ears.

As the car lifted, Theresa had another thought. *Take a neuropharm,* Jackson always said. And Theresa never would, because she had been afraid of losing her special gift of pain, and the place it was supposed to lead her. She had always been afraid of using neuropharms to become somebody else.

Despite herself, Theresa laughed. It came out as a whimper.

She wondered who she would actually find, being whom else, in New Mexico.

The hardest part, it turned out, was hiring the pilot.

Theresa walked into Manhattan East's airfield building on Lexington Avenue. It was a sleek old-fashioned building with wall programming entirely in shifting metals. People hurried past her toward various terminals or various doors. A group of men and women dressed in formal sarongs, laughing and joking. A man in a black holosuit, carrying a remote and a sheaf of printouts. A pleasant-faced elderly woman traveling alone. Theresa had just worked up enough nerve to speak to the woman when a round featureless robocam the size of a human head floated up to her.

"You've been standing still for two minutes, ma'am. May I help you with anything?"

"Oh, yes," Theresa blurted to the floater. "I need . . . I want to hire a private plane. With a pilot. To fly the plane to . . . to New Mexico."

"Our charter-plane booking service can be contacted from any customer terminal, ma'm. If there's anything else I can—"

"But I don't know how!"

"Excuse me, ma'am, while I run self-diagnostics." The robocam whirred softly. "My programming shows no error in sensory functioning. You are a genemod adult?"

"Yes. I'm . . . I'm an adult. But I still don't know how to use a customer terminal." She could feel color flame in her face.

"Would you like me to demonstrate the system?"

"Oh, yes. Please."

The robocam led her to a row of terminals. Theresa could at least recognize a credit-retina scan. She stood docilely against the screen until a pleasant low voice said, "Welcome to Manhattan East Airfield, Ms. Aranow. Desired flight number?"

The robocam said, "Charter plane service, please."

"Certainly," the system said.

Rows of writing appeared on the terminal. Theresa felt her color return; she was such a slow reader. But the robocam said, "Where do you wish to go, Ms. Aranow? And when do you wish to leave?"

"To New Mexico. Near Taos. And I want to leave right now. With . . . with a . . ." How did one ask for a pilot who wasn't too scary? Theresa took a despairing step backward.

"Third flight requirement not understood. Please repeat," the customer terminal said.

"Flying with somebody safe!"

"Three pilots with triple-A safety ratings are available within the next thirty minutes for domestic charter. Rush charges apply. Flying records displayed. Do you wish comlink with any of these three?"

The flying records were more small printing. But there were also pictures: three genemod-attractive faces. But not, somehow, donkey. No, of course not—these were techs. "That one. The woman. A comlink, yes."

The pilot came on-line immediately. She looked in her late thirties, a strong face without makeup, all the beauty in the firm austere planes. Her voice, too, was firm and austere. "Ms. Aranow? You wish a pilot for an immediate flight to New Mexico?"

"Yes. No. I . . . don't know."

The pilot's image leaned forward, studying the image of Theresa. "You don't know?"

"No. Yes, I mean, I do know. I'm not going, I don't need a pilot. It was a mistake." She stumbled away from the terminal. The calm, strong voice stopped her.

"Ms. Aranow, the floater beside you will lead you directly to my plane. We can take off immediately. If you are ill, I can sent a go-'bot for you."

"No, I . . . all right. I'm coming."

She fixed her eyes on the floater, willing herself to see that and nothing else. Just a round gray ball, it wasn't scary, just follow it without thinking . . . like Cazie would.

No, Cazie wouldn't. Cazie would be flying her own plane to New Mexico.

All right, forget Cazie, she couldn't be Cazie, but she needed to be somebody else because she, Theresa, couldn't do this by herself, she could feel herself slipping into panic, who could she be, she hardly *knew* anyone but Leisha and Cazie . . .

And Jackson. *Take a neuropharm,* Tessie. All right, she was Theresa on a neuropharm. She was somebody who was chemically calm, someone who believed the world made sense—

"Hello, Ms. Aranow. I'm Pilot First Class Jane Martha Olivetti."

Theresa was there already. The plane loomed beside them, even though Theresa didn't remember riding the air field maglev from Manhattan East, or crossing the tarmac. Only now did she realize that the field was unshielded, or only peripherally shielded; this was real weather. Cold April wind. She shivered as she climbed into Pilot Olivetti's plane.

"There are tranquilizer patches in the green box on that rack," the pilot said in her calm voice. "EndorKiss in the red, HalluFun in the yellow, Sleep-Ease in the brown."

Theresa looked longingly at the brown box. But most patches, Jackson said, were prepared for Changed bodies. He'd warned her not to use anything not adjusted for her unChanged chemistry.

"No, thank you. Just . . . just a blanket." She was shivering, even though the plane was heated.

Somewhere over hills still topped with snow, Theresa fell asleep naturally. She woke when the pilot said, "Ms. Aranow, this is Taos. Do you want to set down here or at some private airfield?"

"Do you know where the airfield is for . . . for La Solana? Where Leisha Camden once lived?"

Pilot Olivetti turned in her seat and stared at Theresa. "Of course. There used to be crowds of reporters and tourists going there all the time. And lately, people wanting to talk to Richard Sharifi about sending messages to his daughter. But it won't do you any good to go there—Richard Sharifi never comes out. The most you'll get is the standard recorded message."

Theresa closed her eyes. What had she been thinking? Of course she wasn't the first one to try to contact Miranda through La Solana. Probably everybody in the world had already tried—politicians and important people like that. And if Richard Sharifi didn't see them, there was no reason he would see Theresa Aranow. She was a fool.

What would Cazie do?

"We're here now," she said to the pilot. "Go to La Solana."

Pilot Olivetti shrugged and spoke to the plane.

Theresa saw the compound long before they reached it. A pale blue semi-ovoid on the desert floor, it shone as featureless and perfect as a robin's egg. Terry Mwakambe, Miranda Sharifi's most gifted practical physicist, had designed the shield for Leisha. There was nothing like it anywhere on Earth, except around the deserted island of Huevos Verdes, where Miranda and her people had created the Change syringes.

The shield wasn't Y-energy, but something else—Theresa didn't know what. It extended under the ground as well as through the air. Nothing with any DNA content not stored in the security banks got through the blue dome: not birds or worms or microbes. Nor did anything unaccompanied by DNA that *was* stored in the data banks: not 'bots or missiles or rocks. The shield also kept out all but a narrow range of radiation. And nothing that wasn't nuclear could destroy the shield itself.

Theresa walked from the plane to the half-buried robin's egg. Desert sun hit her uncovered head. A small wind stirred the incredible pile of rubble heaped against the shining blue. Stacks of holo cartridges. A child's doll. A tattered American flag. Plastic flowers, bloody handkerchiefs, the bleached skull of some animal, wrecking tools, each bent and twisted. And a sealed, tiny coffin. Theresa's gorge rose. Was it just symbolic, or did the coffin hold somebody's un-Changed baby, dead of a disease that could have been cured by more Change syringes?

A section of blue wall shimmered into a huge screen, ten feet square. It held the image of a man who appeared to be in his forties, although Theresa knew he was actually seventy-seven. The dark eyes above the heavy black beard looked weary.

"This is Richard Sharifi, Miranda Sharifi's father. There is no admittance to La Solana under any circumstances. If you wish to speak a message for Miranda Sharifi, tell the recorder when you want it to start. All messages for Miranda will be beamed to Selene daily. No physical object you leave outside these walls will ever be retrieved or examined. Thank you." The image disappeared.

That was it. Theresa clasped her hands in front of her. "Recorder start."

"Recorder on."

"My name is Theresa Aranow. You don't know me. I'm . . . I'm not anybody. But there are babies dying from not being Changed—"

She stopped. Richard and Miranda Sharifi already knew that. What could she say that might interest them, convince them . . . of what? That people needed help? Who was she to think she could help anyone? Some days she could barely get out of bed in the morning.

But not this day. She tried again.

"I'm not anybody. I'm not even Changed. I wanted . . . I needed to keep what I am because I'm not normal for a donkey, and if I lose that then I lose Theresa. I lose . . . the way I'm supposed to be, to find what . . . I'm looking for."

Something was happening inside her. The rush of competence she'd felt when she was being Cazie returned, only not because she was being someone else. Because she was being the most real, bedrock Theresa. The words rushed out the same way they had when she'd talked to Sister Anne at the convent for the Sisters of Merciful Heaven.

"I could be Changed, and maybe it wouldn't matter. I'm expensive like I am, I know. I have to eat real food. I have to have a house kept free of germs. I have to have clean water. All those things cost money, and if I didn't have so much money, and if my brother wasn't a doctor, then it would be wrong for me not to be Changed because I would be such a burden on everybody else. But I *do* have money, and I *do* have Jackson, and so it would be wrong for me to arrange things so I don't hurt. I have to hurt. Everybody needs to hurt in some way, or they get . . . sloppy. No, that's not the word. Miranda—"

She was talking directly to Miranda, who wasn't even on Earth, but that didn't matter. Theresa rushed on.

"Miranda, I don't know the word for how people get when they can't feel hurt and alone. But something happens to them. When they take those kinds of neuropharms all the time they get so they can't feel *themselves*, and then pretty soon they can't feel other people either. They get like Cazie's friends, and maybe even Cazie herself . . . I don't know. Cazie is good underneath. But she did so many inhalers to cover up her hurt that pretty soon she couldn't see Jackson's hurt, and then pretty soon after that she couldn't see Jackson at all. He's just another piece of furniture in her life, or another 'bot.

"People *have* to hurt. They *have* to let themselves feel the hurt. They *have* to make themselves stand it, and not take it away with EndorKiss or neuropharms or sex or making money . . . it's the only way we know we should do something different. That we should keep on looking harder, inside us and also inside everybody else . . . You can't just go *around* the pain, you have to go *through* it to get to the place on the other side where your soul is . . . oh, I don't know! I'm not smart enough to know! Something went wrong in my embryonic genemod, I'm not smart like Jackson or Cazie . . . but I do know that you have to give us more Change syringes, so babies can live long enough to even feel their own hurt and start to learn from it. Maybe you shouldn't have given us the Change syringes at all. But you did, and now the Livers can't survive without them because we donkeys just dumped them all, and we control the resources. So you have to give us more Change syringes so those children even live long enough to look for what matters.

"But there's something else wrong, too. There's a camp in New York—the state, not the city—that has a new kind of Change syringe. Red ones. And it's doing something to those Livers. They're bonding by pheromones or something in threes, so that if they go far from each other, they die. Really die. And the syringes came with a holo cartridge that has you in it, explaining the syringes are another gift from Miranda Sharifi. The Livers believe that. Only it's wrong.The holo is a fake, and the new syringes just make it even harder for people to feel their own individual hurt and see each other. The triads are all blurred together in a blob, they're not real people anymore, they have the comfort of never feeling alone but unless they can feel alone how can they ever feel their own hurt and then start to go through it to—"

"What new syringes?" Richard Sharifi said.

Theresa blinked. The image on the shimmering blue wall was real-time. Richard Sharifi's sad dark eyes stared at her steadily, waiting for an answer.

"The . . . the new syringes somebody left at the . . . the camp in the mountains in New York, at . . . at . . ." She couldn't remember the coordinates. "Red syringes, and there was a holo of Miranda that wasn't really Miranda . . ."

Richard Sharifi turned his head. He frowned and said, "No—" His huge image abruptly shrank, until Theresa was looking at a screen no more than three inches square. On it Richard Sharifi was replaced by a plain woman with wild dark hair held by a red ribbon.

"Theresa. This is Miranda Sharifi."

Theresa gasped, "Are you . . . are you sending from Selene?"

"Please tell me everything you can about this new syringe and holo cartridge left with the Liver tribe. Start at the beginning, go slow, and don't leave anything out. It's very important."

A second three-inch-square image appeared—Richard Sharifi again, scowling fiercely. He said, "You should know that we have scanned you, your plane, and the area for any recording equipment. Your pilot is not observing you, and even if she were, this screen at that distance is too small for even the most powerful Sleeper zoom lenses to see. If you state to anyone that this conversation ever occurred, your chances of being believed are very low. Your medical records indicate—"

"Unnecessary, Daddy," Miranda said, and now she was scowling, too. The tiny image of Richard Sharifi disappeared.

Theresa blurted, "You're not at Selene at all, are you? You're here . . ."

"Tell me everything about the new syringes, Theresa. Starting with how you happened to be in a Liver camp. No, don't panic—I can't send help out to you. Breathe deeply, look at this screen, Theresa, *look at it*—"

She did, gasping for air, through waves of panicky blackness. Around Miranda shimmered subtle shapes and colors, what were they, she felt a little calmer . . . Subliminals. Theresa breathed.

"Those . . . those are like a Drew Arlen concert!"

An expression of pain, complicated and deep, passed over Miranda's face. "Tell me about the new syringes."

Theresa did, growing calmer as she talked. Miranda listened without ever blinking her dark eyes. Dark like her father's, too dark to be Cazie's . . . But Theresa wasn't pretending to be Cazie. She wasn't even pretending to be Leisha Camden. She was Theresa Aranow.

"Miranda . . . turn off the subliminals. Please. I can . . . can do this. I think."

For the first, and last, time, Theresa saw Miranda Sharifi smile.

When she was done talking, Theresa said, "But if you didn't make the new syringes, who did? Jackson said we donkeys don't have any biotech like that, that sophisticated—"

"Here's what I want you to do, Theresa. Listen carefully. I want you to go home, and tell nobody about your visit here, or the new syringes. Not even Jackson. Also—this is very important—don't speak anything about this into any terminal. Not even if you think it's completely freestanding."

Theresa put out her hand, but stopped short of the tiny image on the blue wall. Her fingers hung suspended. Hot wind stirred the rubble of weathered offerings at her feet.

"Miranda—why did you stop the Change syringes?"

"We made a mistake. We didn't intend—our goal was to make the Livers free of donkey domination. Autotropic. We didn't know they . . . you . . . would so quickly regress to infantile dependence. And now none of us know what the next step should be, because we can't find the equations to predict outcomes with any degree of accuracy. We're all here trying so hard . . ." The holo image shuddered. Miranda raised her hands, let them fall helplessly. "An enormous mistake. When I see the newsgrids of babies dying, of unChanged children suffering, when those pleas are rebeamed from Selene . . . We thought we could control it all for you! Like your 'gods.' We thought . . . we forgot . . ."

Theresa finished the sentence. "You forgot to look hard enough inside yourselves."

"Yes," Miranda whispered. "We did. And we caused chaos."

"But you only meant to—"

"And now we're trying desperately to find a way out of that chaos, a scientific solution you can synthesize yourselves, without us, the right substance . . . a solution you can control, and won't pervert. But, Theresa, we don't think like you, or react like you, or feel like you."

It was a plea. Theresa saw that Miranda—*Miranda Sharifi!*—hurt with a depth of pain Theresa could only imagine. She caught her breath. The two women stared at each other, and something passed between them that, it seemed to Theresa, she had never shared with anyone else in her life, not even Jackson.

She said softly, "Yes, you do. You feel exactly like me."

Miranda didn't smile. "Perhaps. Go now, Theresa. We'll take care of the new syringes that destroy even more freedom than we already destroyed."

The blue shimmering wall went blank.

Dazed, Theresa returned to the plane. The pilot waited, watching a newsgrid. She blanked the screen as Theresa climbed in. La Solana was already out of sight when Theresa finally spoke.

"Do you know how long it takes for a message to get to the moon and back? By the fastest way?"

The pilot glanced at her quizzically. "You mean, if you decided to transmit to Luna City and they answered immediately?"

"Yes. Isn't there a . . . a lag when people are speaking to each other? Of a few seconds, at least?"

"Yes."

"Thank you." Of course, that was human technology. Jackson said the Supers had all sorts of technology that humans didn't. *We don't think like you, or react like you . . .*

"Oh, my God!" Pilot Olivetti said.

"What? What is it?"

The plane suddenly leaped forward with an acceleration that

186 | NANCY KRESS

crushed Theresa against the back of her seat. Then the sky filled with blinding light. The pilot cried out.

The light faded; moments later the plane shuddered as if it would come apart. Roaring assaulted Theresa's ears. The plane righted, and flew on.

The brilliant light was behind her. But the sun was ahead, to the southeast . . . how could that bright a light be where the sun wasn't? Theresa turned to look out the rear window, and saw the top of the mushroom cloud rising above the horizon.

"We took two hundred forty rads," Pilot Olivetti gasped, looking at her screens. "Ms. Aranow . . . prepare to be very sick."

"But . . . but what happened?"

"Someone took out La Solana. With a nuclear weapon. Minutes earlier, and we would be dead."

"But . . . *why?*"

"How should I know? But God, if Selene retaliates . . ." She turned on the newsgrid.

Theresa put her head in her hands. Selene couldn't retaliate. Nobody was at Selene. Miranda Sharifi and all her SuperSleepless had been in La Solana—*we're all here trying so hard to find a solution*—and now they were all dead. They would never give more Change syringes to save dying children, or find a solution to humans' being so dependent on the syringes, or stop whoever was making Jomp and the other triads even more dependent and afraid. Somebody had bombed La Solana to kill Richard Sharifi, or to destroy Miranda's old home, or to attract attention to some cause of their own. The SuperSleepless were all dead.

And Theresa was the only person on Earth who knew it.

INTERLUDE

TRANSMISSION DATE: April 4, 2121
TO: Selene Base, Moon
VIA: Lubbock Enclave Ground Station, Satellite S-65 (Israel)
MESSAGE TYPE: Unencrypted
MESSAGE CLASS: Class D, Public Service Access, in accordance with Congressional Bill
      4892–18, May 2118
ORIGINATING GROUP: "the Carter tribe," Texas
MESSAGE:

To Miranda Sharifi,

    The Carter family ranched West Texas for 250 years, us. We stick together. Now there's no more ranching, it, but we still stick together. I'm Molly Carter, me. I got six kids, seventeen grandkids, twenty great-grandkids, more on the way. But we got no more Change needles for the new great-grandkids. I'm asking you, me, to please send us more.

    My son Ray Junior is taking this cartridge, him, to a radio place in Lubbock to send to you in space.

ACKNOWLEDGMENT: None received

Fifteen

Nothing, Jackson thought, was ever what you expected.

When he'd taken Shockey, Lizzie, Dirk, and Vicki to Kelvin-Castner Pharmaceuticals, he expected a difficult ordeal. He expected panic after panic from the Livers over being in an environment that would have been strange and unsettling to them even *before* they'd breathed in whatever neuropharm had made them so anxious and fearful of anything new. He visualized physical struggles with Shockey to provide tissue samples, and hysterical protest from Lizzie when samples were taken from Dirk. He counted on Vicki to help with these hypothetical struggles. Then, he expected, he and Thurmond Rogers would have a long intense talk about the implications of a drug that was not subject to the Cell Cleaner. The tissue analysis would be a top priority for Rogers, so the report would come swiftly.

None of that had happened.

Instead, his aircar had been met on the roof of Kelvin-Castner, inside the Boston Harborside Enclave, by two high-quality security 'bots. The 'bots had efficiently grabbed everyone but Jackson and fitted them with breathers that had instantly knocked them out. Even Vicki. The 'bots had then loaded the four unconscious people onto floaters and, ignoring Jackson's protests, guided them down an elevator to a lab. Here more 'bots had stripped Shockey, Lizzie, and the baby and had taken samples: saliva, cerebrospinal fluid, blood, urine, feces, and cells from every organ. The samples were extracted with the long nanobuilt needles, their walls only a few atoms thick, of state-of-the-art biopsy. Next had come the scans, everything from skin conductance to brain imaging under various stimuli. No actual person appeared. It was clear to Jackson that this procedure had already been in place.

How long had Kelvin-Castner been abducting research samples from Livers who couldn't, or wouldn't, protest?

Jackson protested. "Thurmond, I want to talk to you!" But all Jackson had gotten was a bland, prerecorded holo: "Hi, Jack. Sorry I can't attend to you personally, but I'm in the middle of something I can't leave. If you want anything to eat or drink while the samples are being taken, just ask the room system. I'll call you when I have anything to report. My regards to your sister."

"Thurmond, damn it . . . room system on!"

"Room system on," the room said. Needles so thin they were barely visible descended simultaneously into the naked bellies of Shockey, Lizzie, and Dirk. Vicki, still clothed, lay on her floater in the corner, breathing whatever her mask supplied her with.

"Give me a priority link to Thurmond Rogers!"

"I'm sorry—this system can provide only recording capability and dietary orders."

"Then link me to the building system!"

"I'm sorry—this system can provide only recording capability and dietary orders."

"This is a medical emergency. Give me the emergency system."

"I'm sorry—this system—"

"System off!"

He could record a blistering message for Rogers. He could remove Vicki's breathing mask and see if she could dip the system. But it was Lizzie who was the dipper, not Vicki, and Lizzie at the moment had a thin flexible probe down her throat, taking cell samples from her bronchial tree. So Jackson did nothing, fuming and pacing for an hour, refusing even to sit in the room's one comfortable chair, out of either anger or ludicrous self-flagellation.

When Kelvin-Castner had taken all the human pieces it wanted, the security 'bots took Shockey, Lizzie, Vicki, and the baby back to the roof, efficiently loaded them into Jackson's car, stripped off their breathing masks, and floated away. A minute later their lungs cleared and they woke up.

"Well," Lizzie said, "what are we waiting for? Aren't we going inside?" And Dirk had cowered against his mother's neck, wailing in fear because the world held more than his mother.

Jackson flew back to the camp, and the three Livers disappeared inside. Vicki said, "I'm not happy about this, Jackson. You should have revived me. I had questions of my own, you know."

"You wouldn't have got any answers."

"Nonetheless." She scowled at him. "Promise me you won't go back to Kelvin-Castner, or even talk to Rogers, without including me. Lizzie's system can multilink us."

"I don't think—"

"I do. Promise me."

And Jackson—out of weariness or resignation or consideration or something—had promised.

Since then, nothing had happened. Four days passed, and Thurmond Rogers neither contacted Jackson nor returned his calls. Theresa spent all her time in the upper-floor study that Jackson wasn't supposed to know about, not appearing even for meals. She left periodic messages for Jackson that she was all right. Jackson paced and fidgeted and forgot to eat, until his body rebelled and he fell asleep naked in the feeding room while his body absorbed the nutrients it needed.

The fourth day, very early in the morning, Cazie called. Jackson didn't answer. He rolled over in his darkened bedroom so that his back faced the wall screen, and let the message record.

"Jackson, come on-link. I know you're there."

All of a sudden Jackson was annoyed. Why did she always assume she knew everything about him?

"Listen," Cazie said, "we need to talk. I just received a private message from an old friend of mine, Alexander Castner of Kelvin-Castner Pharmaceuticals. I think I introduced you once, at some party—do you remember him?"

Slowly Jackson turned over in bed to stare at the screen. In the lower right corner, under Cazie's face, glittered the encryption signal. She was sending to him on a heavily shielded link.

"Alex is contacting several major investment players, very privately. Kelvin-Castner is onto something really big. Something they want to develop very quickly . . . Alex thinks his firm can get an entirely new pharmaceutical system to the patent stage before anybody else. Get this—*it bypasses the Cell Cleaner to effect permanent pharmacodynamic processes.* The applications in the pleasure market alone are staggering. You could eliminate inhalers!

"But Alex doesn't know who else is working on this, or how close they are to applying for a patent, so he has to move as fast as possible. He needs massive commitments of capital, talent, computer time. Jack, TenTech should get in on this, early and hard. It's the kind of opportunity that could move us into the International Fifty. I've pulled together some preliminary figures for you—and for Theresa, too, of course. But we need to commit soon, today if possible—damn it, Jackson, answer the link!"

Jackson climbed slowly out of bed. In the dark he pulled on yesterday's clothes.

"All right," Cazie said, "maybe you're not there. But where are you? I already called that ridiculous woman at your pet Liver camp, Vicki What's-her-name, and she said you weren't there. If you're spending the night with somebody, when you call in for your messages, please contact me on a shielded line at my office at TenTech. If you don't—"

"You'll run me to earth anyway," Jackson finished for her.

"—I'll run you to earth anyway, darling. This is too big to let go."

Jackson left the apartment. In the east, the sun was just beginning to stain the sky pink. The real, actual sun—at the moment the Manhattan East dome was clear. He strode through the roof garden, with its theatrically unfurling morning glories and trumpet lilies, toward his car. He couldn't remember ever being this angry in his life.

Vicki waited for him outside the tribe building, a solitary figure in the pearly April cold.

"The charming Cazie called here first," she said as she got into his car. "I figured something was happening, and I knew you'd remember your promise to take me with you to Kelvin-Castner."

"How did you know that?" Jackson said grimly.

"Because I knew that somewhere deep down you were capable of looking like you do now. Want to tell me what's going on?"

"Kelvin-Castner is trying to create a patentable drug-delivery system out of what they've learned from Shockey's and Dirk's brain scans and tissue samples. They're less interested in finding an antidote for the inhibition anxiety than in the commercial possibilities for the pleasure market of something that bypasses the Cell Cleaner. They've asked TenTech for massive investment."

"Jesus H. Christ," Vicki said, almost admiringly. "Your ex-wife sure picks up the scent fast, doesn't she? Is she part bloodhound?"

"Do you think we should take Lizzie with us?" Jackson asked. "If they deny us entrance, I can't datadip, and neither can you."

"And neither can Lizzie in the half second before the security 'bots hit her. Be realistic, Jackson. She's not a SuperSleepless."

Jackson lifted the car. Vicki said, "Don't you even want to know what I told Cazie when she called here?"

"No."

"I told her that as far as I knew, you were off fucking Jennifer Sharifi now that she's out of jail and since she just happens to have the same coloring as Cazie herself."

Despite himself, Jackson smiled.

* * *

Nothing prevented the car from landing on the roof of Kelvin-Castner. To Jackson's surprise, nothing even prevented him and Vicki from descending the elevator to Kelvin-Castner's top-floor lobby. The lobby was endless baroque variations of a double-helix motif, a precise centimeter over the line into vulgar. Jackson remembered Ellie Lester.

A hostess holo flickered into place a yard in front of him. She was a middle-aged blonde with coffee-colored skin, attractive but serious enough to be reassuring. "Welcome to Kelvin-Castner. How can I help you?"

Jackson said, "Jackson Aranow to see Thurmond Rogers."

"I'm afraid Dr. Rogers is off-site today. Would you like to record a message?"

"Then let me talk to Alexander Castner."

"Do you have an appointment?"

"No."

"I'm afraid Mr. Castner's schedule doesn't permit him time for unscheduled appointments. Would you like to record a message?"

Jackson said to Vicki, "We should have brought Lizzie after all."

"Wouldn't have helped. The second she accessed anything the security system would gas us all. I mean, it's a neuropharm company, isn't it?"

Of course it was. Jackson wasn't thinking clearly. Anger did that. He'd have to be more careful.

Vicki said pleasantly to the hostess holo, "I would like to record a message for Mr. Castner. Or perhaps he'd prefer to have this one real-time. Please tell Mr. Castner that this is Dr. Jackson Aranow of TenTech, Cazie Sanders's firm. That's 'Aranow,' 'TenTech,' 'Sanders'— I'm sure one of those names is in your priority flagging programs as of yesterday. Tell Mr. Castner that Dr. Aranow has retained legal counsel to sue for the tissue samples, plus all resulting patents, taken from citizens Shockey Toor and Dirk Francy while they were unadvised by attorneys. Counsel has already received sworn depositions of all events, plus full knowledge of our current visit. A cease-work injunction from a federal judge against K-C is possible, as is considerable industry attention, which Mr. Castner might find premature. Also tell Mr. Castner that Dr. Aranow and his sister control the voting stock of TenTech, and that no investment commitment can possibly be forthcoming without both their cooperation. Have I engaged your priority flagging programs?"

The holo beamed at Vicki. "Yes, my priority flagging is engaged and transmitting. Would you like some coffee?"

"No, thank you. We'll just wait here for Mr. Castner's reply. Or possibly Dr. Rogers's."

"Dr. Rogers is off-site today," the hostess said. She was still beaming.

"Of course he is," Vicki said. She sank onto a sofa covered in a double-helix paisley print and patted the seat beside her. "Sit down, Jackson. We have to allow a little time for them to hold a council of war to determine who fucked up by contacting Cazie when Rogers was ripping you off."

Jackson said, "We're probably being overheard."

"I certainly hope so."

He sat down and said in a low voice, "Where did you learn to do that?"

Vicki's face grew suddenly weary. "You don't want to know."

"Yes, I do."

"Another time. Ah, such a prompt response. Five points for efficiency."

A wall screen glowed and the image of Thurmond Rogers appeared, smiling stiffly. "Jackson. How are you? I just got in and the building system informed me you were here, and there was some sort of mix-up about not talking to you. Sorry."

Vicki murmured, "Oh, those computer glitches."

"I was going to call you this morning," Rogers continued. A lump of flesh at the collar of his lab coat worked up and down. "We have a preliminary report on the changes in your subjects' brains."

Jackson said, "Then come out and give it to me. In person. I'm not going to assault you, Thurmond."

The image laughed uncomfortably. "Of course not. But I strained my back getting out of my car, and until the Cell Cleaner takes care of it, I'd just as soon not move."

Jackson said evenly, "Then we'll come to you."

"Let me start by telling you what tests we ran on your subjects, and the results. We found . . . is that necessary?"

Vicki had taken a recorder out of the pocket of her jacks and aimed it at Rogers's image. She said, "Absolutely. Let the record read that Dr. Rogers has sealed himself in to the K-C biohazard labs because he's found out something truly alarming about this new neuropharm, and he's taking not the teeniest risk that it might somehow reach his own highly expensive and educated brain. Am I right, Dr. Rogers?"

Rogers looked at her with loathing. "As I started to say, we've run exhaustive analyses on the subjects' medical scans and tissue samples. What we found, Jackson, is only preliminary, but extraordinary. The subjects breathed in a genemod airborne molecule, probably an engineered virus. The molecule itself is unavailable for analysis, having broken down sometime after it reached the brain. We've been able to trace its path, and make very rough guesses at a partial composition from its pharmacodynamic effects."

Rogers took a deep breath. It seemed to calm him, although the lump of flesh still worked up and down at his collar. Jackson wondered what he'd mixed into the air of his office. "The molecule, whatever it was, apparently was designed to affect multiple neural sites as both agonist and antagonist, targeted—"

Vicki interrupted, "And in English comprehensible to lawyers, those terms would mean . . ."

"Jackson, is this *necessary*?"

"Apparently so," Jackson said.

Rogers stared stonily at Vicki. "An 'agonist' activates specific neural receptors, causing them to change biochemistry. An 'antagonist' blocks other receptor subtypes."

"Thank you," Vicki said sweetly. Jackson had the sudden impression she'd already known that, and was making Rogers jump through hoops.

Rogers continued, "The molecule seems to have had high-binding affinity for receptor or receptors in the amygdaloid complex. JEM scans show high recent blood-supply activity there, in areas of the limbic, and in the right temporal area of the cerebral cortex. Apparently the molecule caused a very complex cascade effect, in which the release of certain biogenic amines caused the release of other chemicals, and so on. We've already identified changes in the folding of twelve different peptides, and that's probably only the beginning. There are also changes in the timing of synchronous neural firings."

Jackson said, "Does the sum of your changes point to permanent changes in the NMDA receptors?"

"I'm afraid it does. The changes seem to include alteration of amine creation, including the presence of amines that only appear under pathological conditions. Plus changes in receptor composition, neurotransmitter processes in synapses, and even internal cellular response. Although those particular findings are especially preliminary. There's also significant cell death of the kind mapped for trauma or prolonged stress. The neural architecture itself has been rewired."

Jackson was on his feet and pacing before he knew it. "What data matches do you get for the neural maps?"

"I'm coming to that. The subjects both showed high and invariant heart rate, even while asleep. High skin conductance. Marked stress at the cellular level. Cerebrospinal fluid, urine, saliva, blood—everything shows consistent neurotransmitter breakdown products. The map is of a low threshold of limbic-hypothalamic arousal, high chronic stress, strong inhibition rooted in permanent changes in the primary efferent pathway from the amygdalae."

Vicki said again, "English, please."

It was Jackson who answered her. "The neuropharm—whatever it is—has given Shockey and Dirk the biochemistry of someone born severely inhibited. Afraid of anything new, fearful of separation from familiar people, unwilling to alter known routines because doing that produces painful anxiety."

Vicki said, "Sharon's baby . . . little Callie . . ."

"Yes. It's normal for babies to have stranger anxiety and novelty inhibition at around six to nine months. But then maturation mutes the stranger anxiety, as complex brain functions suppress more primitive ones. But this . . . this is a regression to the inhibition of the most severely inhibited toddler. *Permanently.* And without altering DNA or relying on the ongoing presence of foreign chemicals, both of which the Cell Cleaner would destroy. A natural, pronounced fear of anything new or different."

Like Theresa, Jackson thought but didn't say aloud. A camp full of Theresas. A nation full of Theresas? Were more tribes infected?

"But *why*?" Vicki said.

Rogers looked at her with distaste. "The role of the nervous system is to generate behavior. Obviously someone is experimenting with this kind of behavior."

"That's not an answer."

"I don't have an answer," Rogers said. "What do you expect in four days? Each neuron in the brain can receive up to a hundred thousand contacts from the other neurons they're wired to in pyramid. Plus, there are receptor sites on other organs beside the brain; there are immense individual variations in neural architecture and drug response; there are—"

"All right, all right," Vicki said. "The real question is, what can you do? Can you create a neuropharm to reverse the effects?"

"Jackson," Rogers said, "tell your friend that it's a hell of a lot easier to damage living organisms than to reverse damage. Tell her—"

"—that you had no trouble seeing a fast way to exploit the so-called damage," Vicki struck in. "Study how the neural architecture can be permanently altered to bypass the Cell Cleaner, then adapt it to profitable pleasure drugs. Isn't that what you told Cazie Sanders, hhmmmm? So you must see at least a possibility of finding loopholes in this supposedly unalterable biochemistry."

Jackson said, "She's right, Thurmond, and you know it. Kelvin-Castner should be looking for ways to counteract this."

"We will, of course," Rogers said. "But the enclaves have defenses against missile delivery of biologicals. And individual buildings can be made self-circulating. So can air masks. We might not want to move too precipitously on a counteractive. For the overall civic good."

It took Jackson's breath away. Rogers was saying that donkeys would probably not be affected by the inhibiting neuropharm, if they were careful. Only Livers. And Livers who were inhibited, afraid of novelty, terrified of separation from the familiar—such Livers would be a much reduced threat. They wouldn't attack enclaves looking for Change syringes. They wouldn't attack enclaves at all. They would just live their inhibited, frightened lives in quiet desperation, out of sight and mind of donkeys, until the next generation's unChanged susceptibility to disease killed most of them off.

Vicki said softly, "You son of a bitch."

Rogers grimaced; Jackson guessed he'd let his anger carry him away, and now regretted it. "I don't, of course," Rogers said, "speak in any official capacity for Kelvin-Castner. I don't possess that authority."

Vicki said, in that same soft deadly tone, "And I'm sure as well that Kelvin-Castner—"

"Wait," Jackson said. "*Wait.*"

They both looked at him: one real person, one holo image. He tried to think. "The real question here is *who.* Who created this neuropharm? For what reason?"

"That should be obvious," Rogers said. "It's extremely subtle and advanced biochemistry. The most likely candidate is the SuperSleepless. Miranda Sharifi already remade human bodies; now she's after human minds."

"For what reason?"

Rogers said angrily, "How can we know? They're not human."

Jackson ignored that. "Wait. You said the biochemistry is very advanced. So advanced that it *had* to be the Supers? Or just advanced beyond what the known scientific establishment can achieve now, without absolutely being beyond normal human capacity?"

The holo image was silent.

"Answer carefully, Thurmond. This is vitally important."

Rogers said reluctantly, "It's not absolutely beyond normal humans with what we already know about the brain. But it would take a com-

bination of genius, luck, and massive resources. The easier explanation is Miranda Sharifi. Occam's razor."

"—isn't the only way to shave," Vicki said. "All right, you've laid
out the basics. Now give us printouts of your actual data."

Rogers said, "That's proprietary to Kelvin-Castner."

"If we—"

Jackson interrupted her. "No. That's all right, Thurmond. We don't
need your data. It's replicable from anyone in Lizzie's tribe. Or maybe
by now other tribes as well."

Tribes of Theresas. Afraid of the unfamiliar, reluctant to deal with
strangers, unwilling to do things differently from however they were
doing them when they breathed in the neuropharm. Unwilling to
change. Who would want this neuropharm to exist? Any powerful
donkey group, governmental or private, with a vested interest in protecting the status quo. Which could mean almost any powerful donkey
group that existed. Lizzie's tribe had been the first because of her
demented, public attempt to win an election. They wouldn't be the
last.

Thurmond Rogers's image watched Jackson keenly. "You're right,
of course, Jack. Anyone can replicate our data. Which is why we need
to move so fast on getting a molecule to patentability. Cazie is seeing
Alex Castner at 8:30, along with a few other potential major players. I
can provide you with a suite to clean up a little and the loan of a
business suit in your—"

"Yes, thanks," Jackson said. Beside him, Vicki went still. Jackson
took her hand. "Something for my . . . friend, too. Although she'll
wait in the suite."

"Of course," Rogers said. He looked much happier. He had Vicki
figured out. Jackson could almost hear Rogers's thoughts: *Not my taste
but actually rather pretty underneath and Jackson always did like acerbic
women he married Cazie Sanders didn't he*— Vicki mercifully said
nothing until the hostess holo had shown them to a discreet conference room with a discreet bedroom and bath beyond a discreet door.

"Not in the bioshielded part of the building that Rogers was in," she
commented, randomly opening closets. Inside hung both business
clothes and bathrobes. "What do you want to bet Rogers only attends
the meeting in holo?"

"Could be."

"Although this is a nice enough suite at that." She pressed against
Jackson and breathed directly into his ear, so low that no listening
device could have caught it. "What are you going to do?"

It didn't matter that he couldn't see the monitors; they were there.

He put his arms around her and whispered back, "Let Cazie commit investment funds."

"Why?"

"Only way to find out what they do."

She nodded against his shoulder. It was disturbing holding her in his arms. She didn't feel like Cazie. She was taller, less rounded. Her skin felt cooler. She smelled different. Jackson had an erection.

He released Vicki and turned away, pretending to be busy examining clothing in a closet. When he turned back, he expected to see her smiling sardonically, poised to make some cutting comment. But she wasn't. She stood quietly, somehow forlornly, in the middle of the room, and her face had softened into an expression that on anyone else he would have called wistful.

"Vicki . . . ?"

"Yes, Jackson?" She raised her eyes to his and he saw with a shock that they were wide with naked need.

"Vicki . . . I . . ."

His mobile spoke. "Moonquake from Theresa Aranow. Repeat, moonquake from Theresa Aranow."

"Moonquake" was the family code, left over from childhood, for a high-emergency call. Theresa had never used it before. Jackson opened the mobile. Her image was there, in some kind of small open cabin . . . it looked like a plane. But that was impossible. Theresa couldn't ride a plane.

"J-Jackson!" she gasped. "They're dead!"

"Who? Who's dead, Theresa?"

"Everyone in La Solana! Richard Sharifi!" Suddenly Theresa pulled herself together. "Richard Sharifi. He was in the compound, or at least his recorded image was still there . . . La Solana—"

Behind him, Vicki snapped, "Terminal on! Newsgrid! Channel 35!" A wall screen brightened.

"—nuclear detonation at La Solana, the heavily shielded New Mexico compound that is home to Miranda Sharifi's father, Richard Keller Sharifi. No group has claimed credit for the bomb, which of course violates national and international nuclear bans. The White House has issued a statement of outrage, followed by the Pentagon's immediate dispatching of defense 'bots programmed for minute analysis of the radioactive rubble for any clue as to the bomb's composition, origin, or means of delivery. The energy shield around La Solana was developed by—"

Theresa said, "I'm flying home, Jackson."

"Tess, hold on, you sound funny, you don't sound like yourself—"

"I'm not," Theresa said. Her eyes opened very wide and for a moment she *smiled*. It was the most unsettling thing Jackson had seen in an unsettling day.

Theresa added, in a voice not at all her own, "The pilot says we took two hundred forty rads," and then the screen blanked.

"Jesus Christ," Vicki said softly. "Will she . . . is that enough to kill her?"

"Probably not, but she's going to be very sick. I've got to go."

"What about Cazie?"

"To hell with her," Jackson said, and saw Vicki smile, and knew—just as Vicki did—that he didn't mean it. Not yet. But maybe someday he would. And meanwhile, Cazie couldn't actually commit major investment capital without his consent or Theresa's. Which was, at least, better than nothing.

Although nothing like enough.

Sixteen

When Lizzie awoke, Vicki was still gone.

It was easy to know who was in camp and who wasn't. Everyone gathered at the same time for breakfast under the feeding tarp, and everybody lay or sat in the same place. Some people—Norma Kroll, Grandma Seifert, Sam Webster—even lay in the same position. Day after day. The tribe talked softly as they fed, and then they left the feeding ground in the same order, and set about the same tasks. Bringing fresh soil, with unused nutrients in it. Cleaning out the building. Tending the children, who played the same games with the same toys in the same places. Making things of wood or cloth, or getting the wood or cloth in the forest or from the weaving 'bot. Day after day.

Lunch at the same time, in the same places.

Naps for the children, crafts or holo-watching or water-fetching or cards or exercise. Dinner, in the same places under the tarp. The same stories at night, when the unseasonably cold April kept everyone inside. Would they still stay inside in June, in August, just because it had been the routine in April?

"I can't stand it," Lizzie had said to her mother. Annie replied, "You always was too impatient, you. Enjoy this time, Lizzie. It's safe and peaceful. Don't you want peace, you, for your baby?"

"Not like this!" Lizzie shouted, but Annie just shook her head and went back to the wall hanging she was making of woven cloth, pebbles, and dried flowers. When it was done, Lizzie thought in despair, she'd make another one. At ten o'clock she and Billy would go to bed, because ten o'clock was their bed time. They probably made love the same nights each week. Certainly Shockey and Sharon, in the cubicle next to Lizzie's, did. Tuesday and Saturday nights, Sunday afternoon.

At least when Vicki had been in camp, there'd been someone else to talk to. Vicki was tense, agitated, frustrated, unpredictable. Vicki was real. She paced through the wood paths, mud clinging to her boots, talking out her fear and her hope. Sometimes it seemed to Lizzie that Vicki couldn't tell one from the other.

"We have to wait on Jackson," Vicki had said, smacking one fist into her opposite palm. "Much as I hate doing it, he and his spectacularly obnoxious researcher friend, Thurmond Rogers, are the only way we're going to get to the medical roots of this, Lizzie. It's a medical problem, and it can be fought best with a medical model. Somehow the brain chemistry's been shifted, and we—"

"Wait," Lizzie said. *"Wait."*

Vicki looked at her.

"It's not just a medical problem, it." She heard her own shift into Liver language and hated it. Wouldn't she ever learn? "It's political, too. Some*body*'s doing this, them! It just didn't happen all by itself!"

"Yes, of course, you're right. But we can't deal directly with the cause—we tried that with the election, remember? The best we can hope for is to manipulate the results. Come on, Jackson . . . *call!*"

And apparently Jackson eventually had, because now Vicki was gone. To Jackson's wonderful house in Manhattan East? To Kelvin-Castner in Boston? Lizzie didn't know.

But the worst was Dirk.

"Look, Dirk, a chipmunk!"

That afternoon she'd carried him a little way into the raw spring woods, dressed in his warm winter jacks, his fringe of dark bangs falling across his forehead under the bright red hood. The whole tiny walk, Dirk buried his head in Lizzie's shoulder and refused to look up. Gently she forced him to raise his eyes.

"Look at the chipmunk! Scamper scamper!"

The small creature stopped twenty feet away, looked at them inquisitively, and sat on its hind legs, fluffy tail curled upward behind it. It lifted a nut and began to nibble, its head bobbing comically over its small upraised paws. Dirk looked and began to scream in terror.

"Stop it! Stop it, damn it!" Lizzie screamed in turn, and was immediately appalled and frightened. What was she doing? Dirk couldn't help it! She cradled him tight and ran back to the building. Annie looked up from her wall hanging.

"Lizzie! Where'd you take that child, him?"

"For a fucking walk!" She was angry all over again, now that Dirk, in his familiar surroundings, stopped crying. On the floor he saw the blocks Billy had made for him, the blocks he always played with at this time of the afternoon, and kicked for Lizzie to put him down.

Annie said, "You watch your language, you. Here, come to Grandma, Dirk, this is our block time, isn't it? Come to Grandma."

The baby stopped crying. Happily he began to pile blocks on top of each other. Annie smiled at him from her chair.

Despair took Lizzie.

"Where are you going now, child?" Annie said. "Sit down, you, and talk with me."

"I'm going back outside."

Alarm filled Annie's dark eyes. "No, stay here, you. Lizzie, sit here with Dirk and me . . ."

Lizzie bolted out the door.

The sun had come out from behind gray clouds. She began walking aimlessly, anywhere to get away from the placid, safe routine behind her. Which would go on day after day after day, until everybody died.

Striding the path up the mountain, she kicked at twigs fallen in the winter winds. Would the path just become more and more unused, if it wasn't part of anyone's routine to walk on it? Would the neuropharm spread? Maybe she, Lizzie, would get infected if it came back a second time. And she wouldn't even mind, that was the worst of it. She'd be like Annie, grateful for safety and peace.

Lizzie stopped and punched a birch sapling. *No.* She was eighteen years old, and she couldn't just *give up.* She never had, not in her whole life. There had to be something she could do about this. There had to be.

But what?

She couldn't look for some antidote to the neuropharm; Jackson and Vicki and Thurmond Rogers were already doing that. She couldn't start another election; the way everybody was now, there was even less chance than before that she could get people to vote a Liver into power. This had all worked out pretty well for the donkey candidate!

Was *that* why it had happened? Had Donald Thomas Serrano arranged for the safety-first neuropharm so that a donkey would win the election? But Jackson had said this was a completely new kind of neuropharm, one that the Cell Cleaner didn't eliminate because it must get the body to permanently change the proteins the body itself made. No one would waste a new neuropharm like that on a dinky election for Willoughby County district supervisor.

Unless they were just testing it? Unless *who* was just testing it?

This was getting her nowhere! She was just too stupid to figure anything out. Who did she think she was, Miranda Sharifi?

She was Lizzie Francy, that's who. The best datadipper in the country. Maybe in the whole goddamn world!

All right, she jeered at herself, if she was such a hotshot dipper, why wasn't she dipping? Why was she standing here in the April woods punching baby trees when she should be doing the one goddamn thing she knew how to do? She should, first, protect herself against getting the neuropharm, by finding a place to live apart from the tribe. There were all kinds of abandoned cabins up here in the mountains. Other tribes wouldn't be back from the south until the weather warmed up in a few months. She would be safe enough. She could take a spare Y-cone and her terminal, and spend eighteen hours a day searching the Net for answers.

Without Dirk?

Lizzie's stride faltered. She couldn't take him. If she did, he'd spend his whole time wailing in fear of the new surroundings. And she'd spend her whole time caring for him. Nobody had told her, when she'd so blithely gotten pregnant, how much sheer *time* a baby took. Especially one that was crawling and putting everything in his mouth. She couldn't take Dirk. She'd have to leave him with Annie and the tribe, where he belonged until she could somehow find out what she needed to do to help cure him.

And she would find out. Because she was Lizzie Francy. They—whoever they were!—were not going to defeat *her!*

At a headlong run Lizzie started back to the camp.

She found a foamcast cabin about two miles from the camp. It looked like it had once belonged to a family of Livers, the kind of stubborn people who before the Change Wars had lived alone on the side of a mountain rather than in a government-supported town. When they'd left, they'd taken or burned for heat everything in the cabin. There was no furniture, no plumbing. Lizzie didn't need them. The door still closed snugly and the plastic windows were intact. There was a stream in the woods.

She cleared out the wildlife living in corners: a raccoon, a snake, newly hatching spiders. She moved in a Y-cone, her bedding, and a plastic water jug. Then she sat cross-legged on her bedding, back against the plain foamcast wall, and talked to her terminal.

She started, because she had to start somewhere, with Donald Serrano. The new Willoughby County district supervisor was running his office the same way as had the dead Harold Winthrop Wayland. Nothing in Lizzie's careful tracings of Serrano's financial holdings or personal records led, even indirectly, to a drug company. If that link existed, Serrano had hidden it better than Lizzie could dip. She didn't think the link existed.

Next she tried the major biotech companies. This was much trickier. She didn't want any dipping traced back to her. It took weeks of slow, painstaking work to break all the security codes and get into the deebees. She used phantom searchers, which she constructed in other people's systems chosen at random. The searchers in turn constructed elaborate programs of clones, worms, encryptions, and blind alleys. Lizzie secreted the files thus pirated in yet other randomly chosen systems, and accessed them only through phantoms. She was very, very careful.

But once she had the information, another problem arose: she didn't have the scientific background to know what she was looking at. It did help that she knew what she was looking *for:* any line of development for neuropharms that changed the brain's permanent reactions in the direction of greater fear. A few companies were working on long-lasting pleasure drugs that could evade the Cell Cleaner; nobody, as far as Lizzie could tell, was succeeding.

She paid special attention to Kelvin-Castner. Their data banks were full of esoteric reports on what was being done with Dirk's and Shockey's tissue samples. Every day, it seemed, more researchers joined the team. More equipment paid for, more interim reports filed, more lab notes she couldn't read. The doctors were doing something at Kelvin-Castner, something big and growing bigger exponentially. TenTech was funding some of it. But whether it was just more pleasure-drug research or whether K-C was trying to find a counteragent to the fear neuropharm, Lizzie simply couldn't tell. She didn't have the science.

Every day she trudged down the mountain to see Dirk for a few minutes. There was never any message for her from Dr. Aranow on the camp terminal, telling her what was going on.

Why should he tell her? She was nobody.

She turned next to dipping other Liver camps. This was both easier and harder. The temporary camps, always moving, usually had one or two young people who could exploit a terminal. Some dipped extensively and deeply; some merely scanned other camps' postings. There were few patterns to look for. On the other hand, almost no Liver users knew how to cover their electronic tracks. The data was disorganized, massive, and ragged, but it wasn't encrypted.

She wrote programs to access and analyze dozens of different kinds of data, looking for . . . what? How could you use the Net to notice fear of new things? If people were afraid of new areas, they simply didn't access them. How did you find an absence of subsets of people, across a whole continent?

Slowly, her probability programs began yielding patterns.

A Liver camp in someplace called Judith Falls, Iowa, dipped the accounts of nearby donkey warehouses at exactly the same time every day, for exactly the same duration. The repetitious pattern had not existed before April.

A tribe roaming across Texas sent greetings to exactly the same list of distant relatives in exactly the same order, with essentially the same wording, on the same days every week. Starting April 3.

A town, apparently pre-Change Wars and still occupied by the same people in northern Oregon, datadipped only on Thursday afternoons. Each Thursday, some dipper—whose technique wasn't bad, Lizzie noted approvingly—broke into the same nearby biotech data banks. As near as Lizzie could follow the dipper's tracks, he or she was checking various inventories for Change syringes. There never were any.

Sitting cross-legged on her pallet, Lizzie pulled at her hair. The cabin door stood wide open; spring had given way to an early, abrupt summer, even though it was only May. The scent of wild mint blew in on a warm breeze. Birds, nesting, sang in the leafing trees. Lizzie ignored it all.

Suppose that these Liver camps *had* been infected with the neuropharm, just like Lizzie's camp. Suppose that was why they showed repeated actions—safe, routine actions. Suppose further that they were test sites, too. What good did knowing this do her? Lizzie couldn't travel to Iowa or Texas or Oregon to investigate these camps. And even if she could—so what? She might find that other Livers were lab rats, too. Like her Dirk. But knowing that wouldn't help change anything.

Her neck and back ached from sitting so long, and her left foot was asleep.

She had to figure out something else to try. All right, forget the Livers who'd been infected and the drug companies that might have made the drug. Who else? Who wanted everything to stay exactly the same? Donkey politicians, yes. Shockey's non-election had proved that. But how to find out which politicians could create such a political weapon? No monitor and flagging programs, no Leland-Warner decision algorithms, and no probability equations had yielded anything significant. So now what?

Follow the money. Something Vicki always said. But she'd tried to do that, through the drug-company investments, and gotten nowhere. Or nowhere she could understand. So now what?

Don't start with the end product, the neuropharm, and follow it to the money. Start with the money, and follow it to the neuropharm.

But that was impossible. Lizzie could dip the records of the world's major banks—or most of them, anyway—but she often couldn't follow the transactions she uncovered. She lacked the financial sophistication. And not once had she been able to change anything in any bank records. Well, she didn't need to do that now. The problem was something else: the sheer volume of daily transfers of money around the Earth, Moon, Mars, and orbital accounts. How was she supposed to tell which ones had anything to do with a secret neuropharm developed who-knew-where by who-knew-who? It was impossible.

She couldn't follow the drug development. She couldn't follow the money. All right, then—try again. If those camps in Iowa and Texas and Oregon *were* test sites for the neuropharm, the people who tested would want to know the results. They'd be observing, probably by robocam. Maybe by high-zoom, low-orbit satellite.

Which meant they would also be observing her tribe.

A shiver ran over Lizzie. Were stealth probes, disguised by Y-shields, observing her "hiding place" in the mountain cabin? Did they watch her go back and forth to see Dirk every day? Was someone amused at the idea that Lizzie thought she could escape infection that easily, if they decided they wanted her infected? Worse—was someone, despite all her care, following *her* electronic footsteps as she datadipped day and night?

She got up, stamped her sleeping foot, and went to the door of the cabin. She looked, stupidly, up at the bright blue sky. Of course there was nothing to see. The fresh scent of mint made her remember that she hadn't bathed or washed her hair in days. She smelled like something hit by a maglev train.

She went back inside and sat on her dirty pallet, staring at her terminal.

It didn't have radar capability, especially not if the probes were actually in orbit, and actually stealth. Visual monitoring was beyond her. But she could detect a ground-source data stream within a mile or so radius. If there were implanted transmitters of any kind monitoring the camp, she could find them if she just moved her terminal to various points around the woods. Unless, of course, the theoretical hidden probes found her first and stopped sending.

On the third night, she found it. A steady data stream, heavily encrypted, from a source in a thick pine tree forty yards away from the tribe building. It had a clear scan of the feeding ground. Lizzie wasn't sure what the data were; she couldn't dip the stream. That itself was scary.

But even if she couldn't break the coding—and she tried!—she could at least determine where the data stream went. It beamed itself upward, undoubtedly to a relay satellite in orbit. From there, its destination was theoretically so scrambled it was unknowable. But not to Lizzie. Relay data were old news to her.

She worked at the problem an entire morning, while warm rain pattered on the roof and her heart ached to hold Dirk. Eventually, as she knew she would, she dipped the transmission data.

She gasped and glanced wildly around, although of course there was nobody to see. Then, heart pounding as badly as Dirk's whenever she took him away from his blocks, she shut down her entire system. She even closed and locked the Jansen-Sagura terminal. Sitting cross-legged, staring at nothing at all, she tried to think about implications, and meanings, and safeguards. And couldn't.

The observations about her tribe were indeed being transmitted to orbit. To Sanctuary.

"I have to find Dr. Aranow," Lizzie said to Billy Washington, because she had to tell somebody. She'd found Billy where he always was in the early afternoon, fishing in the creek.

"No, you best stay here, you," Billy said, but more mildly than Annie would have. *Individual biochemical differences,* Dr. Aranow had said. People reacted differently, sometimes very differently, to any drug.

"I can't stay here, Billy. I *have* to find Dr. Aranow and Vicki."

"Speak up, you. I can't hardly hear you."

"No, I'm not going to speak louder, Billy." The monitor was a quarter mile away, but Lizzie wasn't taking chances. "How can I get to Manhattan East Enclave?"

"Man*hat*tan? You can't, you. You know that."

"I don't believe that. You know a lot more than you let on, Billy. You talked to strangers all the time, before we settled here for the winter." She saw the alarm flickering in his eyes at the mention of strangers. "The gravrail doesn't run, it, I checked, but there must be some way!"

Something tugged on his line. Billy pulled it out of the creek, but the line was empty and the bait gone. He stuck another worm on his hook. "You got a baby now, Lizzie. You got no business, you, going off someplace dangerous when you got Dirk to take care of."

"How can I get to Manhattan East?"

"You can't, you."

Even before the neuropharm, Billy had been stubborn.

When Lizzie said nothing, the old man finally said, "You got to talk to Dr. Aranow, you, then call him."

"I can't."

"Why not?"

Because anything that went out over her terminal would be overheard by Sanctuary. She couldn't say that. Billy, the neuropharmed Billy, would have heart failure. "I just can't, Billy. Don't ask me questions."

Again he looked alarmed. Billy jerked up his line, even though there had been no tug, and looked at his worm. He put the line back in the water.

"Billy, I know that you know. How can I get to Manhattan East?"

"You got no business even—"

"How?"

Light sweat filmed Billy's cheeks. Lizzie fought down her impatience. By now Annie would have been in full-blown panic. So would Shockey, that once-swaggering braggart. Individual chemical differences.

Finally Billy said, "A man, he told me last fall, him, that the gravrail tracks east of the river go directly into Manhattan East. But you can't get through the enclave shield, Lizzie. You know that, you!"

"What river? Where?"

"What river? We only got but one, us. The one this here creek flows into."

Only got but one. What didn't exist in Billy's world since the neuropharm just didn't exist. And yet, once, he'd probably been the only one in camp to explore any larger geography.

"How many days' walk?" Lizzie said.

Now he did start to panic. He put a trembling hand on her arm. "Lizzie, you can't go, you! It's too dangerous, a young girl alone, and besides you got Dirk . . ."

His breathing accelerated. Suddenly Lizzie remembered how Billy had been when Lizzie was a child, before the Change, when Billy's heart had been clogged and weak. He'd gotten gasping and dizzy, just like this. Love flooded her, and compassion, and exasperation. "Okay, Billy, okay."

"Promise me, you . . . promise me you won't . . . go alone!"

"I promise," Lizzie said. Well, she wouldn't go alone. She'd take her terminal, plus the personal shield Vicki had left with her.

"Okay," Billy said. His breathing eased. He'd always trusted her word. In a few more minutes, he was absorbed again in his fishing.

Lizzie watched him. His dark eyes, alert in their sunken face, watched the water. He'd taken off his hat so his nearly bald head, fringed with gray curls above his ears, could absorb the soft sunlight. The hat hung on a tree branch. Every day at this time he must make the decision to leave the hat on or take it off. Every day he must place the plastic bucket for fish in the same place on the grass. Every day he must dig the same number of worms, methodically baiting the hook in the same way until the worms were gone. Every day.

What was Jennifer Sharifi *doing*?

Lizzie didn't know. She could datadip as well as anybody in the country, but Jennifer Sharifi was a Sleepless. Not a Super like Miranda, but still a Sleepless. And she had all the money in the world. She was changing the people Lizzie loved, tacking them down to one place and one routine, like they were so many programmed 'bots. Lizzie wasn't going to be fool enough to think she knew why, or what to do about it. Jennifer Sharifi had once tried to force the United States to let Sanctuary secede, and had held five cities hostage to a terrorist virus that could kill everyone in those cities, and had gone to jail for longer than Lizzie's whole life. Lizzie knew when she was out of her depth. She needed help.

It was almost a relief to finally admit it. Almost.

She left that night, skirting the hidden transmitter by walking in a wide circle down the mountain. She stayed away from the old broken roads—that was where Sanctuary would expect people to walk, wasn't it, and so would logically set their monitors? Walking through the woods in the dark, keeping the creek in sight, wasn't easy. Terminal in her backpack, she made slow progress. She couldn't have done it at all if a full moon hadn't shone brightly, aided by what looked like millions of stars. Struggling through the brush, Lizzie tried to stay under trees, in case Sanctuary was using high-resolution space imaging.

Later on, she would wear Vicki's personal shield, and let herself be wrapped in a clear protective energy field that would keep her from being scratched by brambles, stung by insects, frightened of every noise in the brush. But not now. Not until she was farther away from camp. Personal shields set up a detectable field.

Sanctuary couldn't monitor the entire state, could they?

By morning she'd reached the place where the creek joined the river. She was exhausted. She crawled under a windfall of brush that shielded her from sight from above but still let the bright morning sun slant in. Taking off her clothes, Lizzie fed. Then she gratefully turned on the personal shield and slept all day.

When she awoke toward dusk, she wasn't alone. It was summer; tribes of Livers that had spent the winter in the warm south were now roaming back. This tribe sounded small and familial; Lizzie heard several babies crying. Changed or unChanged? She didn't emerge from her hiding place to look. Her biggest danger was not starvation, nor sickness, nor accident. It was others of her own kind. Not all tribes were small, or familial.

At night she started off again. It was much easier wearing the personal shield. Billy had taught her a lot about hiding in the woods—or out of them—and that would help, too.

She'd worry about Manhattan East when she got there.

INTERLUDE

TRANSMISSION DATE: April 20, 2121
TO: Selene Base, Moon
VIA: Mall Enclave Ground Station, GEO Satellite C-1494 (U.S.)
MESSAGE TYPE: Encrypted
MESSAGE CLASS: Class A, Federal Transmission
ORIGINATING GROUP: Internal Revenue Service
MESSAGE:

Dear Ms. Sharifi:

The Internal Revenue Service is in receipt of your personal federal tax return for 2020, which was filed electronically from Selene Base, Moon. However, the return is unsigned. For electronic returns, a manual signature rendered by digital pen or equivalent technology is required by federal law. Therefore, I am attaching electronic Form 1987A for your signature.

Thank you for your attention to this matter.

Sincerely,

Madeleine E. Miller

Madeleine Elizabeth Miller

District Commissioner, Internal Revenue Service

ACKNOWLEDGMENT: None received

Seventeen

Jennifer Sharifi followed Chad Manning into the conference room of Sharifi Labs on Sanctuary. A large U-shaped table arched around three walls, backed by eighteen chairs. In the center of the U, a clear plastic panel, unshatterable by anything short of nuclear detonation, was set into the orbital floor. As Sanctuary orbited, the view beneath the floor changed from black space brilliant with stars to the huge blue-and-white eyeball of the Earth. The panel opaqued automatically whenever the sun flashed into too bright view. Around the edges of the panel curled a decorative border of Arabic design, intricate interlocking geometrics copied from ancient weavings at Kasmir. The border was programmed to change colors to complement the view. It turned the solar system into a rug under Sanctuary's feet.

"Door close," Dr. Manning said. In the large empty room his voice echoed faintly. "Sit down, Jennifer."

"I'd rather stand, thank you. What is it you wish to show me?"

Chad pulled a sheaf of papers from his pocket. That alone was significant: his information, whatever it was, wasn't on-line, not even in the heavily shielded programs of the neuropharm project. And yet Chad Manning was not, as Jennifer well knew, a particularly suspicious person. She knew everything there was to know about Dr. Chad Parker Manning.

Chief scientist for Sharifi Labs, he was the only one of the project team who had not been sent to prison at the same time as Jennifer, for the original attempt to make Sanctuary safe. The inclusion of one outsider on the team had been inevitable. The geneticists imprisoned for treason had lost too much time incarcerated, in a field that still changed rapidly every few years. And the project had to be run from Sharifi Labs: the labs had the equipment for checking Strukov's claims, for detailed analyses of Strukov's results before Jennifer committed the next huge section of her fortune to the Sleeper renegade.

There was no way the secret team could not include Sharifi Labs' chief scientist.

Robert Day, Sanctuary's business manager and another imprisoned hero of the original attempt to free Sanctuary, had chosen Manning from among the Sleepless scientists. Robert had been released from prison ten years before Jennifer. He'd had time to investigate thoroughly, recruit slowly, be completely sure. Dr. Chad Manning was not the scientific genius that Serge Strukov was. A generation produced only one such genius. But as a scientist, Chad was solid, methodical, completely capable of dogging Strukov's scientific footsteps—even if Chad could never have ventured along those same paths first. Just as important, he was completely committed to safeguarding Sanctuary by whatever means became necessary. Jennifer trusted him.

"I've been playing with Strukov's virus," Chad said. "In simulation, of course. And I found something."

"Yes? What sort of something? And is there a reason we're not looking at your simulations?"

"I destroyed them. These are the printouts. Although of course I can recreate the sims if you want to check them."

He unfolded the sheaf of papers. Chad Manning's parents had made him genemod handsome on a fairly uncommon template: sensitive and delicate. He had a thin face, high sharp cheekbones, pale skin, and the long flexible fingers of a violinist. The fingers trembled as he handed the papers to Jennifer.

"The first pages are biochemical equations, models . . . I can go through each of them for you if you like, afterward. Look now at the last page."

Jennifer did. Two identical computer-sketched drawings of protein folds. Below them, a probability equation. The variables were written out by hand.

"The difference is very subtle," Chad said, and she heard the strain in his voice. "See, there—on the farthest left segment. The chromosomal difference is only a few amino acids."

Now Jennifer saw the two drawings weren't identical after all. One small area of one protein fold differed from the other.

"What's most important is that to discover this, you have to be really following an unlikely simulated trail," Chad said. His agitation was growing. "I just sort of stumbled over it. It's not a common mutation, and it's on one of Strukov's proteins that you wouldn't expect to do this . . . but, Jennifer, *look at the equations.*"

The protein folds conveyed little to Jennifer—she was not a microbiologist. But the math was a standard probability equation. The probability of the protein-fold mutation occurring spontaneously within a year's time, given Chad's variables for replication and infection rates, was 38.72 percent.

She said composedly, "What effect would this protein fold have on the virus?"

"It will make it viable outside the human body. And thus transmissible."

"In other words, instead of having to breathe in the virus, which is then destroyed by the Cell Cleaner but not before it sets off the cascade reaction of natural amines—"

"Instead of having to breathe it in, the virus would become transmissible from person to person. It could survive on skin, clothing, hair, in body folds—"

"For how long?" Jennifer asked.

"Unknown. But certainly a few days. And in this form it can enter the body through skin punctures or orifices . . . an infected person can infect others. For at least a few days. That couldn't happen with the previous foldings. Every virus not breathed in from the first strike died a few minutes later. Or, if it was breathed in, it was destroyed anyway by the Cell Cleaner."

Jennifer didn't allow her puzzlement to show on her face. "But, Chad—that's what we've intended all along, isn't it? The second mode of delivery that Strukov is supposed to give us is just that: transmissible by human contact. Why do you consider this a problem?"

"Because if the virus mutates naturally, before Strukov is ready to release his transmissible form, he can't control it."

Jennifer waited. She still didn't fully understand Chad's agitation, but she didn't say so. Never reveal how much you don't understand, not even to allies. She waited.

Chad said, "There are two problems. No, three. If the virus mutates before we're ready, we'll no longer control its spread. The drone delivery schedule—as you know!—was carefully drawn up to avoid attracting scientific or military attention as long as possible. That will no longer be in our control."

"It already isn't," Jennifer said. "Kelvin-Castner Pharmaceuticals happened to stumble across a Liver test site. *You* know that."

"True. But they aren't bringing in the CDC or Brookhaven. At least, not yet. Second, as soon as a virus becomes viable outside the body, it means places like Kelvin-Castner can study the original proteins, not just the secondary effects on the brain. That will give them a big jump forward on finding a vaccine. Or even a reverser."

"But you said finding those would be very difficult, even after the virus is directly transmissible—"

"Oh, it will," Chad said. "It will. But we don't want to give the Sleepers any edge at all. Third, if the virus can mutate this way, with a 38.72 percent probability, and I only found it by accident . . . what *else* might it do? And does Strukov know?"

"Don't tell him," Jennifer said swiftly. "And don't ask him. There's no way to tell if his answer was the truth."

Chad nodded. Jennifer, pondering, studied the clear panel beneath her feet. Stars, cold and remote and sharp . . . but up close, she reminded herself, they were very messy aggregations of violent collisions.

"I want the rest of the team to know about this, Chad. Although you did right to show it to me first, and to destroy the simulations." Sanctuary had its own teenage datadippers. Ordinarily, Jennifer was pleased by that. They were the next generation of systems scientists, and the more ingenious their technique, the better. But not this time. "We have to design a new delivery schedule. A much more rapid one."

"Will the Peruvians be able to accelerate the hardware manufacture?"

"I don't know. That's the real difficulty." Strukov, Jennifer was sure, could handle any shift in plans on his end. "I'll get Robert and Khalid on it."

"All right," Chad said. Jennifer could see that he had calmed down. Her calm had infected him. As it was supposed to.

He held the door of the conference room for her, but Jennifer shook her head. "I will stay here awhile."

Chad nodded and closed the door.

Jennifer gazed at the bordered floor panel. Earth was sliding into view. Clouds over the Pacific Ocean. So beautiful. So treacherous, so morally diseased. But so beautiful.

A sudden desire came over her to once again see Tony Indivino's grave, in the Allegheny Mountains of New York. Tony Indivino, whom she had loved when she was young, as she'd never loved since. Tony, killed by the Sleepers, but not before he'd conceived of Sanctuary, the safe haven for them all . . .

Jennifer destroyed the thought. Tony was dead. What was dead no longer existed. What no longer existed must not be allowed to control the living, even momentarily. To allow that was to risk maudlin and ineffective sentimentality.

Tony was dead. No one who was dead mattered to Jennifer any longer.

No one.

* * *

"I think you should read the reports," Will said. "At least once."

"No," Jennifer said. She moved slightly farther away from his body in their bed. "And I asked you not to bring up the subject again."

"I know what you asked," Will said evenly.

"Then please respect my request."

Will raised himself on one elbow and looked at her. "You run the neuropharm project, Jennifer. That means you should be aware of every factor. The aftermath of La Solana is a factor. The FBI-CIA team has determined that the bomb came in on a trajectory from the Rocky Mountain site, as we expected. They're analyzing every molecule of matter up there. You should at least monitor the reports we've dipped to—"

Jennifer got out of bed. In one fluid motion she put on a pale austere robe. She left the bedroom.

"Jennifer!" Will called after her, and now she heard his anger, that regrettable anger that weakened Will so much as a project member, as an ally. As a man. "Jennifer—you can't go on pretending La Solana wasn't real! It happened!"

Yes, it happened, Jennifer thought, closing the bedroom door on Will's voice. Past tense. It was over. There was no reason to think about it anymore. What was over was no more real now than what had never existed. There was no difference.

Their small sitting room—all personal dwellings on Sanctuary were small—was dark. "Lights on," Jennifer said. Lately, she didn't care for the dark. Sometimes she thought she glimpsed a figure at the edges of dark rooms, a short thick body with masses of unruly dark hair held by a red ribbon. The figure wasn't real, of course. It didn't exist.

Therefore, it never had.

Eighteen

Theresa was very sick. But if she had been Changed, she would have been ever sicker. Jackson found he couldn't appreciate the irony.

Theresa had been exposed to 240 rads. As soon as Jackson raced back from Kelvin-Castner to their apartment, he scrubbed as much of it as possible out of her system. He didn't send her to a hospital; the enclaves no longer had hospitals worthy of the name. Not necessary.

Jackson ordered the equipment he needed by emergency comlink; it reached his apartment at the same time he did. Theresa was hysterical.

"Sssshhhh, Tessie, it's going to be all right. Hang on, sweetheart, it's okay, just help us as much as you can."

"Dead!" Theresa cried, over and over. "Dead . . . dead . . . dead . . ."

"No, you're not going to die. Sssshhhh, Tessie, hush . . ." But he couldn't calm her.

"Sedate her," Vicki said, struggling to hold Theresa's flailing arms. "Jackson . . . it's kinder."

He did. Then he and Vicki worked on Theresa's limp body. He pumped out the contents of her stomach and sent specialized robotic scouring tubes down her esophagus and bronchial tree, up her rectum, into her nose and ears and vagina and across her retinas. He and Vicki scrubbed every inch of Theresa's skin with a chemical compound. Vicki cut Theresa's long fair hair and shaved off the stubble. For that, Jackson left the room. He stood in the hallway and pounded his fists on the wall.

When he returned, Vicki was kind enough not to look directly at his face.

He inserted an endotracheal tube; the lining of her airway was going to slough and swell, and she would need mechanical help in breathing. Next came an injection to make her sweat as much as possible. An IV laced with nutrients and electrolytes. When he and Vicki were done, they stood over Theresa's form lying on her bed, covered with a cotton sheet. Invasive monitors fed to a central terminal, supplemented by green, texture monitor patches dotting her skin. She looked, Jackson thought despairingly, like a skinny plucked moldy sparrow.

Vicki said, "I'll stay, Jackson. You can't nurse your sister through this alone."

"I ordered a nursing 'bot, with radiation-sickness software. It'll be here soon. It had to be shipped from Atlanta."

"No substitute for people."

"Do you know anything about radiation sickness?" he said, more harshly than he intended.

"You'll teach me."

"But Lizzie and Dirk—"

"—don't need me," she finished. "Lizzie can manage fine. And at least nothing novel and innovative is going to happen at the camp."

Jackson didn't smile. He barely heard her. "If Theresa were Changed—"

"I guessed that she wasn't," Vicki said. "But why *not*?"

He ignored the question. "If she were Changed, this would actually be worse. When Miranda Sharifi designed the Cell Cleaner, she didn't take into account radiation sickness. Well, she couldn't cover everything. The Cell Cleaner roots out aberrant DNA. That's how come it catches tumors so early. But Theresa . . ." He couldn't finish.

Vicki did it for him. "Is going to be a mass of mutated aberrant DNA. Jackson, I'm so sorry. Where's the tech pilot?"

"Went home herself, I guess."

"Then let's hope she's related to a doctor, too."

He looked at Vicki angrily. "I'm not a roving humanitarian, damn it! The pilot isn't my patient."

Vicki didn't answer. But she touched his shoulder briefly before saying, "I'm going to get some sleep. You watch her now and I'll relieve you in a few hours."

"Ask the house system to wake you up. Its name is Jones, and the guest-program entry word is 'Michelangelo.' "

"I know," Vicki said, and Jackson didn't think to ask her how she knew.

After an hour, he called the Manhattan East Airfield and sent a message to the tech pilot who had flown Theresa Aranow. He appended a file on treating radiation sickness.

Then he pulled a chair close to his sister's bed and watched her sleeping face while it was still whole.

Vicki crept into the room in the middle of the night and said gently, "Let me sit with her."

Jackson had been half dozing. He had dreamed fitfully. Huge blobs attacked him, trying to engulf his head . . . he realized they had been Theresa's T-cells, being mobilized to fight her own body. He sat up in his chair and said groggily, "No . . . I'll stay here."

"Jackson, you look like shit. Go to bed. Nothing is going to change before morning."

But Theresa was already changing. Radiation burns across her pale skin, sores inside her mouth and on her tongue.

"Jackson—"

"I'll stay."

She pulled up a chair and sat beside him. Some minutes—hours?—later, he woke to find himself stumbling along the hallway to his bedroom, Vicki tugging him along. He didn't remember falling asleep or waking up. She dumped him fully clothed, on his bed, and instantly he sank into restless dreams.

The next time he woke, Cazie was shaking his shoulder, looming over him like a Greek Fury.

"Jackson! I've left you a dozen top-priority messages from K-C—what's the *matter* with you? Don't you realize how important this deal is? And even if you don't, can't you at least do me the courtesy of answering once in thirty-six hours even if you're sulking? God, I can't believe that you—"

"I'd rather you didn't disturb Jackson," Vicki said sweetly from the doorway of Jackson's bedroom.

Cazie turned slowly. Her honey-colored skin paled, making the flecks in her eyes more brilliantly green.

"Jackson needs his sleep," Vicki continued in that same voice of sweet reason. "So it might be better if you left now."

Cazie had recovered herself, always a dangerous mood. "I don't think so . . . Diana, isn't it? Or Victoria? True, Jack looks pretty well done in—you must have given him quite a workout. I'm sure he enjoyed it. But we have grown-up items to discuss now, so if you've already been paid, the building system can call you a go-'bot. Now, Jack, if you like, I'll wait in your study while you shower."

Vicki only smiled.

Suddenly Jackson was sick of them both. He heaved himself off the bed. "Don't be so stupid, Cazie. Theresa is sick. I don't have time to think about Kelvin-Castner until she's out of danger."

Cazie's face changed. "Sick? Seriously? With what? Jackson, a Change syringe—"

"Not this time. It's radiation sickness." He pushed past her and strode to Theresa's room. Cazie ran after him.

His sister lay quietly asleep; no change in her monitor readings. Cazie saw Theresa and gasped. "What . . . Jack!"

"She was in range of the nuclear explosion that took out La Solana." By now it must be on all the newsgrids. Cazie always watched newsgrids.

"*Tess?* Went to New Mexico? That's impossible!"

"I would have said so."

"Oh, my God, Jack . . . I'll stay here and help you nurse her."

This was Cazie at her most genuine, Cazie at her most lovable. She gazed at Theresa with affection and pain. Jackson said, "Vicki's nursing her just fine," and was immediately too wretched to relish his own cruelty.

"All right," Cazie said humbly. She laid one tentative hand on the very edge of Theresa's bed.

Jackson closed his eyes. "Tell me what you want to do about Kelvin-Castner."

"It can wait," Cazie said in a low voice.

"No, it can't. And there's nothing I can do for Theresa this minute anyway. Tell me."

"If you . . . all right. I want to commit five hundred million dollars initially, more on a rolling schedule with go/no-go achievement targets. I sent you the proposed target schedule. We own fifteen percent of gross profits on this project only, with roughly standard liabilities and exposure. The ROI and long-term interlocks—"

"No, not those things. Don't tell me those things. What is K-C going to *do?*"

"Race to get a patentable delivery molecule based on the Liver tissue samples and brain alterations. The first computer models are already running. There are hundreds of possibilities to check on, of course, maybe thousands. But if we get the patentable model, we can use it as the basis of an incredible number of Cleaner-resistant pharmaceuticals. The preliminary applications team has already started brainstorming."

Cleaner-resistant. Jackson had never heard the term before. Maybe the "preliminary applications team" had just brainstormed it.

He took a last look at Theresa's readings and then led Cazie out of Theresa's room. The nursing 'bot floated closer to the bed.

In the hallway, Jackson said, "I'll vote to invest the funding, and commit Theresa's votes, too, on one condition. The first line of research—the *first,* Cazie, with majority allocation of talent and resources—goes to a counteragent for the original neuropharm that affected the Livers. A reverser that will restore their cerebral biochemistry to previous functioning. Without the stranger anxiety and the inhibition toward novelty and all the fucking fear. Is that agreed?"

Cazie hesitated only a moment. "Agreed."

"You can get Alex Castner to agree?"

"Yes." She sounded confident. Jackson wondered suddenly if she was sleeping with Castner. Or with Thurmond Rogers.

He said, "Get it in a contract and send it to me. And I'll want constant recorded progress reports on the counteragent, plus lab records."

"No problem."

"And put in the contract that I'm officially informed the very minute there's any breakthroughs, of any significant kind at all, on any aspect of the entire project."

"You got it. The contract will be at your apartment tomorrow morning. We can record the voting commitment right now. Yours in person, Theresa's by proxy. But, Jack—" Her voice trembled. "How bad is Tessie? Will she . . . will she . . ."

"She won't die." Jackson looked at Cazie. Her eyes, raised to his from her shorter height, filled with sudden tears. "Tess will recover. It'll take a long time, but she'll recover."

"Long term . . . ?"

"Long term, she's going to have to take the Change syringe. It's the only thing that'll keep her from eventual cancers."

"But there aren't any more syringes. Unless you—"

"Of course I have one for Theresa. In my father's private safe. I've always kept one for Theresa."

Cazie's face showed sudden understanding. Of what it had cost him as a doctor to do that, as the public health crisis grew—to watch babies dying and know he could save one more of them. She stepped forward and put her arms around him, and he let her. Her full breasts were soft against his chest. The top of her head fit familiarly under his chin. He was so tired.

In his peripheral vision, he saw Vicki disappear around the corner of the hallway.

* * *

Theresa developed oozing sores over her skull, face, and body. Her tissues swelled until, if she hadn't been on heavy painkillers, the pressure of the soft bed would have been agony. Her firm small breasts turned into ulcerated bags with cracked and bleeding nipples.

She couldn't talk. Her mouth, her tongue, her gums, became as much a mass of ulcers as her radiation-burned body. Sometimes, rising briefly to consciousness, she tried to mumble around the endotracheal tube. Her swollen eyes looked urgently into Jackson's. "Ennh . . . de-de-" He always sedated her. He couldn't stand it.

"Patient's progress within normal limits," the nursing 'bot said pleasantly several times a day. "Do you wish for detailed readings?"

"For God's sake, Jackson, get some sleep," Vicki said, equally often. "You look like something Miranda Sharifi's lab team threw away."

"M-M-M-M . . . de . . . de," Theresa tried. He increased the sedative.

Twice a day, as per contract, lab records arrived from Kelvin-Castner, reams of raw data. Jackson read only the summaries, hastily spoken by Thurmond Rogers. "Jack, we've developed computer models of the most likely protein foldings for the initial molecule, based on most-probable receptor-site responses. Unfortunately, there are six hundred forty-three level-A possible foldings, so the testing is going to take some time and we thought of—"

"That's enough, Caroline," Jackson told his system. "File the reports by date, speaker, and . . . whatever else fits best-retrieval protocol." *And leave me alone.*

"Yes, Dr. Aranow," Caroline said.

"Jack, how is Tess?" Cazie's image said daily, more than daily, he didn't know how often because he never linked with her calls. Once he heard Cazie's voice in another room, talking with Vicki. With *Vicki?* Conflict, sparring, dueling? He didn't go in.

Theresa lost flesh she couldn't afford to lose. Her already thin body grew skeletal, arms and legs like wire clothes hangers, knees and elbows chisel-sharp. Her sores oozed and wept.

The progress reports from Kelvin-Castner, Thurmond Rogers told him daily, didn't seem to progress. The computer models weren't panning out. The algorithms didn't, upon investigation, apply. There were possibilities only, tentative hypotheses later disproved, unsatisfactory animal-testing results. They needed a breakthrough, Thurmond Rogers explained in messages that Jackson watched only until he had their gist. The breakthrough would come, Rogers said. It hadn't yet, however. "After all, we're not Miranda Sharifi and Jonathan Markowitz," Rogers added testily.

"Patient's progress within normal limits," the nursing 'bot said.

"*Sleep.* Your sanity is consumable, you know," Vicki said.

"Possibly a decapeptide, triggering cell response in—"

"De . . . ded . . . mmmm . . ."

"How is she, Jack? How are *you? Answer* me, damn it—"

After a month, Theresa still had radiation burns on her face and body. Her muscles had atrophied. Her sores stopped oozing. Jackson wanted her to eat, even though she wouldn't have any real appetite for weeks yet. To eat, she had to come off sedation.

He and Vicki propped Theresa up against her pillows. Beside the bed, Vicki placed a huge bouquet of genemod flowers, pink and yellow and a deep subtle orange. Then she discreetly left the room. The nursing 'bot prepared a liquid protein, with a straw, that smelled of raspberries. Theresa had always liked raspberries.

"Jack . . . son."

"Don't try to talk, Tessie, if it hurts. You've been sick, but you're going to be fine. I'm right here."

She stared at him fuzzily. Her head was completely hairless, scabbed, burned. But slowly her pale blue eyes cleared.

"M-M-Mir . . ."

"I said don't talk, honey."

"M-Mir . . ."

He gave in. "Let me help. 'Miranda Sharifi.' You went out to La Solana to research your book about Leisha Camden, right? To talk to Miranda's father, because he once knew Leisha?"

Theresa hesitated. The hairless pathetic head nodded slightly. She winced as the back of her skull scraped the soft pillow.

"De . . . ed."

"Richard Sharifi is dead. Somebody bombed La Solana, and he was vaporized." Jackson saw the question in her eyes. "No, the government doesn't know who set off the bomb. It was apparently a drone ground-launched from the New Mexico mountains. No group has claimed credit, nobody's been arrested, and if the FBI has leads, they aren't making them public. And Selene Base hasn't retaliated, or even made any public comment."

"Not . . . at . . . Selene."

"What's not at Selene? Tess, honey, don't try to talk anymore, I can see how it's hurting you. All this can wait until you—"

"De-ed. Miranda."

Jackson gently held Theresa's hand. "Miranda Sharifi is dead? You can't know that, honey."

"Talked . . . to her. Me. Saw . . . her."

"You saw Miranda Sharifi?" He glanced at the monitor. Theresa's temperature, skin conductance, and brain scan were normal; she wasn't hallucinating. "Honey, you couldn't have. Miranda's at Selene. On the moon."

"No!"

"She's not? She was at La Solana? Tess—how could that be?"

Theresa glared at him, watery blue eyes in a hideously deformed head. Then tears started to fall. Jackson saw her wince where their salt touched her skin. "Dead! Dead!"

"Tess, oh, don't—"

"If she says she saw Miranda and Miranda's dead, then it's probably true," Vicki's voice said behind him. "She knows what she saw. And it's the only motive that makes sense for bombing La Solana without taking credit or making demands."

Theresa looked past Jackson, at Vicki standing in the doorway. Theresa nodded, a tremendous effort. Then her eyes closed and she was asleep.

Jackson whirled on Vicki. "Do you know what you're saying?"

"Better than you do, probably." Vicki's face contorted and she left the room.

Jackson didn't follow her. He gazed down at Theresa, who lay propped up, her poor mouth fallen open. Gently Jackson settled her flat on the bed.

He walked the length of the apartment, through the Y-shield onto the terrace. It was apparently dusk; Jackson had lost track of the hours, the days. The trees and flowerbeds in the park below bloomed in full-summer genemod glory. He thought it must be sometime in May.

Theresa said that Miranda Sharifi was dead.

And the rest of the SuperSleepless, too? Maybe. They had usually stayed together, in a pack of their own kind. Maybe because that was the only way they could find anyone who understood them. Or maybe just for simple protection. They stayed together, and hid, and then used all their technology to make the world think they were hiding someplace else, as yet another added protection.

And if Theresa was right, none of it had helped. The haters had gotten them anyway.

The treetops below danced in a sudden breeze. Standing at the very edge of the terrace, Jackson could hear the leaves rustle, smell their cool moisture. In the southeast, just below the moon, a bright planet shone steadily. Probably Jupiter. Or a holo of Jupiter, voted in by the enclave weather committee. *Let's add a planet to the dome programming this month. The children can learn to use the sky-tracking software.*

Jackson saw again the printouts of unChanged Liver children on Theresa's study wall. Dying in bloat and putrefaction from lack of the sanitation nobody needed to practice anymore, or lack of Change syringes, or lack of medical attention.

And now there never would be any more Change syringes. People and groups and governments could send endless messages or even expeditions to Selene, and it wouldn't matter. Unless the Supers had left a huge cache of syringes somewhere for posthumous discovery, there would be no more Changing for this next generation. Or the next. Or the next. Not even for donkey children with sky-scanning software. The biochemistry/nanotech was too far beyond normal humanity, even genemod humanity. You couldn't get to the industrial revolution when you'd only just invented the wheel.

Jackson put both hands on the terrace railing and leaned over. From the street four stories below came the soft sound of a woman's laughter, followed by a man's, smooth and tenor. Jackson couldn't glimpse either of them. The air smelled of mint and mown grass and roses.

Eden, Theresa had once said of Central Park, during her religious phase. She'd been twelve, and had wanted to become a nun.

Eden. For how long?

There were probably syringes hoarded, family by family, throughout the enclaves—one or two here, more there. Newborns would be injected, secretly, before outsiders knew the syringes existed and could steal them. When the hoarded syringes were all gone, the birth rate would drop even further than it had, as parents secure in the Change contemplated the disease and food needs of unChanged infants. Finally, people would have babies anyway, because people always did. Then medicine would revive from a coma feverish with research on pleasure drugs, and donkeys would get along about as well as they always had, behind their Y-shields, which would expand every year as the need grew to put more land under agriculture, under dairy farms, under soysynth factories, under tougher security shields. But the enclaves would adapt. They had all the technology to do so. No expulsion from Eden here.

And the Livers? No need to ask what would happen there. It was already happening. Famine, death, disease, war. And, eventually, they would relearn subsistence-survival skills. Or, if the neuropharm inhibiting tolerance for novelty continued to spread, they wouldn't learn. They'd just cling to old routines designed for Changed bodies that the new generation didn't have. And the donkeys, embittered by the Change Wars and all too aware that Livers had already been economically unnecessary for at least three generations, would do nothing.

Genocide by universal inaction. The Lord doesn't help those who are cerebrochemically incapable of helping themselves. Who are too terrified of change to let anyone else anywhere near them. And who just lost their last extraterrestrial champions.

Jackson breathed deeply of the sweet, artificial air, and closed his eyes.

"Jackson," Vicki said behind him. "Theresa's calling for you."

"In a minute."

To his surprise, he felt Vicki's arms creep around him from behind. Her cheek rested against his back. His shirt grew wet. He remembered that while he'd been thinking of the dead SuperSleepless as mostly a source of Change syringes, Vicki had had some kind of unexplained personal history with them.

He said, not turning around, "You met Miranda Sharifi."

"I met her, yes. Twice."

"What lunatic killed them?"

"Too many candidates to enumerate. The world is full of the disgruntled and the disgusted."

"Yeah. All kinds of losers who resent the winners."

"I'm not sure Miranda was ever a winner," Vicki said. "Not ever. But she and her kind were our one shot at forced radical evolution. Only Sanctuary could have created them, and Sanctuary will never do it again."

And then Jackson saw it. His hands tightened on the railing. The air suddenly smelled noxious. "Jennifer Sharifi killed them. In retaliation for sending her and her co-conspirators to prison almost thirty years ago."

"Yes," Vicki said. "Probably. But the Justice Department will never be able to prove it."

She let Jackson go and stepped away from him. "It's up to you, Jackson."

He turned to face her. "Up to *me?* What the hell are you talking about?"

"You don't think Kelvin-Castner is really aiming their research at a cure for the neuropharm, do you? They don't expect it to filter into the enclaves, because they know it's some other donkey group that must have made it in the first place. In order to render the Livers no political or physical threat, without the nasty business of actually having to wipe them all out. Unless you hold K-C to your contract, they'll just roar ahead with the commercial applications and drag their feet on the counterdrug you contracted for."

"The daily lab records—"

"Have been carefully examined by you, right? Bullshit. You've hardly looked at them."

He was silent, trying to take it in.

"*I* looked at them," Vicki said, "for all the good it did me. I'm not trained; to me they're just rows of charts, gibberish of equations, and models of incomprehensible substances. Jackson, you're going to have to live on top of Kelvin-Castner if you care about a counteragent. *You.*"

"Theresa—"

"—is healing. Dirk and Billy and Shockey aren't. After all"—she raised both hands, palm up, in a humble pleading gesture Jackson had never seen from her and hadn't thought her capable of—"after all, you're a doctor, aren't you?"

"I'm not a medical researcher!"

"You are now," Vicki said. And then suddenly, shockingly, she smiled. "Welcome to personal evolution."

There were weeks of reports. Each day the number of primary researchers grew, starting at seventeen and escalating to an incredible two hundred forty-one at ten different sites around the country. Everyone had sent copies of everything to Jackson: every recorded conference, every procedure, every speculation, every version of every electronic model. Variances in absorption rate, bioavailability, protein binding, receptor-subtype mechanisms, efferent nerve equations, Meldrum models, gangloid ionization, ribosome protein synthesis, Cell Cleaner interaction rates—no one person could possibly have processed it all. As he tried, Jackson began to suspect that was the point.

He also began to suspect that some of what he'd been sent was bogus. But he didn't have the time, the expertise, or the patience to determine exactly what.

Sitting at the terminal in his study, scanning printouts, he realized that the only way to wade through all of this was by using programs written to search for specific patterns, specific lines of research. Or possible research. Or maybe a direction that research could go, perhaps. Such customized programs didn't exist. And Jackson, no software expert, couldn't write them. Let alone dip the records he suspected he wasn't getting from Kelvin-Castner.

"Send for Lizzie," he told Vicki, wearily.

"*Lizzie?* She doesn't know anything about brain-chemistry research."

"Well, neither do I. Or at least, not enough. Call her and tell her I'll send a car for her right away. She's going to have to help me write specialized intent–software. If she can't do that, she can at least dip K-C's closed records. God knows she's good enough at dipping. I don't want to bring in an outside dipper who might resell the information. At least, not yet."

Vicki's eyes gleamed. "All right. And, by way of information, Jones says that Cazie is on her way up to see you."

Jackson looked up from the toppling piles of printouts all over his antique Aubusson. Vicki's face was carefully neutral. Once more he could feel her arms around him, warm and solid, beside the terrace railing.

Maybe help from Lizzie wasn't the only way through.

He said quietly, "Cazie. She's been here regularly, hasn't she? To see Theresa."

"This time she wants to see you."

"How do you know?"

Vicki smiled sourly. "I know."

And then Cazie was there, striding into his study as if she owned it, electric blue dress rustling and dark curls swirling, a vivid presence igniting the dim room to a dangerous glow that seemed capable of consuming the nonconsumable plastic printouts. Cazie scowled. "Jack! If I could see you alone . . ."

Vicki murmured, "Only if you can see past yourself," and left the room.

Jackson stood, for the fragile advantage of height.

"How are you, Jack?"

"I'm fine." He waited. This was going to be it, then. It really was. He wondered if Cazie realized.

"And Tessie?"

"She's progressing right on schedule."

Cazie's smile was genuine. "I'm so glad! Our Tessie . . . remember how we used to think of her as the child we hadn't yet had? Unearned sentiment, but not totally false." She moved a step closer to him. He could smell her perfume, like flowers in animal heat.

Jackson said, "Kelvin-Castner isn't developing the counteragent. And I can prove that you know it."

It was his only real shot—catch her by surprise, counting on the fact that she didn't expect duplicity from him, or unsubstantiated accusations, or lies. She trusted him, even though she'd always let him know he couldn't trust her. He was Jackson: solid, honest, dazzled by her. Easy to fool. Easy to control.

He watched closely. She was good—just a slight widening of the huge gold-green eyes, an involuntary change in the shining pupils. It was enough. Jackson suddenly felt punched in the stomach.

Cazie said evenly, "That's not true, Jack. You've been sent the lab reports every day."

"They're faked. All the effort in understanding the permanence factor is going toward its use as a basis for a pleasure drug."

"You haven't had time for that kind of analysis. And even if you had, you're wrong. Come over to K-C and see for yourself. Thurmond will show you—"

"—actual experiments. Yes, I don't doubt it. A few kept for show. Cazie . . . how could you? You know what this new neuropharm did to the Livers in Vicki's camp. What it could do everywhere. No one able to adapt, to modify their daily routines. When the Change syringes are all gone and kids can't count on the Cell Cleaner to zap every harmful organism they pick up, or on trophoblastic tubules to feed them, nobody will be able to innovate enough to relearn how! Within a generation—"

"Oh, God, Jack, you'll never change, will you? You just gaze at your tiny specialty, the sacred medical model, and never even glance at the larger picture. Look up—literally! The Livers don't exist all by themselves, some little helpless endangered lizards alone on a barren desert! They have Miranda Sharifi as guardian angel. With a whole host of SuperSleepless seraphs and cherubs. Miranda will fly out of Selene when she's goddamn good and ready, burn a few bushes and hand down a counteragent, and that'll be that. K-C doesn't have to do anything for Livers. And there's no reason why we should."

"Well, there's the little fact that you promised *me.*"

Cazie looked at him. God, she was beautiful. The most desirable woman he'd ever known. Beautiful, smart, tender when she felt like it. His wife—once, anyway—with everything Jackson had once thought that word meant. Something under his ribs twisted sharply. It physically hurt to know that he'd never hold her in his arms again.

"Jack—"

"Tell Thurmond Rogers, my old university pal, that I'm moving into Kelvin-Castner. Immediately. With a datadipper and a lawyer. I'm going over every report personally, visiting every lab in the biohazard complex, fucking *haunting* him with consultant experts. And if—"

"You can't bring outsiders into K-C! Nondisclosure—"

"—if I don't find substantial, scientifically valid progress, *daily,* toward a counteragent to the inhibition neuropharm, I'm tying up K-C in contract-violation lawsuits that will prevent old Alex from getting a patent until the millennium. Even if I bankrupt TenTech in the process."

Cazie stared at him. It seemed to Jackson that suddenly she stood behind a Y-shield, invisible but unbreakable. His shield, or hers? Bleakly, he realized that it no longer mattered which.

She had always been quick. She said softly, "You're through with me this time, aren't you, Jack? For good."

"Tell Rogers what I said."

"Something's changed in you. You really would sacrifice TenTech for this quixotic gesture. Why?"

"Because you're incapable of seeing that it's not a gesture."

She said, not moving, "I never pretended to be anything besides what I am, Jack."

He said painfully, "No. You never did."

Suddenly Cazie threw back her head and laughed, a high full laugh with no hint of hysteria. Jackson felt something then, a quick flash of old fear—*I can't let her go*—and felt just as clearly the moment it died, leaving him empty.

She said lightly, "I'm going to visit Theresa now."

He stood there after she left, waiting. Now Vicki would come in, with some sardonic, provocative remark. That was how it went: he quarreled with Cazie, Vicki listened at doors, then she came in and poked the wound. That was how it went.

But this wasn't just another routine quarrel with Cazie. And in a few minutes Vicki did come in, but not to poke. She was pulling a sweater over her head, her hair made wild by her roughness, her eyes not focused on him at all.

"I'm taking your car, Jack. Lizzie's gone."

"Lizzie? Gone where?"

"Annie doesn't know. But Lizzie left the camp a week ago and hasn't called since. Two strangers, genemod, came looking for Lizzie right after she'd gone. Annie was terrified of them, of course."

"A week—listen, Vicki, I can't go with you, I have to go to Kelvin-Castner—"

That distracted her for just a moment; the cold determination on her face lifted and her eyes gleamed. For just a moment.

Jackson finished, "—but I can let you have a gun. A Larsen-Colt laser that—"

"You don't have any weapons comparable to what I can get," Vicki said with the same efficient coldness, and left Jackson staring after her as she left the study cluttered with printouts he hadn't yet read.

INTERLUDE

TRANSMISSION DATE: May 13, 2121
TO: Selene Base, Moon
VIA: Dallas Enclave Ground Station, GEO Satellite C-1867 (U.S.), Satellite E-643
     (Brazil)
MESSAGE TYPE: Encrypted
MESSAGE CLASS: Class C, Private Paid Transmission
ORIGINATING GROUP: Gregory Ross Elmsworth
MESSAGE:

Ms. Sharifi—Undoubtedly you know who I am; I wouldn't insult your intelligence by suggesting otherwise. The people of the United States chose to reject my bid for the presidency, but that does not mean that I still don't stand ready to serve this great country of ours any way I can. I therefore am prepared to offer you one billion dollars— a third of my private fortune—in return for a complete scientific explanation of your Change syringes, sufficient for commercial duplication. I will make this information, without charge, freely available to all pharmaceutical companies in the United States. Although your own fortune is of course large, I can't believe you will be indifferent to my offer.

    Addresses and encryptions to reach my lawyers are attached.

    Let history fondly recall both of us.

                          Sincerely,
                          Gregory Ross Elmsworth
                          Gregory Ross Elmsworth
                          Elmsworth Enterprises International, Inc.

ACKNOWLEDGMENT: None received

III

MAY 2121

It is impossible for such a creature as man to be totally indifferent to the well- or ill-being of his fellow-creatures, and not readily, of himself, to pronounce, where nothing gives him any particular bias, that which promotes their happiness is good, and what tends to their misery is evil.

—David Hume, *An Enquiry Concerning the Principles of Morals*

Nineteen

Lizzie shrank back farther into the shadows of the building. The tribe was just around the corner. No, it wasn't a "tribe"—a tribe had rules and order and kindness. This was just a . . . a . . . she didn't know what.

The scum of the Earth, them, she heard inside her head, and it was her mother's voice. Who had Annie been talking about? Nobody like these people—there'd been nobody like this in East Oleanta or Willoughby County. Lizzie couldn't remember who Annie had called scum. She couldn't remember anything. She was too scared.

"My turn, me," a man's voice said. "Get off her, you!"

"Hold your horses, I'm getting . . . All yours."

A third voice laughed. "Didn't leave much, did you, Ed? Hope Cal don't like them feisty, him."

"Fuck, she ain't even breathing!"

"Sure she is, her. Climb on, Cal."

"Christ!"

"You go last, you, you take wet decks."

Lizzie fingered her belt, with its reassuring slight bulge of the personal-shield casing. The shield was on. She could see its faint shimmer around her hands. The men out there couldn't hurt her, even if they caught her. The most they could do would be knock the shield around awhile, with her in it like sausage in a casing. Lizzie remembered sausage. Annie used to make it. Sausage . . . what was she doing thinking of *sausage?* The girl out there was being . . . and there was nothing Lizzie could do to help her. She couldn't even help herself by hiding inside this building she cowered behind. The building, like all the others in the abandoned gravrail yard, was Y-shielded. She pressed her own shield tight against the building's shield.

The other girl screamed.

Lizzie closed her eyes. But she could still see the girl inside her eyelids. She could see all of it: the girl tied naked on the ground, the four men, the rest of the tribe a little way off. Other women, ignoring what was happening because the girl had been stolen from another tribe, wasn't one of their own. And children, glancing at the four men, curious . . .

How could they? How *could* they?

"You got enough," one of the men said. "Come on, we gotta move out, us."

"Give him a minute, Ed. Old guys need time, them."

A bark of laughter.

What if one of those curious children came around the edge of the building and saw Lizzie? She could grab him and knock him out before he called to the others.

No, she couldn't. A little boy, like Dirk would be in a few years . . . she couldn't. How impenetrable was a personal shield, anyway? She'd been wearing Vicki's for two weeks now, and she didn't really know. It kept out insects and raccoons and rain and brambles. Those were the only tests she'd given it.

"Come on, Cal!" one of the men shouted. "We're moving out, us!"

Slowly the tribe straggled past Lizzie's building. Seventeen, twenty, twenty-five. They wore ragged jacks and carried tarps and water jugs. No Y-cones, no terminals that she could see. Four filthy, Changed small children, but no babies. When they were all out of sight and sound, Lizzie ventured around the corner of the building.

The girl was dead. Blood from her cut throat drained into the ground. Her eyes were wide open, her face contorted into terror and pleading. She looked about Lizzie's age, but smaller, with lighter hair. In one ear was a small tin earring in the shape of a heart.

I can't bury her, Lizzie thought. The ground was hard; it hadn't rained in a week. Lizzie had nothing to dig with. And if she stayed here much longer, she'd lose her nerve for the bridge. Oh, God, what if those people were going over the bridge? If they caught her on it?

No. She wouldn't let that happen. She wasn't as helpless as this poor girl had been. And it wouldn't be a good idea to bury her even if Lizzie could. The girl's own tribe might come looking for her, and it would be better if they knew what happened to her than if they had to wonder forever if she was still alive. That would be intolerable. If it were Dirk . . .

She thrust the obscene thought away, knelt on the bloody ground, and untied the girl's hands and feet from the crude wooden stakes. She pulled the stakes from the ground; she could spare the girl's people that much. Grateful for the shield protecting her from contact with the streaming blood, Lizzie lifted the girl's body and staggered with it to the shadow of the building. She rolled the body against the Y-dome and covered the torso with a shirt from her backpack, knotted loosely around the girl's waist to keep it from blowing away.

Then she set out for the bridge, before it got too dark, or she got too scared.

She knew exactly where she was. Although she didn't dare use her terminal to open a link of any kind that could be traced, she could use it to access information in the crystal library, including detailed atlases. This was the New Jersey tech yard of the Senator Thomas James Corbett Gravrail. Of course, the gravrail had stopped running during the Change Wars. But the shielded buildings were still here, probably with the trains inside, and nothing could destroy the maglev lines themselves. Shining twin lines of some material Lizzie couldn't identify, they'd run all the way here from Willoughby County. They ran across the bridge spanning the Hudson River into Manhattan; they would run, according to her atlas, north to Central Park and straight to a ground gate of Manhattan East Enclave.

And then what?

First, just get there.

Lizzie stared at the bridge, and then at the sky. About three hours until sunset. She could cross under cover of dusk, hide on the other side. The trestle bridge itself provided little cover. It was narrow, no more than ten feet across, with no visible protrusions or supports. How did it stay up? Probably the same way the gravrails had stayed up. Neither physics nor engineering much interested Lizzie—only computers. Still, she should gather all the information she could before the crossing.

The Hudson shimmered bright in the sunshine. By the river, half-hidden by an embankment, Lizzie found a patch of weedy ground. She drank from the Hudson, turned off her shield, and stripped. As she lay on the ground to feed, she raised her head every few seconds to be sure no one approached. The sun felt good on her bare skin, but she couldn't let herself enjoy it. As soon as her Changed biochemistry signaled satiety, she jumped up, dressed, and turned on the personal shield. Then she settled into work with her computer. By sunset, she knew as much as was in her crystal library about the Governor Samantha Deborah Velez Memorial Gravrail Trestle.

At the eastern end of the trestle, in the deep shadow of a building, Lizzie listened as hard as she could. An hour ago she'd heard people start across the bridge. But now there was no one in sight, and all she heard was the cry of wheeling gulls and the lapping of the river against the shore. She dropped to her hands and knees and started to crawl across the bridge, presenting as inconspicuous a silhouette as possible.

The bridge was 2.369 kilometers long.

Darkness set in more quickly than Lizzie had counted on. Darkness was a cover, of course, but she was afraid of crawling across the unlighted bridge. Not of falling off, but of . . . what? She was just afraid. Of everything.

No, she *wasn't*. She was Lizzie Francy, the best datadipper in the country, the only Liver to even try to reclaim political power from the donkeys. She would not be afraid. Only people like her mother were afraid of everything—even before the neuropharm.

Stay home, child, where you belong, you. Annie's voice again. God, she'd be glad when she was too old to hear her mother's voice in her head. How old was that? Maybe as much as thirty?

Then she heard something else. People, crossing the bridge from the Manhattan side.

Lizzie crawled forward even faster. Now she could see their light, a bright Y-energy torch, bobbing in the distance. How far? The wind must be blowing toward her; it carried their laughter. Men's laughter.

It should be here soon, soon, it had been a while since the last one . . .

She felt it in the darkness, the small dark bump at the edge of the bridge, meant to be used in making repairs. The techs attached their floaters here, then activated the energy shield that temporarily augmented the width of the bridge for easy maneuverability. The shields could hold several tons of equipment, if they had to. They could also bend at any needed angle. Lizzie had read everything about them in the crystal library—which did not include the activation codes. And she hadn't dared open a satlink to try to dip the information from the gravrail corporation's deebees.

Now, she didn't have any choice.

"System on," she whispered. "Oh, God—*system on.* Minimal volume."

"Terminal on," the computer whispered.

She worked as quickly as she could, muttering feverishly to the terminal, eyeing the torchlight ahead. It seemed to have stopped. Occasional wordless voices blew toward her on the wind. Raised voices—an argument. Good. Let them argue, let them fight, let them all throw each other off the bridge . . . What if they threw her off the bridge? She didn't know how to swim.

Stay home, child, where you belong, you.

"Path 74, code J," Lizzie tried. *Come on, come on* . . . It had to be a simple code, maybe even a standard industrial one, easy for all techs on rotating crews to remember. Not too many contingencies or automatic changes; they'd hamper an emergency. It had to be fairly simple, not all that deeply secured . . .

She had it.

The torch was moving forward again. Lizzie seized her terminal and backpack in her arms. She laid a hand on the dark bump and spoke the code. Soundlessly—thank God it was soundless!—the bridge extended itself over the water, a clear platform of energy disappearing into the darkness.

Lizzie hesitated. It looked so insubstantial. If she crawled out on it and it just let her drop through into the river far below . . . but that wouldn't happen. Y-energy wasn't insubstantial. Y-energy was the surest and most solid thing left from the old days, before the Change Wars, when life had been safe.

The voices crystallized into words. *Hurry up . . . Where's . . . can't never . . . Janey girl . . .*

They might be all right. They might be just normal people, crossing a bridge. Or they might be like those animals at the tech yard. Lizzie looked again at the almost-invisible shield, closed her eyes, and rolled onto it. She whispered code, and felt the shield curve, move, and swing her under the bridge for inspection and repair.

Cautiously Lizzie opened her eyes. She lay inches under the trestle, the underside of which was pocked with bumps and panels. Probably some of those were terminals. For once, she felt no desire to datadip. She groped with one hand along the edge of the energy shield supporting her, trying to feel the place it met the bridge. As far as she could feel, the whole shield had swung neatly underneath, detectable from the top only if you happened to be looking in the dark for a bridge extension made of energy field.

Above her, people straggled past.

She waited several minutes after the last vibration in the bridge. Then she spoke the code to swing the extension back, followed by the one to close it up.

On the east side of the bridge the gravrail divided. One line ran south, along the western shore of Manhattan, on a narrow strip of land between the river and the dome of Manhattan West Enclave. The other veered north, to skirt the enclave and, eventually, Central Park. That way, Lizzie knew, were the ruins of Livers' New York. Not too many people lived there now; broken foamcast and fallen stone didn't provide much to feed on. Those that did remain tended to be dangerous.

She had no choice. This was the way to Dr. Aranow.

Wrapped in her personal shield, Lizzie hid under a thick bush until morning. She felt fairly sure she wouldn't be seen. But she couldn't go to sleep for a long time.

In the light, New York was even worse than she'd imagined.

She'd never seen anything like it. Yes, she had—those history holos that Vicki had insisted she study in the educational software, before Lizzie grew old enough to put her foot down and study only the software she wanted. The holos had shown places like this one: burned, fallen piles of rubble with weeds straggling through them. Streets so blocked you couldn't be sure which direction they'd once run. Scattered twisted metal separated by black glassy areas where some weapon had fused everything into smoothness. Lizzie had always assumed the holos were made-up, like the literature software Vicki had made her watch. Or if not made-up completely, then data-enhanced.

But this broke-down city was *real*.

She moved cautiously through the ugly ruins, listening. A few times she heard voices. Immediately she hid, shaking, until the men had passed. She didn't see them, and was just as glad.

People lived in some of the ruined buildings. She saw a woman carrying water from the river, a man braiding rope, a Changed child chasing a ball. And then an unChanged baby, carried by a little girl of about ten.

The Changed girl was dirty, half-naked, hair matted with debris. But her skin shone with health, and she clambered strongly over a pile of rubble, the baby clinging to her chest. He—she?—looked over a year old, the age of Sharon's baby, Callie. But this child's legs were shriveled and weak-looking, his belly swollen, his arms like sticks. An open sore on his leg oozed pus. When the little girl set him down, he mewed and held up arms that almost immediately dropped helplessly to his side.

That's how all babies would look soon, if Miranda Sharifi didn't make more Change syringes, and if Sanctuary spread the fear neuropharm. Just like that.

The older girl set the child down, and he immediately fell over. His bones had no strength.

Lizzie moved away from the children. It would have been better to wait until they left the area, but she couldn't stand to wait. Carefully she made her way across Manhattan, keeping direction by the gravrail even when she had to skirt north of it to avoid people. To the south, both ahead and behind her, she could see the towers of Manhattan West and Manhattan East, separated by the broad expanse of the park. The towers shone in the sunlight, and bright splashes of genemod color bloomed on their terraces under the enclave Y-shields. Aircars flew in and out of invisible gates in the invisible dome.

By mid-afternoon, she'd reached the northern ground gate for Manhattan East Enclave.

It was surrounded by a sort of ruined-village-within-the-ruined-city. Of what Lizzie guessed were the original foamcast buildings, half were intact and empty, still surrounded by impenetrable shields. The other half were rubble, burned or bombed or hacked into ragged chunks by sheer brute force. Around and between, people had constructed shacks of board, foamcast debris, sheet plastic, even broken 'bots. Well, tribes everywhere made do with what they found. But these shacks were also broken and ruined—some patched, some not—as if there had been a second Change War here. And a third, and a fourth.

Lizzie saw no people, but she knew they were there. A dead campfire, the ashes still undisturbed. A worn path, free of weeds. A bouquet of unwilted wildflowers from some child's game. And, most puzzling, a framed picture of a man in very old-fashioned clothes, stiff ruffles at neck and wrists, holding some sort of jeweled book. How had *that* gotten there? She stayed hidden, within sight of the enclave gate, and waited.

Suddenly a chime sounded.

Immediately people rushed out of hiding from behind rubble, out of shacks, even from an underground tunnel. Livers, but not dressed like any Livers that Lizzie had ever seen. They wore donkey clothes: boots, tight little shirts, full trousers, rich coats. But only in bits and pieces— nobody had a complete outfit. The people—women, children, a few men—didn't look dangerous. They gathered around the enclave gate. The chime sounded again.

If Lizzie wanted to see what was happening, she was going to have to gather with them. Cautiously she edged into the small crowd. They stank. But no one paid her any particular attention. So they weren't really a tribe, who knew each other and stuck together. They were just a bunch of pathetic people. She jostled to the front of the group.

The enclave dome was opaqued gray for fifteen feet up, clear after that. Probably the residents didn't want Livers peering in at them, spoiling the view of their pretty gardens. The gate, a black outline on the gray energy field, suddenly disappeared. Everyone rushed inside the enclave.

It couldn't be this easy!

It wasn't. Inside was another sealed dome, full of . . . what? Piles of clothing, boxes of stuff. Lizzie saw a doll with a broken head, some mismatched dishes, a scratched wooden box, some blankets. Then she understood. The donkeys in Manhattan East Enclave were giving away the used things they no longer wanted.

People snatched objects from the piles, the boxes, each other. There was a little pushing and shoving, but no real fighting. Lizzie watched carefully, trying to see everything, both dome structure and discards. Clothing, pictures, toys, bedding, flowerpots, furniture, plastics—nothing electronic or Y-energy, nothing that could become a weapon. In three minutes the dome was picked clean, and all the Livers ran away with their new discards.

Lizzie waited, her heart starting a slow hammering in her chest.

"Please leave the dome now," a stern 'bot voice said. "Today's giveaway is over. Please leave the dome now."

Lizzie stayed where she was, fingering her personal shield.

"Please leave the dome now. Today's giveaway is over. Please leave the dome now."

Outside, someone screamed something unintelligible. The Livers froze for a horrified moment, then started running.

"Please leave the dome now. Today's giveaway is over. Please leave the dome now." And then, just like that, she was outside. The rear energy wall had unceremoniously pushed her forward, closing itself, so quickly that Lizzie tumbled on her face in the dirt.

The Livers still screamed and ran, disappearing into their dens and holes. Some weren't quick enough. The band of raiders, mostly men but a few women too, burst on them and started grabbing the donkey discards, knocking people down, shouting and hollering as they stomped with heavy, stolen boots on bodies and faces.

Lizzie rolled back toward the dome that had just ejected her. She understood now why the shacks had been repeatedly destroyed, repeatedly rebuilt. The price for living near the enclave's used bounty was that others would take it away from you, with varying degrees of viciousness.

She scrambled to her feet and started sidling along the dome. Useless—she was the most visible, best-equipped target in sight. Two men converged on her.

"Backpack! Grab it, Tish!"

It wasn't two men but a man and a woman, a woman as tall and broad-shouldered as a man. With deep purple eyes under thick, thick lashes. *Genemod.*

The beautiful donkey eyes leered at Lizzie, grabbed for her, encountered the personal shield. "Fuck! She's shielded, her!" The voice was pure Liver.

Tish outweighed Lizzie by at least thirty pounds. She knocked Lizzie sideways, and Lizzie felt herself fall against the energy dome and slide down it. She cowered and whimpered, groping inside her boot. Tish dropped to her knees beside her, the purple eyes bright with the joy of torture, and began to shake Lizzie by the neck like a dog with a bone.

"So I can't get inside there, me . . . I can still shake you till your neck breaks, it, right inside your safe little shield . . ."

Lizzie pulled Billy's rabbit-skinning knife from her boot and shoved it up and under the woman's breastbone.

She'd sharpened the knife every day, during the long daylight hours of hiding. Even so, she was surprised how hard it was to drive the blade through muscle and flesh. She pushed until the long blade was buried to its handle.

Tish's beautiful eyes widened. She slumped forward on top of Lizzie, her arms settling around Lizzie like an embrace.

Lizzie shoved her off and looked wildly around. The man who'd told Tish to grab Lizzie's backpack was across the clearing, fighting with one of the few men left alive near the enclave. Tish's partner seemed to be winning. And there were other raiders around, in a minute another one would attack . . . Lizzie had only a few moments.

She didn't hesitate. If she thought, she'd never be able to do it. But Tish was too heavy for Lizzie to lift, she couldn't carry that muscular body . . . but she didn't need the whole body.

Shaking, Lizzie knelt beside Tish and pulled out the silver teaspoon she'd stolen from Dr. Aranow's dining room. She'd had some weird idea that once inside Manhattan East, she could show it to the house system, convince "Jones" that she belonged there . . . not likely. But now she grasped Tish's right eyelid with her right thumb and index finger, pried the eyelid wide open, and slid the spoon under the eyeball. Gasping, she scooped the eyeball out of its socket. She pulled her knife from Tish's body; immediately blood spurted over her in jets, running down the outside of the energy shield. Lizzie sliced through the nerves and muscles tethering the eyeball to its empty socket.

She turned, groping for the black outline of the enclave gate. Blood smeared between the outside surfaces of the dome's Y-shield and hers. Embedded in the gate outline was a standard retina scanner, set to admit any genemod configuration. An emergency measure: a tech could get caught outside, an adventurous adolescent could be stranded. Lizzie knew about it from datadipping.

She pushed Tish's eyeball against the scanner, and the outer dome gate opened. It closed behind her, just ahead of the raiders screaming for her death.

Lizzie collapsed to the floor and heaved. She couldn't vomit; she'd had no mouth food in weeks. But there was no *time*. How long did a dead eyeball stay fresh enough to fool a scanner? Such information wasn't in the deebees.

Staggering to her feet, she held Tish's purple genemod eye to the second scanner. The inner gate opened, and Lizzie lurched through.

She was inside Manhattan East.

Specifically, she was inside a warehouse of some kind, with heavy-machinery 'bots standing motionless around the walls. Good. No cop 'bots until she left the building, which would be heavily shielded and locked. That could wait. Lizzie lay on the floor until she could breathe normally.

When she could stand, she turned off her personal shield. Tish's blood slid off onto the floor. Lizzie turned the shield back on, then realized she was still holding the eyeball. It wasn't bloody; all the blood had come from withdrawing the knife from Tish's body.

Tish had never used her genemod eyes to enter the enclave. Why not? She must have known what she was. But when she tried to shake the life out of Lizzie, Lizzie had felt the reason for Tish's exile. Tish's hands had circled Lizzie's neck; Tish's body had pressed hard against Lizzie's. And through Tish's clothing, Lizzie had felt the hard lumps in the wrong places, the misshapen breastbone, the asymmetrical ribs. Tish's skeleton must have gone wrong in the womb. Naked, she would look grotesque. Lizzie thought of how donkeys insisted on physical perfection, and how long Tish must have dwelled with Livers to have that accent. Vicki always said that hating yourself was the worst kind of hatred. Lizzie had never understood what Vicki meant.

She shuddered and dropped the purple eyeball. Her gorge rose. But still, she couldn't leave the thing here, for a maintenance 'bot to find. She forced herself to pick the eyeball back up and put it in her pocket.

Then Lizzie started patiently to dip the inside security locks on the warehouse.

It took her almost half an hour. When she was finished, she stepped out into Manhattan East Enclave. She stood on an immaculate street bordered with genemod flowers, long slinky blue shapes that yearned toward her. Lizzie jumped back, but the flowers were soft, flaccid, harmless. The air smelled of wonderful things: woodsmoke and newly mown grass and spices she couldn't identify. The towers of Manhattan gleamed in sunset, the programming on their outer walls subtly keyed to the colors in the sky. From somewhere came the low (artificial?) hooting of mourning doves.

People actually lived in this beauty and order. All the time. They really did. Lizzie, terrified and exhausted and enchanted, suddenly felt that she might cry.

There was no time. A cop 'bot zoomed toward her.

Frantically she dug in her pocket for Tish's eyeball. It had grown softer, slightly squishy. Lizzie's gorge rose. She held the disgusting thing in front of her right eye, squeezing shut the left, but the 'bot didn't even try for a retina scan on the decaying purple eye. Somehow, it already knew she didn't belong in Manhattan East. Lizzie saw the mist squirt into her face, screamed, and slumped backward onto the genemod flowers, which wrapped their soft petals lovingly around her paralyzed limbs.

Twenty

J ennifer Sharifi, dressed in a flowing white *abbaya,* stood in the conference room of Sharifi Labs. The other members of the project team called this "the command center," but Jennifer disliked that name. The team was a community, not an army. Through the clear bordered floor panel, stars shown beneath her feet.

However, Jennifer gazed not down but at a row of five holoscreens. The conference room had been transformed. Gone were the long curved table and eighteen chairs. Banks of computers and consoles filled the large space, with team members moving quietly among the machines. Jennifer herself remained motionless. Only her eyes moved, flickering from screen to screen, taking them all in, missing nothing.

Screen one: the "tribal" camp in Oregon, on hidden-frequency monitor. Livers walked on the rocky Pacific beach in mid-afternoon fog, because these particular Livers always walked on this particular beach in mid-afternoon. Today, however, the heavy ugly Liver faces were clearly upset and frightened. The Livers huddled together ten feet from the surging ocean. Surrounding them, donkey reporters shouted questions. Robocams recorded.

"The newsgrids have finally discovered one of the test sites?" Eric Hulden said, walking up beside her. "Slow enough, aren't they?" Eric was one of the new ones, the few Sanctuary youngsters Jennifer and Will had added to the project in its later stages. Without stopping the back-and-forth flickering of her eyes, Jennifer smiled. Eric was tall, strong, perfect as all the Sleepless were perfect. More important, he was cold, with the coldness necessary to understand and control the world. Much colder than Will. Still, if Jennifer smiled directly at Eric, his eyes would deepen their genemod blue. He was ninety-six years her junior.

But all that could wait, until the project was over.

Screen two: newsgrids from Earth. The left side of the split screen ran the United Broadcast Network, the most reliable of the donkey channels. An announcer with the flashy genemod handsomeness of a Spanish grandee said, "In a major data-atoll coup on the Singapore Exchange, the stock of Brasilia-based Stanton Orbital Corporation rose to . . ." Nothing in the newscast mentioned a strange neuropharm altering Liver behavior. Nor did the flagging program on the right side of the screen, which constantly scanned the world's major newsgrids in several languages. So far, the project's luck was holding; Strukov's virus had not mutated on its own.

"The neuropharm is still just a local story in Oregon, then," Eric said. "Donkey fools."

"Not completely local," Jennifer said calmly. "Just underground." She gestured toward the next two screens.

Screen three: Jennifer's chief scientist, Chad Manning, gave his six-times daily summary of the progress at Kelvin-Castner on replicating Strukov's neuropharm. Kelvin-Castner was thoroughly monitored, in ways the stupid Sleepers would never detect. Chad received streams of data, which he analyzed and reduced to terms intelligible to Sleepless who weren't microbiologists. Kelvin-Castner was proceeding slowly— far too slowly to do them any good.

Screen four: the pirated monitoring of government progress. This was more problematic. The federal agencies were much better at security than corporations like Kelvin-Castner. Neither Jennifer nor her communications chief, Caroline Renleigh, was sure how complete their pirated information really was. But as far as Sanctuary could discover, the government labs at Bethesda, although they had "in protective custody" Livers infected by Strukov's virus, hadn't yet succeeded in replicating or countering it. And the FBI hadn't succeeded in establishing any solid evidence about the La Solana bombing. As far as Sanctuary could discover.

Miranda would have found out for sure.

Immediately Jennifer destroyed the thought. The thought did not exist, and never had. Her eyes flickered among the five screens.

Eric Hulden put a hand on her shoulder. "I came to tell you that Strukov linked. He wants to strike Brookhaven in an hour. Is that all right with you?"

"Fine. Call in the entire team for the viewing."

"All right, Jennifer." A part of her mind noticed how he said her name. Firmly, coldly. She liked it. But all that could wait.

Screen five: empty. It was used for communications from Jennifer's agents on Earth. They were Sleepers, informants against their own kind, highly paid and little trusted. Anything that Jennifer needed to know about came through here, instantly.

As Eric walked away, the fifth screen brightened into a formless glow. Audio only. The encryption integrity code appeared along the bottom of the screen. The transmission came from one of her agents in the United States. "Ms. Sharifi, this is Sondra Schneider. We've located Elizabeth Francy."

"Go ahead," Jennifer said composedly, but she felt her chest lift. That little Liver had been surprisingly hard to find. After Sanctuary had caught her electronic stumbling across Sanctuary's data beam from the Liver camp in Pennsylvania, the Francy girl had disappeared. Hard as it was to believe, one of the most debased class of Sleepers had apparently realized what she'd found. She knew that Sanctuary was connected somehow to the neuropharm that had infected her pathetic "tribe." Elizabeth Francy had apparently also realized that if she opened a comlink through any satellite relay or ground station, Sanctuary would locate her. She'd been off the Net, out of visible surveillance, hidden somewhere in the barbarous countryside. Jennifer had hoped she were dead.

"Elizabeth Francy is in custody of Manhattan East Enclave security," Sondra Schneider said. "She apparently made her way to New York and through an enclave ground gate. A half hour before her arrest, the gate was opened by a donkey retina scan nowhere in our data banks. I can't explain that. A 'bot from the enclave's security franchise, Patterson Protect, classed her as suspicious, and moved to sedate and capture. Our Net-wide flagging program picked up the girl's name from the routine police-net queries to other franchises."

Jennifer said swiftly, "How long ago?"

"About ten minutes. They'll give her a truth drug soon, if they haven't already. But that's off-Net, of course. We can't access."

"Do we have an agent inside Patterson Protect?"

"Unfortunately, no."

Jennifer considered. Lizzie Francy must have gone to Manhattan East in search of either Victoria Turner, her quasi-adopted mentor, or of Jackson Aranow. But why? To tell them what she'd discovered about Sanctuary's monitoring her infected tribe, of course. If the local police franchise thought her worth truthing—and they would, of course, they'd want to know how a Liver had penetrated Manhattan East—Lizzie would tell them. She'd tell them, too, about Sanctuary. But would they believe her? The drawback to truth drugs was that if the subject believed that lies were truth, lies were what the drug elicited. Would the Sleepers believe that Elizabeth Francy was deluded?

Perhaps not. Especially if Jackson Aranow supported the Liver girl's assertions.

Damn it, it was less than an hour until Strukov's most important test!

Jennifer stood very still, appalled at herself. She didn't have such flashes of anger. They were unproductive, weakening. Jennifer Sharifi didn't become angry. She became cold, and hence effective.

The moment of anger had never happened.

"Ms. Schneider," she said calmly, "I'll take care of this. Pull all of our agents out of Manhattan East, unobtrusively, during the next forty-five minutes. Make sure they understand that they must leave immediately. I'll take care of the rest." Strukov could go ahead with the Brookhaven test, but Jennifer would instruct him to change the second target to Manhattan East. That would take care of the problem of Elizabeth Francy.

"Understood," Sondra Schneider said. The fifth screen blanked. Jennifer's eyes flickered regularly among the other four.

Livers on the Pacific beach, huddled in fear against donkey reporters . . .

The UBN newsgrid and Net-grid flagging programs, both ignorant of the inhibiting neuropharm . . .

Streams of data from Kelvin-Castner—data accumulating too slowly to unravel the tangled skeins of Strukov's molecules . . .

Frustrated investigative reports from the FBI on the nuclear explosion at La Solana . . .

Miranda's cold face on screen five . . .

Jennifer's body jerked in shock. There was nothing on screen five. There had been nothing since Sondra Schneider blanked. Miranda was dead. Her image had never existed.

"There you are," Will Sandaleros said. "Jenny, look at this."

She looked at Will instead. His face was flushed with excitement. He held out to her a portable terminal, with a CAD model of a 'bot on it.

"The Peruvian delivery drone. The bastards finally released the detailed design to us, which contractually they were supposed to do weeks ago. It's somewhat interesting. It—"

"I've already seen it," Jennifer said. "Weeks ago."

"They showed it to you? The detailed version? And you didn't tell me?"

Jennifer merely stared at him. Now his face, moments ago flushed from what he considered his triumph over the Peruvian contractors, paled at what he considered his betrayal by her. More and more, Will was absorbed by these petty power struggles. He got upset over them, he compromised his objectivity and his effectiveness. He lost sight of the project's overwhelming, sacred mission.

"Excuse me, Will, I have things to attend to. Strukov launches in less than an hour."

"You knew I wanted the drone design, that I've been badgering those sons of bitches—"

"A Sleepless does not 'badger,' Will." Jennifer saw Eric Hulden, across the room, watching them.

"But you knew—"

"Please excuse me."

Will's hand tightened on his terminal. "All right, Jenny. But after today's tests, you and I are going to have some personal discussion."

"Yes, Will. We are. But after the tests." She walked gracefully away from him.

The rest of the team arrived in the conference room in ones or twos. The mood was quiet, subdued. This was too important for hilarity, or for the kind of irresponsible heat that Will showed. This was the culmination of Jennifer's life.

She was finally going to make Sanctuary truly safe for Sleepless.

They had been despised, persecuted, resented, harassed, and even killed (always, always, she remembered Tony Indivino) for over a hundred years. The Sleepers hated her people because Sleepless were smarter, calmer, more successful. Better. The next step in human evolution. So the losing species had tried to render the Sleepless impotent in the world. Only Jennifer Sharifi and Tony Indivino had seen coming that inevitable long-term warfare. Now only Jennifer was left to make her people safe against the enemy's so much greater numbers.

When all members of the project team had gathered, Jennifer moved among them, murmuring words of thanks, praise, encouragement. Strong, competent, cold people. The most effective and loyal in the solar system.

Jennifer had chosen not to make any sort of speech. Let the event speak, eloquently, for itself. Evidently Strukov had made the same choice. Without preamble, the main wall screen brightened as the cam mounted on the Peruvians' drone activated itself.

Below their feet, through Sanctuary's clear floor panel, Earth drifted into view.

The drone flew low and leisurely over Long Island, New York.

Slowly the dome of Brookhaven Enclave grew in the distance, dominating the new spring grass, abandoned roads, and wrecked Liver towns of Long Island. The drone angled upward and now Jennifer could see inside the enclave dome. Simple, gracefully proportioned buildings. Houses. Shopping complexes. Entertainment areas. Government buildings. And Brookhaven National Laboratories.

Brookhaven was the ideal site for the first high-security test of Strukov's virus. Small enough (as Taylor Air Force Base would not have been), isolated enough (as the Pentagon would not have been), secretive enough (as the Washington Mall Enclave would not have been). And because of the Brookhaven National Laboratories, shielded as completely as any government installation anywhere. If Strukov's drone could penetrate Brookhaven's Y-shields, it could penetrate anyone's.

Except the one that had shielded La Solana . . . Jennifer destroyed the thought.

The drone flew through Brookhaven's triple Y-shield as if it weren't there. The drone burst into speed and zoomed to just under the top of the inner dome, and the picture disappeared.

"It's in," Chad Manning breathed. "We're in."

"Drone disintegrated," Caroline Renleigh said. "Brookhaven is of course equipped for biological warfare. There have to be security systems signaling, tracking, aiming . . . How did the Peruvians even—"

"Response signals might have been electronically delayed at their sources," David O'Donnell reported from his security console.

The screen brightened again. This time the picture was jumpy, distorted; Jennifer realized it represented microsecond intrusions into the Brookhaven security computers themselves, time-sharing the Brookhaven monitors in noncontinuous bursts to better evade detection. There was no sound. The screen split. The top showed grim security specialists at banks of machinery. The bottom displayed data taken from the enclave computer.

"They know they've been penetrated," Will said, standing behind her. "They know there might be a biological agent . . . they're sealing the labs . . ."

"Too late," Jennifer said, studying the data on the bottom half of the screen. "At least, for everybody not sealed in when it struck."

Will exulted, "We can afford to have a few escape infection. It isn't like they're going to be able to detect what hit them." His mood had changed. If she turned around, she'd see Will excited, arms twitching and eyes shining. She didn't turn around.

The printed data on the bottom half of the screen said:

> STATUS SUMMARY: OUTSIDE PENETRATION TYPE 7C
> BROOKHAVEN MECHANICALLY SEALED RF-765
> AIR SAMPLES TAKEN FOR ANALYSIS—PROGRAM 5B
> MEDICAL ALERT RECOMMENDED

"Won't do them any good," Will said, chuckling.

Jennifer kept her face immobile. Will tended to underestimate the enemy. There were some quite good people at Brookhaven, for Sleepers. Not as good as the Peruvians, but still competent. Sydney Goldsmith, Marianne Hansten, Ching Chung Wang, John Becker. Unlike the pathetic Liver test sites, the Brookhaven team would easily locate the unbreathed virus in their automatic air samples, even with its low concentration and short half-life. They would bond it with a radioactive marker and have lab animals breathe it in. The gas would enter the bloodstream and circulate for a few minutes before being both lost in the breath and destroyed by the Cell Cleaner.

Before that happened, the parts of the brain most active at that particular time would receive the greatest blood supply. The marker would clearly pinpoint the amygdalae. Then the researchers would switch to both brain scans and cellular tests. They would launch a dogged examination of Strukov's long and twisted skein of cerebral events.

But long before the Brookhaven researchers could unravel that skein, they would no longer want to. The newness of the research would make them vaguely uneasy. It wasn't familiar enough. Anxiety would fill them whenever they thought about the novelty of the situation. For a while they might fight the anxiety, but then it would grow. The Brookhaven researchers—and, eventually, all of the domed enclaves in the United States—would choose the known over the unknown. It would just feel too unsettling to mobilize for any new research effort.

And then Jennifer Sharifi and the rest of the Sleepless really would be safe.

Will was pouring champagne. Jennifer never drank—it made her feel in less than perfectly cold control—but this time she couldn't stay outside the circle of her people. They'd done it. They were safe.

She raised her glass. The room quieted. In her calm, low-pitched voice Jennifer said, "Thanks to the efforts of everyone in this room, we have finally won. The Sleepers have had their own biochemistry turned against them. In the next hour, drones will penetrate the Pentagon, Washington Mall, Kennedy Spaceport, and Manhattan East enclaves. No Sleeper will die. But no one will ever be able to threaten us again, except in those ways we already understand and can counter. We will be in control, if only because there will never again be any unknown devils unleashed against us. Let us therefore drink to the devil we know."

Laughter. Drained glasses. And then Strukov's face appeared on the main screen.

"Ms. Sharifi. You and your people, without doubt, now celebrate the successful penetration of the Brookhaven. I, too, am pleased; I was very eager to see if we could accomplish this. But I cannot permit—"

"Oh, my God!" David O'Donnell said from the security console. "Launch. Code sixteen A. Repeat, *launch.*"

"—you to continue with this project. I, too, am a Sleeper, of course. And although I feel no loyalty to my own kind, I am, naturally, as self-protective as they. Or as you. So—"

Brilliant light exploded under their feet, somewhere between the floor panel and the rotating planet thousands of miles below.

"Sanctuary's countermissile array destroyed," said David O'Donnell. "Launching backup."

"—so no more of the Peruvian drones will fire themselves. And since we both know from the experience of La Solana that only the nuclear can destroy completely, I fear it is the nuclear I myself am forced to use. Do you know La Rochefoucauld on superiority? *'Le vrai moyen d'être trompé . . .'*"

Safe, Jennifer thought numbly. *I thought we were finally safe.*

"'. . . c'est de se croire plus fin que les autres.'"

"Countermissile array number two destroyed," David O'Donnell choked out.

Jennifer took a step forward. She thought for an uncontrolled moment that Strukov's face on the wall screen had been replaced by Miranda's.

Sanctuary orbital exploded in a burst of brilliant lethal light.

Twenty-one

Lizzie woke in a small bare room, no more than eight feet by four feet, with windowless foamcast walls. Three walls. She sat up on the bed, which was only a platform jutting from the wall, and looked for the missing wall. A woman sat on a chair, facing her. Behind the woman, who wore a blue uniform, stretched a featureless corridor.

"Hello," the woman said. She was beautiful like Vicki was beautiful: genemod. Black, black hair, brown eyes, skin like clean snow. The fourth wall, Lizzie realized, was a Y-shield.

"You're in Manhattan East Security Headquarters, Patterson Protect Corporation, legal franchisee. I'm Officer Foster. You're Elizabeth Francy, and you were picked up for breaking and entering, criminal trespass. Would you like to tell me how you penetrated the enclave?"

Lizzie patted the outside of her pocket. The purple eyeball was gone, which meant Officer Foster already knew how she'd gotten in. Lizzie stared silently.

"Ms. Francy, you don't seem to understand. Manhattan East is private property. Patterson Protect is fully authorized to deal with intra-enclave police matters. We also can involve the New York Police Department—if we choose to do so. Criminal trespass is a felony charge. And murder is a capital crime." She held up Tish's eyeball. "Patterson Protect can—and will—use truth drugs, as authorized under the law."

"I didn't murder anyone! And I need, me, to see someone in here. Dr. Jackson Aranow. To tell him something important!"

"Dr. Jackson Aranow," the cop said, and sat silent. Lizzie guessed a system was speaking information into her ear mike. After a moment, she said, "Why do you—"

The door somewhere in the corridor behind her flung open. Running feet. A boy appeared, no more than fourteen, dressed in the same uniform, "INTERN" blazoned across the collar. His face showed excited shock. "Officer Foster! Come quick, the newsgrid—"

"Daniel," the cop said tonelessly.

"—says that—"

"Daniel."

"—somebody blew up Sanctuary with a nuclear bomb!"

Slowly Officer Foster rose. She followed the boy down the corridor, but not before Lizzie had seen her parade of successive expressions: shock, calculation, pleasure.

Blew up Sanctuary.

Lizzie leaped off the sleeping platform. Her legs didn't falter; whatever neuropharm the security 'bot had used didn't leave lingering effects. She ran her hands over the Y-shield that formed the fourth wall of the cell. No openings. No machinery on this side of the shield. No way out.

Blew up Sanctuary. Who? Why? With all the Sleepless inside? It might have been Miranda Sharifi, at war with her grandmother . . . but why now? Could it somehow be connected with the fear neuropharm?

None of it made any sense.

And Lizzie was tired of trying to figure it out. Tired, angry, scared. Of walking to New York to find Vicki and Dr. Aranow. Of being attacked by Livers and donkeys and 'bots. Of being threatened with arrest for murder. Even of datadipping. She was a *mother*. She belonged home with her baby. And as soon as she found Vicki, or Dr. Aranow, or *anybody* to turn this mess over to, that's exactly where she was going.

"Hey!" Lizzie yelled, experimentally. No one answered. Officer Foster didn't return.

Lizzie started in on the standard spoken codes, to see if she could get any sort of building system to respond to her. Nothing happened.

She settled in to wait.

An hour passed. Wasn't anybody going to come back to question her? Wasn't anybody left in New York? What if whoever blew up Sanctuary sent a bomb to Manhattan East . . . well, then she'd never know about it before she was dead. But what if somebody had set off the fear neuropharm here? Would the cops just go home and stay there, afraid of anything new, leaving Lizzie in her cell just to rot?

Everything in here was synthetic. Nothing was consumable.

But there had to be a 'bot to bring something to feed on. And water. And a place to piss . . . She spied the hole in the floor.

Another hour dragged by. Lizzie tried to think carefully, to plan. All right, if no one came and nothing happened by the time she counted to a hundred . . . all right, two hundred.

Time up.

"Uhhhuhhhhuhhh!" Lizzie shrieked. She grabbed a few nose hairs in her right nostril and yanked. It hurt tremendously. Immediately mucus flowed from her nose, her heart began to pound, and she could feel the color rise in her face. She yanked more nose hairs, tears streaming from her eyes and snot from her nose. Then she began to breathe in quick shallow pants, until she started to hyperventilate. She threw herself on the narrow foamcast floor.

"Medical assistance required," the cell said. "Abnormal respiratory pattern. Blood pressure abruptly elevated by forty points over thirty, heart rate one-thirty, brain scan shows—"

A medunit floated through the Y-shield. It was a kind she'd never seen before, even back when Liver towns *had* medunits. A small arm with a patch shot out toward her: another tranq. Lizzie leaped onto the sleeping platform, grabbed the medunit, and yanked it up with her, upending it and hoping to hell that she was holding it so that no 'bot arms could reach her. And that the alarm it was undoubtedly sending to the building system had no people around to answer it.

"Open medical comlink!" she yelled at it, and recited Dr. Aranow's AMA code, just as she'd dipped it from his personal system. God, it had to open! The thing was a medunit, wasn't it? It had to be linked to official records.

"Official medical link open," a female voice said calmly. "Recording. Go ahead. Dr. Aranow."

"Link me with my home system!"

"This unit is not equipped to do that. You have opened an official medical link recording channel. Please proceed."

"Fucking damn!" Lizzie yelled. What if the unit activated physical defenses? She started to reel off the security overrides she'd dipped on various government systems, all of them, hoping one would open the channel that she knew was possible, *must* be possible, even official donkey links always had back doors to allow the system to be used for something besides what it was designed for . . .

"Link opened," the female voice said, and a moment later a male voice: "Yes, Dr. Aranow?"

Jones. Dr. Aranow's house system. Lizzie took a deep breath to calm herself.

"Jones, please tell Dr. Aranow he has an emergency call from Lizzie Francy." She continued to hold the medunit as far away from her body as she could, even though it had stopped trying to slap her with a tranq patch. *"Ms.* Lizzie Francy."

"Dr. Aranow is not currently available. Would you like to record a message?"

"No! Don't . . . I mean, I need him, me! Link with his personal system!"

"I'm sorry, this system cannot do that on outside orders. Would you like to record a message?"

She didn't have a high-priority link, and this patch-pushing 'bot wouldn't have the ability to create one. Now what?

"Please respond in the next fifteen seconds. Would you like to record a message?"

"No!" Lizzie said desperately. "Let me talk to the doctor's sister!"

"Just a moment, please."

And then a weak, frightened voice, "Hello?"

"Ms. Aranow!" Suddenly Lizzie couldn't remember Jackson's sister's name. She could see her, slim and elegant in her flowered dress, holding Dirk in her arms, tears running down her pale terrified face. Lizzie could even remember the sister's personal system's name—"Thomas"—and, of course, all the access codes. But she couldn't think of the donkey girl's first name. "Ms. Aranow, this is Lizzie Francy, Dr. Aranow's . . . friend. With the baby. I'm in jail in Manhattan East Enclave! Please tell Dr. Aranow and Vicki Turner right away to come get me, it's an emergency!"

"In . . . jail? With . . . with the *baby?"* Ms. Aranow started to say.

The medunit suddenly started to push toward her, some sort of time-delayed follow-through, the 'bot arm again snaked out with a tranq patch . . . "Tell the doctor! Tell Vicki! Come get—"

The medunit bucked with a sudden urge of energy. The patch connected with Lizzie's wrist. Immediately blackness took her; she didn't even see the medunit float out of her grasp to hover beside her body, slumped half on the platform and half off.

Theresa lay trembling in her bed. That Liver girl was in jail. With her *baby.*

She saw, as clearly as if she gazed at the walls of her study and not of her rose-pink bedroom, the newsgrid holos of Liver babies, crippled and crumpled and starving and dying . . .

No. She was being ridiculous. Lizzie's baby wasn't dying. That baby was Changed. But the little thing was in jail, in a cell someplace, and *something* had happened to its mother to cut off the comlink like that. Had somebody hurt Lizzie Francy? And the baby?

Theresa had never seen a jail. But she'd watched history holos, and movies. Jails in those were filthy, horrible cells that smelled bad and held dangerous people who hurt other people. But surely jails weren't like that anymore? The cleaning 'bots wouldn't let them stay filthy. But the rest . . .

She sat up against her pillows. The sores on her hands and body had closed up. She could eat, and talk, and even walk a little, with crutches. She'd had a floater, but Jackson had sent it back because, he said, using the floater didn't help rebuild her muscles. Twice a day the nursing 'bot coached Theresa through the physical rehabilitation software. But getting up was an effort, and feeling her hairless head made her cry. Jackson had removed all mirrors from her rooms. Much of the time, Theresa lay in bed and spoke notes, hours of obsessive notes, to Thomas. About Leisha Camden. About the Sleepless. About Miranda Sharifi.

She spoke to her system now. "Thomas, have Jones place an emergency call to my brother at Kelvin-Castner!"

"Of course I will, Theresa."

But it was Cazie, scowling and rumpled, who answered her call. "Tess? What's wrong? Why the emergency call?"

"I need to speak to Jackson."

"So you said. But why?" Cazie drummed her fingers on an unseen table. Her black hair needed combing, and there were smudges under her eyes. She looked distracted and upset. Theresa shrank back against her pillows.

"It's . . . private."

"Private? Are you all right?"

"Yes . . . I'm . . . yes. It's about somebody else."

Cazie's gaze suddenly focused sharply. "Who else? Did a message come for Jackson? This isn't about Sanctuary, is it?"

"Sanctuary? Why would Jackson get a message about Sanctuary?"

Cazie's gaze veiled again. "Nothing. So who's the message from?"

"What about Sanctuary?"

"Nothing, Tessie. Listen, I didn't mean to snap at you, when you're so sick. Go back to sleep, pet. Jackson's in the middle of an important meeting here and I don't want to interrupt him, but I'll tell him you called. Unless there's something important you want to tell me, so I can pass it on to him?"

Theresa looked into Cazie's eyes. Cazie was lying to her. Theresa knew it—how? She didn't know. Yes, she did. Theresa had pretended to be Cazie, and now she could tell when Cazie was pretending. A shift in her voice, a look in her golden eyes . . . Jackson was not in a meeting. Which meant Cazie was keeping Theresa away from Jackson. As well as away from something about Sanctuary. And Cazie had never liked Jackson's helping that girl Lizzie and her baby . . .

"N-no," she faltered. "Nothing . . . important. Just a message from . . . from Brett Carpenter. That man that Jackson plays tennis with. About a match."

"But you said it was an 'emergency.' "

"I . . . I guess I just wanted to talk to Jackson. I'm kind of lonely."

Cazie's face softened. "Of course you are, Tessie. I'll have Jackson call you the minute this meeting is over. And I'll come by tonight to see you. I promise."

"All right. Thank you."

"Now you rest like a good girl and get all better." The link blanked.

"Thomas," Theresa said. "Newsgrid flag, last twenty-four hours. Anything on Sanctuary."

She didn't need the flag. The screen lit up with current news, and Theresa watched the holo of Sanctuary blowing up, listened to the shocked newscaster, saw the simulation of the missile's path, heard President Garrison's angry denunciation of the nuclear terrorists who had not yet named themselves.

"Repeat," Theresa said to Thomas, even though the word came out a choked whisper and the salt tears hurt her radiation-burned skin. The newsholo repeated.

So they were all dead. Miranda Sharifi—dead at La Solana, along with all the strange and inhuman Supers who had changed humanity into something different. Jennifer Sharifi—dead on Sanctuary, along with her brilliant, powerful people who controlled so much of the world's money in ways Theresa had never understood. Leisha Camden—dead seven years ago in a Georgia swamp. All dead. All the people genemod for never having to sleep, all the people who, Jackson said, were once supposed to be the next step in evolution. All dead.

But Lizzie Francy and her baby were alive. In jail in Manhattan East Enclave. *Tell the doctor! Tell Vicki! Come get—*

Theresa couldn't do it. She was too weak, too frightened.

Please tell Dr. Aranow and Vicki Turner right away to come get me, it's an emergency!

She could do it if she became Cazie.

Theresa closed her eyes. The tears stopped. Jackson had no idea—nobody did—how often in the last month Theresa had become Cazie.

Lying in bed, hurting even through the painkillers, struggling to push herself through the physical rehabilitation program, making herself think about the explosion at La Solana without panic and seizure—Theresa had practiced being Cazie. Being someone who was not afraid, who was able to decide what she had to do and then do it.

She became Cazie now.

Gradually Theresa's breathing slowed. Her hands stopped trembling. More important, she could feel the difference in her head. Like a newsgrid changing channels, almost. Her *brain* felt different. Could that be? But it was how she felt.

Theresa swung her legs to the floor and reached for her crutches. The nursing 'bot floated to her bedside. "Do you need help, Ms. Aranow? Would you prefer a bedpan?"

"No. Deactivate," Theresa said, and the part of her that was still Theresa—there was such a part, only if she thought too much about that she'd lose the part that wasn't—heard the decisiveness in her tone. Cazie's tone. In Theresa's still-hoarse voice.

Don't think about it.

She struggled out of her nightgown and into a dress. It hung on her thin body. Shoes, jacket. In the foyer she caught a glimpse of herself in a mirror.

No. Oh, God, no . . . that bald head, her? Sunken eyes, burned scabbed skin stretched over the skull . . . her? The tears started again.

No. Cazie wouldn't cry. Cazie would know it was only temporary, she was getting better, Jackson said so . . . Cazie would wear a hat. Theresa took one of Jackson's and jammed it down over her ears.

"Manhattan East jail, look up the coordinates," she told the go-'bot that the building had called for her; she tried to scowl like Cazie. She'd had to wait for the go-'bot for nearly fifteen minutes. But she'd stayed Cazie the whole time.

"Yes, Ms. Aranow," the go-'bot said. Theresa opaqued the windows and closed her eyes, to avoid glimpsing herself in window reflections.

The go-'bot left her in front of a building near the enclave shield's east wall. A few people hurrying by stopped on the sidewalk and stared at her. Theresa ignored them. Chin high, hands clasped tightly together, she told the retina scanner in the deserted atrium, "I'm Theresa Aranow. I'm here to see a . . . a prisoner. Lizzie Francy. Or whoever is in charge here."

"You're not registered as an attorney, Ms. Aranow," the building said. "Or as a close relative of the prisoner."

"No, I'm . . . can I talk to a human, please?"

"I'm sorry, we're in an emergency state just now. All Patterson Protect personnel have been deployed elsewhere. Would you care to wait?"

An emergency state. Of course. The attack on Sanctuary . . . people must be afraid the next bomb could fall on New York. If she hadn't opaqued the go-'bot window, she would probably have seen people streaming out of the enclave by air. No wonder her building had taken so long to get her a go-'bot. And maybe the startled-looking people outside hadn't been startled by her weird looks after all, but by their own fear. This bolstered her.

"I don't want to wait," she said. "I want to take Lizzie Francy out of here. What do I have to do for that?"

"Are you requesting Public Records?"

"Yes." Was she? Why not?

"This is Public Records," a different system said. "How may I help you?"

"I want . . . I want to take Lizzie Francy home. With me."

"Francy, Elizabeth, citizen ID CLM-03-9645-957," the system recited. "Apprehended 4:45 P.M. May 18, 2121, at 349 East 96th Street by Patterson Protect security 'bot serial number 45296, licensed to Manhattan East Enclave for official operation within the enclave dome. Placed under enclave detention, Patterson Protect franchise headquarters, 5:01 P.M., detaining personnel, Officer Karen Ellen Foster. Grounds filed for detention: breaking and entering, criminal trespass. Current legal status: enclave action only, NYPD not notified. Current detainee status: in custody, alert, no registered attorney."

Theresa repeated stubbornly, because she didn't know what else to do, "I want to take her home."

"Detainee has not been placed under NYPD arrest. Patterson Protect does not have extended detention rights without NYPD notification. No notification has been filed for Francy, Elizabeth, citizen ID CLM-03-9645-957. However, arrested person does not have authorization to remain within Manhattan East Enclave unless she is under the recognizance of a registered resident."

"She's my . . . guest." Was that good enough? Cazie would think it was good enough. Theresa said, more firmly, "My guest. Mine. Theresa Aranow."

"Let the record read that in the absence of Patterson Protect notification of charges to NYPD, detainee Elizabeth Francy, citizen ID CLM-03-9645-957, has been released under the recognizance of Theresa Katherine Aranow, citizen ID CGC-02-8736-341. Thank you for your patronage of Patterson Protect."

Theresa suddenly panicked. "And the baby! Let me take the baby home, too, Lizzie's baby, I forget his name . . . the baby!"

The system did not respond.

Theresa closed her eyes, fighting for control. Cazie would not panic. Cazie would wait and see if Lizzie came out of one of these doors carrying the baby. Cazie would wait, and then decide what to do next . . . *She was Cazie.*

"Ms. Aranow?" Lizzie said. *"Theresa?"*

Theresa opened her eyes. Lizzie stood there, without the baby. She stared at Theresa from wide shocked eyes, and Theresa remembered how she must look. She said, "Where's . . . where's the baby?"

"Baby? My baby, you mean? Home with my mother, him. Why?"

"I thought—"

"What *happened* to you?"

And at that, Theresa crumpled. She wasn't Cazie. Now that someone else was here, someone stronger . . . now that Lizzie had reminded Theresa of how she looked . . . now that she'd succeeded in getting Lizzie out . . . she wasn't Cazie anymore. She was Theresa Aranow, and she could feel her breathing start to go ragged and could watch her scrawny arm clutch at the disheveled Liver girl who for all Theresa knew might be the only other human left in an enclave about to be hit by a nuclear bomb. Theresa moaned.

"No, don't do that here," Lizzie said from far away. "God, it's just like Shockey, isn't it? And you never even breathed a neuropharm . . . come on, don't fall, lean on me . . . no, wait, I need my terminal back—building system! I want the backpack, me, that I come in here with!"

Theresa's weakened legs gave way. Her crutches clattered to the floor, and she with them. Later—how much?—she felt herself half dragged, half carried, outside. Dumped into a go-'bot. Held firmly around the shoulders.

"Come on, girl, it's all right. Come on, girl," Lizzie was saying, over and over. "Don't be like this, you. You can't be like this, I need you!"

I need you. It got through to her. *I need you.* Like people needed Cazie, like people needed Jackson . . . but not Theresa. People never needed Theresa because she was always the one doing the needing.

Not this time.

She concentrated on once more being Cazie. Her breathing slowed, the streets came back into focus, her fingers unclutched Lizzie. The *click* went on in her brain.

Lizzie was staring at her. "How did you do that?"

"I can't . . . explain."

"Well, don't then, you. We have more important things. Where can you make this thing go so we can talk?"

"Home!"

"No. Probably monitored. What's all that woods?"

"Central Park. But we can't—"

" 'Bot," Lizzie said, "go into Central Park and stop someplace private. With a lot of trees, and no people within a hundred yards."

The go-'bot whizzed through the streets of the enclave, entered the park, and stopped under a huge maple near the East Green. With one hand Lizzie dragged Theresa away from the go-'bot. With the other she carried a purple backpack, which she opened on the grass to pull out a terminal. The go-'bot whizzed off.

"I wanted it to wait!" Lizzie said. "Oh, never mind, we'll call another one. I have to find Dr. Aranow right away, I'll have to take the risk of a call—"

"Jackson's at Kelvin-Castner," Theresa said. She wrapped her arms around herself; her wasted body felt cold and exhausted. "But you can't reach him. Cazie's intercepting his calls, even emergency ones. She didn't want me to know, but . . . but Sanctuary was bombed and destroyed."

Lizzie didn't answer. She didn't look surprised. But then she said slowly, "Are you sure?"

"Yes." Theresa felt the tears start again. "I saw . . . the news-grids."

"Who did it?"

Theresa could only shake her head.

Lizzie demanded, "Why are *you* crying? There were only Sleepless on Sanctuary, right?"

"Leisha . . . Miranda . . ."

"Miranda Sharifi's on the moon. At Selene. And who's Leisha? Never mind, let me think, you."

Lizzie sat over her unactivated terminal, silent. Theresa fought for control of herself. She was Cazie . . . she was Cazie . . . no, she wasn't. She was Theresa Aranow, sick and weak and exposed in Central Park, and she wanted passionately to go home and go to sleep.

Lizzie said slowly, "Sanctuary made the fear neuropharm that infected my baby. And my mother, and Billy, and . . . all of them. At least, I think it was Sanctuary. They were monitoring my tribe afterward, with heavily encrypted and shielded data streams, and I don't know how they'd even know we were infected if they hadn't done it.

Only . . . only if they're all dead, all the Sleepless . . . God, Theresa, don't cave in now, you!"

"I want . . . to go home."

"No, we can't. I have to find Dr. Aranow. If we can't call him, we'll have to go there, us . . . Look, I'll call a go-'bot on my terminal. Just hang on."

Theresa didn't. But she didn't panic, either; she was too exhausted, clear down to her weakened bones. She tried to tell Lizzie that a go-'bot wouldn't take them to Kelvin-Castner in Boston because the go-'bots couldn't leave the enclave, but she was too exhausted to form the words. The last thing she remembered was falling asleep on the grass in Central Park, genemod and fragrant, while she wept wearily for the Sleepless, who were all gone and would never come again.

Twenty-two

Jackson sat in the atrium of Kelvin-Castner on a white marble bench, surrounded by white marble columns, a decorative pool filled with milky white water, and his lawyer. The surface of the white water was occasionally broken by darting silver fish, genemod and shining. The white columns were subtly laced with silver threads. The last time Jackson had sat here, the lobby had been all paisley double helixes. Somebody had reprogrammed.

Jackson's lawyer, in severe black business coat buttoned to his chin, was costing TenTech triple legal fees for "immediate, exclusive, and overriding service." Jackson had summoned him from Manhattan's best law firm an hour before, causing several other cases to be postponed. For this situation, Jackson didn't want a TenTech lawyer. Who might have slept with Cazie.

"They can't keep us waiting out here indefinitely, can they?" he demanded.

"No," said Evan Matthew Winterton, of Cisneros, Linville, Winterton and Adkins. He was genemod for a certain kind of eighteenth-century handsomeness: long bony aristocratic face, sharp deepset eyes, delicate long fingers with tensile strength. Winterton flicked through a handheld terminal in write mode. "Contractually, you have guaranteed physical access to the premises as well as the data. Not, however, to the person of Alex Castner. He doesn't have to see you."

"But Thurmond Rogers does."

"Yes. Although the wording here in section five paragraph four is ambiguous on a few points . . . Why didn't you come to me in the first place, to have this drawn up?"

"I didn't know I'd need you. Or anyone like you. I trusted Kelvin-Castner to do what they said they'd do."

The lawyer just looked at him.

"All right, I was a fool," Jackson said, and hoped the building was recording. Let Cazie and Rogers know that he knew it. "I won't be a fool again. Which is why I've hired a systems expert on the same basis as you."

"You can have a systems expert," Winterton said, with the patience of someone who's already said it several times. "A systems expert to write flagging, data-organization, and data-summary algorithms. What you can't have is a systems expert to dip private corporate records, unless you have sufficient evidence for a court order that Kelvin-Castner is in violation of contract. I've already explained, Jackson, that you don't have such evidence."

No. All he had was the look in Cazie's eyes, to which years of watching had attuned him as sensitively as a brain scan. Not the sort of thing that led to a court order. It led only to truth.

"However," Winterton continued, in his pedantic style that Jackson suspected covered the instincts of a killer shark, "if your professional examination of the data offered, plus that of the systems expert, shows sufficient cause to suspect that Kelvin-Castner is not complying with contractual promises of disclosure, then a *subpoena duces tecum* is certainly possible."

So Winterton, too, expected the building to be recording. He was warning Castner.

The wall brightened and a holo of Thurmond Rogers appeared, smiling warmly. "Jackson! I'm so glad you finally dropped by to see our progress personally!"

"No, I don't think you will be," Jackson said. "This is my lawyer, Evan Winterton. A systems expert is en route from New York, along with two medical consultants. We're going to be going very carefully over your data, Thurmond, to be sure you're in contractual compliance."

Rogers's smile didn't waver. "Certainly, Jackson. Standard procedure when there's this much at stake, isn't it? You're more than welcome."

"Then let us in."

"Now, Jackson, this is a level-four biohazard facility. The air is sealed, you know that, and we have U.S. Installation A decontamination procedures. No researcher has left the building since the start of the project. Once in, you're in. But Alex Castner has authorized complete terminal facilities for you in the unsealed portion of Kelvin-Castner. The rooms are quite comfortable. So if you'll just follow my holo—"

"No," Jackson said. "My team will use the comfortable facilities, but I'm coming inside. To the labs."

Thurmond's face turned grave. "Jackson, that's not advisable. Particularly with your sister so sick and susceptible to infection. She's not Changed, is she? Cazie told me. Although the neuropharm isn't transmissible in its current form, there's no guarantee that a version might not mutate, or even be deliberately created, that is transmissible by direct contact."

"I'm coming in," Jackson said. "It's in my contract."

"Then I can't stop you," Rogers said, and from the lack of hesitation Jackson knew that this had been discussed before he even arrived. *If he insists, legally we have to admit him,* someone had decided: Castner or K-C counsel or even judicial-probability software. "But of course you'll have to go through decontamination procedures, and quarantine before you can leave again. If you'll both follow the holo, I'll conduct you each to the appropriate corridor for—"

The holo froze.

At the same moment, Winterton's comlink shrilled. "Code One call, Mr. Winterton. Repeat, Code One call . . ."

Winterton said, "Go ahead. By cable, please." Only then did Jackson notice the thin, insulated wire running discreetly from the collar of Winterton's coat to his left ear. His law firm's Code One calls must come in heavily encrypted. But once the remote in his pocket had unscrambled them, the data was vulnerable to field interception. Unless it traveled to his brain not in any radiated form but by old-fashioned insulated cable. Sometimes, Jackson reflected coldly, the old-fashioned method was the best. Such as visually inspecting K-C's experiments for himself.

Evan Winterton's long aristocratic face suddenly trembled. The deepset eyes widened, then closed. Jackson understood that he was looking at an extreme emotional reaction. Thurmond Rogers's frozen holo abruptly vanished.

"What is it?" Jackson said. "What's happened?"

Winterton took a moment to answer. His voice sounded scraped. "Someone has blown up Sanctuary."

"Sanctuary?"

"Nuclear. From the outside, missile trajectory originating in Africa. The President has declared a national alert." Winterton stood up, took a pointless step forward, and began flicking rapidly through his remote, still listening to the ear implant. Jackson tried to take it in. Sanctuary gone. And La Solana as well. All the Sleepless, or pretty close to it . . . but only Theresa and Vicki and he knew that. The rest of the world thought Miranda Sharifi was safe at Selene Base.

"Who . . . ?"

"Doesn't matter," Winterton said, and Jackson saw that to him, it didn't. Cisneros, Linville, Winterton and Adkins must have many clients who dealt, directly or indirectly, with Sanctuary. Jennifer Sharifi's tangle of corporations, lobbyists, investors, holding companies, and data-atoll activities would of course need a legion of lawyers, both Sleepless and, as blinds, Sleepers. Every financial institution in the world would react to the massacre at Sanctuary. The legal implications would take decades to unravel.

The Livers didn't have decades. Not if the neuropharm spread.

"I'm sorry, Jackson, I have to leave," Winterton said. "Urgent business at my firm."

"I've retained you!" Jackson said. "You're obligated to stay until we—"

"I'm sorry, but I am not," Winterton said. "As yet we have nothing in writing. If it weren't for the overriding need at my firm . . . but surely you see that this changes everything. *Sanctuary* is destroyed."

Not even Evan Matthew Winterton, Jackson noted as the lawyer left, could keep the note of awe from his voice.

Jackson stared into the atrium pool, with its clouded white water. The silver fish darted and leaped ceaselessly. Their metabolism must be genetically accelerated, to keep up that activity level. He wondered what they ate.

Sanctuary is destroyed. This changes everything. And, in Vicki's voice, *It's up to you, Jackson.*

He didn't want it to be up to him. He was one individual, not particularly effective in the world, and his professional training had only underscored his belief that no one individual made much difference. Science argued against it. Evolution was never interested in the individual, only in the survival of the species. Brain chemistry shaped the individual's choice of actions, no matter how much that person might believe in free will. Even the great scientific discoveries, if they had not been made by the men and women who made them, would eventually have been discovered by somebody else. When the slow accretion of tiny bits of knowledge reached critical mass, then you got steamships, or relativity, or Y-energy. The individual wasn't really important for radical change. Perhaps a Miranda Sharifi was the exception—but Miranda Sharifi had not been human. And there were no more like Miranda Sharifi left.

And Jackson didn't *want* this. He wanted to live quietly with Theresa, and to be able to love Cazie again, and to practice medicine, conventional medicine, the kind he'd been trained for before these Sleepless started remaking the world. As it happened, he couldn't have any of those things, but they were nonetheless what he wanted.

Or did he?

If he had wanted to practice conventional medicine, he could have joined Doctors for Human Aid, left his comfortable enclave, and practiced among the Liver children dying for want of medical care. If he had really wanted Cazie back, he wouldn't have opposed her on TenTech's role in adapting the neuropharm delivery targets. If he had wanted to live quietly with Theresa, why wasn't he there now, doing that, in their apartment overlooking the carefully guarded Eden of Central Park?

Welcome to personal evolution.

He stood. The silver fish continued to cavort frantically in their white pool. Probably their genemod metabolism didn't permit them to stop.

"Building," Jackson said, "tell security I'm ready to begin decontamination for the sealed biohazard labs."

A remote holo of Cazie appeared at his elbow. Jackson had just emerged from Decon, dressed in a disposable suit of Kelvin-Castner green. The suit wasn't in any way protective. Maybe K-C wasn't concerned about what might infect him as much as they were about what he might have carried in with him. Or maybe he would have to go through yet more Decon before he inspected the biohazard labs supposedly re-creating the inhibition neuropharm. If there were any such labs.

Cazie's holo—projected from inside Kelvin-Castner, or outside?— said, "Hello, Jackson. Despite everything, it's good to see you again in actual flesh."

Her manner was perfect. Not seductive—she must sense he'd moved beyond that susceptibility. Not cold, not accusing, not ingratiating, not falsely friendly. Cazie spoke gravely, quietly, with just a shade of regret that things could not be different, a shade of respect for Jackson's right to do what he was doing. Perfect.

"Hello, Cazie." Astonishingly, he felt for her a sudden stab of pity. Because he felt nothing else. "Shall we get started?"

"Yes. There's a lot to show you, and someone will be here soon to do that. But while you were in Decon, a complication arrived."

" 'Arrived'?"

"Your friend Victoria Turner. With that Liver girl, the mother of the juvenile tissue samples. Ms. Turner is demanding to be admitted wherever you are. Demanding it somewhat vociferously, I might add."

The Cazie projection looked at Jackson meaningfully, sudden vulnerability in her holographic eyes. Deliberate, or genuine? He'd never been able to tell, with Cazie. And now it no longer mattered.

He considered rapidly. "Admit Vicki through Decon. She can assist me in my inspection. Put Lizzie in the outside room with the systems experts from New York—are they here yet?"

"No. But I'm afraid Ms. Turner can't blithely walk through Kelvin-Castner proprietary labs just because you have a—"

"An assistant inspector is in my contract. Read it again."

"A trained assistant, not some amateur—"

"Vicki once worked for the Genetics Standards Enforcement Agency. She's trained in espionage. Now show me where I can link with Lizzie immediately. While Vicki's in Decon."

Cazie bit her bottom lip, hard enough to draw a single bright drop of red blood. Then she said coldly, "Go down this corridor and through the last door on your left." Jackson understood that Cazie had absorbed the changes between them, and moved on. That single drop of holographic blood was the only acknowledgment that he would ever see. Or possibly that Cazie would let herself feel.

The door led to an alcove-sized room with a standard, self-contained, building-system terminal. Jackson said, "Call to Lizzie Francy, on premises."

"Dr. Aranow! Don't worry about Theresa, she's back home and asleep."

"Theresa? Back home? What are you talking about?"

Lizzie grinned. Jackson saw that she was bursting with excitement and self-congratulations. She looked a mess: bits of grass—very green, very genemod grass—in her hair, her face dirty, her screaming yellow jacks more rumpled than he thought plastic jacks could look. She was a vivid, youthful, disorderly smear in the pristine Kelvin-Castner work cubicle, and Jackson felt his spirits lift just looking at her.

"I walked to Manhattan East Enclave to see you, because I have something important to tell you that I couldn't open a link for—"

"Then don't say it here."

"Of course not," Lizzie said scornfully. "Anyway, I got into Manhattan East all by myself, I'll tell you how later, and then a security 'bot picked me up and took me to jail. I faked a medical emergency and forced the medunit to open up a link to your house, only you weren't there, so I talked to Theresa, and she came down to jail and got me out—"

"*Theresa?* How could she—"

"I don't know. She does something weird with her brain. Anyway, when Theresa got too scared I took her home and used your system to call Vicki, who it turned out was out looking for me. She brought me here, because she said you needed me. But I wanted to tell you first that the nursing 'bot says Theresa's fine, and she's asleep. And Dirk is fine, too—I called my mother."

Jackson felt dizzy. Lizzie—a Liver, scarcely more than a child—had walked two hundred miles to New York, dipped what was supposed to be an impenetrable energy shield, subverted the Patterson Protect security equipment, and sat there eager to pit herself against one of the world's major pharmaceutical companies . . . *The individual wasn't really important for radical change?*

"Listen, Lizzie. I need you to write flagging programs for a list of key word combinations I'm going to give you, to search all Kelvin-Castner records. Copy everything flagged for me to look at later, with double-flagging clearly indicated."

Lizzie stared at him, looking puzzled. What he was asking her to do was something anyone basically familiar with systems could do. He spoke the next words very slowly and carefully, looking directly into her eyes, willing her to understand.

"This is very important. I need you to do what you do best."

She got it. Jackson could tell from her smile. What she did best was datadip fast, confusing her tracks as she went, so that even the K-C systems experts who would be following everything she did would be constantly one move behind her. She'd find hidden data that matched his flagging combinations faster than they expected, and she'd copy it to her own crystal library faster than they'd believe possible. Especially than they'd believe possible by a dirty teenage Liver.

And after she'd done it, Jackson would have sufficient cause for a *subpoena duces tecum* of private K-C documents.

"Okay, Dr. Aranow," Lizzie said cheerfully, and he would swear she looked so wide-eyed and dumb just to throw off the K-C observers. She was *enjoying* this, the little witch.

Jackson wasn't. He let Cazie lead him to the first of the K-C labs and introduce him to the junior lab tech (a status insult, of course) appointed to explain the research to the intrusive outsider. Jackson prepared to hear streams of irrelevant summaries, to examine ongoing irrelevant experiments, and to wonder behind what sealed doors the real work was going forward, in directions that would not do anything to make little Dirk less afraid of the trees outside his front door.

Dip hard, Lizzie. *Dip fast.*

* * *

By midnight, Jackson's head ached. For hours he'd concentrated on the research he'd been shown, trying to discern behind it the shadowy outlines of what he wasn't being shown. He hadn't eaten. He hadn't taken in sunlight. Brain and body couldn't take any more.

For the first time, he realized that Vicki hadn't joined him.

"This particular series of protein foldings looked promising at first," said the senior researcher that Jackson had insisted replace the junior lab tech as his guide, "but as you can see from the model, the gangloid ionization—"

"Where's Victoria Turner? My assistant, who was supposed to show up here hours ago?"

Dr. Keith Whitfield Closson, one of the leading microbiologists in the United States, looked at Jackson coldly. "I have no idea where your people are, Doctor."

"No. Sorry. Thank you for your time, Doctor, but I think we'd better resume in the morning. If you'd just point me in the direction of my quarters . . ."

"You'll need to call the building system for a holo guide," Closson said, even more coldly. "Good night, Doctor."

The building led him to his room, a nondescript rectangle designed for comfort but not aesthetics. Bed, closet, bureau, chair, terminal. Jackson used the room terminal to call Lizzie.

She sat alone in the same room as hours ago, a table by her elbow strewn with the remains of mouth food. Her hair stuck out all over her head, evidently pulled at in the throes of battle, and her black eyes gleamed. She didn't look even remotely tired. Jackson suddenly felt old.

"Lizzie, how are the flagging programs coming along?"

"Fine." She grinned. "I'm getting closer and closer to a really good flag. Oh, and Vicki said to tell you she's on her way through Decon and will be there to talk to you soon."

"What took her so long?"

"She'll tell you herself. Sorry, Jackson, I have to get back to work."

It was the first time Lizzie had ever called him by his first name. Despite himself, Jackson smiled ruefully. Lizzie now considered them equals. How did he feel about that?

He was too tired to feel anything about anything.

But when he came out of the shower, dressed in complimentary pajamas of Kelvin-Castner green, Vicki sat on his lone complimentary K-C-green chair.

"Hello, Jackson. I invited myself in."

"So I see." Was his room monitored? Of course it was.

Vicki looked even more exhausted than Jackson felt. Instead of the Liver jacks he'd always seen her in, she wore a pants and tunic of K-C post-Decon green. She said, "I've been to your house, that's why I wasn't here earlier. Don't look so alarmed, Theresa's fine. But I have a lot to tell you."

"Maybe not—"

"—from across the room. Yes, you're right, darling."

She got up from the chair, walked toward him, didn't stop. Not until she'd pushed him back onto the bed and stretched full-length beside him did she stop. She put her mouth directly over his ear and whispered, "You could act as if you meant it, you know. Monitors."

Jackson put his arms around her. She was presumably trained for this kind of thing; he was not. He felt embarrassed, ridiculous, exhausted, and horny. Her body felt light and long in his arms, different from Cazie's tiny voluptuousness. She smelled of Decon fluids and very clean female hair.

She covered his ear with her mouth. "Lizzie left the tribe two weeks ago because she discovered high-intensity monitors there. She traced the data stream back to Sanctuary. They were responsible for the neuropharm. No, don't react, Jackson. Stay amorous."

Sanctuary. Responsible for the neuropharm. Why? To keep power from shifting unpredictably to unpredictable Livers.

"More," Vicki breathed. "Something strange is going on at Brookhaven National Laboratories. An information shutdown. After Sanctuary blew, and Lizzie felt safe dipping again, she went into the government deebees. I'm guessing, but I think Sanctuary tried to extend the neuropharm to the enclaves before somebody blew them up. The newsgrids are assuming it was Selene, but if what Theresa said was true, Selene is empty and Jennifer Sharifi killed Miranda before Sanctuary was hit. So somebody else destroyed Sanctuary. No, don't show any reaction, Jackson. Act natural."

Act natural. What the hell was that? Jackson didn't know anymore. *Selene is empty* and *Jennifer Sharifi killed Miranda* and *somebody else destroyed Sanctuary.* His arms trembled. To still them, he pulled Vicki closer and pressed his mouth against her neck. "And . . . and Theresa?"

"Get comfortable, Jackson. It's a complicated narrative. Something has happened to Theresa, and I don't really understand what. Or how."

INTERLUDE

TRANSMISSION DATE: May 20, 2121
TO: Selene Base, Moon
VIA: Denver Enclave Ground Station, GEO Satellite C-1663 (U.S.)
MESSAGE TYPE: Unencrypted
MESSAGE CLASS: Class D, Public Service Access, in accordance with Congressional Bill
           4892-18, May 2118
ORIGINATING GROUP: "the town of Crawford-Perez"
MESSAGE:

We counted, us, on you, Miranda Sharifi. You was supposed to save us, you. Now it's too late. Three babies are sick, them, already. And it's your fault.

Who are we supposed to look to now, us? Who?

ACKNOWLEDGMENT: None received

Twenty-three

Theresa awoke from a deep sleep to find herself back in her own bed, with no clear memory of getting there. Had Lizzie Francy brought her home, in a go-'bot? That must have been what happened.

And she, Theresa Aranow, had gotten Lizzie out of jail.

Theresa lay quietly, marveling. Her back ached, her skin itched, her bald head burned. All her muscles felt watery. Yet she had forced herself to leave the apartment, go to a jail, and free a strange girl she'd only seen once in her life. Despite her dread and doubts and anguish, which were no different than they'd ever been. Her brain was no different. Only, somehow, when she pretended to be Cazie Sanders, it *was*.

Not pretended to be Cazie. Became Cazie. For a little while anyway, and in her own mind.

Did that mean that if she could somehow change her brain, anybody could? Without more syringes from the Sleepless? Who no longer existed.

The nursing 'bot floated to her bed. "Time for physical rehabilitation, Ms. Aranow. Would you like to eat first?"

"Yes. No. Let me think, please."

Theresa stared at the 'bot. For six weeks she'd heard Jackson or Vicki give it instructions. She knew the words.

"Do a brain scan, please. Print results."

The 'bot moved into position, extended four screens around her head, and whirred gently. Theresa lay still and thought about the night last autumn when Cazie had brought her friends around, those frightening, cold men wearing rags and bees and breathing from inhalers. When the printout issued from the 'bot, she laid it on her pink-flowered bedspread.

"Now do another brain scan in exactly five minutes."

"It is not usual to do two scans so close together. Results don't—"

"Do it anyway. Please. Just this once, all right?"

She was pleading with a 'bot. Cazie would never plead with a 'bot. Theresa closed her eyes and became Cazie. She was striding into the jail, insisting on taking Lizzie home . . . she was at the Manhattan East Airfield, arranging for a charter plane . . . she was facing Cazie—Cazie facing Cazie!—telling her to treat Jackson better, telling Cazie what a good person Jackson actually was, telling Cazie *off*—

The nursing 'bot whirred.

Theresa closed her eyes. When she was just Theresa again, she studied the two printouts, trying to compare them. She didn't know what the diagrams meant, or the numbers, or the symbols along one side. Most of the words were too hard for her to read. But she could tell that all of those things differed from one paper to the other.

So it was real.

Her brain worked differently when she was being Cazie. When she was *choosing* for it to work differently. She could choose to change its chemistry, or electricity, or whatever things these scans measured. It was real.

The nursing 'bot said pleasantly, "Time for physical rehabilitation, Ms. Aranow. Would you like to eat first?"

"No. Deactivate. Please."

Theresa got out of bed. Her legs felt shaky, but she could stand. No time for a shower, though—she didn't want to waste her strength. Even though she'd look like a scruffy beggar . . .

She paused. A beggar. Someone with no power to command, no power to hide, no power to trade. No power to look scary with.

She pulled off her nightdress and walked unsteadily to Jackson's room. From his closet she took pants and a shirt, and used scissors to rip and cut them. From a pot of genemod flowers, big showy purple blooms that Cazie must have given him, Theresa took soil and rubbed it into Jackson's clothes. The soil was probably genemod for all kinds of things, but it still dirtied the pants and shirt. They were too big for Theresa; she tied them on with string.

When she looked at herself in the mirror, she wanted to cry. Bald burned head, sunken face, dirty ragged clothes, trembling and weak . . . No, not cry. Exult. This was her gift, and she was finally going to use it.

"Follow me, please?" she told the nursing 'bot, relieved when it did.

She managed to get to the roof, into the aircar, and all the way to the Hudson River camp without being Cazie. She was saving it. When the car had landed out of view of the Liver camp, she took a deep breath and began.

"Ms. Aranow," said the nursing 'bot on the seat beside her, "it really is time for physical rehabilitation. Would you like to eat first?" Theresa ignored it.

She was a beggar, a beggar with the gift. The gift of needing these frightened people. The gift of needing to be fed, to be welcomed, to be taken in. She was hungry, and weak, and she needed them. She brought the gift of need, to save them.

"Ms. Aranow, it really is—"

She was a beggar, a beggar with the gift. The gift of needing these frightened people. The gift of needing to be fed, to be welcomed—

"Ms. Aranow!"

"Stay here for half an hour, and then follow me."

She wasn't Theresa, she was a beggar. A beggar with a gift. The gift of needing—

The walk to the camp nearly finished her. The camp looked deserted, but the beggar knew better. She squatted outside, in full view of a window, and began to cry. "I'm so hungry, I'm so hungry . . ." And she was. Theresa was hungry, the beggar was hungry, Theresa was the beggar, with her gift.

Eventually the door opened, and an old woman peered fearfully around its corner, hugging the door.

"Please, ma'am, I'm not Changed, I haven't eaten, I'm sick, I'm so hungry, don't leave me here . . ."

The woman's fear was heavy on the air; the beggar could smell it. But her old face creased with compassion. The beggar saw that the old woman, in her long life, knew well what it meant to be hungry, and sick, and alone.

Slowly the old woman crept around the door. And with her, the two people to whom she must be bonded, another elderly woman and a young girl whose heavy features resembled the second woman. One carried a bowl, another a blanket, a third a plastic cup. Ten feet from the beggar they stopped, breathing hard, taut with fear.

"Please, please, I can't move anymore . . ."

Fear warred with memory. The old women, who remembered the unChanged days of hunger and sickness, briefly became the people they'd been then. And moved toward Theresa, the stranger in need.

"Here, now, how come you're not Changed, you? Eat this, go on . . . Look at her arms, Paula, they're like sticks, them . . ."

Plastic bowl and spoon. A mess of gluey food, looking like oatmeal but tasting of wild nuts, slightly bitter, incompletely masked by too sweet maple sugar. The beggar wolfed it all.

"She's starving, her . . . Paula, she can't hardly move, we can't leave her here, us . . ."

From around the edge of the heavy door crept Josh and Mike and Patty, clinging to each other's hands. Jomp. Feebly, the beggar raised her bald, scarred head. They didn't recognize her. "Not *Changed*, her? Jesus Christ—"

"It's starting to rain, she can't stay, her, out here like that . . ."

Mike picked her up. The beggar winced as her tender skin was hoisted into his arms. He carried her inside, the others trailing behind.

A dim, strange room, unfamiliar faces peering at her in fear . . . Her throat started to close and her heart to race. But she wasn't Theresa. She was the beggar. The beggar with a gift. They needed her to need them.

The unChanged child, the same child she'd seen before, in another life, watched her from behind her mother's legs. So it was still alive. And older; the beggar could see now that it was a little boy. His nose streamed snot. His crippled left arm, shorter than the right, dangled from his shoulder.

"Thank you," she said to the circle of faces. A few shrank back, but the rest nodded and smiled. "Now will you let me give you something, because you helped me?"

Immediate alarm. Something different, something new. The beggar wondered, deep in a part of the brain that was someone else, how all their brain scans changed with her words.

"You can do this, accept this," she said. "It's just a 'bot. You've all seen 'bots, lots of times."

The door to the building had been left open. The nursing 'bot, following its instructions, followed the beggar. The unChanged child, who had not seen 'bots lots of times, began to cry.

"It's a medunit," the beggar said desperately. Maybe if she spoke like them . . . "A medunit, it. Like we used to have, us. It can't Change that baby, but it can give him medicine for his nose. It can fix his arm, it." And, again, "You can do this."

"Do what, us?" Josh said. He was still the most intelligent, and the least afraid. The beggar spoke directly to him.

"Do something new, Josh. You can do it, you, if it's a good thing, and you really want to. I can teach you how, me."

She was going too fast. Josh paled and took a step backward. But she also saw the quick gleam of interest in his eyes, before it was lost in fear. He could do it. He could learn to make different brain chemistry by pretending to be a person who was different. Maybe not all of them could, but some could. Like Josh. And maybe that would be enough.

A man was backing away from the nursing 'bot, dragging his two partners with him. "No, no, we're fine, us. Take it away, you!"

But the mother of the crippled child stood her shaky ground. Theresa reached out and, with a corner of her torn and muddied shirt, wiped the baby's nose. The mother let her, although her hand tightened on the little boy's good shoulder. Still, she let the beggar, who ended up with snot all over her hand, touch her child. She had a reason to fight the fear.

Take a neuropharm, Tessie. It's a medical problem.

With that thought, she was Theresa again. Theresa weak, Theresa frightened, Theresa in a strange place with strange people. She felt her breathing grow uneven. But she had been the beggar, she had come here, she had made a difference . . . and next time she would be the beggar longer. Would teach others to do it, only not now, she was so weak, she was afraid but these others understood fear, they would take care of her . . .

She had time for just one more thought before blackness took her. Theresa's thought, not the beggar's: *Only partway a medical problem, Jackson. Only partway.*

When she came to herself again, Theresa lay on a strange bed in the dark. No, not a bed: a pile of blankets on the floor, spread over pine branches. She could smell them, and they rustled underneath her. Irregular walls loomed on either side of her.

The Liver camp. They had put her to bed in one of their own sleeping places. Theresa remembered everything. Immediately she closed her eyes and tried to become Cazie. Only Cazie could get her out of here without panicking. She *was* Cazie, she was fierce and small and fearless, she was Cazie . . . the now-familiar *click* happened in her brain.

She rose quietly in the dark and groped along the closest wall. It ended in a heavy blanket hung as a curtain. After she pushed it aside, there was more light, glowing from a Y-cone in the center of the cavernous floor. The room smelled of unwashed, sleeping people. Cazie crossed it as swiftly as her battered body permitted. Halfway to the door, the nursing 'bot floated up to her. "Ms. Aranow, you've missed two sessions of physical re—"

"Quiet!" Cazie whispered. "Don't talk! You stay right here."

The 'bot whispered, "I am not programmed for override reassignment, Ms. Aranow. I must stay with you."

The stupid thing was bonded to her. Like Jomp. Cazie scowled. "Then follow me in half an hour. Like before."

She hobbled to the door and opened it quietly. The moon was full and high. Cazie started along the path beside the river, to the aircar. It took every bit of Theresa's strength, borrowed and made and natural and a final strength that could only have been a gift, to make it.

"Oh, God," a voice said. "Oh, Theresa!"

Vicki Turner. Vicki's voice. But what was Vicki doing on the roof of her apartment building, in the cold night? Theresa, heavily asleep before the aircar landed, blinked and shrank back against the seat.

"Look at you, Theresa. Where did you go? Those rags . . . don't you have a hat? Come on, let me help you . . ."

"I was Cazie," Theresa said. "And the beggar."

"What? Come on inside, you're shivering. I've been waiting here for you to come home because I had no idea where to look, I didn't even dare tell Jackson you were missing. No, Tessie, let me hold you up, here's the elevator . . ."

She was asleep again. She was dreaming, she must be, strange shapes with huge teeth were chasing her across a genemod garden where all the trees hated her, she could feel their hatred coming to her in waves and she couldn't understand what she'd done to make them want to destroy her—

"Theresa, wake up, it's just a dream. You screamed, you've been asleep for hours . . ."

Her body was burning up. The shapes had set her on fire. Her head ached. "I don't . . . don't feel so good."

Vicki, standing beside her bed with one hand on Theresa's shoulder, went suddenly still. Theresa turned her head and vomited onto the pillow.

Vicki waited until she was finished. "Come on, Tessie, slide out the other way . . . no, you won't fall, I've got you, we're going into the bathroom . . . There. Theresa, listen, this is very important. Where's the nursing 'bot?"

"I . . . left it." She let Vicki wipe her face with a cool cloth. So cool. She was burning up, the sharp-toothed shapes had set her arms and legs on fire and now flames danced along them, dry and hot.

"Left it where? Where, Tess?"

"The . . . camp."

"A camp? A Liver camp? You gave the nursing 'bot to a Liver camp?"

"I was . . . the beggar." Her stomach heaved and she vomited again.

"At the camp. Theresa, was there any Liver there who was un-Changed? Did you touch anyone who was sick?"

"The baby. His nose . . ."

"What about his nose? How sick was he?"

But she couldn't answer. The bathroom jumped and swirled, and she vomited again, thin black bile in ropy gobs.

Then she was back in bed, but the bed was clean. Vicki held a pan under her mouth whenever the dry heaves came. Theresa's head pounded from the inside, so hard she could only see in flashes, and the flashes sent hot lances through her eyes. She saw that the room was a mess. Holes in the walls, furniture knocked over . . . Had Vicki done that? Why had Vicki done that?

"Where is it, Tess? Think, darling. It's important. Where is it?"

"What?" Theresa said, because Vicki's face looked so urgent and intense. Like Cazie's face. No one could stand against Cazie. Not even Jackson. Only Theresa couldn't be Cazie because she was too weak, too hot, she hurt too much—

"Where's the safe, Tess? Your father's private safe. I know he had one because I once heard Jackson say so—come on, Tessie, stay with me. Where's the safe?"

Safe. She wanted to be safe. All her life she'd wanted to be safe, and she never had been . . . *Take a neuropharm,* Tess. But that wouldn't make her safe, she'd always known that, she'd needed something more, something bigger—

"Where is your father's private safe?"

"I think . . . master bathroom? . . . the wall behind the toilet . . ." Vicki ran off. Only then did Tess realize that the torn-apart room wasn't hers but Jackson's, she lay in Jackson's bed and not her own. Jackson's room that had once been her parents'.

From the bathroom came a tremendous crash. Jones immediately said, "Ms. Aranow, there's a plumbing problem in the master bath. Would you like me to summon a building maintenance 'bot?"

"Yes . . . No . . ."

More crashes. Something heavy hit something else, hard. Theresa cowered in Jackson's bed. Vicki came back in, covered with water.

"All right, it's an old-fashioned mechanical look. Completely unde-tectable by any electronics. You open it with numbers. What's the code, Theresa? . . . Three numbers . . . Theresa! Stay with me!"

"Don't know . . . call Jackson . . ."

"I can't get through. Kelvin-Castner has cut him off electronically, and he probably doesn't even know it. I can't get through to Lizzie, I don't know enough about systems . . . wait a minute. *Systems.*"

"I'm . . . am I . . . dying?"

"Not if I can help it," Vicki said grimly. "And not if your brother is as sentimental and naive as I think. Jones, calendar information!"

Theresa winced. Vicki sounded exactly like Cazie. But how could that be, *Theresa* was Cazie . . .

Jones said, "What dates would you like, Ms. Turner?"

Vicki ran into the bathroom, yelling to Jones, "Jackson's birthday. Theresa's birthday . . ."

Theresa was dying. But she couldn't die, she had to sing vespers with Sister Anne. Vespers and matins and . . . what came next? Something else. The unChanged Liver baby with the snotty nose was going to sing with her. She'd promised him . . .

"The date Jackson graduated from medical school," Vicki yelled.

If Theresa died, the little boy with the runny nose would die, too. *You can't, Jackson,* she argued with him, ghostly by her bedside. *You can't stop me. I can show them how . . . Don't you see, it's a gift? It's always been my only gift. Need. You needed me, to take care of.*

Vicki stood beside her, with something in her hand. She'd stopped yelling. In fact, Theresa could barely hear her. Vicki's voice came from someplace very far away, still sounding like Cazie. "The code was his wedding date, damn him for futile tenacity. His wedding date to that narcissistic succubus. Theresa, listen—"

The thing in Vicki's hand was a Change syringe.

"Listen, Tess. Jackson told me he had this put away in his safe for you. For when you someday reversed your decision about Changing. You've picked up some disease from that unChanged kid in the Liver camp; it must be a fast-mutating virus—there's all sorts of microbes coming out of the woods now that the host population is without vaccines. Tess, I gave you antivirals from Jackson's supply but it doesn't look like any of them are working. I don't know what I'm doing with medicine, the nursing 'bot is gone, I can't reach Jackson. It has to be the Change syringe—"

Theresa shook her head. Tears burned her eyes.

"Tessie, you'd have had to have it sooner or later anyway, because of the radiation you took in New Mexico. The cancer curves . . . I'm going to inject you, Theresa. I have to."

"G-g-g . . ." She couldn't get the word out. Gift. Her gift. It would be gone if she Changed, you had to struggle to gain your soul . . .

they said so . . . all the great historical people that Thomas had quoted for her . . .

"I'm sorry, Tess." Vicki gripped Theresa's arm and raised the syringe.

"Beggar," Theresa gasped. "Gift . . ." She closed her eyes, and fever danced along her body and burned her soul. Gone.

She felt nothing. When she opened her eyes again, Vicki still held the syringe above Theresa's arm.

"Tessie—" Vicki whispered. "Do you really want to die instead? I can't make you do this . . . yes, I can make you. But I shouldn't, it should be your choice . . . damn you to hell, Jackson! This should be your problem!"

Tess said, *"My* . . . problem."

Vicki stared at her. "Yes. Your problem. Your choice, your life . . . God, Tess, how can I not . . . all right. Your choice. Should I inject you? If I don't, you might die—but I don't *know* that you'll die. If I do inject you, you might or might not have your brain chemistry altered in some ways . . . I don't know, I'm not a doctor!"

Her brain chemistry altered. But Theresa could already do that! She could be Cazie, could be the beggar, could make herself control her own brain . . . at least a little.

Enough to be Theresa.

Even if her body was Changed. She was more than her body. But hadn't she always known that? Wasn't that what she'd argued about so hard with Jackson?

"Tess? You're smiling like . . . God, honey, your forehead is burning up . . . I don't know what to do!"

"Inject me," Theresa said, and thought, at the moment that the needle plunged in, and through the bright hot whirl of fever, that Vicki was different from Cazie after all: Cazie would never have said she didn't know what to do.

The slim black syringe emptied into her wasted arm.

Twenty-four

When Vicki finally stopped speaking, Jackson lay silent a long time. Her body beside his on the narrow Kelvin-Castner guest bed no longer distracted him, and he certainly no longer felt sleepy.

He believed her. Even though some of the events she'd just whispered into his ear seemed incredible. Theresa—his Theresa—bailing Lizzie Francy out of jail? Going alone to a Liver camp to give them the nursing 'bot? *Choosing to be Changed?*

And yet he believed Vicki. But, then, he'd always believed Cazie, too, right up until he came to Kelvin-Castner . . .

"I have something to show you," Vicki said, and now it was her voice that drowsed. "Proof, of a sort. But it can wait until morning. I am spectacularly sleepy. Worn out with Lizzie and Theresa, the children of the next age . . ."

"The what?" Jackson said, more harshly than he'd intended, because he felt so disoriented. Theresa, choosing to be Changed . . . Theresa, Changed. Would she still need him?

"Children of the new age," Vicki repeated, almost mumbling. "Self-appointed . . ." She was asleep.

Jackson eased himself away from her limp body and off the bed. Sleep was impossible. The room, ten by ten at the most, had no room to pace. And if he used its terminal, he might wake Vicki. He didn't want Vicki awake. She'd only hit him with additional emotional right hooks—that's what she *did*—and he'd already been hit too many times today.

How many brain-rattling punches were too many? And why the hell was he the one receiving them?

Soundlessly Jackson opened the bedroom door, closed it behind him, and padded barefoot in his borrowed pajamas down the unfamiliar and institutional-looking hallway. At the end he found a small, empty lounge. Of course it was empty—this was the middle of the night. The lounge held a sofa, chairs, table, servebot—all as institutional as the hallway—and a flat-screen terminal.

"System on," Jackson said.

"Yes, how can I help you?" An anonymous program, for waiting technicians or bored insomniac guests. Undoubtedly limited access. It was enough.

"Newsgrids, please. Channel 35."

"Certainly. And if there's *anything* else Kelvin-Castner can do for you, please don't hesitate to ask."

"—in eastern Kansas. The tornado brushed the Wichita Enclave, which immediately activated high-security shields. In Washington, Congress continued debating on the controversial airport-regulation package; the Senate vote is scheduled for tomorrow morning. In Paris, the Sorbonne Enclave saw the first performance of Claude Guillaume Arnault's new concerto, *Le Moindre*. The venerable but irascible, much-feted composer did not—"

"Internal communications," Jackson said. The newsgrids didn't have anything fresh on the destruction of Sanctuary. And the inhibition neuropharm wasn't yet major news, merely an isolated phenomenon, a local curiosity among backward Livers.

Fools. The enclaves were all fools.

"Yes, how can I help you?" the program said. "With which internal department would you like to link?"

"Not a department, an individual. Lizzie Francy. She's a guest user somewhere in this building. In the bio-unshielded portion."

"Certainly. And if there's *anything* else Kelvin-Castner can do for you, please don't hesitate to ask."

Lizzie's face came on the screen. Her wiry black hair stuck out in twenty different directions, hirsute vectors. Her black eyes gleamed with excitement, despite the deep shadows underneath. "I just tried to link with your room."

"I'm not there," Jackson said inanely. "Only Vicki is. She came from my and Theresa's—"

"I know," Lizzie said hurriedly. She raised both hands to her hair and pulled, creating even more hair vectors. "I woke her up. Jackson, I need, me, to come into you. To see you, me, in person. Now."

"Lizzie, it's bioshielded here. If you come in, you can't leave for—"

"I know, I know! But I have to come in, me. Now."

Jackson looked more closely. It wasn't excitement shining in Lizzie's eyes. It was fear. And her speech had reverted to Liver.

"Lizzie, what—"

"Nothing yet. I can't dip this system, me. It's too hard. But I don't like it here, me, by myself. I want Vicki. I want to come in, me!"

Lizzie, Jackson saw, was trying hard to look pathetic. A teenage girl alone in the middle of the night in a strange place, who wanted her surrogate mother. Except that this was Lizzie Francy, who had walked to New York alone, had broken into a supposedly impenetrable enclave, had dipped more donkey corporations than Jackson could probably name. The pathos was faked.

The underlying fear was not.

He said, "Dirk—"

"I know that if I come in, me, I'll be in quarantine a few weeks. But I want Vicki, me! And I can't dip this fucking system!" Tears filled her black eyes.

Bewildered, Jackson said, "All right. I'll tell a holo to lead you to Decon. Thurmond Rogers gave me the code. The whole process takes about an hour. But you can't take your terminal through, Lizzie."

"My diary is on here! And Dirk's baby pictures!" And she started to cry.

"Lizzie, sweetheart—"

"I want Vicki!"

So, all at once, did Jackson. Vicki might know how to deal with unexpected hysteria. *Lizzie,* of all people, wailing and throwing a tantrum for her mother . . . But Vicki wasn't even her mother. And Jackson didn't believe that Lizzie hadn't dipped the Kelvin-Castner system.

"Come on in, Lizzie," Vicki said beside him. "Leave your terminal. Isn't the information you're concerned about backed up at Jackson's?"

"No! If I try, it might be zapped!"

"Then carry your personal system—you've unlinked it from K-C already, haven't you? Of course you have—carry it outside the building. Through the door behind you, turn left at the end of the corridor, continue to the fire exit. Right outside are seven people in a van. Give them your system, and they'll safeguard it while you come in to me."

Jackson blinked. *A van?*

Immediately the screen split, and Thurmond Rogers said from the other half, "No proprietary data can be physically removed from Kelvin-Castner. Ms. Francy has been analyzing K-C systems, and—"

Vicki interrupted him. "Two of the six people in the van are bonded shield-security agents. They have appropriate equipment for encasing Lizzie's system in such a way that it cannot be opened without retina scans from her, Jackson, and two Kelvin-Castner officials present at the sealing. One official could easily be you, Thurmond."

"Even so, you can't—"

"One of the people in the van is a lawyer. He has a court order to safely remove any Kelvin-Castner records that may be pertinent to Dr. Aranow's legal contract with Kelvin-Castner."

"That's only contractual if—"

"Another person in the van is a microbiologist. She is prepared to examine Lizzie's data before sealing and declare, as legally valid expert opinion, that it is indeed relevant to Dr. Aranow's contract. Unless, of course, you don't wish her to examine the data."

Thurmond Rogers stared at Vicki with hatred.

"Go now, Lizzie," Vicki said. "It's a short walk, and no one will stop you. There's a homer stuck inside the collar of your jacks; the people in the van will track you when you move out of sight of K-C monitors. Dr. Rogers will tell the building to open the door for you, and to let you back in. *With* a witness from the van accompanying you. Go now, honey."

Lizzie, her eyes still gleaming, picked up her terminal and her ugly purple backpack. She hugged the terminal tightly to her chest and walked out of link range. Vicki drew a deep breath and held it until a strange male face flashed onto the screen. In the middle of the night, the stranger looked crisp, combed, and calm. "Elizabeth Francy is with us outside, Ms. Covington. With the system. Sealing of her system to begin as soon as the Kelvin-Castner team appears, unless Kelvin-Castner prefers Dr. Seddley to examine the data."

"Rogers?" Vicki said.

Thurmond Rogers's hatred had not cooled. But he had himself under control. "No examination at this time. I'll be at the east fire door immediately, accompanied by Kelvin-Castner security."

"Certainly," the well-groomed male face said, and Jackson thought inanely of the anonymous guest system that had turned on the newsgrids for him. "Ms. Francy, accompanied by Agent Addison, is returning into the building." Both halves of the split screen blanked.

Jackson looked at Vicki. She was barefoot, and her hair was rumpled from sleep. Fine strands strayed across her left cheek. She looked young and defenseless. He said, "Who's Agent Addison? And the other three people in the van?"

"Bodyguards."

"How did you know to—"

"That's what I do," Vicki said. "Or what I once did. Although of course I didn't pay for all this. You did."

"How—"

"Lizzie dipped all your personal account numbers long ago. But she's an ethical little creature, in her own way. I'd swear she's never used them." Vicki smiled. "Can't say the same for me, clearly."

Jackson put his hand on Vicki's arm. Not a grip, but not a caress either. "What has Lizzie dipped?"

"I won't know until she tells us. Or until her terminal is unsealed. But I'm more interested in why she wanted to come into the bio-shielded area to speak to us in person."

"Will the agent—bodyguard—whatever he is—stay with her through Decon?"

"Like fused atoms." Vicki spoke to the air. "And the agent carries subcutaneous continuous transmitters. Among other augments."

"So we wait," Jackson said. "Until Lizzie's through Decon."

"We wait," Vicki said. "System, instruct a servebot to bring coffee."

"Certainly. And if there's *anything* else Kelvin-Castner can do for you, please don't hesitate to ask."

Vicki just smiled.

It took an hour for Lizzie and Agent Addison to go through Decontamination. Jackson drank two cups of coffee and watched Vicki get ready to lob another grenade. By now he knew the signs. She drank her own coffee slowly, deliberately, and watched the newsgrids. Finally he said, "What specifically are you waiting to hear?"

"Anything about Brookhaven." Vicki spoke naturally, which meant she didn't care if they were overheard. She shifted position on the waiting-room sofa, curling her legs under her.

"Brookhaven National Laboratories? What about them?"

"I don't know. But Lizzie's monitor program picked up an anomaly. The program scans transmissions from selected governmental agencies to flag marked differences in volume, frequency, priority, or encoding. Information from Brookhaven to nearly everyone else showed an anomaly." Vicki uncurled her legs and crossed her knees.

"An anomaly? Some significant changes?" Jackson said.

"A significant lack of change. The same volume, frequency, priority, and encoding every day."

"You mean—"

"The inhibition neuropharm has penetrated an enclave shield. And not just any enclave—a government laboratory that's supposedly bio-safe." Vicki shifted her weight again. "Of course, Kelvin-Castner already knows this, I'm sure. Damn, I just can't get comfortable."

She stood up from the sofa, stretched, yawned, and smiled at Jackson. For once, he saw what he was supposed to do. He said, "Come get comfortable with me."

She crossed the room to his chair and settled onto his lap. The screen droned out routine news at a volume, Jackson suddenly realized, slightly higher than normal. Vicki's lips nuzzled his ear. She said softly, "I want to show you something," and unbuttoned her shirt.

Hormones surged in Jackson's chest. But then he saw drawings on her chest.

Vicki murmured, "Fewer monitors here, probably, than in your room. Even so, turn to the left. More. There."

Their bodies formed a closed triangle with the padded back of the chair. Vicki bent her head, and her hair screened the enclosed space from the ceiling. She unfastened more buttons.

Her breasts were smooth and pale. Smaller breasts than Cazie's, but firmer, with a sweet high lift. On the upper curve of each was a sketch in nonsmearable ink, the kind used for indelible signing and dating of off-line lab records. Such pens lay all over Kelvin-Castner. Vicki must have drawn on herself after she came through Decon. Jackson peered at the sketches; there was barely enough light to decipher the inked lines. And Vicki's scent, the fragrance of her skin and breath, clouded Jackson's brain.

Until he realized what he was looking at.

Two crude sketches of brain-scan printouts. The one on the left breast was Theresa's. Even drawn upside-down and rough, Jackson recognized it. He had looked at those particular graphs daily during Theresa's illness, and frequently throughout the years before. They were the graphs of chronic cerebral overarousal, especially in the more primitive parts of the brain that controlled emotion. The limbic, hypothalamus, amygdalae, brain stem reticular formation, rostral ventral medulla—all overaroused.

The ascending reticular-activating system—ARAS—which reacted to neural input from many other parts of the brain, showed especially frantic wave activity: low-amplitude, high-frequency, intense desynchronization. Alarm signals constantly traveled to Theresa's cortex, which thus constantly thought of the world as an alarming place. This information in turn traveled back to the ARAS, which reacted with even more frantic electrochemical activity. Electrochemical danger signals alerting thoughts of danger that in turn alerted more electrochemical stress responses. The vicious circle, which Theresa had never let Jackson interrupt with neuropharms.

The second set of rough graphs was entirely different. In fact, it was unlike any brain scan Jackson had ever seen. The ARAS and primitive graphs showed only normal arousal, the kind associated with steady, purposeful, realistic action. But the input *from* the cortex to the ARAS was intense. And parts of the brain showed a veritable electrical storm. These were in the brain sections associated with intense nonsomatic activity: epileptic seizures, religious visions, imaginative delusions, certain kinds of creativity. Such graphs were most often seen in visionaries in locked wards: people who believed they were Jesus Christ or Napoleon or General Manheim. But to combine that pattern with the control and clarity of high-amplitude, low-frequency alpha waves, usually a product of intense concentration or biofeedback . . .

"Whose is the second scan?"

Vicki said, "Theresa's."

"Impossible!"

"No, it's not. They're both Theresa. One scanned before she put herself in a mental state to do something difficult for her, and one after. I don't know exactly how she accomplishes it."

"I wish I could see the spinal segment readings!"

"Well," Vicki said acidly, "there's only so much room on my breasts. Unlike some other people's. So I memorized only the parts of the two printouts that looked most different from each other."

"But how could Tess—"

"Lower your voice, Jackson. And look like you're actually nuzzling me; we're still on monitor. I said I don't know how Theresa does it, but I do know what she told me she thinks she does. Theresa changes her brain scan by pretending to be Cazie."

Jackson was silent. Theresa. Pretending to be Cazie. And capable of inducing, at least temporarily, the kind of brain-activity pattern that belonged to another, entirely different temperament. Plus the activity of intense imaginative creativity bordering on the delusional. She must start with controlling her thoughts in the cortex, which changed the information feeding back into her autonomic nervous system . . . All experience of emotion, after all, was essentially a story that the brain created to make sense of the body's physical reactions. Tess had found a way to reverse the process. She was telling herself some sort of story, telling it in her conscious brain, that was altering her more primitive physical reactions. Right down to the neurochemical level. She was controlling her physical world by sheer imagination and will.

Jackson hadn't known his sister at all.

He said haltingly, "I'll want to replicate this . . ."

"Of course. But not now." Vicki rebuttoned her shirt, but she didn't move away from him. Nestled on his lap, her breath warm against his neck, she said in a different voice, "I'm a little afraid of you, you know."

"I'll bet."

"You don't believe me. You think you're the only one afraid of feeling very much. Well, fuck you."

Abruptly she stood. From her words, Jackson had expected her to look angry, but instead her face showed hurt and uncertainty. And at that moment, Jackson realized that this was the woman who could replace Cazie in his life.

Immediately the realization filled him with terror. *Another* bitchy, bossy woman? Mocking him at every turn, struggling to control him, knowing what he was going to say before he said it . . . Vicki's scent, somehow stronger now that she no longer sat so close to him, filled his nose and throat. She had left the bottom three buttons of her shirt unfastened. Deliberately? Of course. Resentment filled him at the manipulation.

Vicki's vulnerability lasted only a moment. Then she looked again like Victoria Turner, controlled and competent.

Victoria Turner. Not Cazie. That was his confusion, not hers.

It was Theresa who was Cazie.

Jackson laughed aloud. He couldn't help it; the whole critical, ludicrous situation suddenly struck him as unbearably funny. Or maybe just unbearable. Theresa. Brookhaven. The renegade neuropharm. Kelvin-Castner. Sanctuary. The world was blowing up, on both micro and macro levels, and he, Jackson, had chosen as his object of fear a woman who said she was just as afraid of him, except that he was too afraid to believe her, and she was too afraid to believe that he was too afraid . . . "Vicki—" he said tenderly.

Their eyes met across the drab room, the newsgrids blaring. The moment pulled itself out like taffy, stretched and sweet.

"Vicki . . ."

"You have guests on their way in," the system announced brightly. "Ms. Francy and Mr. Addison will arrive in ninety seconds. Shall I show them in?"

"Yes," Jackson said. He welcomed the reprieve, at the same time that he was disappointed by it.

"Certainly. And if there's *anything* else Kelvin-Castner can do for you, please don't hesitate to ask."

Addison was a tech, clearly chosen not only to be threatening but to look it. His head brushed the ceiling; his arms bulked twice Jackson's in diameter. And probably augmented as well: muscles, vision, reaction time. He surveyed the room professionally. Beside him Lizzie looked like a very small, very scrubbed, very fearful doll dressed in Kelvin-Castner green disposables. She threw herself at Vicki and clung. Jackson expected to hear Vicki making maternal cluckings, but this was not happening.

"Come on, Lizzie," Vicki said, "reassemble yourself. You can't tell me that the all-conquering datadipper gets tearful over a little deep lavage. You've gone deeper into government holes than Decon scrubbers just went into yours."

Lizzie laughed. Shaky, but still a laugh. Vicki's bawdy tartness had braced Lizzie. Jackson would never understand women.

"Now," Vicki said, "sit down right there and tell us what you found. No, ignore the monitors. It's fine if K-C knows that we know what we know. Do you want some coffee?"

"Yes," Lizzie said. She looked calmer. Her hair, with no time to pull at it since Decon, lay flat and clean against her scalp. Addison finished his survey of the room and took up a position between Lizzie and the open door of the alcove.

Vicki said, "So what *do* we know?"

Lizzie sipped her coffee and made a face. Jackson realized she wasn't used to the real thing. He sat down across from her, watching quietly.

"We know that Kelvin-Castner made a probability model for research on the fear neuropharm that . . . that Dirk has." Lizzie's voice faltered for only a moment. "I can't understand most of it. But it looks like a program would furnish data to Dr. Aranow along a pre-set path. Some points on the flag had bolstered Lehman-Wagner equations for realiability . . . depending on what Dr. Aranow asked, the decision tree furnished consistent data. I think. What I *could* tell was that every branch of the tree ended in inconclusive equations."

Jackson said calmly, "How do you know the data wasn't actual?"

"The dates on most of the stuff was in the future."

"Projected experiments . . ."

"I don't know," Lizzie said flatly. "How would I know?" Jackson saw that he mustn't argue with her; her confidence might deflate again as suddenly as it had ballooned.

Vicki said smoothly, "None of us will know until the terminal is unsealed and you can examine the data directly, Jackson. But it certainly sounds like a tool for contract smashing, doesn't it?"

Jackson said, "It does." A large cold rage was rising in him, quietly, like black, still water. Had Cazie known?

Lizzie said, "The probability model was cross-referenced with a bunch of stuff about you, Dr. Aranow. A customized psych program." Lizzie blushed.

So Cazie had known.

Jackson rose, but after he was on his feet, there was no place to go. Lizzie clearly wasn't done. His cold black anger seeped higher.

Vicki said, "Good work, Lizzie. But that's not all, is it? Why did you want so badly to join us in the biosafe area?"

Lizzie's hand shook. The rest of her coffee spilled. "Vicki—"

"No, say it. Here. Now. So everybody knows what K-C knows."

Lizzie's hand still shook, but her voice was steady. "There were other probability models in the deep data. Simpler ones, so I could understand them, me. They showed various probabilities of mutation of the original neuropharm. Or maybe not the original, it, maybe something it makes. That part was hard. But the models for different paths . . . the models . . ."

"Give me the Tollers average," Jackson said coldly. "The average probability was for direct transmission of the infection, wasn't it? From person to person, through Nielson cells in bodily fluids. What was the Tollers probability?"

Vicki said, her voice scaling upward in surprise, "You knew?"

"I guessed. I hoped I guessed wrong. But this kind of delivery vector is notoriously unstable, mutates all the time . . . Lizzie. What's the Tollers probability for mutation to an airborne form that could survive independently, outside either laboratory cultures or the human body?"

"Point oh three percent."

Low. The designer—whichever the hell Sleepless it *was*—of the original vector—whatever the hell it was—had at least done everything he could to prevent uncontrollable, worldwide airborne infection. At least he had done that. "And for mutation to an independent form capable of direct human-to-human transmission?"

Lizzie whispered, "Thirty-eight point seven percent."

Better than a one in three odds. So now, Jackson thought, they knew. The inhibition infection might end up passed from person to person, through blood. Saliva. Semen. Urine? Maybe. Probably. A thirty-nine percent chance. To get that high a possibility, the lab samples must be mutating like crazy.

Vicki said to Lizzie, "You were afraid you might get infected yourself, out there. Then you'd never be able to help Dirk. So you came into the bioshielded area with us."

Jackson said, "Even if the mutation has already happened—which isn't likely—she wouldn't have contracted it if she'd just stayed away from people. She'd have needed to come in direct contact with blood or have sex or—Lizzie, what is it?"

Lizzie whispered, "Or touch eyeballs?"

"Eyeballs?"

"Dead ones, I mean, me. Oh, Dr. Aranow, I done touched . . . oh, God, what if I got it? Dirk! Dirk! Is there a test, what if I got it, me, what if I got it!"

The girl was hysterical. Jackson remembered that Lizzie was eighteen years old, and had just come through horrors Jackson couldn't imagine. Lizzie sobbed, and when Vicki led her down the hall and a door somewhere closed behind them, Jackson was glad for the sudden silence.

It seemed a long time before Vicki returned, although it probably wasn't. Her genemod violet eyes looked tired. It must be some godawful early hour of the morning.

"Lizzie's asleep."

"Good," Jackson said.

Vicki stood three feet from him, not trying to touch. "So what happens now?"

"Kelvin-Castner scraps the fake data tree and does the research for real." Jackson looked at the silent screen. "You hear that, you bastards? Now you have a motive. It's not just Livers who inhale some weird compound. They've got it at Brookhaven, don't they? Shielded enclaves can get the infection. *You* can get it. Better find a reverser."

He waited, half expecting to see Thurmond Rogers or Alex Castner or even Cazie. The screen stayed blank.

Vicki said, "So now we're all on the same side, looking out for the same interests. How cozy."

"Right," Jackson said bitterly.

"Except," Vicki continued, "you and I and Theresa know something the rest of the world doesn't. Miranda Sharifi and the Sleepless can't get us out of this one. This time, no miraculous syringes from Sanctuary or Eden or Selene. The Supers are all dead."

Jackson stared at her.

"No, we shouldn't keep it secret, Jackson. We need to tell K-C. We need to call the newsgrids and the government and all the people counting desperately on Miranda Sharifi to rescue us one more time. Because K-C isn't going to get any help from the sky. And the government has to break into Selene to verify missing persons. And people might as well stop beaming messages to Miranda, because there won't be any *dea ex machina* this time. The *machina* broke down, and the *dea* is dead. Jackson . . . please hold me. I don't care who's watching."

He did. And although Vicki felt warm in his arms, it didn't really help. Not really.

"Jack," Cazie said from the terminal screen, her face grim, "tell me what you think you know about Miranda Sharifi and Selene."

He went over it for Cazie, in the middle of the night. He went over it for Alex Castner, also in the middle of the night. He went over it for the FBI and the CIA late the next morning—late because, it turned out, Kelvin-Castner did not call the feds until K-C had had a board meeting. Jackson was grateful for the prolonged sleep. For the FBI and CIA, he had to go over it a lot.

After that, he tried to push the investigation out of his mind. He spent his days with the data Kelvin-Castner now freely gave him. No reason not to. As Vicki had said, now they were all on the same side.

The twenty-first day of his quarantine, the last day, and he had worked his way through all the data K-C had. He didn't go into the labs themselves; he was not a trained researcher. He confined himself to the medical models, which were inconclusive. Maybe a reverser to the neuropharm could be found. But they didn't yet know where, or how.

Or when.

The cold black anger stayed with him. The anger wasn't because devising a cure was hopeless. It wasn't hopeless. Nor was the anger because someone had created this dangerous and cruel neuropharm, unknown in nature. For four thousand years men had created poisons unknown in nature to incapacitate each other. Nor was the anger because Kelvin-Castner had put its own profits ahead of public good, until the public good suddenly became identical with its own good. That was how corporations worked.

On the twenty-first day, as Jackson was leaving K-C for a brief trip to see Theresa, Thurmond Rogers stopped him just short of the security lock into the bio-unshielded part of the building. Thurmond Rogers in person, not holo or comlink. "Jackson."

"I don't think we have anything to say to each other, Rogers. Or are you a messenger boy for Cazie?"

"No," Rogers said, and at his tone Jackson looked closer. Rogers's

skin, genemod for a light tan meant to contrast with the golden curls,
looked blotched and pasty. The pupils of his turquoise eyes were dilated, even in the simulated sunlight of the corridor.

"What is it?" Jackson said, but he already knew.

"It's gone to direct transmission."

"Where?"

"The Chicago North Shore Enclave."

Not even among the Livers. Someone had gone outside North
Shore—or someone else had come in—and contracted the
neuropharm from blood, semen, urine, saliva, breast milk. It was in
non-inhalant form.

He said crisply to Rogers, "Behavior of the victim?"

"Same severe inhibition. Panic anxiety at new actions."

"Medical models?"

"All match known effects. Cerebrospinal fluid, brain scans, heart
rate, amygdalae activity, blood hormone levels—"

"All right," Jackson said, meaninglessly, since it was not all right.
But all at once he knew why he was so angry.

"It's the same thing, over and over," Jackson said to Vicki. They sat
side by side in his aircar, lifting off from Boston. This month the
Public Gardens below them bloomed yellow: daffodils and jonquils
and roses and pansies in artful genemod confusion. The dome of the
State House gleamed gold in the late afternoon sun, and beyond the
dome the ocean brooded gray-green. After a month in front of terminals, Jackson's fingers felt awkward on the car console. He set it for
automatic and flexed his shoulders against the back of the seat. He
was very tired.

Vicki said, "What's the same thing over and over?"

"People. They just go on doing the same thing over and over, even
if it doesn't work."

"What specific people are we talking about here?" Vicki laid her
hand on Jackson's thigh. He covered it with his own, and immediately
thought, *Where are the monitors?* Twenty-one days of holding back,
self-conscious about being observed . . . Only there were no
monitors in his aircar. Or were there? The car had been sitting for
three weeks under the Kelvin-Castner dome. Of course there were
monitors. And anyway, he was too tired for sex.

"All people," he said. "Everyone. We just go on doing whatever
we've always done, even if it doesn't work. Jennifer Sharifi just went
on trying to control everything that might threaten Sanctuary. Mi-

randa Sharifi just went on relying on better technology to lift up us poor benighted beggars who have to sleep. Kelvin-Castner just goes on following profits, no matter where they lead. Lizzie goes on datadipping whatever system's in front of her. Cazie—" He stopped.

"—goes on performing for whatever audience feeds her hunger for applause," Vicki said, more tartly. "And what about you? What do you go on doing, Jackson?"

He was silent.

"Didn't think of applying your own theory to yourself? Well, then, I will. Jackson goes on assuming that the medical model can explain everything about people. Profile the biochemistry and you understand the person."

He glanced sideways at Vicki. Her eyes were closed; Jackson was suddenly sorry not to see their pure violet. She had removed her warm fingers from his. He said, "You sound like Theresa."

"Theresa," Vicki said, not opening her eyes, "is learning to do something different. Very different."

"It's still just a biofeedback control of the brain chemistry that—"

"You're a fool, Jackson," Vicki said. "I don't know how I can be so much in love with a man who's such a fool. Watch Theresa when she learns that the inhibition neuropharm is transmissible. Just watch her. And meanwhile—car, land there, in that soonest clearing at two o'clock."

The flowers in the clearing weren't genemod. The grass was rough, smelling of wild mint. The air was a little too cold, at least for naked bodies. But Jackson discovered that he wasn't nearly as tired as he thought.

Afterward, Vicki clung to him, her long body imprinted with marks from grass and weeds, smelling of crushed mint. He stroked her goose-pimpled skin. Against his shoulder, he felt her lips curve into a smile.

"Solely biochemistry, Jackson?"

He laughed, feeling too good for annoyance. "You never give up, do you?"

"I wouldn't appeal to you if I did. Solely biochemistry?"

He wrapped his arms around her. They had to return to the aircar; this scraggly field was hard ground. Also exposed. Also blanketed with biting insects. In addition, he had to see Theresa, get back to Kelvin-Castner, launch the legal fight to get K-C to share data with the CDC now that the neuropharm had moved from random terrorism to public health crisis . . .

Vicki's voice held sudden uncertainty, that unexpected quality that emerged in her at unexpected times. "Jackson? Biochemistry?"

He held her tighter. "Not biochemistry. Love."

And that both was, and was not, the truth. Like everything else.

EPILOGUE

NOVEMBER 2128

All strangers and beggars are from Zeus, and
a gift,
though small, is precious.
—Homer, *The Iliad*

Jackson waited beside the ugly bulk of a destroyed building, his equipment well back in the shadows. The usual procedure. The building had been foamcast, which meant it couldn't burn, but everything else had been done to it. Smashing, ramming, looting, maybe even shelling. Old destruction, starting to be covered by the mutated form of kudzu covering the rest of St. Louis, possibly the ugliest place Jackson had ever been.

In the last seven years, he'd been a lot of ugly places.

Theresa and Dirk had finished their readying and started their walk forward. Dirk, eight years old and new to readying, clung tightly to his mother's hand. Lizzie, of course, had not needed to ready; she'd never contracted the inhibition virus. But she was guiding Dirk, who over the past year had made tremendous progress in sustaining another persona—he called his "Treeboy." Dirk had learned readying with the adaptability of the young, apparently still present under the panicky inhibition artificially hardwired into his amygdalae. "Treeboy," created by imagination but neurochemically real, was braver and freer than Dirk was. Jackson had the brain scans to prove it.

Theresa led the way. Theresa, dressed in the most ragged of all three of their pathetic rags. Theresa, whose fair hair, grown out from baldness, was the most matted of the three. Theresa, with the emptiest hands, for whom this was harder than for anyone else.

Theresa, who was finally happy.

The three beggars approached the semi-whole building where the infected tribe camped. All the Livers, of course, had fled inside. Theresa, Lizzie, and Dirk squatted in front of the closed door and began to beg.

"Warm clothing, please. Oh, please give us some warm clothing if you can spare it, the nights are so cold . . ."

They would stay there, Jackson knew, for days, if days were necessary. This time, he didn't think they would be. The beggars had a child with them. All the inhibited, in and out of the enclaves, were more likely to open to women and children. The Order of the Spiritual Brain—Jackson hated the name, but it had been Theresa's choice—had three thousand members across the country, not counting affiliated doctors and corporate sponsors, but only twenty-eight percent were male. Still, the number was growing. The Order was growing.

Almost as fast as the inhibition was spreading.

Still, the major pharmaceutical companies—Kelvin-Castner, Lilly, Genentech Neuropharm, Silverstone Martin—were close to a reverser. They might have been closer still if the inhibition plague had been easier to transmit. But the human race had been lucky. If one person in a camp or enclave got it, usually everyone did, due to the poor sanitation and feeding habits of the Changed. But transmission between camps and enclaves was slow, because once infected, the inhibited neither became nor received visitors.

Theresa was changing that.

"Please, just a warm coat . . ." little Dirk begged.

Sometimes the camp would just open the door and throw out whatever was being begged: clothing, a jug of water, a spare Y-cone for warmth. The beggars didn't go away. The one thing about religious orders, Jackson thought, awaiting his part in the shadows, was that they were persistent. Nuts, maybe, but persistent.

And, sometimes, effective.

The door of the Liver building opened a crack. A man squeezed through, followed by a child. Jackson switched his eyes to zoom augments. The child wasn't Changed. Jackson studied the bare, inflamed patches on the side of her scalp: rounded lesions, crusty in the middle and scaly at the edges. Most likely ringworm. But otherwise the little girl looked healthy, if inhibited. Although not as inhibited as some others. The renegade neuropharm, like every other drug, affected different people differently. There were even a few cases of natural immunity, studied eagerly by the pharmaceuticals and the CDC.

The little girl ducked behind the man's legs, but peeped out between them at Dirk.

Treeboy smiled.

Maybe Jackson wouldn't have to wait too long to do his part, after all.

The equipment stood ready, loaded onto a floater. Medicines, nursing 'bot. And, most important, holo cartridges to play on the camp's very own terminal, a terminal they were used to, that was a part of the usual routine. Theresa would start them with the holos on medical care for the unChanged children. Even the most inhibited would try something new when their children's lives were at stake. The more unChanged children were born, the more desperate the inhibited became—and that need was the key to getting into their lives.

Once in, Theresa would gradually introduce the holos on readiness. She, herself constantly afraid, would teach them to overcome fear by imagining a different self. Then, later, they would learn the biofeedback techniques that could make that different self neurochemically real. Temporary—but real. And ready when you needed it.

Or until somebody found a medical solution to the same problem. A medical solution would of course be simpler, easier, faster. Just take a neuropharm. With the right neuropharm, you could become less fearful, more fearful, more lusty, more hopeful, less angry, more lethargic . . . anything. But Theresa and her disciples weren't using neuropharms. So the question wasn't, as Jackson had always assumed, *how neurochemically driven were humans?* The question was, *why were they ever driven by anything but neurochemicals?* Why—and how— could men and women choose against their own fear, lust, hope, anger, inertia? Because clearly they could choose that. Theresa was doing so, right in front of his eyes. So not—*isn't man just a bunch of chemicals?* Rather—*how could man ever be anything else?*

Jackson didn't know the answers. He was, after seven years, still uneasy with the questions.

He blew on his hands; it was getting colder. Jackson turned on the Y-heat filaments woven fluidly into his clothes. Theresa, Dirk, and Lizzie vanished inside the building; a good thing, too, since beggars' rags carried no Y-heat weaving. Nor personal shields. The beggars wore remotes monitored by the backup doctors and nurses—themselves backed up by carefully concealed, highly equipped security 'bots. In the seven years of Theresa's Order of the Spiritual Brain, the security 'bots had only been needed three times. The inhibited were not notable fighters.

The sun began to set over the rubble of St. Louis. Another night vigil. Jackson sighed, activated the Y-shield tent, and moved the floater inside it. He called Vicki.

"Hello, Jackson. How is the assault going? Has Troy fallen yet?"

Jackson grinned. "We just wheeled in the wooden horse. Don't let Lizzie hear you call it that."

"People in the grip of temporary religious mania have no sense of humor. Even seven-year temporary mania. How are you, love?"

"Lonely." Jackson looked more sharply at Vicki's face on the small portable screen. "How are *you?* You look . . . something's happened."

"Yes," Vicki said. Her violet eyes reflected light, like purple wine.

Jackson said, "Someone's found the reverser."

"No. Not that. Although K-C keeps saying how close they are. Something else—clearly you haven't been watching the newsgrids. The Chicago School of Medicine has made an announcement."

"An announcement? Of what?"

"Egg and sperm. Frozen for seven years, unknown until they arrived by time-activated 'bot last week."

A slow pounding filled Jackson's ears. In the distance, beyond the shadows, the door of the Liver building opened again. "Egg and sperm. Whose?"

"You can guess, Jackson. All of the SuperSleepless. Miranda Sharifi, Terry Mwakambe, Christina Demetrios, Jonathan Markowitz . . . all the dead geniuses that we normals didn't know how to engineer for ourselves."

Jackson said nothing. A small figure slipped out the camp door into the long twilight shadows.

Vicki said, "The Chicago School of Medicine is where the original Sleepless were engineered one hundred twenty-five years ago. Leisha Camden, Kevin Baker, Richard Keller . . . Miranda Sharifi must have had a sentimental streak after all."

"So it will start all over."

"If they fertilize, it will. The debate will be fierce. Do we need more *dei* from rediscovered *machinae*? Or are we better off blundering along alone?"

The small figure was Dirk. On zoom, Jackson could see that the little boy was terrified, exhilarated, proud of himself, longing to run back inside. Dirk waved frantically for Jackson to come to the building.

"Vicki, I have to go. They're ready to let me inside."

"Already?"

"Already. Theresa's getting very good at this."

"Saint Theresa. All right, Jackson, go convert. I love you." The screen blanked.

Now Dirk waved both hands. Jackson put away his comlink, waved back, and summoned the floater. The equipment to teach people to take back their own lives was ready: medicine, teaching holos, nursing 'bot, seeds, crystal library. All following the chemically inhibited Dirk, who had turned himself into Treeboy, who had become a beggar because only with empty, open hands could any of them reach each other.

Dr. Jackson Aranow moved forward with his gifts.